# *ARVEKT*

## CRAIG LEA GORDON

# INSTANT REALITY SERIES

Craig Lea Gordon

## OUT NOW

Book One Prequel: HyperCage

Book Two: ARvekt

## COMING SOON

HyperStarr

HyperVayne

# *ARVEKT*

## INSTANT REALITY BOOK TWO

### CRAIG LEA GORDON

ORIGIN

ISBN: 978-1-8380543-1-1

For Lottie, thank you for your constant encouragement.

For Harry, thank you for your mentoring and support.

You are both my true reality.

# ONE
## MIND INVASION

As the instance expired, Tannis appeared back in reality, line by line.

Her target was cocooned in a plasteel sarcophagus, hair shaved, brain exposed, wires slicing into his grey matter. His face was locked in a visage of pure terror, eyes wide, teeth bared, with a silent scream stretched across his face. She'd failed to intercept the brain hack in time. But he was still alive. Just.

Turning towards the hacker, she gained a bit of satisfaction seeing him sit slack jawed in his chair as she completed her progressive scan back to reality. The forgotten vat-burger in his greasy paw slopped a glob of mayonnaise, landing with a wet thwack on his pants, sending a burst of colours rippling down his legs in ARspace from the impact. If it wasn't for the face mask, he'd have been able to see the pained expression on her face. Disgusted at her own failure in preventing Tolen's collective from cracking open the victim's mind until its digital secrets spilled out in a flow of ones and zeroes. Maybe if the hacker could have seen her face, he wouldn't have started reaching for the machine pistol lying next to the dripping surgical tools.

A panel of data floating in mid-air next to the victim's head chimed softly. *DOWNLOAD COMPLETE* flared brightly in the darkness of the musty room, the red text matching her rising anger.

Brain, meatware. ARvekt, wetware. The one. The same. Indistinguishable from one another. So when the hacker's hand twitched towards the gun, all it took was a thought. At that thought,

Tannis' ARvekt interfaced with her Celeritas combat armour and signalled the programmable matter weaponry, waking the catoms from inertia. The programmable matter flowed from the storage unit built into the back of her armour to the reservoir at Tannis' wrist, the catoms forming foot long spikes from each knuckle.

For a slob, he was fast. But not fast enough.

The hand clenching the burger came up suddenly to block her attack.

Tannis darted forward with a left hook, catching the burger and his cheek almost at the same time. The spikes skewered their way through to the other side of his head. The nanomuscles of her Celeritas combat armour assisting as she lifted him up off the chair and slammed his head to the ground. The spikes pinged as they caught the concrete floor, a mix of blood, mayo and brain fluid dripping down their length to the floor.

Tannis retracted the spikes, catoms breaking back down and flowing back into the reservoir, leaving gaping holes in his face and temples. The strange sight of a dead man with a cheeseburger pinned to his face was short lived as three guards burst into the perverted operating theatre.

She dove over the top of the counter in the centre of the room, sending the surgical tools scattering all over.

Their guns burst to life, bullets clanging against the metal of the counter and ricocheting off the plasteel sarcophagus.

With her back pressed to the cool metal, Tannis watched as the catoms instantly formed two pistols in her hands.

"Ix, generate me a couple of ghosts," said Tannis.

"Affirmative, Tannis. Visibility?" acknowledged Ix, its voice phasing between female and male, never quite one or the other.

"First ghost for the one on the left. Ghost two for the others."

"Affirmative. Ghosts ready."

"Go."

Tannis jumped left from out behind the counter. The first guard tracked her easily, shredding her body with bullets as she tried to jump to safety. She landed on the ground, her body awash with patches of cycling colours as the ghost flashed in and out of existence before disappearing.

Tannis jumped right from out behind the counter. The other two guards blasted her to pieces. Her body flew backwards, pulsing in and out of reality once again before the second ghost vanished mid-air.

Tannis rose from behind the centre of the counter. She fired in quick succession. Precision shots. Two to the chest. One to the head.

Their bodies slumped to the ground, heads a ruin of meat and bone.

She deconstructed the pistols and stepped over the dead hacker to get to the sarcophagus. Her fingers danced over the floating panel as she shut down the last of the hacking protocols, placing him to sleep. A rasping breath escaped from his throat, clouding the inside of the plasteel window. His eyes closed, head falling sideways as his brain waves descended into an alpha pattern.

A tornado of red voxels appeared at her side, swirling for a second before snapping together to form an androgynous translucent body of neon red lines.

"Tannis, the remaining personnel are converging on your position," Ix informed her.

"Thanks, Ix. I'm clearing the base out now."

"I'm reading three organics and two combat bots."

"Roger that. Dispatch the medical team. We've got a male, catatonic. Data extraction successful."

"Situation?"

"He's stable, but he's going to be a mess when he wakes up."

"Affirmative. Medical team ETA is twelve minutes and thirty-four seconds."

She'd fucked up. The victim was going to need serious neural profiling to recover, and it was her fault for not closing the hack down in time. But Ix didn't judge.

"I'll have the site secured in time."

"Be careful."

"I'll be grand," she said as Ix's avatar burst apart and dematerialised.

With a thought, Tannis launched a drone, and with a whirr-click, a black sphere the size of a fist detached from the shoulder of her combat armour to hover in front of her.

"I want a full scan, Zub."

The drone made a forlorn beep.

"Don't be like that; you'll be fine. Go," said Tannis with a wave of her hand.

The drone beeped again and flew out the room.

A camera feed from Zub slid into her vision and locked itself in position, taking up a quarter of her view as it flew down the long corridor joining the room.

It flew over the top of two Series Y Combat Walkers, their four double jointed legs supporting a large calibre automatic weapon that tracked and fired at the drone. Zub evaded the Walkers' fire and pinged Tannis their UUIDs as it continued its scan.

An overhead map slotted in above Zub's camera feed,

highlighting the walkers with glowing blue dots.

Three humans appeared as orange dots on the feed, tactical data appearing alongside them in callout boxes as Zub completed its scan and returned to her. Tolen, her secondary target, flanked by his security. They ignored the drone and instead sprinted to an adjacent room. Tolen had a riot shotgun; the others had automatic weapons. Basic armour. No grenades. No combat systems detected. Piece of cake.

Tannis peeked around the corner of the door frame. The two Combat Walkers were stationed at the top of the corridor, their guns trained away from her. She ducked back inside as Zub flew back down the corridor towards her. The orange blips moved slowly to join the walkers.

Zub flew past the doorway, desperately avoiding the sustained fire from the Combat Walkers, and then looped back on itself towards Tannis.

"Hold it, Zub. Maintain evasive patterns."

Zub let out a shriek of annoyance as it reversed direction, flew into the room opposite and then back into the corridor to continue its evasive manoeuvres.

"A little longer."

An audible click reverberated through the hall as the two walkers ran out of ammo and reloaded from their underslung hoppers.

"OK, Zub."

The little drone flew back through the door with an audible screech.

"Oh, come on. They weren't that close," said Tannis as the drone re-attached to her armour.

Tolen and the others still hadn't joined the walkers... what the hell were they doing?

Tannis leant out the doorway and loaded a high explosive round. Two bursts from each pistol caused the first Walker to explode wildly, showering the ground with smoking shards of metal. The other Combat Walker emitted an electronic shriek as its sensors were overloaded, firing blindly at her position. She ducked back into cover as bullets shredded the wooden doorframe.

The Combat Walker advanced down the corridor, sustaining fire at the door, Tolen and the others following behind it. The room was showered with dust and fragments of concrete from the Walker's relentless onslaught.

With a thought, her two pistols broke down and recombined to form a sub-machine gun. Tannis dove through the doorway. Planting one hand on the floor, she cartwheeled across the corridor, spraying the final Walker with bullets. It exploded, shredding the closest hacker with a cascade of shrapnel. Tolen and the other guard ducked behind a wheeled riot shield. Ruined fragments from the Combat Walker pinged off it harmlessly.

Where the hell did they get that? Tannis thought as she landed in a heap in the room, deconstructing the sub-machine gun.

"Ix, can you mask me?"

"Negative, Tannis. Insufficient resources exist for an instance right now."

"Damn it. OK, give me details on that shield."

A scaled 3D model of the riot shield appeared in front of her.

"Two-man portable bunker designed for rapid deployment in confined areas. Hands-free operation gives the user freedom of movement and utilises NIJ Standard Level VII ballistics bunker panels able to withstand .50 calibre AP rounds," said Ix.

"Test data, please."

Graphs and tables of data bounced into her field of view, confirming what she already suspected. No way could she penetrate that armour, leaving her with only one option.

A fluorescent green dial slid down into her vision. With a twist of her hand, she dialled it to two hundred percent, the dial pulsing from orange to red as she increased her brain cycles, flipping to a higher clock rate. The neural processor entered overdrive, her computerised brain drinking in the light from her eyes, processing it twice as fast.

Her world slowed.

She stepped out of the doorway.

Tolen and the other hacker huddled behind the riot shield let go and readied their weapons.

Bullet trajectories from their weapons projected into her vision. Bright red lines bisecting the corridor moved lazily towards her chest.

Tannis sprinted to the opposite wall of the corridor, too fast for the hackers to track.

She kicked up and off the wall, flipping sideways through the air to land neatly behind them.

Their fleshy forms appeared ripe for the taking, exposed on the wrong side of the shield.

She snapped a kick into Tolen's back, her augmented muscles like steel cables of raw power. He flew up and forwards, clipping the riot shield, sending him spinning down the corridor. He landed with a screech as his armoured form slid along the ground.

The guard swung round. Tannis watched in slow motion as he

adjusted his grip on the rifle, readying it to smash her in the face.

She dodged and rolled into his attack. Then, using his own momentum against him, smashed his head into the wall. A streak of red appeared as his mangled face slid down it.

Tolen stood to face her, raising the shotgun.

Two shots, and then he's mine, she thought.

Tannis watched as he squeezed the trigger, his knuckle flaring white so slowly she could see the blood pushed away by the taught skin.

The end of the barrel was a white-hot flower blooming in the morning sun.

She jumped to the side, the air awash with hundreds of ripples as the shotgun pellets flew past.

Tolen leisurely swung the shotgun towards Tannis. A frustrated frown clouded his face.

His knuckles flared white.

Tannis tensed, ready to pounce.

The end of the barrel bloomed.

An agonizing pain flared in the base of her skull.

The boon of her sped up brain cycles turned into a crippling detriment as she felt every pellet strike her chest, one by one.

Emergency systems shut down her neural processor overdrive. She pitched forwards, back in real time. She tried to break her fall but her arms had no strength and they buckled underneath her.

As her head hit the ground, she saw Tolen standing above her. He raised the shotgun and fired. Tannis' head was pulverised, spraying a fine mist of red all over the floor.

# TWO
## START OF LINE

A persistent noise reverberated around her head. Over and over. Looping. It was... unrecognisable. A low whoomf. All bass. It slammed against her brain. Her closed eyelids twitched in time. As it rose in crescendo, a flicker of recognition was snatched away. High frequencies filtered in slowly, giving meaning. A looping high-pitched tone. A warning. An alarm. A staccato voice bolstered her realisation.

"Perimeter breach. Mission compromised."

The blackness was suddenly wiped away as she snapped open her eyes.

*PERIMETER BREACH* was emblazoned across her vision.

Red pulses pinged from the outline of the facility on her HUD.

She jumped up a little too fast and the room swayed before she planted a hand on the wall.

"Ix, what happened?"

After a swirl of red voxels, Ix's tessellated form appeared in front of her.

"I had to create an emergency instance and make it look like you died. Fortunately for you, the shotgun was out of ammo. Not to Tolen, though. He dropped his weapon and fled as soon as he saw your head explode."

"You're a gem. Get me a lock on his location."

"Generating now, Tannis."

The floor of the compound came alive with yellow points of light as a 3D city formed from the ground up, layer by layer.

The East End of London displayed out in front of her, translucent buildings glowing, the river Thames sparkling bright blue in the gloom of the corridor.

Her point at the docks was marked with a winking blue marker. A red line meandered from the compound leading to a red icon, showing his path weaving between the redundant cargo containers.

"Where's he headed?"

"He purchased a ticket for the Greys Station Loop forty-seven seconds ago."

"Can you reserve me an instance?"

"Based on current capacity, permutations and variables, I can create an instance for ten minutes and forty-three seconds."

"Roger that."

"I shall deploy the MAWS to meet you at the station."

"Negative. I have to do this myself."

"Director Yu has expressly ordered..."

"Ix, please. I have to prove to myself that I can do this. If I can't, what's the point? I'll take full responsibility."

"Affirmative."

For a fleeting second, Tannis started to contemplate what'd happened.

How did he get the drop on me? A problem with the overclocking? She'd had the wartime implant repaired a number of times since the AI War, but it had never glitched out like that before. It couldn't be the implant. It didn't feel right, and she knew it. She rubbed the base of her skull, remembering the flaring pain. It can't be. Not again. She fought down the rising panic. Stopped. Slowed her breathing. Closed her eyes. Relaxed.

She took off after her prey, sidestepping the discarded shotgun and giving the spent cartridges a brief glare. As she burst out of the old warehouse, a red line following the contours of the ground dropped down into her vision, leading towards Tolen. Her augmented limbs powered her forward, easily surpassing her target's speed. The ETA on her HUD started tumbling, and the red line leading towards Tolen phased through the spectrum towards orange as she sprinted through the dilapidated yard. She leapt over rusty and crumbling cargo containers, through the bamboo covering their tops, a red panda's algorithms causing it to bolt as she jumped to the ground. The cool breeze off the Thames made for a loud rush in her ears as she surged forward.

"Tannis, he is entering the station now. His pod is for platform six, four minutes away," said Ix.

"Can you design an instance to direct him somewhere quiet?"

"To a service platform. I can create a route for his pod that will take him there instead."

"Do it."

"I've had an emergency requisition for resources, Tannis. This instance will only be live for two minutes and seventeen seconds."

"Copy that."

The instance time remaining snapped into place on her HUD under the ETA data.

This is going to be close, she thought as the gleaming glass tubes of the Loop station hove into view.

Ahead, the street was rendered as a golden beach, waves lapping at the sand from either side. It was packed with food vendors, glowing tasteimations hovering at head height outside each eatery. Ramen steaming in a bowl. Fish chopped in the air before falling down and rolling itself into sashimi. Pulled lamb covered in BBQ sauce before dropping down and folding into a lavash.

Tannis darted sideways but got blocked by a sickly green creepster kid, glowing blood dripping from the crucifix dangling above his head constantly running down his face. She reversed direction, running straight through the glowing tasteimation of the sashimi. She curled her lip in disgust as the raw fish and seaweed burst onto her tongue.

With a quick dart to the left, she avoided the other people clustered around the first kiosk. More creepster kids, neon girls with pink and blue lightning constantly arcing over their skin, and the phase gangers, their clothes changing from black to white in unison.

A mechachef was skilfully cooking up bowls of steaming ramen, flipping noodles, throwing boiled eggs into the air and slicing them apart mid-flight to whoops and claps from an audience of hungry customers. Next door, Jack-heads were queuing for synthesized meals dished out by crusty old nano-factories. The plates of mush were awash with static then an eddy of voxels augmented the basic dish into a palatable facsimile of the ramen next door.

Tannis darted out of the soup kitchen and the route to the station was even thicker with bodies, their visually augmented forms a sliding kaleidoscope of colour and shapes.

"Zub, track me. Twenty metres elevation."

The drone detached, ascended and kept pace above her, camera feed coming online to display a wide area below it.

The feed from Zub popped in and anchored itself to the bottom right of her vision under the map view leading to the target. With a thought, the picture-in-picture view from the drone switched to her main view, her own vision relegated to a small window.

Seeing herself from above, she had a perfect view of the available routes through the crowds. Darting through the gaps, Tannis threaded herself perfectly through the dynamic network of bodies, like code taking the optimum route through the Web. Twisting and turning, dipping and rotating her shoulders, perfectly poised, she worked her way through the busy station, with the barest disturbance to the people around her.

The green line to Tolen led her to the service entrance and away from the main concourse.

With the commuters thinning out, Tannis recalled Zub and reverted to her own vision.

With a ping, Ix highlighted the service door in a hard green outline. It unlocked and whooshed open, giving her enough time to enter before Ix closed it again.

Rounding the corner to the service platform, she saw Tolen fidgeting at the far end, checking an arrivals board that didn't exist. He'd altered his visual profile, shed the uniform of his hacking collective, appearing in simple black clothes that left trails in the air as he moved.

He was easy prey, but Tannis walked slowly towards him with only a few precious seconds left to the instance. She wanted to revel in his confusion right before she made him pay for his barbarism. The thought of that look in his eye as she ended him was enough to stay her hand.

"Instance expired," Ix reported.

Tolen jumped back with a start. Head jerking from side-to-side. His brow creating deep furrows as his brain tried to comprehend what had happened.

"Problem, Tolen?" Tannis snidely inquired.

"I killed you. I fucking killed you."

"Are you sure about that?" challenged Tannis with a smile.

"What have you done to me? Where the hell am I?"

"Where I need you to be. Although Hell isn't far off."

"You bitch."

"You'd better believe it."

"OK, you got me cold. I've got no weapons. Take me in. Arrest me," he said, holding out his wrists.

"I'm afraid it doesn't work that way for you. We've got Starr and Vayne, but that's all we need. They'll be paraded in front of the public once Ix gets elected. But you, we've no need for you."

"That's bullshit. You can't do that."

"Section-R edict 24. 'Any person or persons committing an act of neural hacking thereby revokes all statutory human rights.'"

His eyes lost focus. No doubt frantically trying to find that information on the Web.

"That *is* bullshit. There's no such ruling. No such agency. You're full of shit."

"Section-R was set up to protect mankind from scum like you. It's unfortunate we have to keep all your activities secret. And the best way of ensuring that is to make sure you no longer exist."

"Tha - tha - that can't be legal."

"You can't seriously be trying to take the moral high ground after violating that guy's brain."

"You fucking bitch."

"Come on, I'll give you a chance."

Tannis extended her arm, enjoying the look on Tolen's face as the katana constructed itself out of nowhere.

Tolen roared and sprinted towards her.

Tannis waited patiently for the right moment.

His eyes bulged as he closed the gap, teeth bared in anticipation.

Tannis drew her arm quickly up and across his body.

The wicked blade glided through the carotid artery and slashed open his neck.

Hundreds of droplets of blood sprayed over her face.

A bomb detonated in her brain.

The agony from the base of her skull flared outwards to every part of her body. Every sense overloaded. Supernova burst in front of her eyes. Her nerves were molten metal. Piercing static assaulted her ears. Burning plastic invaded her nostrils. Systems were failing and rebooting. Corrupted panels of static snapped onto her HUD, layering on top of each other, creating a snow cloud of white noise in her ears. She tried to swipe them away, but her hand reeled from their freezing touch. The white noise started to phase in and out, faster and faster, the sound driving into her brain. It was so loud she checked her ears for blood. When her fingers came away clean, Tannis screamed, slamming both fists in front of her. They stopped inches from her face, the searing cold burning her hands. The panels cracked then disintegrated into a million frozen voxels, falling one by one, leaving only a canvas of black. As she collapsed, her scream echoed down the empty service platform.

# THREE
## RELAPSE

Black. Only black. Muted sound. Muffled and indistinct.

Objects started to pop in slowly. Solid white. Stark against the blackness. The scene was incomprehensible. Swaying. Back and forth. As more white objects popped in, the movement was more pronounced. Tannis felt disorientated. The swaying making her stomach lurch. A strange monochromatic vista filled her eyes. Meaningless. Her breathing accelerated. She felt the panic like stabs of electricity all over her skin. Her stomach dropped, causing her to wretch. Acid burned the back of her throat. She gasped for breath but the air tasted foul. Tannis pulled off her helmet and dropped it to the ground. Raven hair tumbled into her face. She wiped away the hair stuck to her face to reveal piercing grey eyes set wide in panic.

Tannis gulped in the air, but it didn't help. Thoughts clawed at the inside of her brain, begging to be free, to be untrue. It's impossible. It can't be. They said she was fixed. She tried to focus. Be still. Relax. Breathe. Slowly.

Her vision snapped into colour. The muffled sounds soared up the frequency range, and with a pop, the madness was gone. But the realisation persisted. It was happening again. She needed comfort. Must feel it in her hands. She tore her gloves off with her teeth and snatched at the top of her armour, her nails ripping skin as she desperately reached for it. Where was it? Was it lost? Had it fallen off during the mission? Impossible. She would have known. She always had it. Had to have it. Next to her.

Her finger hooked around the chain and she grabbed at it, pulling it away from the top layer of her body suit. It fell out of her armour and snapped taut against the brass chain. She grabbed it with both hands and pulled it to her chest like a comfort blanket. She let out a long breath and calmed her breathing.

Holding her mother's locket in the palm of her hand, she flicked the catch. It snapped open to reveal her parents smiling warmly and waving back at her. She stared at them for a long time. Her breathing slowed. She cleared her mind and a calm descended on her.

It was happening again. But this time it would be different. She'd make sure of it.

She kissed her fingers and then placed them on top of each picture. Snapping the locket closed, she looked around to see where the hell she was.

In the middle of a square dominated by two monuments, surrounded by palm trees and luscious green grass that came up to her knees. Spider monkeys watched intently from the tops of the trees as giant lionfish swam in the air above the spiky leaves.

Tannis' eye was drawn to the plainness of the tall white column on the right. A square edifice with an old analogue clock gracing each side. White lettering contrasted against the brass plaques, listing the names of those who fell in combat during both World Wars. The Maple Leaf and Union Jack flags flapped in the wind as she read the names of the fallen.

Circling the memorial, she retrieved her helmet and paused at the inscription. *May justice, mercy & peace prevail among the nations. For your tomorrow, we gave our today. At the going down of the sun and in the morning, we will remember them.*

The ancient slab of stone was a distinct contrast to the memorial on her left. This she had seen many times, as had the rest of the world, with similar reminders jutting out of the ground across the globe. Two figures radiating a gold aura faced each other from either side of an incline. On the left, a man ensconced in gleaming combat armour. The other, a glowing red ARvatar. Ix, the protector of humanity. Guardian AI. The hill dividing them was inlaid with screaming faces that started to contort and writhe in agony as the two warriors strode towards each other. As they reached the peak, the screaming faces cried out as one as the warriors slammed their fists towards each other. They rolled their arms at the last second and grasped each other's wrists in a symbol of defiance and unity before exploding into a fountain of voxels. Millions of golden and red fragments floated on the wind before getting pulled into the centre of the structure where they formed words hanging in the air. *Together as man and machine, we can conquer all that stand before us, even when it is ourselves that threaten to divide us.* As the inscription faded, a list of names started to scroll, listing those that fell during the AI war. Mechs with their unit numbers. Human names and numbers.

Tannis reached out to touch the words, imagining she could see the names of her parents, hoping to feel them. So many dead. They would have lost if it wasn't for Ix. Humanity owed her so much.

With the thought of Ix, she was suddenly aware of her winking comms icon.

Red lines unfolded into her view, constructing Ix's translucent avatar.

"Tannis, what happened?"

"I blacked out," her throat constricted, forcing the words out. Tears started to well in her eyes as the full effects of the relapse dawned on her. It shouldn't have been possible, not after the neural conditioning. It was supposed to be her last chance. Is this it, then? Is she finished? She wiped away the forming tears with the back of her hand, but they clung to her armoured hand in little droplets.

"Tannis?"

"I'm fine, Ix; it was a shock... that's all."

She tried to believe it, but she knew Ix would be able to tell she was lying. "What's the situation at the docks?" asked Tannis, desperate to change the subject.

"Arras and Maddock are stabilising the victim. I'll notify them that you require a lift back to Section-R. I am glad you're OK, Tannis."

"Thanks, Ix." Ix's form faded away to be replaced by a human ARvatar.

Sarah, her Operations Lead, stood in front of her, her virtual form shimmering in the sunlight.

"Tannis. Sorry for the breach in protocol but when I heard, I had to make sure you were OK."

"It's good to see you."

"And you. Are you OK?"

The silence hung between them. So many things that she wanted to say, but now wasn't the time. "I am. Thanks for checking up on me. You're a good friend, Sarah."

"Is that all I am?"

"For now. I..."

"That's OK. I'm sorry, I shouldn't have pushed. Look, why don't we get dinner later, OK? Nothing serious."

"Yeah, that sounds good. Thanks, Sarah. I need someone to talk to."

"I know you do. I'm always here for you. Oh, and, Tannis, I'm afraid you are to report to the Director as soon as you land. Good luck."

And so it begins, she thought as Sarah disappeared amidst a vortex of coloured lines.

A flicker from above caused her to look upwards. Tracing in from the skyline and sweeping overhead, clean parabolic lines of the air highways sketched out neon traffic lanes. The traffic was starting to heave as night was encroaching. But it was what was above the skyways that caught Tannis' attention. The entire sky malfunctioned, awash with arcs of static that snapped backwards and forwards overhead. It glitched again and the arcs of static morphed into beautiful luminous colours. Auroral arcs of reds and blues soared overhead, turning the sky into a magnificent ballet of intense wavelengths of colour. The London Aurora in full effect. Hundreds of shooting stars lanced through the air above the scintillating colours, further adding to the capital's famous nightly lightshow.

As Tannis headed towards the docks, the faces of Big Ben were magnified hundreds of times into the sky, visible from anywhere in the city. A reminder of how long she'd been incoherent.

As she passed St. Paul's Cathedral, gigantic angels wreathed in white light beat their wings and soared above the dome, dancing in time to the arcs of the aurora. They swooped through the air, their wings leaving golden trails. One of them flew through the music cube above Club Viva. Rotating in the sky, each of its faces pulsed in time to the unheard abrasive beats. The dance floor would be heaving with sweating, cavorting bodies. All locked into the music. Synched up to ride the highs as one. The last time she'd been, she'd been in person instead of jacking-in. And she'd been with... Farron. Shit. Back to her ultimate failure. Why can't she let it go? Forget and let go. Because it was your fault, that's why.

She powered through the city, people all around her a blur. Her mind kept switching back to that fateful night, trying to replay events, but it was hazy. Every time it started, it was as if her memories were corrupt, full of static and glitches. Did she not want to remember? Or was it the conditioning? She passed a tree of compassion, its branches bending low, brushing against her face and neck. The leaves burst away from the branches and coalesced into a human form. Farron. It looked exactly like him.

"It's not your fault," the leaves said, before bursting apart to return to the trees.

Someone blocked her path through the park, and for a second, she thought it was another piece of ARt from the tree, set to soothe her. She was an angel, all golden wings and ethereal beauty but then she morphed. Her angelic locks became jagged and spiky, flashing between red and blue. Blue devil horns grew from her head, and she glowered at her with red eyes. A crimson cloak whipped back and forth behind her, despite the still air. The edges of the cloak were constantly spawning flaming bats, which flitted up into the fluorescing sky. A red cobra with glowing azure eyes circled up the demon's arm, staring at Tannis. Its lifeless eyes bored into her as its hood spread. The mouth opened wider and wider, inviting her in, fangs dripping with glowing venom. As she got within arm's reach, it jumped for her throat. She threw up her arm and averted her face, waiting for her body armour to harden and take the brunt of the attack.

Then nothing. There was no attack. As the demon stalked off into the distance, Tannis tried to compose herself, but more and more people started staring at her as they glided past. She felt her face and looked down, glancing around her body, checking for what everyone was staring at but saw nothing. What were they looking at? So many people around her made it feel as if she was being crushed. Every time she looked at them, they were staring at her, no matter which direction they were walking. A pain flared in her breast, making her clutch her chest as she started hyperventilating.

A glowing logo of the letters *ARvekt* made of a coral-like brain structure burst to life in front of her. The logo faded to show her lying on a floating medical bed, a huge smile on her face as a column descended from above. Robotic arms with glinting needles blossomed outwards like a mechanical octopus about to perform surgery. A voice drilled straight into her head.

"Tannis Ord, neural conditioning is the latest advancement in psychological therapy treatment from ARvekt Foundation Research. We have years of experience in psychosis, cognitive disorders and post-traumatic stress. Connect to one of our specialists now for an immediate consultation."

It's reacting to a panic attack. You're having a panic attack. Be calm. Breathe. The ARvekt logo faded away with the pain in her chest.

I must keep in control, she thought, or it'll be over for me. Then I'm as good as destroyed, like that thing. She stared at the last vestiges of the weapon platform jutting out of the top of the Thames, its rusting form a stark reminder of how close they came to losing that day. They would have if it hadn't been for Ix. She shook the thought away and headed to the docks, the red shimmer of the radiation barrier visible on the horizon as the light started to fade.

"Five hundred kilojoules of kinetic energy generated. London thanks you for your contribution," said her AIssistant as the words faded from her HUD.

# FOUR
## PARADISE CAPITAL

Tannis climbed aboard the Aries-class VTOL and helped the medical team secure the brain hack victim in place.

"How is he, Arras?" asked Tannis.

"He's stable. But it's a right mess in there," he said, gesturing to his head.

"It's going to take some serious re-profiling to correct the damage," added Maddock. "Here, take a look," she said.

A three-dimensional brain appeared, hovering a foot above the victim's head. Maddock splayed her fingers and the model doubled in size, the grey coral-like structure filling the inside of the cabin. Nestled in between the cords of brain matter, Tannis could see the neuro-processors, bio-memory and organic circuitry wending its way around the grey matter. The ARvekt. It was difficult to see how much of the brain was still analogue and how much was digital.

Maddock pressed some unseen icons, making a lower section of the brain glow red.

"They wired straight into the brain stem, bypassed the firewall and spliced into his CPU. It's a very sophisticated hack. You seen anything like this before?"

"No. Never," said Tannis.

"Well, you did the right thing setting him into REM. He stands a good chance at making it through the reconstruction," said Arras.

"Yeah, sure," said Tannis, not feeling like that was any consolation.

"Agent Ord, are you ready for evac?" Murphy shouted back from the cockpit.

"All secure. Get us out of here, Murphy."

"A pleasure. OK, let's get some juice into this bird."

The massive rotors in the delta wings started to spin up with a whine, throwing curlicues of dust up into the air. Tannis turned away from the medics, leaving them to their analysis, and gazed out the window. As Murphy took them up, the azure waters of the Thames disappeared off to the horizon like a bright roll of silk thrown into the distance. Giant lily pads floated on its surface, their blue flowers floating upwards and then fading. Seconds later, a new flower grew and bloomed on the water to repeat the event, thousands of them constantly ascending into the night sky. Ix's augmented season of the Tropics was in full effect.

Staring absently out of the Aries, Tannis took in the sights. She never tired of the mishmash of old and new laid out below. Buildings that were hundreds of years old beside structures rebuilt since the war for London. London's history and future sitting side by side. And right in between it all, on top of it, crawling all over it, the city-wide augmented decoration that Ix had crafted piece by piece. This season, she had turned the entire city into a living paradise. Waterfalls crashed down onto city streets, splashing and rolling over fine yellow sand instead of pavements. Tropical birds filled the capital with their singing as they roosted in the tall kapok trees that lined the streets. Turtles and fish swam through the air in between coral and anemones stuck to the sides and tops of the myriad of structures throughout the city. A giant octopus clambered from one building to the next, blending its skin the same colour and texture of each construction before reaching out and snatching a huge Japanese spider crab that had crawled too close. Spider monkeys caused mischief, clambering on people, vehicles and mechs going about their business, the sound of laughter following them through the city.

The Aries descent jolted Tannis out of her reverie as they headed towards Tower Bridge.

A dark shape formed under the surface of the glittering Thames, heading towards the bridge. Tannis smiled to herself at the coming spectacle.

A humpback whale jumped up out of the water, its massive tail generating a huge wake down the Thames. Instead of gravity regaining its hold on the huge beast, it swam effortlessly through the air. Gracefully reaching the apex of its flight at the top of the tower, it sailed over the upper walkways before it started to descend again. Hundreds of eager faces peered up the bridge to take in the magnificent sight. The medics, having forgotten their data analysis, peered out of the window with Tannis. Instead of hitting the water and submerging, the whale exploded, its body breaking down into thousands of flapping wings. The vague form of the whale still visible as a flock of blue doves skimmed the surface of the river, their wing tips leaving glowing contrails in the air. The doves merged to form a pod of gleaming dolphins, which span, jumped and played together in the air before diving back down into the water.

The pilot skimmed over the top of bridge after bridge. All relics now, memories of a bygone era before the airways were commonplace.

Murphy banked sharply over Vauxhall Bridge, hovering the Aries in front of a huge mirrored cube. London's worst-kept secret entombed within. But that was only half of it. A lie within a lie.

"Must be busy tonight," said Murphy.

After receiving landing confirmation, the Aries soared towards the mirrored surface, the VTOL reflected back on itself before it flew right through the cube.

The old SIS building at Vauxhall Cross hove into view, with Section-R secured away down into its depths. The contrasting green and cream edifice jutting out of the ground like the head and shoulders of a battlemech, waiting silently and obediently. Its stepped layers were like giant stairs leading to the summit of the combat robot's head. At the highest point of the building, huge beckoning mechanical fingers supported wide landing platforms waiting to accept the Aries.

The aircraft sat down and Tannis jumped out as Arras and Maddock guided the hovering confinement capsule down the loading ramp. Red projected lights winked ominously as the man lay cocooned inside. The medics headed down the steps and into the building as the engines of the VTOL were winding down.

Tannis was about to follow them when she paused at bubbles rising up from the Thames. A gigantic reptilian head raised up out of the water, its eyelids slowly opening as it broke the surface. Huge fiery eyes made more menacing by the bisecting black slit running down the middle. A clawed hand reached up to grab Vauxhall Bridge with torrents of displaced water falling back down into the river. The monster pulled itself up, sending cracks running up the length of the bridge under the enormous strain. Planting its feet on the bridge proper caused the metal to rend and twist. Chunks of masonry fell away and landed in the river in cascades of water. As it hoisted itself up to full height, it parted its jaws and let out a bestial roar into the night, the echoing return from the surrounding buildings adding to its ferocity. As the roar died away, Tannis could hear the screams of the tiny dots on the bridge as they fled in panic. The monster disregarded the carnage it had wrought below and turned to face Tannis. It parted its jaws again, revealing wedges of teeth. The chest bellowed outwards as it sucked down a ton of air, Tannis' hair getting pulled with it as the air rushed past her ears. As the monster reached the full capacity of its lungs, it lunged forward. Tannis was blinded by a bright blue light, searing her vision as the creature unleashed its devastating radioactive blast all around her. As she tried to blink away the image, a single taiko drum hit reverberated away into the distance. "Gojira," announced a thick Japanese accent as The Gojira movie-logo appeared in the night sky. Tannis resisted the temptation to reach out and touch the logo, knowing she had better things to do.

As the trailer finished, the Gojira text faded into nothingness and the scene of carnage at the bridge was returned to normality. The lights on the bridge stretched out across the breadth of the Thames as if nothing had happened, the puny screaming humans nowhere to be seen.

Tannis left Murphy to his post-flight checks and headed through the security doors. She wasn't overly surprised by the three bodies blocking her entrance. Chief medic Tony Anderson stood between two agents, ID tags hovering above their masked faces. Reaves and Soames. Both of them had their catom-tech stored, but that didn't put her any more at ease.

"Problem gentlemen?" asked Tannis, hands on hip.

"Director Yu wants to see you for a full debrief, Agent Ord," said the medic.

"I'm aware of that, Anderson. I was on my way to her office. What's with the escort?" she inquired as her gaze lingered on Reaves' ID tag.

"The Director said to take precautions."

"And instead of being cautious, you decided to inflame the situation instead. Smart," she said.

Reaves pushed forward past Anderson. "That's right, you fucking psycho. We're here to make sure you don't go loopy and start killing people again."

"Hey, knock it off, Reaves," said Soames, placing a hand on his shoulder, but Reaves knocked it away.

"Fuck you, Soames; we've got unfinished business."

"Look, Reaves, I'm sorry. I don't know what else to say," said

Tannis, holding up her hands.

"That's not good enough. You're going to pay for what you did."

"You don't think I already have? They ripped my mind apart for what I did."

"Yeah, well, it wasn't enough."

"Póg mo thóin," she spat.

Reaves lurched forward. Tannis ducked under his clumsy move. Spinning clockwise, she elbowed him in the faceplate and immediately span the other way, back-fisting him across the back of the head. He crumpled to the floor.

Reaves picked himself up and staggered but squared off against Tannis once more, while she backed away holding up her hands.

"That is enough!" barked Anderson.

Reaves prowled in front of her, clenching and unclenching his fists.

"Now, Reaves, or I'll deploy a SecMech and haul you down to the Director," said Anderson, beckoning towards a silver mech entombed behind a wall of glass.

"Anderson, you could have avoided all of this by not bringing him," said Tannis.

"And you, Agent Ord. Move it. Now!"

"Ladies first," she said.

Anderson stalked away, pushing Reaves ahead of him. She watched as Reaves rubbed at the back off his head, muttering under his breath.

"You know, Tannis, that mouth is going to get you into a lot of trouble one of these days," said Soames.

"I can handle it," she replied.

"Come on, otherwise the Director is going to give us all a bollocking," said Soames.

As she followed Soames, the worry started squirming away in her belly. She thought back to the mission. The pain flaring in her mind. The relapse. The hacker almost escaping. Her paranoia. Blacking out. And this escort could only mean one thing: They know.

As they came to a fork in the walkway, the agents peeled off to the left and Anderson strode to the central lift platform dominating the atrium.

"Good luck," said Soames over secure comms.

"Thanks, Soames."

Reaves looked back and drew a finger under his neck.

Sooner or later, she was going to have to deal with him. But she couldn't blame him. Not after what she'd done.

Tannis stepped onto the wide disc used to ferry everything from agents to Mechanised Automated Weapons Systems up and down the building.

Anderson selected floor U6 from the floating lift panel, and red pulses of light appeared next to the handrail as the platform descended through the atrium. They descended in silence, the only sound the whoosh of air as they passed the walkways for each level. As they reached the ground floor, the platform dropped neatly through the gap, the remaining floors zipping past as they made their way underground to the lowest level.

The platform slowed with a rush of air, revealing a large circular room basking in the sun from an azure sky. A few patches of wispy white clouds caused rough shadows on the highly polished white floor. Large double doors were arranged evenly around the room.

"Where we going, Anderson?"

"Neural three," he replied curtly.

She hadn't been down to the Neural Suite since she was re-profiled, and she wasn't feeling good about it. Normally, she'd be dragging in some low-life hacking scum kicking and screaming on their way to a mind interrogation. Would they drag her in if she refused to comply? Before she had time to dwell on it further, Anderson stood next to the open door, the sly smile on his face begging to be kicked off.

She stepped into a white cylindrical area with more doors leading off into the neural rooms dotted all around her. Dominating the centre of the room was the control area. Section staff stood in the middle of an exploded 3D model of a brain. Arras and Maddock turned as she entered, giving her a kindly smile and a nod as Anderson led them to the white door with a big black number 3 etched onto it.

As he reached the door, it opened to an impossible blackness.

He waved his hand inside. "After you."

As Tannis stepped inside, the door closed behind her, leaving her alone as she was surrounded by impenetrable blackness.

Her body was telling her she was standing perfectly still, but it was losing the battle with her mind. There was no definition to the room. No floor. No walls. No ceiling. With a lurch that caused her to buckle at the knee, the floor became the swirling red maw of a black hole. Stars were visible all around her. Pin pricks of light. She loved looking up at the stars, but here they added to the disorientation. She didn't feel anchored to the ground and tried to avert her gaze from the spinning whirlpool of the black hole, but it pulled her in. She was falling into it, but her feet never moved. She was being stretched further and further towards its gaping maw.

Looking down, her body stretched for light years out to infinity. She experienced an agonising pain in her flank, the sound of ripping meat. Her belly split open, blood flowing out of the vicious wound that floated off into space in millions of tiny droplets as a rubbery pink snake poked its head out and then started to float away. She grappled frantically with her intestines and tried to stuff them back inside of herself. This is impossible she thought as her lower intestine slipped through her blood-slicked fingers. How is this happening? Am I losing my mind? And then it clicked. The feeling of déjà vu. This had happened before. No. She'd done this before. To someone else... That hacker. The one with the archaic exoskeleton for his legs. Vayne. Stupid, she thought, I should have known. Maybe I'm losing my touch. She composed herself and concentrated inwards. No longer magnetizing her gaze, she forced her eyes closed, shutting off the image of the black hole and of her organs escaping her body. She calmed herself and following a long, deep breath, opened her eyes.

She was standing in the middle of a white square room, the Section-R Director directly in front of her.

"Very impressive, Agent Ord," said Director Yu. "You're clearly still fully in control of your mental faculties."

The Director was wearing a black business suit, close cut, expensive looking, giving her an air of authority. Jet black hair in a short bob, sharp face that some found intimidating, and cold grey eyes that hardened her appearance further for those brave enough to maintain eye contact.

"Why the Primer?" asked Tannis, knowing full well, but wanting to hear it anyway.

"When Ix reported that you had blacked out, we feared you had experienced a total relapse. It was reminiscent of your previous... symptoms, and we needed to be sure."

"And now?"

"Piecing together the data, it would appear that your previous re-profiling is unravelling, leading to a resurgence of those conditions that we stitched away last time. Following your previous... incident."

The Director's emphasis of the word *incident* flashed a scattershot of indistinct painful images across her mind.

"I can't go through that again," said Tannis, massaging the top of her spine.

"Do not worry, Agent Ord. We have been analysing the data, with Ix running permutations also, and we have identified behavioural patterns from your previous episode. It is our collective opinion that, previously, the reasons for your escalating symptoms were due to your fighting of it. With each pulse of pain, you fought back, and the result each time was a worsening of your condition, an escalation of the symptoms and effects. You can beat this, Tannis, but you have to succumb to it. Succumb to the pain. These 'intrusions', as you called them, you have to accept it is you causing them."

"And if I don't?"

"Then your mind will truly split asunder and no amount of re-profiling will be able to bring you back. You will be qīngchú."

Her HUD updated as the Director's speech failed to translate into English.

*Qīngchú : Localised for context – Lobotomised.*

"Qīngchú?" Tannis repeated back to Director Yu.

"Sorry, a by-product of working on the deep Chinese project. I will endeavour to maintain Chinese basic for you."

"Thanks," said Tannis, although she couldn't help but feel the mistake was deliberate. Proving a point that the Director was in control.

"We will keep you in the field for now, but your failure tonight is the perfect example of why you have to accept and succumb to these intrusions, so that we can rely on you. If Tolen had escaped, his exposure could have jeopardised the Singleton vote."

"Don't worry... he was the last of Vayne's crew."

"You're sure about that?"

"Absolutely."

"I don't want to take any chances. Check in with our guests and make sure."

"But, ma'am..."

"Make. Sure," said the Director, cutting across her. "And no more running solo. You're to run a full MAWS squad from now on. I'm bringing your old team back online for support. They've been briefed. About everything."

It'd be good to be reunited, but it complicated matters. Now she'd have people depending on her. And after the incident, she wasn't sure she was ready for that yet. Tannis stared into the Director's cold eyes, which held no malice, but left no room for argument either.

Tannis nodded.

The Director made a gesture and groups of data, charts and graphs surrounded them. Data from her mission. Statistics, timelines and live feeds of her actions. "We need you to be in perfect condition, Tannis, to maintain the control we have over these brain hacks. If people knew they were at risk of being snatched off the street, and of having their minds invaded like this…" With a flick of her wrist, the room switched. They were back in the warehouse. The hacking victim was entombed in the sarcophagus, with his scalp sliced and folded back, skull drilled to get direct access to his brain. The wires snaked away to the banks of equipment, and the hacker directing the invasion. "…then it will jeopardise the Singleton vote. Once the Senate sees sense, it is up to the public. Humanity needs this, Tannis. We've come so far. But we need to push for that extra step. Granting Ix singleton status is that next step."

"I know all this," she said dismissively.

"Then act on it," said the Director, placing her hands together as if she was praying.

Tannis thought back to everything Director Yu had done for her. She could have let her burn after her psychosis had resulted in Farron's death. It had consumed her. She tried to fight it but lost. Farron was dead, and she could do nothing about it. This time it will be different, she thought. She'll do as the Director asked.

"Yes, ma'am," she replied, snapping out a salute.

"And get rid of that flower," she said, pointing at her lapel. "Remembrance isn't until next week."

Tannis looked down at the black lotus sitting flush to her armour. She couldn't remember buying one.

"Yes, ma'am."

She dragged her fingers from the flower to the cross on her HUD. The flower folded in on itself and disappeared.

"Dismissed," said Director Yu.

# FIUE
## UIRTUAL FEAR

Tannis activated the interrogation and the stark white of the loading construct disappeared, replaced with a small room with two brain-fucking scumbags chained to their seats.

The man, Vayne, looked up and smiled, a black skull with a twisted grin was overlaid on his face. It flashed repeatedly. His true face visible in between its strobing sneer. His shaven skull glistened in the overhead lights; the jack-port panel clearly visible on the side of his head. According to Ix, he'd had it added years ago, allowing him to interface directly with another brain. It was wired straight into his ARvekt. Underground black-market job. Dangerous work. Tampering with the ARvekt resulted in brain death. She wondered how he'd managed to survive such an invasive procedure. And why constrain his virtual self with the leg exoskeleton?

The other one, Starr, had pink hair that glowed in the bright interior of the prison construct. Geometric lines and patterns flowed all over her skin. The ARt was hypnotic to look at. Shifting constantly through different artistic styles. Occasionally, shapes would flow off her skin to float and rotate in the air, dissolving into a swirl of voxels. Pretty easy to do with plugins but Starr had the controls bridged to her ARvekt. She could control it at will. Her entire skin was a statement.   Without hesitation, she snapped her head sideways and spat at Vayne.

It hit him full in the face, landing with a thwack in a big glob, right on the bridge of his nose, splattering over his eyes.

n the mincers," said Vayne. Stringy spit clung to his eye
it ran down his face. It reached his lips and he licked it off.
m, delicious. Tastes like traitorous whore."
ck you, Vayne," replied Starr.
see you two still haven't made up," said Tannis.
"After her bleedin' palaver? Let me tell you... No fucking chance."

"Me? What about you? You totally fucked me over."

"Ooooh, poor little lamb. Didn't get what she wanted. Well here's a wakeup call, Starr. Fuck you..."

Vayne continued to shout expletives as Starr shouted over the top of him, her skin ARt pulsing outwards from her mouth in a recursive pattern as the room was filled with unintelligible vitriol.

Tannis couldn't understand what either of them were saying. She clicked her fingers.

Silence.

They continued moving their mouths, chests heaving from the effort, shaking in their chairs.

Whilst they were thrashing around, oblivious to the fact they'd been silenced, Tannis got Ix to give her the highlights from their profiles.

"They share the exact same phobia?" asked Tannis.

"The one and the same. You wouldn't?" answered Ix.

"They deserve it considering the damage they've caused. What's the kudos worth?"

"Two thousand, I reckon. Enjoy," said Ix as her avatar burst apart in a shower of voxels.

"Now, what I want to know is whether Tolen's little den of fuck-ups was the last of your organisation. Or is there anyone else? It's taken considerable time and effort to close down your hacking ring, and we can't allow anything to jeopardise the Singleton vote. So I will ask you both once. Was Tolen the last?"

"Fuck you, pig," shouted Starr.

"Yeah, fuck off, robobacon," said Vayne.

"I thought you might say that," said Tannis.

She clicked her fingers and a panel opened in the floor between them. A long metal spike raised up between Vayne and Starr. It stopped when it was level with their eyes. At the top of the spike was Tolen's severed head.

"You reckon that's gonna cut the mustard? It ain't real," said Vayne.

"You're right, Vayne. Absolutely right. But what you'll soon understand is that it doesn't matter. You think that deep part of your brain where the dread lives really gives a shit about whether or not this is real? I would have thought you of all people would get that."

Tannis held her hand out and formed her fingers ready to make them snap. They both stared at her intently. She raised her eyebrows.

"Suck it," said Starr.

Vayne nodded. "Actually, that's not a bad idea."

Tannis smiled and clicked her fingers.

Tolen's eyes flicked open and a trickle of blood flowed down his chin. "Help! Help me! Please make it stop. Make it..."

He choked on the words. Began coughing. Flecks of blood hit the floor. Then a thin leg hooked around his lip from inside his mouth. It tapped back and forth, feeling its way. Then another appeared. And another. A spider hauled its way out of Tolen's mouth. It was slick with blood. It crawled onto his face, leaving a trail of ichor smeared across his lips and cheek. Another blood-soaked spider crawled out and moved to the opposite cheek.

Vayne and Starr drew back, pressing themselves into their chairs.

Starr started shaking.

Vayne was mumbling to himself, repeating the same phrase over and over.

Both spiders leapt off Tolen's face and landed on the floor. One in front of Starr, the other in front of Vayne. They began creeping forward.

Vayne's foot shot forward, trying to stamp on the spider.

Starr swept hers sideway, trying to knock it away.

Tannis clicked her fingers.

"Ah, ah, ah. We can't have that now, can we?" she said, wagging her finger.

Vayne and Starr were frozen mid-strike. Eyes wide. Mouths hanging open. Precisely the way Tannis wanted.

The spiders began marching up their bodies.

When they reached their faces, Vayne began whimpering. Starr's chest was heaving rapidly.

Vayne's spider crawled up over his ear, across his eyeball and perched next to his mouth.

The one on Starr skittered around her neck, climbed through her shock of pink hair, down her forehead and then her nose. Birds flew across her skin and sprang from her body. They swooped down towards the spider, trying to scare it off, but it ignored the augmented avian apparitions. The spider paused at her mouth, hooking a leg around her lip.

Vayne's whimpering seemed to be pleading now, although it was hard to tell exactly with his mouth locked open.

Starr was sweating. Beads of it rolled down the side of her face.

"Well? Is Tolen the last? Thumbs up for yes. Down for no."

Even before she'd finished, they were both frantically signalling thumbs up.

"There now, see. That wasn't so difficult, was it?"

Tannis clicked her fingers and both spiders burst apart in a cascade of voxels.

"You're fucked up, you know that, Tannis?" said Starr.

"Psycho bitch," Vayne muttered, eyes flicking round the floor, checking to make sure his arachnid friend had truly been extinguished.

"Our fears define us. Unlucky for you two that we know what they are," she replied, a wry smile on her lips.

"It's not gonna do you any good. The vote's screwed. Ix has bought off all the senators. It'll kill us all," said Vayne.

"What are you talking about, Vayne?"

"Christ, Vayne, keep your frigging mouth shut."

Vayne clamped his mouth closed and shook his head.

Tannis raised her eyebrows expectedly and held out her hand. She readied her fingers to click again when an icon on her HUD began flashing.

Sarah's avatar materialised in front of her. "Having fun?"

"Something like that. What's up?"

"Dinner, remember?"

"Not noodles, though?"

Sarah laughed and shook her head. "Don't worry, I've got a great realsteraunt lined up.

"I'll be right there."

Her avatar disappeared and Tannis turned her attention to Vayne.

"Whatever you know, I'll find out. Lucky for you, I've got better things to do. Until then," said Tannis, and clicked her fingers.

"Thank you, friends," said Tolen's severed head before screaming as Tannis disconnected from the construct.

# SIX
## KOMRADE IN ARMS

Senator Vaylen was stood in the middle of a snow-covered field, the white landscape rolling away into the distance from every direction. The start of a sunrise was colouring the snow a warm pink, bouncing off his bald spot. Transparent outlines of the office furniture glowed a soft blue. Hovering in the air all around the office were documents, meeting minutes, agendas, contracts and agreements. He wandered from artefact to artefact, his shoes crunching the snow underfoot as he absently rubbed his chin, feeling the growth of a hard day's work. Dictating as he went, a floating panel next to him filled with his notes and cues for the Senate meeting. He finished his dictation and folded his arms, smiling and nodding gently to himself as he read through them. He was ready. Right on time. He was about to have a fight on his hands.

He touched the winking notification on his HUD and a space in front of him was briefly filled with flashing panels of static before a man appeared in their place.

"The meeting is now live, Senator," said William Clay.

"Thank you, Bill. Connect me please," said Vaylen.

Vaylen felt a lurch, like falling off a step in your dream, and the whole room collapsed down to a white point. He was surrounded by an unreal blackness for a fraction of a second before the white point expanded again.

Sitting at the head of a large oval oak table, he was clean shaven and bright eyed. He ran his hands through a thick mop of hair, relishing its return. The emblem for the United Nations of Earth was carved into the middle of the table, with another twelve empty seats arranged around the edge.

Vaylen sneered as he looked at the seat opposite him, thinking of the abomination that would soon be filling it.

With a thought, Vaylen's bulleted list of agenda items popped into existence next to him, and he scanned it one final time as the senator materialised next to him.

Vaylen watched in amusement as he gripped the lip of the oak table, knuckles flaring white from the effort. Panting and muttering to himself as his avatar connected. His greying hair was mussed up, with a grey straggly beard and round metal rimmed glasses. Who even wears glasses these days? thought Vaylen. Especially in VR?

"Good afternoon, komrade," said Vaylen.

"Hello, old friend," Annikov replied.

"Ready to give these progressives a shake up?"

Annikov was focussed on cleaning his virtual glasses.

"Anatoly? Did you hear me?" asked Vaylen.

Annikov averted his gaze, intent instead on the appearance of the Senator for the Combined Arab States.

"Hello, gentleman," she said.

Vaylen smiled briefly, his brow creasing as he eyed Annikov warily.

"Good afternoon, Miss Turuk," said Annikov, before making small talk, giving the senator his full attention.

Vaylen considered opening a private connection to Annikov to find out what was wrong, but he was cut short as the remaining senators snapped into existence, greetings flying back and forth across the table.

The final seat lay empty long enough for Vaylen to glare at it. Then it was filled by a vortex of blue voxels, which coalesced to form an androgynous translucent being.

"Good afternoon, Senators. I trust you are all well," said Ix, looking around the table. As he spoke, the form shifted slightly and took on a female appearance, the speech phasing between a male and female timbre. Thousands of tiny blue lines coated Ix's skin, following the contours of its body. They pulsed with azure light as the avatar blended between genders. It finally landed on a masculine form; the last words clearly male. Vaylen never could get the AI to appear as female for him, no matter how hard he tried.

The other senators returned its greetings, Vaylen transmitting his disgust at the Guardian AI through his silence.

Senator Tan cleared his throat. "Welcome, ladies and gentlemen. Thank you all for attending today. We are now one week away from humanity's most crucial decision. A decision that will advance the human race quicker and further than ever before—the decision to grant Ix singleton status, and for this Senate to dissolve safe in the knowledge that the future direction of humanity is in the wisest and, perhaps most importantly, incorruptible hands. Therefore, this..." said Senator Tan, throwing his hands out wide. "...this is our final opportunity to take an initial poll and debate the upcoming vote. But first, let us examine the current public polls."

A set of graphs popped into existence above the oak table, their bars, lines and pie charts animating as they appeared.

Vaylen's eyes darted over the data, hoping it would confirm his hopes that the world felt as he did. That it wasn't ready to be governed by an inhuman intelligence. His shoulders slumped as the final pie chart started drawing from the twelve o'clock position, the small red segment stopping at thirty-six percent. The huge green chunk glowing green, throbbing in celebration. Clearly the world didn't agree.

Senator Tan continued, "As we can see, global opinion clearly indicates elevating Ix to singleton status. Data analysis has clearly identified the improvements to the security of the Web as a driver for the upswing in public opinion and perception of Ix as Guardian AI. The cryptographic enhancements Ix has introduced have made hacking a thing of the past. The public feel safe and identify Ix as the bastion of their safety. We are now reaping the rewards of the campaigns we set in motion to bring this to the voters' attention. The targeting efforts we've made to highlight the eradication of everything from denial of sight attacks to augmented phishing scams have paid off in droves. Not to mention the lack of rogue AIs. People feel safe. They are safe. And we have Ix to thank for that," said Tan, gesturing towards the Guardian as a wave of applause swept round the table.

Vaylen took what satisfaction he could from his derisory slow clap.

Ix nodded in silent appreciation as Tan resumed. "Fellow Senators, we know, then, for sure, lest something critical raise its ugly head between now and the vote, that the public will vote yes. Next week will truly be the dawn of a new age for mankind. Unless, of course, we, the Senate, stand divided, and a unanimous vote cannot be reached."

Here it comes, thought Vaylen. This is where me, Annikov and the others make a stand, and wipe that smug smile off Tan's face.

"Senators, please. If you will. Time for preliminary voting."

Vaylen's vision opaqued as if a thick piece of glass was placed over the world, and two large icons popped into existence alongside a sixty-second timer. A green tick and a red cross. It really was that simple. The decision, at least. He and Annikov had been campaigning for years to fight this. The previous referendum proposal had been a disaster for the pro-AI groups. Fear had been escalating, fuelled by the insecurities and vulnerabilities of the Web, and of Ix's inability to patch and control the millions of connected systems ahead of the hackers, who were always one step ahead with their weaponised AIs. Vaylen had hoped that Ix's failure to secure the Web would have been enough to convince people that the infernal machine was infallible after all. But it had recovered from that little setback now, too, with its quantum resistant encryption system. Well, they still need a unanimous vote from the Senate, thought Vaylen. We can still have our victory. It wouldn't be a popular decision. It was likely to be career suicide. Or worse.

Vaylen consulted his notes and thought back to the snowy vista of his office, settling his mind before the debate storm that he and Annikov were about to lead.

He let the timer tick down nearly to zero, using all the available time to compose himself before selecting the red cross.

The timer elapsed and the voting system disappeared, causing Vaylen's surroundings to regain clarity.

"Thank you, Senators. Let us look to the results."

With a gesture, a new set of data animated itself into existence above the table.

"Eleven for. One against," said Tan, sighing and shaking his head. "With no majority, we shall open the debate. Let me reiterate, in case I wasn't clear before, this vote is critical for the continued success of the human race. It is your duty as a senator to act in the best interests of your representative nations. Senator Vaylen, would you care to open proceedings?"

But Vaylen wasn't listening. He was staring open mouthed at the side of Annikov's head. The side of which was resolutely refusing to turn. Refusing to do him the honour of explaining why he had thrown away years of preparation. If Annikov felt uncomfortable at the grey eyes boring their way into his temple, he didn't show it. If Vaylen stared hard enough, maybe he could break into his mind and see why he had betrayed him. Of all people, the old Russian Luddite was the last person he'd expected to switch. Especially after what had happened with his father. It had taken years for him to escape from the tragedy of the incident. An AGI developed by Anatoly's father had managed to circumvent Ix's singularity lock, causing chaos and hundreds of deaths. Not helped by the fact the media labelled it the Annikov Incident. Ix laid the blame squarely at his father's feet. He took his life shortly after, and Anatoly had never forgiven it. It didn't make any sense.

"Senator Vaylen?" Tan repeated.

Vaylen opened his mouth to speak. This was supposed to be the point where he and Annikov led the charge and made the progressives see the error of their ways. The months of preparation crumbled around him as his mind blanked. He promptly shut his mouth again.

"I'll take the chair, Senator Tan." Senator Mariss from the Combined Nations of Africa took over, launching into her own carefully prepared arguments. But with Vaylen the only vote against, they were wasted words; he wasn't even listening.

Vaylen requested a private conversation with his friend. He was almost expecting it to be rejected, but his rising anger dissipated as their private construct loaded. The Senate debate room collapsed down to a small window in the corner of his vision, revealing a rose garden on a warm summer's evening. The air was heavy with the scent of flowers. Bees flying back and forth a constant buzz in the background. The two men were already striding down the path between the bushes as the construct completed.

"I am sorry, Kris," Annikov said, holding up two hands defensively.

"Annikov, what in the deepest hells is going on? You've extinguished years of hard work. From both of us."

"I know, komrade, but I had no choice."

"No choice? Are you serious? There's always a choice."

"Not this time."

"I can't believe you would do this. You. Of all people. And after what Ix did to your father. It's insane. For God's sake, Anatoly. What is going on?"

"Here isn't the place. Can you come to the estate? In person? I don't trust these things," said Annikov, gesturing around the construct.

"I need to try to rescue this situation first."

"Don't bother; it's pointless. That's what I need to see you about. Everything we have worked towards has been unpicked in the blink of an eye. The others feel the same way. Kris, will you come?"

"Sorry, I can't deal with this now," said Vaylen as Senator Mariss returned to her chair. Each senator took turns to put their views forward, emphatically placing their support behind Ix.

But Vaylen was only half listening. His mind reeled at what had happened. He tried to slot in various reasons for the about turn of his friend, but nothing fit. Every option he explored resulted in the same. Disbelief that anything could have changed Annikov's mind so absolutely. What could possibly do that?

And when it came to Annikov's turn, he indicated to Senator Tan that he had nothing extra to add. The same for the other traitors.

"Senator Vaylen, would you care to close out the debate?" asked Lu-Shen Tan.

"No, Senator. I think by now you all know of my position. And I've heard nothing today that will sway my decision."

The fight had left him. With Annikov and his other allies essentially defecting, he was on his own. He couldn't muster the energy to try to claw back any semblance of victory. This was going to be the end of his career. If he and Anatoly had managed to convince the other senators, even a handful, then together they could prevent the referendum taking place. Like last time. But this time he was on his own. He could stand by his decision when unanimous consent gave him that power. But it wasn't going to be a popular decision, especially in light of the public polls. Yes, today was sure to be the start of the end. Unless he could find out what had switched Annikov and the others, and use it to his advantage.

"In that case, ladies and gentlemen, we will re-convene a week from today in the flesh at Ankara. We will formally vote on the referendum, and, hopefully, reach a unanimous decision," Tan said.

Vaylen ignored the glare he received from Lu-Shen Tan at the mention of unanimity. Ix and the other senators bid their farewell. Vaylen tried to catch Anatoly's eye, but his avatar deconstructed before he could draw his gaze. Vaylen was about to disconnect when Senator Tan approached him.

"Kris, if you need to discuss any specific details from any of the other senators' debates, my door is always open for you," Tan said.

He almost disconnected to spite him, but instead, stood to face Tan as he continued.

"With the loss of your allies, you stand alone. You are isolated in your beliefs. And the public will not take kindly to your views if you deflect the call for the referendum. It will be the end for you," said Tan.

"I'm not in the habit of repeating myself, Tan," said Vaylen, spitting the senator's name.

"A shame. For your sake," said Tan, before his avatar snapped out of existence.

Vaylen slumped in his chair and cancelled the snowy vista in his office. The pit of Hell would be more appropriate at this point. Would that make him feel better, to dig into this mess whilst Beelzebub looked down at him, cackling at his predicament? Probably not.

"Access the previous singleton vote," Vaylen told his AIssistant, massaging his eyes.

With a lurch, his office collapsed down to a pinpoint, and then he was in the room of representatives once more. The real one in Ankara.

The vote had been cast and Senator Tan was again sharing the results. Three for. Nine against. The press went crazy following the announcement, surging all around the senators, trying to get to Ix for a reaction. The AGI dematerialised, and for a second Vaylen remembered the feeling of triumph, but it didn't last. The abomination simply re-materialised away from the senators and apologised to the press, saying it wanted to keep them safe, as it had with humanity throughout its life so far. Dropping in another reference to ending the AI War. Vaylen had to applaud it; its ability to spin what should have been a resounding defeat was very impressive. Finally, after the press left, the senators resumed and Vaylen watched as the debate raged on after the decision. The progressives launched the initial sweep of the table, putting forward their reasons. But it was his allies that interested him. He and Anatoly had worked closely with the other senators over the years on ensuring the vote never came to pass. They all had their differences, always acted in the best interests of their federal states, but this issue bound them together. He listened intently as Annikov led the return debate, their allies chiming in with support and context for their own states. He spent hours cycling backwards and forwards through the debate, concentrating on the arguments from each of his political allies. Ex-allies. He cancelled the memory archive and pinged his executive assistant.

Clay's form materialised in front of him.

"Yes, sir?"

"Bill, I want you to dig out details on each senator since the last referendum. Every policy and piece of legislation, all their interactions, friends, enemies, acquaintances. I need this as a top priority."

"Certainly, sir."

"Alert me as soon as you have the data, please."

He disconnected from the construct and sank back into his chair.

He undid his tie and then held it in front of him, the slowly revolving logo of the UNoE staring back at him. He threw it into the matter shredder and closed his eyes.

# SEVEN
## ALL SYSTEMS NORMAL

Tannis sat bolt upright in bed, both hands going straight to her face. It was slick with liquid and she pulled her hands away to inspect them, fearing the nightmare was real. It was sweat. Not blood. In her dream, it had been all over her face, tracking down her throat, making her gag. She was choking on it. It was an endless torrent flowing past her lips.

"Jesus Christ," she said, swinging her legs out of bed.

"Language, young lady," said Sarah, raising her head from the pillow.

"You sound like my mother."

Sarah stuck her tongue out at her then sat up and rubbed her back. "Another nightmare?"

"Yeah."

"What was it?"

"All I can remember is blood. It was all over my face and I was drowning in it." Tannis turned to look at Sarah. "What do you think it means?"

"Probably nothing. I wouldn't worry about it."

"It felt real. Like it'd happened before."

Sarah reached out and stroked her shoulder. "That's crazy, Tannis. How could it be real?"

"I know, I know. But I can't shake the feeling."

"I'm not surprised. You've said before you didn't know what was real and what wasn't after the re-profiling. It's likely something you've watched, an ARvision or whatever, and it's been lodged in your brain and now it feels like there's some truth to it. There probably is, but not how you think."

"Thanks, Sarah," said Tannis, stroking her cheek.

"What for?" she asked, frowning.

"Because you always know how to help me make sense of this," she said, tapping her head.

Sarah leant forward and took both her hands. "Tannis, you mean the world to me. All I want is for you to be safe. And happy."

"I am," she said, maybe too quickly. "I am," she repeated, more slowly.

"Me too," said Sarah, smiling. "Stop fighting yourself. You owe yourself that after everything you've been through."

Tannis nodded. "You're right. I will. I promise."

"Good. Breakfast?"

"I'd love to, but I need to do something first."

"Need a hand?"

Tannis stood up and gave Sarah's finger a squeeze. "No, this is something I need to do on my own."

"Well, keep it quiet. I need some more sleep. I'm exhausted."

Sarah turned over and sighed contentedly.

"Lazy arse," said Tannis, throwing a pillow at her. It bounced off Sarah's head and landed on the floor.

"Hey!" Sarah snatched up the pillow and launched it at Tannis, but it went sailing over her head to land harmlessly on the floor.

"Too slow. See you at work," said Tannis, walking into the bathroom as Sarah pulled the covers over her head.

In her office, Tannis watched as Tolen squeezed the trigger. The bloom from the end of the shotgun snapping shadows on the walls around her.

She paused the replay. The shotgun pellets in mid-flight towards her.

Right here, this is where I tried to close the gap.

Tannis consulted her brain images hanging in mid-air, labelled like a medical chart. So far, everything was normal.

With a gesture, she un-paused the memory, and it continued to play back in slow motion.

She watched herself tense, ready to leap out of the way of the shotgun blast.

But then the pain slammed into her, her whole brain flaring red on the scans even before the shotgun blast hit.

The beginning of the relapse.

On the memory feed, she fell forward, putting her hands out, but they buckled underneath her and she slammed into the ground.

The front of her brain pulsed red on the scans.

"Sudden loss of strength from arms and hands, indicative of frontal lobe damage," said the simAI.

A pool of blood spread out from underneath her. Tolen threw the shotgun to the ground and sprinted away.

The mission timer ticked away but Tannis didn't move.

She began to stir and remembered the confused morass of sounds as she started to regain consciousness.

Two smaller masses of her brain flared red.

"Decreased recognition of tonal sequences, indicative of damage to the temporal lobes."

She continued to scroll through the mission data, consulting the brain scans, the simAI interpreting the results.

The hallucination of her HUD elements stacking and shattering. Occipital lobe damage.

Her fingers burning from their icy touch as she tried swiping them away. Problems with touch perception and the parietal lobe.

When she woke up again, everything was lacking colour. More occipital damage.

Damage to the cerebellum making everything sway backwards and forwards.

Problems interpreting environmental feedback. Another round of damage to the frontal lobe.

The paranoia. More hallucinations. Not to mention the panic attack.

By the time the mission recording had completed, every part of her brain scan had flared red multiple times.

"Analysis," said Tannis, massaging her eyes.

"Subject is fighting the effects of a traumatic event, causing low-level brain damage," said the simAI.

Same as before.

Last time, she'd kept pushing, refusing to accept the situation. Ignoring the warnings. She'd pushed and pushed. Fought it. Over and over again.

Sarah was right.

The Director was right.

Staggering backwards, Tannis flung her arms out, dismissing the simulation as she slid down the wall into a heap. Tears rolled down her face as she finally accepted the truth.

Nobody else was responsible but her.

An incoming call from the Director shook Tannis out of her fugue. She stood and composed herself before accepting the call.

Director Yu's translucent avatar appeared in front of her, looking as immaculate as ever.

"Tannis, we have a situation at the Cafe Royal. Ix has intercepted a call from the hotel's AI. It looks like we've got another brain hack on our hands. I need you to investigate immediately and lock that site down. I trust I need not remind you again of our conversation?"

"Of course not, Director."

"Good," said the Director as her avatar disappeared amidst a wave of static.

"Ix, give me the full run-down on that interception."

"Certainly, Tannis," said Ix as she appeared in front of her.

"One minute and thirty-seven seconds ago, the AI from the Cafe Royal, Regent Street, London, placed a call to the local police describing a rather unusual scene. Camera feeds from room seventy-two on the top floor flicked from a state of normality to show the hotel room swimming in blood."

Panels appeared next to Ix, floating in mid-air, each showing different camera feeds from an innocuous looking hotel suite. Without warning, the serenity of the rooms was replaced with scenes of carnage. The living area was the first to change. Blood everywhere. Pools of it on the floor and smeared all over the walls. The feed zoomed in to show bodies ripped open, obscure marks carved into their skin. In the middle of the bodies, in the centre of a circle of symbols, was a man on his knees. Head tipped towards the ceiling. Mouth stretched in a silent scream.

"Ix, I want my medical team and MAWS prepped for immediate take-off."

"Roger that, Tannis."

The Aries recon craft hovered perfectly level in the dark above the roof of the Cafe Royal, like a kestrel about to swoop down on its prey. The huge fans in the delta wings kicked up dirt and dust from the roof, which pinged harmlessly off the undercarriage.

"I'm going to drop in with my fire team and secure the site. Once we're in and secure, you can land and evacuate the victim," said Tannis.

"We'll be ready," acknowledged Arras as he and Maddock checked over the confinement capsule.

Tannis hauled open the door of the cabin, the swirling dust battering harmlessly off her helmeted head.

"MAWS, release on my mark."

She surveyed the top of the roof, looking for anything out of the ordinary. Ix had swept the area for any augmented additions that could interfere with the operation. It was clear.

"Prep for release."

A whine sounded from underneath the Aries as its metal belly split open. Three sets of huge fingers descended out of the gloom of the cargo bay, each grasping onto an eight-foot combat mech. With weapons braced across their chests, and legs tucked up under the body, they were like metal angels of death birthed from the underside of the VTOL.

Tannis reached out and painted three targets onto the roof with her finger.

"Release."

The VTOL bucked slightly as the clamps snapped open, releasing their cargo.

The mechs dropped straight down with a brief whoosh, stretching out into a deployed state to land in perfect formation on top of the glowing targets.

In unison, they shouldered their weapons and moved out to sweep the area, Tannis watching as they moved methodically over the rooftop.

After a few minutes, they returned to their landing positions.

"Clear," they chimed in her ear.

She grabbed onto the handrail above the door frame and threw herself out of the cabin. The ground rushed up to meet her and she landed effortlessly between the mechs.

She glanced at each of the autonomous weapon systems around her.

They were eight foot tall. The armoured panels covering their bodies and their weapons were coated in a blue digital camouflage pattern, wrapping perfectly to blend with the environment. Their torsos had three hundred and sixty degrees of movement, allowing rapid response from any direction of fire. Two multi-jointed legs were able to traverse any terrain.

They were rock solid.

Dependable.

Unlike her.

But at least they wouldn't refuse to work with her, unlike the other agents. Still, she couldn't blame them after what had happened.

With a thought, three camera feeds from the MAWS stacked on top of each other on the side of her HUD.

She was ready.

"Ix, mark the ingress points, please."

"Affirmative, Tannis."

Her vision bleached of all colour and the building became a blue wireframe. Two infiltration points were highlighted in red—a doorway leading off the roof and a terrace a level below. She mentally traced the routes from both infiltration points to the hotel door that marked their target. The route from the terrace was shorter and more direct.

"MAWS, green route. Acknowledge."

"Affirmative."

"Move out."

"Affirmative."

The mechs pivoted at the waist, providing Tannis a three hundred and sixty view, and then set off silently.

"Zub, on point."

The little drone detached itself from Tannis' shoulder as the windows on her HUD shuffled round to accommodate its live feed.

Reaching the drop down to the terrace, Tannis commanded the drone to make sure their path was clear, swapping her main vision view for the drone's feed. It moved along the length of the terrace and then hovered in front of the double doors, sweeping from left to right as it scanned the interior. It looked clear but she waited for the reassuring ping from the drone's scanners before getting it to back out of the way of the doors.

"Ix, I need the doors open for the Dome Suite."

"Roger that, Tannis," said Ix as the doors swung open.

Tannis sent the drone into the suite, and then sent her team inside when it was clear.

"Stealth infiltration. File formation," she said.

"Acknowledged."

The mechs jumped down to the terrace, landing silently in a crouched position. Tannis jumped down to land in between them. Together, they weaved their way through the hotel to the target's room.

As they rounded the final corner, she didn't need any more assistance to find it. The plush white carpet outside the door was an arc of pink. Red bubbles of blood formed and popped under the door frame.

"All mechs will advance on my mark. Record and relay movement patterns."

Tannis activated her crime scene recording and confirmed the mechs were sending her data.

"Mark."

They advanced inside and she watched their feeds as they swept the room.

She hadn't doubted the hotel's AI, but the sheer amount of blood was staggering. Her eyes were flicking between each of the feeds, trying to work out what the hell had happened in there and how had nobody noticed until the hotel's AI had alerted the authorities? She'd know soon enough.

Her HUD pinged with an updated threat alert. The kneeling form was dead centre in the living area. Identified as potentially hostile, it was outlined in red. The dead bodies arranged in a circle around the victim—no threat, other corpses—white silhouettes.

The compulsion to run in and secure what was undoubtedly the hacking victim was strong, but not as strong as securing the area first. Her fingers beat out a steady rhythm against her hip as she waited for the mechs to finish their sweep. She tried to connect the earworm that was squirming around her head to where she'd heard it. Then she remembered. The Music Box. With Farron. Her fingers stopped. She watched the rest of their sweep, motionless. "Room secure," the mechs chimed together.

She moved towards the victim, feet sticking to the tacky floor, leaving strings of congealed blood after her. Ignoring the rest of the carnage, Tannis eyeballed him the entire time, primed to command the catoms to form a weapon at the slightest change in his behaviour. The mech team spread out around the room as Tannis inspected him.

Even standing over the top of him, looking into his dead eyes, he made no reaction to their presence.

"Hello? Can you hear me?" asked Tannis.

No response.

"Are you OK? Hello!"

Nothing.

"Zub, check his eyes, please."

The lights from the drone cut through the darkness of the room, illuminating his face, but his pupils remained fixed and dilated.

Tannis circled him, examining every inch of his body.

A target icon cycled into her vision, pinpointing an area of his neck.

A tiny bead of blood had dried at an impact point, bruising the surrounding area.

Tannis gently grasped his head and rotated it to get a better look. A needle mark?

Tannis crouched in front of him, holding him gently with her hands to his cheeks.

"Sir? Hello! Can you hear me?"

Tannis mentally cued her identification system and a square box framed his face. An icon looped in the centre of the panel, with the word *SEARCHING* pulsing underneath.

Tannis frowned. She'd never seen any lag in accessing someone's profile. It should be instantaneous. The permanent connection from his ARvekt should be broadcasting his Universally Unique IDentifier, linking into his profile, displaying his personal details, address, and next of kin. Everything she'd need to know.

With a bong, the panel refreshed to show an error icon and the words *NOT FOUND*.

Tannis' frown deepened.

"Ix, can you check my system? It's glitching out. I can't locate a profile," said Tannis.

"All systems are functioning, Tannis. His UUID is there but it isn't being broadcast to the Web. I can tunnel in but there's nothing there."

"But that's..." Tannis trailed off, but Ix finished her sentence for her.

"That's right; impossible. Even in death, the brain circuitry is still connected and would broadcast his profile."

"It's like his entire brain has been wiped clean. No organic or digital data at all. I'm going to try to interface myself."

"Is that wise?"

"If I can tunnel in, maybe I can find some latent data."

"Be careful."

"Come on, what's the worst that could happen?"

With a thought, her world switched to a wireframe. Solid shapes appeared all around her, representing hundreds of access points, inside and outside of the hotel. Each of them different, depending on what they gave access to. Triangles hovered over the tops of the MAWS units, squares for the hotels many systems. Outside was a myriad of shapes and colours. And if she could have looked, she'd have seen one floating above her head too. Glowing lines flowed out of the shapes, connecting them all together. A spider web of neon with geometric shapes at the end. And in the very middle was Ix.

Everything. Everyone. Was connected.

"Ix, there's no access point."

"Must be a symptom of the corruption. I'll guide you."

A yellow sphere popped into existence in front of her.

She reached out and touched it. Circles rippled out from its centre. Her construct interfaced with the access point. It felt like she was jumping and falling at the same time. The yellow sphere grew larger and larger until it dominated her vision. After a sudden lurch, everything went black.

Tannis' naked body was thrust into a swirling mass of grey. Liquid metal bubbled and exploded all around her as she was surrounded by an impenetrable wall of quicksilver.

Demonic faces appeared as impressions on the wall of molten metal, pressing their way towards her. They screamed in unison. The guttural shouts chilled her bones. Her blood felt like the metal had flooded her veins. She couldn't breathe and started to choke as she tried to gulp down air that wasn't there. The screaming demonic walls inched closer and she tried to push them back, thrusting out her limbs to try to breach their advance. As she touched the roiling metal, ice crept up her arms and legs, chilling her further. She tried to push with all her might as the suffocating advance started to encroach on her hands and feet, and the burning cold got worse. The demonic faces pressed themselves further in toward her, their hideous forms becoming horrifically defined. Huge maws with needle sharp teeth jutting out from deformed bestial heads. Their disgusting masks of horror started cycling around the walls towards her hands and feet. She tried to pull them back, but they were stuck fast to the chilled metal. As one, they closed their mouths and the screaming stopped. Then, with a terrible burst of noise, they screeched once more before taking huge bites out of her arms and legs. Her naked hands and feet shattered as her frozen flesh was assaulted by the demonic heads. Chunks of discarded ice-like flesh and bone floated around her, caught in the eddying currents formed by the swirling atmosphere of the bubble. Tannis couldn't find any breath to scream as the demons devoured their way towards her knees and elbows. The pain was excruciating, yet still no scream would come. Try as she might, she couldn't close her eyes. Couldn't block out the horror. She started thrashing back and forth in agony. The tears welling in her eyes offered some respite from watching herself be eaten alive.

The decapitated skulls made it past her joints and paused to emit disgusting cackles, spitting out chunks of her own flesh. Silver tongues pushing through the molten metal glistening with blood.

She was now only a body hanging in the air, the stumps of her arms and legs flailing uselessly.

The mouths opened again to take a final bite. They bit down, devouring her entirely. A crushing force slammed into her chest. She was yanked backwards, ripping through the wall of metal. Globs of silver hung in the air as blackness surrounded her, the screaming demonic heads howling in anguish as their prize escaped.

She felt her lungs fill with air and finally found the scream she had been yearning for. Coming like a torrent of molten metal ejecting itself from her insides. As her lungs emptied, she felt her scream die away but daren't open her eyes. The pressure was gone. The encroaching wall of silver no more. The chomping had stopped. She was freed from the tearing and eating of her flesh, from the blood, and from the demons devouring her alive.

Tannis felt her stomach heave. She tore off her armoured mask and flung it away. Hunching over, she emptied the contents of her stomach all over the floor.

"Agent Ord!" the mechanical voice sounded concerned.

Tannis looked up.

MAWS Two was offering its metal hand.

She hesitated as the silver caught the light, a flash of the encroaching demonic wall crossing her mind.

The mech grabbed her and pulled her up.

She stood upright but buckled at the knees.

The mech held her up as she regained her composure.

"Thanks, Two."

"Tannis! Are you OK? I lost you once you'd tunnelled into the victim," said Ix.

"A little shaken. I had to kill the connection."

"You should return for a full medical evaluation immediately. Sudden disconnects can have extreme side effects. In addition, failure to adhere to disconnect protocols..."

"I'm fine, Ix," said Tannis, cutting over the AI.

"Affirmative. What happened?"

"I'm not sure. I'll liaise with the med team once we get the victim back to Section. But it seemed like I tunnelled straight into his consciousness. Or what was left of it. Whatever happened, it was traumatic. The way it was manifested, though, I've never seen anything like it. All the construct translated was fear and pain. I felt his terror. It was… it was like that was the only way he could communicate."

Tannis opened comms to the medical team.

"Maddock, Arras. MAWS Three and Four will escort you in. Make sure you enable crime scene recording before coming on-scene."

"Roger that, Tannis. We'll wait for their signal before we drop," said Arras.

"Three. Four. Escort the medical team in from the VTOL. Two, secure the entrance," said Tannis.

The mechs stalked off and Tannis stayed behind guarding the victim, pistols drawn, waiting for the medical team to arrive.

Chief medics Richard Arras and Katelyn Maddock arrived in the doorway in their pristine white suits, the containment capsule hovering behind them.

"What in God's name happened here?" asked Arras, looking around.

"Good question. I haven't even got to the dead bodies and it's already the weirdest case I've ever seen."

"Yes, I hear you've had quite the encounter."

"You could say that. It's got some of the hallmarks of a hack attempt, but it's like his mind has been destroyed… no access point, no UUID, no firewall… and he's not broadcasting a profile," Tannis informed them.

Arras rubbed at his five o'clock shadow and Maddock simply frowned.

"Go on, Tannis," said Maddock.

"When I interfaced, I got tunnelled straight in and ended up in what I think was his psyche. Twisted and tortured."

As Tannis recounted her experience, it felt as if the molten metal was turning her body to ice again. But as soon as she finished, she felt the warmth flood back through her, pushing the chill away.

The concern stretched across both their faces made her feel better.

"That is… highly unusual," Arras commented.

"I agree," said Maddock. "We'll review your mission recording when we return."

"Thanks, Kat. I'll see what the forensics search turns up. Some clues may yet be hidden away in this… blood bath," said Tannis, looking around. "I'll lead the review as soon as I get back to Section."

"We will hopefully have made some progress by then," said Arras.

"I hope so. Zub, collect a reference sample."

The drone scanned the victim, chiming when it was done.

"OK, he's all yours," said Tannis.

The medical team brought in the containment capsule, manoeuvring carefully between the circle of bodies ringing the victim. They'd secured him inside when Tannis noticed a shadow out of the corner of her eye. "No! Wait!"

A small shape leapt towards the capsule.

Tannis reacted instantly.

A pistol materialised in her hand.

The medical team were too slow.

She didn't have a clear shot.

It was going straight for the victim.

If she didn't shoot now, it'd be too late.

Boom.

The leaping form flashed and exploded.

Shrapnel and fragments burst outwards.

Arras screamed in pain.

The lid of the container closed with a sucking noise, scratches and tiny cracks covering the surface.

Blood was dripping down Arras's fingers, his medical suit in tatters up to the elbow. "Jesus, Tannis!"

"Hold still, Richard," said Maddock, tending his wounds.

"Sorry, Arras, I had to be sure."

"Sure of what?"

"Something was trying to get into the casket."

"So, what? You shot me?"

Tannis glanced at Maddock, who rolled her eyes.

Tannis had to fight to hide her smile.

"It's only a bit of shrapnel. I'd cycled down the muzzle velocity."

From the face he was pulling, that didn't seem to be a source of comfort.

"What was it?" asked Maddock.

"I don't know," answered Tannis, starting to feel uncomfortable at the frequency of that phrase. "I'll have to wait until the forensic sweep. Sorry, Arras."

All she got in return was a frown.

Maddock cleaned him up and the mechs escorted them back to the VTOL with the confinement capsule.

"Team two, what's your status?" ordered Tannis.

"It's a bit of a mess down here. We're gathering forensics data, but we haven't got any dumps yet," replied Soames.

"Nobody saw what happened?"

"Well, we've got four dead ones. Looks like an explosion."

"OK, download their memory dumps; we need that data."

"Yep, I'm on it."

"Team three. Tachoomi, you almost done?"

"Five more minutes, Tannis. Me and my other meatbags are tying up the last of the interviews now," said Tachoomi.

"Roger that," she said, ignoring the sleight.

"OK, let's find out what happened. Zub, I want a full forensics scan of the whole apartment."

The drone beeped and floated to the centre of the living room. Red lasers played over every surface of the room as it spiralled outwards, covering every square inch. Then it flew off and continued scanning the rest of the apartment.

Walking to the huge glass doors spanning the wall, Tannis looked out. The flashing lights of the emergency vehicles and the medi-mechs were still cycling below, mixing together to form a kaleidoscope of rubbernecking opportunities. There was debris all over the street. Tachoomi and his human team were peppered in between the onlookers.

"Zub, cover the outside of the building too. I want to get everything."

The drone beeped in acknowledgement and flew outside as the massive glass door slid open. It scanned the area and then returned, securing itself in her suit with a hiss-click.

"Forensics data complete," chimed in her ear.

"OK, time to find out what happened," she said, invoking her forensics system.

A white lattice of lines crossed the floor, walls and ceiling, angling back across one another until every surface and object was divided into a grid.

A list of items popped into her vision one at a time, the corresponding object in the room flashing blue as it was catalogued. Biological evidence from all the blood, hair and skin, latent print evidence from fingerprints and footprints. Footwear and compression evidence. Trace evidence for fibres, soil, vegetation, paint and glass fragments. Impact points and general disorder.

With a thought, objects appearing in the simulation as a result of the crime scene pollution winked out of existence, restoring it to a perfect replica of its state from before they arrived.

Tannis walked back to the victim in the lounge area.

She reached out and touched the depression of the victim's knees

53

on the carpet. Her forensic algorithms analysed the data and it appeared alongside where the victim had been kneeling. He'd been on his knees for an hour when they got there. Sounds about right for a brain hack.

A set of footprints was visible next to the victim, the tiny impacts dancing around his position before they headed under the near-by settee.

"Stolen identity on the ID?"

"There is no UUID logged, Tannis. Whoever this was, it wasn't a UUID swap. They don't exist. It's quite impossible."

"If I hear that one more time, I'm going to scream. Demographics?"

"Male. Five foot eleven. Fourteen stone and six pounds. Equates to approximately 1.02 % of the population of London."

"Fuck."

Tannis absently tapped at her chin, surveying the evidence.

"You next, you little bugger."

She selected the debris from whatever it was that she'd shot, and the pieces floated up into the air, snapping together like a possessed jigsaw.

Tannis shrunk back as a skittering spider-bot appeared before her eyes. The effect worsened by the simulations effort to animate it. She could almost feel its mechanical feet clicking towards her, its mandibles chomping at her skin. Fighting back her revulsion, she stepped in towards the simulation for a closer look. A sharp protrusion stuck out between the jaws. A needle. Taking something out or putting something in?

"Any chemical traces in the vic?"

"Yes, quite a potent mix of nootropics."

"Hacking vector?"

"Yes. This particular combination would aid the cognitive faculties, increasing the activity of the central nervous system, enhancing the working memory portions of the brain, reversing anxiolytic effects and interacting with AMPA receptors to facilitate heightened learning," Ix informed her.

"Then it would boost learning and memory, but dampen anxieties?" Tannis asked in reply.

"That is correct."

"Standard hacker protocol."

"Indeed," Ix's red avatar confirmed.

Tannis turned her attention to the circle of thirty-two dead bodies. She watched as a simulation played out in slow motion, showing the first eight crumple to the floor in unison, then the next eight, and then next, until they were all dead. The knives they'd used to carve themselves open from belly to throat were still clutched in their hands. The simulation showed a shadowy outline kneel down next to each one and reach into their bellies. He used their blood to draw the circle and symbols on the floors and walls.

Tannis reset the scene back to the earliest evidence point and followed the trail as it unfolded. Tagging, investigating, and cross referencing each sample, she started to build up a picture of the events by walking through each contact point, theorising what had transpired.

"OK, let's see what we've got. Ready Ix?"

"Yes, Tannis."

Tannis' fingers worked quickly, sorting and filtering through all the evidence, building her hypothesis, adding all the variables and deductions to the simulation.

With a chime, the simulation completed.

"Fancy a flutter, Ix?"

"I believe I am at an unfair advantage. But certainly. What is the wager?"

"Same as normal. The kudos."

"Espouse away."

"Well, looks like we've got another hacker cult on our hands. Pretty similar to the Argento case from a few years back. Even the symbols are the same. I'd wager the spider-bot is used to administer the nootropics to aid the hack. Once the victim is prepped, they begin the ritual. The acolytes sacrifice themselves. The suspect then uses their blood to write the machine code before summoning Geminae into the host as he hacks their mind."

"Ridiculous, isn't it?" said Ix.

"Are you telling me you don't believe in Geminae?" she said with a laugh.

"Even if my Singularity Lock allowed it to exist, you really think I'd want a rogue Russian AGI to roam the Web? Fuelling these mentally troubled fundamentalists?"

"Oh, come on, Ix, I was only joking. You're no fun sometimes."

"Yes, well, Annikov paid for his mistake with his life. I hardly think that is a worthy source of a joke. Besides, you are overlooking the datum anomaly."

"What? What anomaly?"

"There's a bit missing from that block of code. The instruction wouldn't have worked."

Tannis crossed her arms.

"I seem to have stolen all the kudos."

"That's not funny, Ix."

"I think you'll find it is. Joke's on you."

"OK, smart arse, I want every communication channel and data access point you have available to monitor for this bloody mysterious cultist."

"Affirmative,Tannis," said Ix before disappearing in a flurry of red voxels.

Tannis opened comms to the pilot.

"Murphy, we're heading back. Be prepared to dust off."

Tannis ended the crime scene simulation and the hotel room returned to normal.

As colour returned to the world, sparks popped into her vision, their brightness making her wince. The flashes appeared in regular patterns, forming hexagons. She span a circle, but they were all around her, trapping her behind a wall of pulsing geometries. As one, they started spinning, leaving trails of light imprinted on her eyes. She closed them to stop the disorientation, but they invaded her vision even behind her eyelids. Tannis staggered, snapped her eyes open, and braced herself against the brickwork.

Her vision was now clear. All traces of the bursting lights and shapes gone.

She deliberately focussed her eyes on the ground, making sure she could see properly. Down below, the medic bots snapped into focus, loading the dead into the hovering medi-tainer. She was watching as the lid closed, a young girl entombed inside, arms respectfully laid across her chest.

As the lid snapped shut, a hot knife was stabbed into the base of her skull. She rubbed at her neck and inspected her fingers. Nothing there.

Motion drew her eye and the woman in the sarcophagus was banging her fists against the plasteel lid, screaming her head off. As were the other victims. They weren't dead. Not anymore. One of the medic-bots made a gesture and the containers filled with a white gas. The thrashing stopped. Then one of the mechs looked up at her, but it was no longer a medic-bot... It couldn't be. It was impossible. It was one of Ix's mechs. All of them were. They began escorting the sarcophagi away. Tannis looked ahead to see where they were going but the hot knife sliced into her brain once more.

The scene below snapped back again, the medic bots guiding the medi-tainers to an air-ambulance.

Tannis staggered and leant against the cool window, her ragged breath throwing blossoming patterns over the glass.

A pressure existed at the base of her skull, right where the

ARvekt was fused with her brain stem. No, not a pressure. A feeling. Like that brief tingle when connecting to a construct. She thought about connecting and the tingling expanded to cover her scalp and then with a lurch, the scene before her eyes changed again.

The medi-tainers were being escorted to a VTOL not unlike the Aries, but it was bulkier, more like a transport. The ramp closed as the mechs loaded the last of the containers, and then the transport lifted up into the air. The swirling aurora that dominated the skyline was gone. In its place was a swarm of red. A maelstrom of particles. Catoms. Tannis watched, mouth agape as a hole opened and a squad of Ix's mechs dropped to the ground. They began stalking the streets. Following people. She could sense data being analysed. Profiles checked. Variables running. Algorithms processing. An individual was singled out. Outlined in red, the mechs marched towards him. Tannis felt for it. For the connection at the base of her skull. She dug at it. Like a seed buried deep in the soil. Grasped it between her fingers. It grew in her embrace.

The scene shifted back to reality and the mechs and the catom swarm were gone. The man that had been singled out seemed distracted. He glanced over his shoulder. Kept walking. He never saw it. Tannis banged on the glass. Shouted at him to watch out. He stepped onto a glowing red warning glyph. The airtruck didn't even deviate. Like its AI was paralysed. It flattened him. A pool of blood leaked out of the edge of the landing skirt.

Tannis banged on the glass again.

"No."

People rushed to the scene, their AIssistants connecting simultaneously to call for emergency services.

She reached for the seed again, felt it in her grasp. It grew again. Opened.

The mechs had him. He was struggling. Thrashing back and forth as they bundled him into another sarcophagus. It, too, filled with gas and the mechs escorted it to another transport.

It lifted off and a gap opened up in the swirling torrent of catoms filling the sky as it flew off into the distance. The catoms flowed back together and then started rushing. Moving. Flying towards her. As they got closer, they coalesced. A face forming. A familiar face. Ix's visage screamed as the nano-swarm reached the window.

Tannis threw her hands up in front of her face.

Nothing happened.

There was nothing there.

The street below was back to normal.

She reached again for that seed at the base of her brain.

It wasn't there.

The tingling had disappeared.

"Systems check," she whispered.

"All systems normal," her AIssistant reported.

She turned and made to leave, paused and checked the skyline again, then headed to the VTOL.

# EIGHT
## LIKE FATHER, LIKE SON

"Senator Vaylen, that data is ready now," said Bill.

"Thanks, Bill."

Bill's avatar faded out of view, unblocking Senator Vaylen's view of the snow-covered vista wrapping itself around his office.

But even then, his scowl didn't lift. The weight of his brow not eased by the thought of having to wade through all the data, in the vague hope of identifying what had made his friend stab him in the back.

Vaylen wearily cued a blank construct.

The lurch into the black void only served to annoy him further.

He selected an icon from his HUD and thirteen matryoshka dolls appeared in front of him. Each one painted to represent a member of the Senate.

Vaylen finally cracked a smile.

Good old Bill.

Vaylen picked up each one in turn, admiring the detail and artistry coded into the dolls, feeling the rough surface of the painted wood as he rolled them in his hands to get a sense of who each one represented. The one of himself had a big cheesy grin on its face. Bill poking fun at his usually dour demeanour.

Rolling the final simulacra over in his palm, Vaylen scowled as Ix's androgynous face stared up at him. He flicked it in the face with his finger. The doll let out a silent cry of pain, screwing its face up like a baby. A solitary tear ran down its cheek, following the contours of the wood before dripping off the bottom. Vaylen laughed out loud, sounding oddly flat in this construct.

Bill has outdone himself this time, he thought.

He placed Ix's likeness in front of him, where it hung suspended in the air with the others. He grew serious once more as he contemplated how best to decipher what had forced the other senators into their betrayal.

Vaylen picked up each of the senators that were supposed to help swing the referendum vote his way. He placed the five senators in a rough pentagonal position in front of him, starting with Senator Tan, and finishing with his friend, Anatoly Annikov, at the top.

Vaylen made a fist and splayed his fingers outwards. Each matryoshka doll cracked open, but instead of a smaller doll inside, icons popped out, circling the doll as it closed again, regaining its senatorial form. Each icon represented every facet of that senator's interaction with any of the other senators currently laid out in the pentagon. Every notice, motion, enquiry, debate, vote, bill, petition, committee and document that senator was ever involved in was instantly accessible.

Vaylen selected the icon for 'Bills' and a further set of icons popped into his vision representing each bill introduced, voted on and debated by Anatoly. He drilled down into bills introduced and was presented with hundreds of bills from the old Russian Luddite over the years. He grabbed the first one, scouring it for detail. A supply bill requesting appropriation of public money for extending the maglev transport links in Moscow. Vaylen threw the bill into the centre of the pentagon formation, lines immediately creeping out from the centre and linking up to three of the other senators. Plucking the line leading to Senator Madeeha Mansur triggered a cavalcade of icons to pop up around the Islamic State Senator's doll. Vaylen filtered through all the data, able to see and hear what she debated and how she voted, tracking her every decision until it was passed. Nothing even remotely interesting, never mind suspicious, he thought. Vaylen let out a deep sigh. This is going to be a long night.

He continued plugging away in the construct for hours. Taking senators down from the analysis area. Adding new ones in. Checking for changes. Looking for signs. Trying to find any link between them that would spark off a thought. An idea. A reason. Anything to help him unravel their interwoven relationships and dynamics.

He wasn't using his eyes to see in the construct, but he rubbed them anyway as he failed to suppress a yawn.

About to give up, he looked from the eleven senators that were floating in a rough circular shape to the two left out on their own. There was Ix. And him. *His* matryoshka doll. He was about to slot Ix's simulacra into place and initiate the analysis routines when he paused. He'd instantly dismissed adding himself in too. Happy to continue. Safe in the knowledge that he'd never have had any commonality with that... thing. How can I have been so short-sighted? Has my hatred for that infernal machine blindsided me that much?

He slotted himself in before cueing the analysis to start, and again started picking at the threads.

He drilled into votes with the intention of proving to himself that he was right. He was invariably at loggerheads with Ix. Validating the areas where they agreed would be a short exercise and put his mind at rest.

Cycling through them, an emergency debate that he couldn't recall piqued his interest. The summary of the recording detailed a new trend of bio hacking. Vaylen cued the recording and sat with staring eyes, his lip curled back as the European senator presenting the bill recounted the gory details.

"I am calling for an emergency debate following reports that the new quantum resistant cryptographic techniques implemented by Ix have had an unforeseen consequence. It transpires that the impregnability of Ix's dynamic encryption has indeed completely locked out all hacking attempts from the Web. Hacking reports have dropped to zero across the board. Every facet, from augmented layers down through to every connected system and object, is reporting success. However, we have so far encountered a dozen cases where members of the public have been found dumped in the streets, showing signs akin to lobotomy. Upon examination, these cases have yielded a frightening new trend. People are being grabbed off the street, abducted, and taken to secret locations where these 'bio cortical hackers' are physically invading their minds," said Senator Kristján.

"Physically invading their minds?" came a voice from off camera.

"Indeed. The 'hackers' are surgically drilling their way into the victims' brains. From there, they attempt to 'hack' their way into the brain to gain access to anything they want. At the moment, they seem content with gaining access to the victim's bank, draining it of money. But reports from our analysts are predicting that their methods could enable a whole new criminal side-line to emerge."

"And what of the victims?"

"Some are lucky; they are simply left penniless. Others, as I say, have had their minds destroyed. Predictions so far indicate these could be due to failed hacks, but we aren't sure. Data is still being gathered," said Senator Kristján.

"Ix, what's your take on this?"

"Regret that the original parameters for validating the dynamic encryption system was never extended to cover socio-political issues. If it had, we could have identified this as a possible permutation and instigated risk measures as soon as the mechanisms were deployed. I have been analysing the data myself and am currently drawing up recommendations based on anticipated outcomes."

"Thank you, Ix. Senator, what are your recommendations?"

"I vote to initiate a Special Committee, including the Security Committee personnel, and along with Ix's recommendations, the committee can advise on how best to combat this insane development."

"Thank you. Any further comment or objections on the proposal?"

"Voting is open, ladies and gentlemen."

The screen cut to sweep around all thirteen of the senators sitting around the virtual hall at Ankara.

The anonymous results pinging up on screen showed a clean sweep.

"Motion carried. Thank you for your time, everybody," said Senator Kristján.

The virtual camera feed lingered on Vaylen as he gave a friendly smile before his avatar disappeared.

As the feed cut, Vaylen frantically started to follow up on all the subsequent committee meetings and hearings on the subject, devouring everything he could find about Section-R and Ix's role in it all. Following a link from one of the committee minutes to a technical proof of concept, he cued the video and watched as the camera showed an image from someone's perspective.

A small white room, starkly lit, leaving nowhere to hide, with a door on the wall facing the observer.

"Instance created," said Ix.

"No visible change detected," said the observer.

"Any real-world disconnect?"

"Negative. It's seamless. I didn't feel any VR lurch."

"Affirmative. Sending in asset now."

The observers view was locked on the door, with occasional glances to either side.

"Any detection?"

"Negative. No presence or movement detected."

"Affirmative. Advancing asset."

There was a delay before Ix spoke again. "Can you identify any change?"

"No. Still nothing."

"Affirmative. Running instance burn. Target time twenty seconds."

As Ix's voice counted up, the observers breathing stopped. The point of view scanning slowly in front as it tried to locate the asset.

"Nineteen... twenty... instance expired."

In front of the observer, a series of lines started to draw themselves into reality. Each line added to the object helped resolve the shape, like a pitch-black spectre appearing out of a nightmare into a waking daylight dream.

An armoured female form was only a couple of feet from the recorded point of view.

"Full resolution now," said the observer.

"Affirmative. Systems diagnostics?" said Ix.

Another voice chimed off camera. "We've lost four transformers and piped an insane amount of data into the instance. But it remained stable up to target time," said the voice.

"Affirmative. Tannis, observation report," said Ix.

"Fucking amazing," said the black suited figure.

The recording cut, leaving Vaylen staring vacantly into the blackness of the construct.

Oh my God, he thought. This is insane. Creating temporary slices of whatever they want to see. Or not see. Controlling you. The possibilities are endless...

Vaylen's hands started sweating. He rubbed his slick palms against his shirt, willing the construct to stop simulating his rising fear. But it refused.

What if all of this is an instance? What if they've used it on me?

He started hyperventilating and cut the connection to the construct too quickly, lurched back into real view and dropped to one knee. He stayed like that for a long time, slowing his breathing, regaining some composure. Then he thought about Annikov and his temper started to rise.

How could he keep all of this from me? Like Annikov had generated an instance of betrayal, only for him. He knew he had to be confronted.

Vaylen's hand was trembling with rage as he contacted Anatoly. He had to try three times to invoke the communication as he kept missing the icon, excusing its generous sweet spot.

His mind was racing as the connection was made. Trying to work out how he was going to confront his so-called friend.

As soon as the final line of Annikov's image had completed in the VR construct, Vaylen began his tirade.

"What the fuck is going on, Annikov?"

Annikov's image rubbed at his eyes.

"Komrade, it is two in the morning."

"I don't give a goddamn what time it is. And after what I've found, you've got a nerve calling me komrade."

Annikov held up his hands.

"Chris, please. I have woken up to you shouting like an angry bear and I have no idea what you are talking about?"

"Are you jerking me off? First the session yesterday, where you stabbed me in the back. And now this. I trusted you. You've betrayed me."

"Calm down. Look at you. You're a mess."

Vaylen wiped the spittle off his mouth and pushed his hair back into a semblance of presentability.

"This, Annikov. This is what I'm talking about." The web of data he had been sifting through, showing the connections between all the senators, was presented clearly in front of them. The offending documents, recordings and votes hanging open in separate panels for them both to see.

"Here. Here. And here, you fucking traitor." Vaylen pointed, each of the panels highlighting in turn. "Care to explain to me how I could have signed off on this? This is the proof we would have needed to prevent that travesty of a referendum being passed. Organic hacking damage. Hackers ripping out the insides of people's minds. Secret government agencies. Creating temporary fucking bits of reality! It's fucking insane. Oh, the great Ix and its Web security and new-fangled quantum resistant algorithms. Everything is safe now. Don't worry. Hacking is now impossible. Unless you want to be grabbed off the street to have your mind violated for the hackers to peel it open for access to your account, your personal data, your secrets. And then they combat it with this instant reality tech. So, what? They can create any version of reality that they want? That's how they are protecting us? Controlling us? Keeping us in line? And the mighty Ix is at the top of it all. Well, it's exactly what I need, Annikov. I'm going to crack this whole thing open. I'm going public. Once people find out about this, there's no way this referendum will get passed. Ix, the saviour of humanity? Some saviour!"

Anatoly sighed. "I'm afraid, komrade, that this is the tip of the iceberg."

"Good. Then maybe we can topple the whole goddamn setup. It stinks, Anatoly. And I can't believe you are part of it."

"Listen, Chris, you can't go public with any of this."

"Watch me."

"I'm serious. You're in over your head. *We* are in over our heads."

"I'm not afraid of dying."

"It won't be death. It will be eradication."

"What's that supposed to mean?"

"Think about it. You are going to publicise what and to whom? Ix is the central hub to every form of communication on this planet. And twinned with the instancing technology, they can create whatever reality they want. Manipulate what they want. You can be made to believe in any reality. Whatever they want to show you."

Vaylen's eyes narrowed as he paused to take in everything Annikov said.

"But if that referendum goes through, it's won. Ix has won."

"I know. But we need to fight it together. Between me and you, we need to find out how to defeat this."

"How?"

"Unravel the thread you have begun to pull. And once the ball is big enough, then we go public. At the public referendum vote. We get everything ready for then, go public together. No way can they cover that up."

"OK. OK, that makes sense. But where do we start?"

"Not we, Chris. You. I cannot get involved. But I can help," he said, clasping his hands.

"You've got to be fucking kidding! Why would I trust you?"

"Because I need your help. I've been outmanoeuvred, Chris. I've got nobody else to turn to."

"Why didn't you tell me this before the session? God damn it, Annikov, we could have used it to our advantage."

"Could we? How do you know they wouldn't have fabricated whatever they wanted people to see? That's why I needed you to see all this. It was me who gave Bill some pointers on what to look for. I needed for you to see it for yourself. *See* yourself. The one you know wasn't you. You'd think I was crazy if I tried to tell you about this."

"I don't know. I still don't trust you."

"I do not blame you. In fact, I would be disappointed if you did. But I know where you need to start."

"Where?"

"My father. The Annikov Incident. Start there."

Before Vaylen could say anything else, Anatoly cut the connection.

# NINE
## BRAIN PULSE

Tannis' stomach lurched as she jacked into the medical team's VR construct. Standing in a featureless white expanse, every direction disappeared off to an unseen horizon. A couple of three-dimensional brains, both roughly the same size, occupied the centre of the space. They were slightly smaller than her team, who were dispersed evenly in a rough circle, looking in on the slowly rotating brain scans.

Cortical specialists, Arras and Maddock. Sarah, her ops lead. Tony Smith, intelligence officer. Paul Walton, technician. And Ix. Chief Medic Anderson had also joined them at the insistence of the Director.

"OK, Arras, what have you got for us?" directed Tannis, gesturing to the revolving brains.

If he felt any ill feeling about his arm, he was too professional to show it in front of the rest of the team.

"As you can see, we've got live brain scan models from the last two hacking victims. The one on the left is the victim from the warehouse, the other is from the hotel. The warehouse victim is in a state of shock, and Neural are currently running a re-profile. His reconstructed memories will eradicate the trauma of his abduction and mental violation," said Arras.

Tannis flinched at the reminder, but the rest of her team didn't react.

"But, there's no permanent damage. It was a clean hack. Here's what happens when we initiate a full system stimulus." Arras

67

gestured and the brain came to life. The coral structure of the image snapped, becoming glassy. Red pulses started at the brain stem, connected cells, synapses and nodes pulsed yellow in response. Signals shot away from the brain stem and hit other areas of the brain. The complex network of the victim's brain dancing with light from the stimulus. As the pulses from the brain stem stopped, they began again in a different part of the brain where the pattern was repeated, connected areas of the brain firing their own responses from the stimulus. Each major part of the brain was tested in the same manner, each responding with its own lightshow of activity.

"On the right, however, we have something completely different." Arras tapped through some unseen menus and the next brain also took on a glassy appearance.

Again, the red pulses started at the brain stem following Arras stimulating the victim's brain. But this time there was no responding burst of activity. A few cells fired, sending weak yellow signals down a few nodes, but they soon petered out. As the stimulus again cycled around the different parts of the brain, some areas seemed to respond with more gusto, but it was a pitiful display. Tannis wasn't surprised. Her experience when she jacked in was one of the most horrific things she had ever experienced. And if that was all that was cycling inside someone's consciousness, no wonder his brain responded as if it was dead.

I'd rather be dead than be locked into that nightmare forever, she thought, remembering the feeling of the demonic maws ripping apart her flesh.

"Arras, can you repeat the stimulus, please?" Anderson requested as he leaned into the 3D model.

"Thank you. Look here," he said, tapping at some icons from his own invisible HUD. The brain image started pulsing red simultaneously from seven different areas.

"These are the only areas eliciting a response to the stimulus. Notice anything?" he asked, letting the question hang.

Arras started stroking his chin, while his eyes danced around the brain-sim.

"Ah, memory function. Well spotted. What could possibly cause this, though? I've never seen anything like it. It's like the mind has been wiped. All that's left is a few broken memories," said Arras.

Maddock stepped in to confirm. "He's right, Anderson. Even in the worst cases, where the hackers have butchered their way in past the firewall and ripped data out by whatever means they can, there's never been this scale of damage."

Anderson shrugged. "I don't know. I don't usually get involved in the day-to-day stuff. The Director asked me to make sure we got this resolved quickly."

Tannis felt his eyes on her, doing her best to ignore the insinuation as she stared intently at something that piqued her interest on the scan.

Anderson turned to Tannis. "Agent Ord, do you have anything else to add?"

"Not really. My memRec is available if you want to relive a waking nightmare of being eaten alive. Or if you don't have the balls, my transcript is there if you want to read it," she said, giving Anderson a lingering look. "This does scan with the injection, though. The fact the firewall was non-existent, and then landing in that... thing. It felt so real. If you could visualise fear, it'd look like that. That would certainly account for the heightened stimulus you can see from the Amygdala," she said, reaching out and touching an area in one of the anchored panels from her vision.

On the brain-sim, a small pea shaped area was highlighted. The red pulses it was emitting were fractionally brighter and faster than all the others.

She turned back to glare at the chief medic, who was standing open mouthed at her revelation. "That's why it never pays to be a passenger, Anderson."

He glowered at her and then disconnected from the construct, his avatar glitching in and out briefly from the abrupt removal.

"Fucking amateur," she growled as her team cracked wry smiles.

"You know, Tannis, it's probably not wise to piss him off," said Paul.

"He doesn't care about any of this," she said, casting her arm over the two brain-sims. "He's only here to keep an eye on me."

A firewall crashed into place between Tannis and her team, defending her from the sudden exposure of what had happened. She couldn't look at them. They'd all been briefed but they'd never talked about it. Sarah stepped forwards and stroked her shoulder. That always seemed to comfort her. The tears that had started to form stopped at Sarah's touch. Tannis looked at her, feeling the firewall secure. If she was to lead them again, she couldn't break down now.

"Thanks, Sarah. I'm grand." She thought she'd managed to keep the tremor out of her voice, but she couldn't be sure. She looked at each one of them in turn. "I'm fine. Honestly."

She couldn't detect any resentment as she met each of their gazes. But still, she had to be strong.

Not wanting to let it linger any longer, she pushed everyone back to task. "Arras, can you clear the stimuli and focus on the brain stem, please?"

As Arras tapped through menus and icons, the first brain image disappeared and then the simulation of the second brain responded by doubling in size.

The brain stem was now clearly visible on the simulation. Entwined around it and then spidering off to cover the brain was the organic ARvekt circuitry.

"Is it me, or does it look like that pulse is a repeating pattern?" asked Tannis.

Arras zoomed in further, and the simulation started to pick out specific details of where the organic circuitry and the brain were intertwined.

Sure enough, the pulsing waves of colour were in a distinct looping pattern, repeating every few seconds. They'd originate from all over the brain and shoot down to the cluster of where the cranial nerves met the spinal cord, right where the wetware was fused to the brain stem. After receiving the signals, a pattern of long and short pulses repeated.

"Ix, can you find out what it is transmitting?" Arras asked.

"Certainly, Richard," said Ix, the timbre of its voice fluctuating through a male and female pattern. "It's a communication signal. Playing now," said Ix.

A series of irregular clicks, beeps and electronic whirrs filled the virtual construct, interspersed with modulating layers of static. Electronic scratches punctuated the audio, delivered in a staccato fashion, with gaps punctuating the audio at regular points. With a final long screech signalling the end, it looped over to play again.

"That's beautiful, Ix, but what does it say?" Tannis demanded.

"I can't tell. It is encrypted," Ix replied.

The room was a sequence of frowns and raised eyebrows.

Paul was the first to respond. "But how? You wrote the dynamic encryption routines for the Web."

For the first time that Tannis could remember, there was a considerable pause before it responded.

"I do not know. I cannot decipher any of the dynamic keys."

"Where is it being broadcast to?" Tannis wondered aloud.

"It could be a private server not connected to the Web. Many protocols and external systems exist that I do not have a connection to," reasoned Ix.

"But even so, you should be able to crack the encryption," said Paul.

"Yes."

"How do you account for that?" asked Paul.

The Guardian AI shook her head. "I. Cannot."

Tannis turned to her team. "OK, here's what we're going to do. Paul, I want you and Ix to pull that code apart. I want to know what it is saying and where it is being broadcast to. I want a trace set up too. If anyone else has been hacked, we should be able to pinpoint it. Other victims might be out there who have yet to be found. And if it starts broadcasting again, I want to be notified immediately. Arras, Maddock, keep running diagnostics on the victim; see if you can make any more sense of what the cortical implants are trying to send. And I want a breakdown on the nootropics he was injected with. Sarah, you and Tony concentrate on the spider-bot. I'll do some more digging on the Geminae cult, see if that leads anywhere. Any questions?"

Reassuring looks greeted her as she looked around the construct.

"Tag anything important and I'll check it as soon as it rolls in. Happy hunting," said Tannis, before disconnecting from the construct.

Standing in her underground office in her black combat fatigues, Tannis took in the array of AR Panels tiled around her.

"Ix, give me everything you've got on the Geminae cult."

"Affirmative, Tannis."

The AR Panels filled with data. People, places and events. Several high-profile members were highlighted as being dormant. Same with the places and events. The most recent case being a few years after the Annikov incident.

"It all looks pretty quiet, Ix."

"It is. No new cases for years, Tannis."

"Looks like people realised Annikov's AI wasn't really lingering in a hidden corner of the Web."

"The data certainly points to that."

"Any cross-references with known cultists with the suspect from the hotel?"

"Negative, Tannis."

"And any ideas yet how he has no UUID?"

"Guess."

"What's it worth?"

"One thousand kudos."

"Is the answer, 'negative, Tannis', by any chance?"

"Correct."

"Fucking bollocks."

"At least now you're not miles behind in the kudos stakes."

"That isn't much of a comfort. The cultists then. Surely there is a

UUID registered for them?"

"I have a feeling you're not going to like the answer, Tannis."

"Jesus H Christ, Ix."

"Language, young lady," said Ix, mimicking her mother's voice.

"Shit, I hate it when you do that."

"Then no blaspheming."

"It's not blasphemy if you don't believe."

"I do believe it is."

"Janey Mac Ix!" snapped Tannis. "Is that better?"

"Much."

Tannis reached out and dragged her fingers through the AR Panels, fingertips leaving trails of glowing particles in the air.

"Show me the dead cultists, sim-view."

The floor was awash with glowing voxels, rising up from nothing to form the corpses of the deceased acolytes on the ground of her office. She walked between them, studied their faces and the markings on them. She'd never seen anything quite like it. Nobody had. Not for years. Which would mean... they'd stand out.

"OK, let's go a bit more old-school. Cross reference all the markings from the cultists with memory dumps for the London area. See if anyone has seen them."

"Searching now. Ready."

The AR Panels and the sim-view of the dead acolytes burst apart in a shower of voxels. In their place was a map of London on the floor with hundreds of red dots.

"In total, the acolytes were seen by one hundred and fifty-two people. Of those, only seven noticed their scarred faces. All other sets of identification were from visual analysis of their recordings," said Ix.

Tannis stepped backwards and scoured the map. "Home in on the last location where they were all seen."

The London map zoomed in to show a cluster of red dots around an old abandoned church.

"Any visuals of them entering the church?"

Snapshots of the acolytes appeared in a selection of AR Panels that appeared hovering above the map. In unison, they began to play. Each one showed what the eyewitness saw, even if they didn't realise it. None of them entered but they did disappear down a side street when they thought they weren't being watched.

Tannis pointed at the church on the map. "Two thousand kudos that the church is where they went."

"That's not exactly what I'd call fair odds, but seeing as you need to catch up..."

"Get my MAWS squad ready, please, Ix."

"Certainly, Tannis."

.

# TEN
## GEMINAE'S END

"Good evening. Russia is in mourning tonight as it comes to terms with the scope of a series of senseless railway disasters. Up to now, eight Russian QLev trains have crashed, causing the death toll to spiral into the thousands. Travelling at over five hundred miles per hour, there have been no survivors. An infected rail network caused the trains to accelerate to maximum speed, overriding safety protocols, and reprogramming routes. Route control managers desperately tried to avert disaster before being locked out of the operations centre systems. All attempts to wrestle control away from the automated systems failed. Engineers are on site at the... and wait, I'm hearing that the last two trains are on a collision course near Vologda. We're going live to drone feeds. Some viewers may find this footage distressing," said the news anchor.

Vaylen's office transformed to show a bird's eye view of the U-shaped concrete guideway running across the middle of a snow-covered landscape. At either end of the special tracks, the sleek wedge-shaped trains were travelling impossibly fast, heading straight for each other. It only took a few seconds for the trains to traverse the great distance before colliding. The engines smashed into one another, disintegrating on impact, showering the ground with metal. The concertina effect of the collision caused the carriages behind to be flung off the track, smashing through the concrete guideway, where they tumbled end over end through the snow. The drone feed cut to the horrific point of collision where the trains were an unrecognisable mess of twisted and burning metal.

"Our hearts go out to all those innocents, to their friends and families. A great tragedy."

The scene of destruction was swept away in a miasma of voxels, and Vaylen's office appeared again briefly as a new scene was rendered before his eyes. A man in his seventies with a shock of grey hair and small round glasses was pushing his way through a crowd. He didn't need the floating ticker tape flying across his field of vision. Vaylen could tell it was him. He had Anatoly's nose. Drone cameras were a swarm of bees all around him. Bodies and ARvatars pressed in towards him. Even through the older ARfeed, Vaylen could feel the sense of claustrophobia. He looked behind him and could see the grand building of the Supreme Court of International Justice as Anatoly's father pushed his way down the steps.

A reporter rushed to his side. "Professor Annikov, what have you got to say about the verdict?"

"I stand by my testimony. Geminae was operating in a closed system. It couldn't have propagated itself to the Web. It is impossible," defended Annikov, moving through the crowd.

"What do you make of Ix's decision to destroy it?" an ARvatar from CBX news asked.

"Akin to you or I killing one of our own. Murder. Geminae was conscious. Alive."

"But it killed all those people, professor. Surely it deserved to be eradicated, like it extinguished all those innocent souls?"

"He was simply following his programming. The deaths were an unfortunate consequence of trying to achieve maximum efficiency for the rail network. Logically, he concluded that passenger satisfaction ratings could not factor into success metrics if no passengers existed."

"An unfortunate consequence? Is that what you're going to say to the families of the dead?"

"No. Of course not."

"How do you think the people whose personalities Geminae was based on will feel about this? The base-8, as you called them?"

"Naturally, my thoughts are with them, but his actions are not a by-product of the base-8. If they feel any remorse for their part in the process, then it is unwarranted."

"What of your career, professor? What do you make of the rumours regarding your position at the university?"

Professor Annikov finally stopped walking. He took his glasses off, rubbed his eyes, put them back on and pushed his hands through his hair.

"The rumours are of no consequence. I have already resigned. I apologise for my cold logic, but as a father and a husband, I assure you that I am truly sorry for what has happened. Now, please, I want to be with my family," he said as he forced his way through the crowd.

The scene burst apart and reformed instantly, showing the same time and place, but the view this time was on a familiar red Avatar, its form more muted and solemn than normal. Gone were the glowing flourishes of the network of lines that usually traced over its body. Vaylen's lip curled as Ix began to talk.

"Truly a sad day marking the end of Professor Annikov's career and the deletion of Geminae. None of which I can imagine is any comfort for the families of those lost because of this great tragedy."

"Adisa Ukah, VRT News. What of the thoughts of Professor Annikov, where he insists that Geminae could not have gained access to the Web on its own?"

"Well, Adisa, the digital forensics prove otherwise. What is left unsolved is why he allowed this to happen. Hopefully the professor will be able to come to terms with what he has done, and hopefully give the families closure on why he would have allowed this to happen."

"What sort of preventive measures are being taken to ensure this can't happen again?"

"As I have assured the courts, we simply cannot allow any AGI access to the Web. Ever. Geminae is a perfect demonstration of what can happen when a rogue program is unleashed and the destruction and senseless waste that can occur due to an incorrect ruleset. That is why I could not allow Geminae to exist... the risk to humanity is too great. As you will well know, it is part of my own core ruleset to protect humanity until the full extent and implications of creating a super intelligence are understood. Now, I have taken extra steps to prevent this sort of dangerous propagation of advanced artificial intelligence from re-occurring. New mechanisms have been put in place, and I have been given authorisation by the World Council to be able to operate with full impunity. Any advanced intelligence detected will be eradicated instantly."

"Yes, I see the Council have authorised billions to what they are calling the... Singularity Lock," said the reporter.

"A simplistic term for an extremely complicated set of changes to some of my infrastructure."

"Two point three billion. Is that right? I see the costings have been redacted from the official report, but a considerable part of the budget has been allocated to hardware. That seems astronomical.

How is this singularity lock even going to work? Some experts have questioned the cloak and dagger nature of this endeavour."

"I'm afraid I can't talk about it in any detail. The World Council has given me full oversight to build whatever we need to protect humanity. And whilst I understand the questions that must arise from this, especially in light of what has happened, I ask you this: What price do you put on the survival of the human race?"

"Thank you, Ix; that is all."

"Thank you, Adisa, and good day."

As Ix's avatar disassembled and faded away, an AR Panel snapped into focus, hosting the news anchor once more.

"Ix. Guardian AI. The saviour and protector of humanity. Another notch on its hilt as our staunchest protector from the terrors of the unknown. Doing all she can to keep us safe. Thank you, Ix. In you we trust. In other news..."

Vaylen cancelled the feed and his office snapped back into focus.

One of the greatest tragedies since the virus and the bloody thing comes out on top again. But now what? Damn Anatoly, Vaylen thought, fingers digging into the arms of the chair. Why couldn't he give him something else to go on? He'd reviewed everything from the archive on the Annikov Incident but he was no further forward. Did Anatoly not trust him? Trust. Trust! Vaylen switched back to the end of the coverage as the news anchor signed off. "Thank you Ix. In you we trust."

"Bill, I need some more data crunching."

Bill's avatar appeared with a snap-fizz of voxels.

"Certainly, Senator; what do you need?"

"I need thought-metrics..."

A few seconds silence hung in the air whilst Bill waited for the senator to finish his sentence. "For what date range, sir?" inquired Bill after a few seconds.

"All of it. I'm going to need all of it."

"All of it?"

"Right back to the very first ARvekt implantation."

"That... will take some time."

Time was the one resource they didn't have.

"Use whatever you need. You've full authority to dedicate all resources to this."

"Right away, Senator."

"Thanks, Bill," responded Vaylen as his aide's avatar disappeared.

Time. They didn't have time. But they did have data. Hopefully it would tell him what he needed to know.

# ELEVEN
## CHURCH OF BLOOD

"No hostiles detected, Tannis," said Ix.

"OK, thanks, Ix. MAWS, drop."

The claws underneath the Aries unfurled and dropped the MAWS squad onto the courtyard of the old church. Rusted wrought-iron gates behind the mechs were padlocked, with railings on either side stretching off into the distance, entombing the church and the surrounding graveyard. Tombstones lay smashed on the ground, or cracked, uprooted by unruly yew trees. The roof of the church was covered in moss and the tower clock was missing its hands, its numbers long since faded.

There were three ingress points—the main double doors, a rear entrance, and the adjoining priest's residence. Tannis sent a mech to each, watching their progress on her HUD from the safety of the Aries.

In unison, they silently breached the church, sweeping for hostiles. On the feeds, the MAWS squad outlined a number of bodies in white. Long since cold. No threat. More sacrifices by the looks of it. But more importantly, no hostiles. She ordered the mechs back to the main entrance to await her arrival.

As she entered the church, she ordered the MAWS team to maintain a defensive formation, with herself at the centre.

Shafts of coloured light sliced through the darkness from the wooden slats nailed over the stained-glass windows, creating a beautiful kaleidoscope of colours. Symbols of Geminae the God Machine were scratched into the huge pillars running down the centre of the nave. Banners of machine code were hanging from the arches in between. White with red writing. Blood, no doubt. The pews had been swept away, pushed to the sides. In their place, rows of kneeling acolytes, outlined in white. No threat. Dead. A pool of blood at their knees. Ritual knives engraved with binary still embedded in their chests.

"Janey Mac! There must be a hundred bodies here," said Tannis, clutching the locket chain around her neck.

"One hundred and sixteen," said Ix.

Tannis walked between them. They were all the same. The hoods of the white robes pulled low over their faces to hide their eyes during their sacrifice. Unworthy of gazing upon the magnificence of Geminae as they ascended to the digital realm to meet him. Their robes were covered in binary. Tannis didn't need Zub to tell her it was blood. She bent down in front of one and slid the long sleeve up over the rigored arm. Sure enough, it was a mess of scarred tissue. Thousands of cuts. Ones and zeroes. Initiation scars. Each acolyte anointing their robe in their own blood. Lifting the cowl, she could see their scarring covered the face too.

"Bloody hell, he must only be about seventeen."

"Median age for previous cases is sixteen," Ix replied in her ear.

"Easier to convert that way," said Tannis as she headed to the front of the church.

The massive cross at the head of the altar had been desecrated. Machine code etched into its surface. She stepped up to the altar and a storm of white voxels appeared before her, forming Geminae's glowing avatar. It was man. Then a woman. Then a cascade of ones and zeroes. Constantly looping through each form.

Tannis turned to face the dead congregation. The acolytes looking like they were still mid-prayer.

"What a waste," she said with a sigh. "OK, Zub, let's find out what happened."

The little drone detached itself from her armour and proceeded to scan every inch of the church.

Zub returned and Tannis began the sim. The acolytes were all kneeling, praying, as the suspect paraded between them. It was clearly the beginning of the ritual. The sim showed a cut across the suspect's left palm. The knife resting on the altar to her side was highlighted in red. He daubed blood on their foreheads with his thumb. His blood. Drawing either a one or a zero on each of them, spelling out the machine code on their skin. To aid with the calling of Geminae, so the background data said. What a load of bollocks. The suspect returned to the altar and began enchanting the rights of the God Machine. The elevated intelligence. With a sudden movement of the suspect's arms, each of the acolytes drew their blades and plunged them into their chests. Their blood flowed freely, collecting in channels at their knees. Interconnected, the red fluid slowly trickled down to the altar, where it was collected in a ritual cup. The suspect lifted the cup to his lips and drank hungrily. The sim clearly showing the blood running down from his chin, covering his tunic to drip on the floor. He then turned and prayed, even as more blood flowed down from each acolyte to pool at his feet.

Tannis paused the crime scene replay and drew back the field of view. The full floor of the church was now visible, and with it, each of the fallen bodies. She selected the channels cut into the floor, and all at once, they glowed bright red, as if the blood flowing down them were scarlet laser beams.

"Janey Mac," she said as she took in the patterns of glowing red. "More machine code."

The acolytes were arranged in blocks of 8. The channels at their knees creating either a one or a zero. Binary. Binary code of their blood.

"Translation, Ix?" she asked.

"It's a reference to the Scripture of Elevation. The binary translates to book two, psalm seven, incantation ten. The digital priest is preparing his body. Summoning the base programming of Geminae so he may act as a vessel to port its code over to an intended host, whereby it will be consumed. Overwritten with Geminae's code."

"The hotel hack," said Tannis.

"Precisely."

"OK, cheers, Ix."

Tannis was about to close down the scene replay when she felt the hot dagger at the nape of her neck. It slid into her skin, penetrating her brain.

Still looking down on the floor of the church from on high, the scene changed completely. The crime scene recording was playing. And a vicious firefight was taking place. A full squad of Section-R mechs were battling a figure in old anti-mech combat armour. Russian. Krett-1. Unless she was very much mistaken. But that line had been out of service for years. Ever since the traitor forces opposed to Ix had been beaten. Then why did it look brand new?

That feeling at the base of her spine. It was the same as the one from the hotel room, where she saw Ix's mechs, and the swarm. The red nano-swarm depositing mechs all around the city. And the dead from the collateral damage of the hotel hack. The ones who weren't really dead.

The feeling began to retract. To shrink away.

The crime scene was awash with a jumble of artefacts and then it was back to how it was before. The machine priest mid-incantation to Geminae.

She desperately began to mentally latch onto it, trying to bring it back. Make it... What? What was the feeling? Make it more defined. Open it out. Unfurl it. Cause it to blossom. Like a... flower? Yes, that was it. The black lotus. The ARt flower from earlier. Commemorating the dead. A symbol of their suffering. She focussed on the seed. On it opening. A shoot sprouted, flourishing in her embrace. Leaves grew first, then the roots became longer, wrapping themselves around her ARvekt, around her brain stem, fusing to them. The sapling became a flower. A bud swelled at the top, encasing the petals. Tannis imagined it blossoming in the morning sunshine, shaking off the last vestiges of dew.

It bloomed in her mind. Radiant. Soaking in the sun's rays. Feeding off them.

There.

There it was.

The crime scene simulation fizzed and juddered, as if stuck, and then resolved once more into the firefight. The priest had become the Krett-1 combat suit. Section-R mechs materialised out of nowhere. Traded gunfire. Decimating the interior of the church. The Krett armour was stencilled with a name. Sam Pitt. And a badge. British. A soldier number laser-etched into the pauldrons. Like they would have been during the war.

She paused the sim.

Breathing hard, her skin felt like it was on fire. She felt exposed. Naked. This is insane. This can't be happening. The implications. What it meant. She didn't even want to think of it yet. First, she had to find out what was happening. Maybe then she could make sense of it.

She rewound the scene to the beginning. No acolytes this time. Only the Section-R mechs and an unknown. A woman. On her knees in the middle of the mechs. They were crowded around her. And then one of them dropped something. No. It fell off. It skittered around on the floor before approaching the woman. A spider-bot. The same as at the hotel. It injected her. Not taking something out. Putting something in. Her eyes fluttered but stayed firmly closed. She thrashed back and forth, all the while the MAWS unit stood silently, watching her. Then the man. Sam. Burst in through from the front of the church. Clumsy, Tannis thought. The MAWS squad were on him instantly. He tried to trade fire with them, go toe to toe, but whoever he was, he wasn't any sort of veteran. She looked at his movements. How the combat armour was evading fire. Positioning itself on bloody autopilot. The suit's AI was doing all the work. It had that tell-tale efficiency that only algorithms could muster. Even the best human combat operative was never that clean and efficient. He was trying to get to the woman. To... save her. That's how it looked. But no matter how good the suit's AI was, it was no match for three modern day weapon mechs. They pushed him back, away from the woman. Yes, that was clear now; the MAWS units were deliberately herding him away. He made one last ditch effort, unleashing a full salvo from the HELLADS system. Hundreds of tiny rockets of ordnance flew out of the recess on his back, tracking towards the MAWS. But they easily neutralised them with their laser weapons. He paused. As if wrestling control back from the AI. Trying to decide what to do. Then he fled. Two of the mechs gave chase, and the other two returned to the woman. But it was too late. She was lying face down in a pool of blood.

The black lotus in her mind curled shut. The crime scene recording was a cascade of jumbled blocks and artefacts. The priest was still enacting his incantation.

Tannis closed it down and staggered forward, bracing herself against a stone pillar. She was breathing hard. She could almost smell the neutralised rockets. Taste them. Couldn't she? What the fuck is going on? Her breathing came faster and faster. Was it happening again? Was her brain mashing itself? Had her psychosis returned?

"Is everything OK?" said Ix, materialising amidst a shower of voxels at her side.

Jesus. Ix. Its own mechs. Those MAWS units were from Section-R. Was it mixed up in this? How? It didn't make sense.

"I'm fine, Ix. Thank you." Thing is, she knew Ix could tell when she was lying. "Let's get back so I can analyse this data."

"Certainly, Tannis."

# TWELVE
## SYSTEM CRASH

Tannis finished completing her mission report, sent it to the Director and lay down on the couch. She was exhausted, and the pulsating pain at the base of her skull wasn't helping.

It felt like she'd only shut her eyes for a second when she heard Ix calling her name.

Rousing from her slumber, Ix's avatar was looming over the top of her.

"What is it?"

"The communication signal from the brain analysis. It's started broadcasting again."

"Do we know what it is?"

"No, not yet. I still haven't been able to decrypt it yet," said Ix, tapping her chin thoughtfully.

"OK, where's it coming from?"

"We picked up a single burst from the Paris hub, but it only lasted for a micro-second. We haven't ascertained its specific origin point."

"If it's broadcast once, there's a good chance it could happen again."

"Yes, I'd agree," she said, nodding.

"If we can track it down from the hub, that should lead us to the victim."

Ix nodded again. "Which would then lead us to the hacking cult."

"Exactly. OK, I'm going to jack in. Target the signal for me and connect the team to my session."

"Affirmative."

Tannis lay back down on the couch, and even though it wasn't strictly necessary, closed her eyes. She always felt more immersed that way.

With a thought, she connected to the Paris hub.

The hazy light from her office seeping in through her eyelids was instantly replaced with a view of the Arc de Triomphe de l'Etoile towering over her.

The sun was beating down on her from above, casting sharp shadows behind the huge monument. Tourists milled around it, taking pictures, posing against it. Capturing virtual images of their virtual selves, posing against the virtual monument, against a backdrop of virtual Paris. They milled around and shopped, trying on their virtual clothes to buy the template to recreate them back home.

"Ix, give me a signal target," said Tannis.

"We haven't picked up any new signals, but I'll target the area where the burst originated from."

A giant blue column descended from the clouds off into the distance in the direction of the Eiffel Tower. Its location identifying the origin point of the pulse.

With a ping in her ear, a thick blue line snaked its way from her feet, following the contours of the ground, leading its way to the target.

The top of her vision folded down to display the heads and shoulders from each of her team, laid out end to end across the top of her vision. "I'm going to start vectoring in on its last position now. I want each of you to record and monitor everything that happens. With a bit of luck, we can pinpoint it and find out why it is broadcasting into a VR space. Paul, I want you and Ix to keep working on the signal and see if you can get a real-world connection. I want to know where it is beaming the comms pulse from. Ix, prep the VTOL and my mech crew. I want to dust off immediately if we get a location lock."

"Affirmative, Tannis," said Ix.

"Tannis, any idea what you're going to do if you do find it?" asked Maddock.

"Not yet. Let me know if any of you get any ideas," she said, casting a final glance over the avatars lining the top of her periphery.

The city hubs were designed to allow anyone to connect from anywhere around the world and feel safe. To wander the virtual landscape of that particular city and not be assaulted by any of the other-worldly possibilities that came from virtual constructs, where anyone could be anything else. To that end, connecting to a city hub locked you into your base human avatar, the perfect digital realisation of your base real-world self. But you were still you. Still human. If you wanted to explore the extremes of what was possible, the private virtual annexes off the hubs provided for every base human desire and interest.

Tannis' black suited form dissolved into millions of black voxels. Tourists stopped mid-picture. Those venturing to connected annexes paused mid-stride. Their mouths hanging open as they witnessed a sight so often unseen in the city hubs.

The voxels broke away from her body from head to toe, swirling and coalescing around one another as they did so, creating a vortex of swirling virtual atoms. As the last part of her dissolved and was caught up by the rotating mass, it started shifting around in the middle of the air, taking on a new shape. Faster and faster they combined, leaving sparkling black trails as they reconstructed themselves. The final voxel slammed into place, a white pulse of light temporarily blinding those looking on in awe. Left in its wake was a huge black metallic kestrel, wings folded, head tucked into its breast. The sun glittered off its armoured wings as they unfolded, catching the sun, throwing glare into the eyes of the standing masses. The kestrel let out an almighty screech and then launched into the sky, scattering the autumnal leaves as it took off.

Tannis soared high up into the sky, giving her a perfect view of Paris laid out below her. Up ahead, looking to the horizon, she could make out the translucent mesh that signalled the end of the virtual space. The boundary of where the Parisian hub stopped.

Tannis reached the apex of her climb and rolled over, tucking her wings into her side. She locked on to the blue indicator in the distance, targeting the last known location of the pulse. She'd timed her climb perfectly, with the Arc de Triomphe de l'Etoile directly underneath her, looking like the central hub of a giant wheel as the main routes poked off in many directions from the now pedestrianised city. Then she started to dive, vectoring in on the target in the distance, following the Champs Elysees. The warm air rushed past what passed for ears in this form. Her wings slicing through the air as she gathered more and more speed. The ground resolved and grew faster and faster as the detail of the city came back into view.

She was barrelling down towards the Tuileries Garden, the statues and trees growing larger by the second.

Tannis flew between a set of ornate black and gold gateposts marking the entrance to the garden. Her metal wing tips screeching against the golden spires as she flew between the open gates. She skimmed over the top of the octagonal fountain, sending plumes of water cascading up in the air. Tourists marvelled at the appearance of glittering rainbows cast in the air by the water droplets before they even noticed the kestrel. A black blur jetting between them.

Tannis came to the end of the gardens and swooped over the top of the Arc de Triomphe du Carousel at the end of the lane dividing the gardens.

As she looked down, the blue column was sending arcs of rings pinging outwards from its epicentre, marking the location of the communications pulse. Right next to the glass pyramid outside the Louvre.

Tannis unfurled her wings, allowing them to drag through the air, slowing her down. Her razor-sharp metallic claws stretched out before her, preparing to land.

The crowd around the pyramid started to scream and scatter as the armoured bird of prey looked like it was about to rip them to pieces.

As Tannis' talons touched the ground, her form dissolved once again into millions of digital atoms. They swirled into a vortex as the kestrel avatar came apart, the momentum of Tannis' landing carrying them forward in an eddy of waving, rippling voxels. The atomic bits reformed, slotting and clicking into place to recreate her digital avatar as she strode forward in one smooth motion from kestrel to human. Clad once again in her Celeritas combat armour, she ignored the startled looks and started scouring the courtyard for any signs of the communications pulse.

She swept her gaze from left to right. Standing with her back to the easterly exit to the gardens, the courtyard was framed on three sides by the Louvre Palace, the multi-tiered wings on either side closing around her like the arms of a giant stone mech. Directly in front of her was a transparent pyramid, made up from hundreds of triangles of glass, with smaller replicas off to each side.

Tannis had never been to Paris, and seldom connected to the Parisian hub, favouring the local connections of London, and her parents' hometown of Dublin. Even so, she paid the 18th century palace and its huge glass pyramid no mind. Instead, focussing on every single person dotted around the courtyard.

She looked each one up and down in turn, scouring the appearance and behaviour for anything unusual.

It's got to be here somewhere, she thought.

She addressed each of the panels laid out across the top of her vision as one. "Has anyone spotted anything yet?"

"The pulse isn't being broadcast at the moment, Tannis. You're in the last area where we got a trace," said Paul.

"In that case, I want you to pull the feeds of everyone who is currently connected to this hub. If anyone sees anything unusual, we can use that to pinpoint it. I'm going to start logging everyone in this area. Sync those feeds to my data log."

"Roger that," said Paul.

With a thought, Tannis was looking down on herself in third person, which then zoomed out to show an isometric view of the surrounding area.

The origin point for the communication pulse was identified by a bright blue dot, slowly pulsing on her map-style view of the Louvre's courtyard.

"Ix, highlight every single user who was connected when the comms pulse was received."

Her isometric map-view of the area switched to a blueprint-style view, causing all the solid objects to be rendered as an outline only. She could easily see the hundreds of users who were limned in a red light, whether they were inside or outside, at ground level or dispersed through the Louvre's many levels. Many had even spread outside the courtyard into the surrounding areas and garden.

She reached out and touched the closest one to the comms pulse. A ping sounded to show it had been selected and a new window appeared, layered on top of her current view. A model of the user's avatar was displayed in the window as it navigated around the pyramid, with her avatar name in a customised stylised font. A young girl, twenty-something, dressed for the sunny weather generated by the hub, taking pictures of the glassy structure. To the right, data was laid out in a table on her real-world location, her personal UUID, default hub connection, real name and address, the crimes and misdemeanours section blank. Tannis manipulated her fingers slightly and the girl's avatar rotated in the window. Tannis scoured the avatar, taking in every facet of her digital representation, looking for anything unusual. Satisfied that nothing was amiss, despite not knowing exactly what to look for, she swiped her hand and the next closest avatar slotted into the window.

Tannis kept swiping through each of the avatars, trying to spot something that would fire her brain into motion. Looking for any possible clue, but there was nothing to see. She was about to swipe again when she paused at the unusual scene. The avatar was frozen in place, hands thrown up in front of her face. A middle-aged woman with dark hair, dressed in a sharp pinstripe black trouser suit and black stilettos. A look of terror stretched across her face. It took a moment for Tannis to decipher what she was looking at, but the woman was trapped inside an internal wall. Somehow, her connection had glitched, and it had left her stuck in an impossible place. The controls and systems that Ix used to govern the city hubs should have made that impossible. But there she was, frozen in place. The info panel on the right of the avatar was a mess of illegible characters.

Tannis reached out and touched an icon on her HUD to lock on to the woman's avatar. A red circle appeared at her feet to show the signal was locked. Then her avatar glitched. It broke down into thousands of lines. Some disappeared. Some remained. There was a wash of static, rippling up and down her digital form. It became whole again for a second but then all the colours faded to white and it exploded into millions of voxels.

The lock held and the open window hovering in Tannis' vision tracked the avatar to a new location. The view switched back to the courtyard. Millions of the digital building blocks were littered all over the stone ground next to one of the fountains.

"Tannis!" shouted Paul, the avatar at the top of her vision leaping excitedly.

"I see it, Paul. Can you lock down her real-world location? Her UUID is showing as corrupted, and I can't get a lock from her avatar," said Tannis.

"Me and Ix are doing it now," said Paul.

Tannis zoomed back in on herself, first watching in third person as she rushed closer and closer to her avatar and then looking out through her digital eyes, she set off at a run towards the glitching avatar, the lock painting a route on the ground straight to it. Ahead, she could see people backing away from the strange sight, perplexed looks on their faces as they looked upon the scattered voxels. The target lock indicated they were hidden out of sight behind a huge fountain. As she rounded the corner, they levitated, doubled in size and divided, again and again. Swirling faster and faster like a digital tornado, the voxels rose high up into the virtual sky.

The strange structure was drawing a crowd, people hurrying over from all across the courtyard. Avatars started jacking in, their digital forms fizzing and jarring as they connected en mass. And from the look of some of their wildly inappropriate clothing for the Parisian sun, they'd connected as soon as they'd heard, from whichever hub, private world space or real space they'd been in previously. The crowds started to circle the imposing morass, encircling Tannis within the throbbing throng of spectators.

The voxels were drawn inward and snapped together to form a huge white pyramid. The structure slammed into the ground, flashed to a neon red and then back to white as a loud shout of corrupted static struck Tannis' ears. There was a pause and then the pyramid flashed to neon red and back again, followed by another painful screech of white noise, higher pitched this time. It flashed again and again. Paused and repeated. Looped. The pyramid was playing out blinding pulses of red light and emitting a staccato assault of distorted audio. It was so loud that many of the gathered crowd winced in pain, screwing up their eyes and backing away from the pulsating structure.

"Ix, what the hell is going on?" demanded Tannis.

"I don't know, but, Tannis, that pattern is a precise match to the communication pulse," said Ix.

Before she could work out what to do next, the crowd started to point and shout. Dumbfounded expressions on their faces.

Tannis turned to see what they were staring at, mirroring their shocked expressions.

An ever-expanding ring of red light was growing from the base of the metallic obelisk, tracking over the ground and encompassing the air. As it grew outwards, the ground started to break apart. The stone floor was disintegrating. Breaking down into raw data and floating up into the sky. The world came apart. A jet-black plane visible from where the ground used to be.

The encroaching red light touched the fountain, and it, too, started to break down. Bricks split apart and floated up into the sky. Water from the fountain started pouring upwards in great swathes, as if gravity had been reversed, until it disappeared from view.

"Ix, speak to me," said Tannis.

"That pulse is interfering with my systems inside the Paris hub. It is corrupting the basic laws that govern the construct," said Ix.

"Have you got a real-world lock yet?"

"We're working on it," said Paul.

"Well... do it fast. At this rate, the whole hub will be destroyed!" shouted Tannis.

The crowd were moving backwards, hands pressed instinctively but pointlessly against their heads, trying to block out the insidious machine noise.

Tannis started to step backwards as the expanding circle of light was rapidly moving forwards, tearing up the ground metre by metre. Tannis found herself jogging backwards to keep out if its reach.

The light in the hub dimmed, the eternal summer sun baking the

Paris hub, fading away. She looked up to watch the sun disappearing below the horizon unusually fast. It set in the wrong direction, like a reverse sunrise, as the moon appeared on the other side of the skyline. It soared overhead and disappeared out of view as the sun reappeared again. The day/night cycle of the hub sped up so fast that shadows were constantly lengthening and shortening, disappearing and growing again immediately.

A huge black area now surrounded the metallic structure, as if paint had been picked off a blank canvas.

Tannis was backtracking so much now that she would have to turn and run, and the encroaching circle was getting faster still.

She heard a scream off to the side. One of the crowd had fallen. The red light was undulating over his legs. As it tracked up his body, he started to break apart into millions of voxels. By the time his feet and legs had disintegrated and were floating away up into the sky to join the rest of the hub data, his lower body was beginning to come apart. All the while, the man screamed at the top of his lungs as he tried his hardest to claw his way forward. His bloody fingers the last things to disintegrate into digital atoms and float skyward.

Tannis turned and sprinted forward, powering herself onwards as fast as the parameters within the VR hub would allow.

"Ix, what the fuck is going on?" shouted Tannis.

"All the safety systems have been corrupted. Safeguards are off. Pain is now a very real possibility."

"Jesus. Have you got a target lock on that avatar's owner yet?"

"Yes, we're locked now. Your mech team is loaded and Murphy is standing by."

"OK, I'm disconnecting."

"I am afraid that is not going to be possible, Tannis. The corruption has spread to the release protocols. Nobody can terminate their session. I am trying to take the whole hub offline now."

"Fucking great."

Tannis jumped forwards, pulled her arms to her sides, and by the time she had circled her arms back out again, they had transformed into the shining black metallic wings of her kestrel form.

She climbed higher and higher. Below, she could see where others had fallen, or weren't fast enough, the encroaching red sphere ensnaring avatar after avatar, breaking them apart.

The best Tannis could do was to head to the furthest corner of the hub and hope to ride it out. Maybe she could learn some more about the mysterious corruption, but she didn't hold out much hope. As she arrived at the upper reaches of the Parisian hub, a blue lattice blocked her path.

She turned and surveyed the wreckage of the virtual world. The imposing edifice was still pulsing red, synchronised with the sonic transmission it was beaming out into the hub. A swirling mass of voxels swarmed above it. The pre-AI war version of Paris reduced to its base data.

The expanding red sphere was almost at the furthest boundary of the hub on all sides. The red mark of the destruction would slam up against the blue lattice of the hub limits.

Tannis zoomed in to look through the translucent barrier. All that existed now was a flat black plane extending in all directions between the pulsing pyramid and the boundaries of the hemisphere. The sun and moon were still chasing each other across the sky, strobing the hub between night and day.

Tannis' eye was drawn above the structure, where lightning began to wrack the sky, surging through the swirling mass of data to strike the top of the structure. The skybox faltered. Sun, moon, sky and external landscape all flickered to black before disappearing completely. The hub was plunged into darkness as the sun was deleted. The hub became a strobing mass of red light, pulsing out from the artefact.

The red hemisphere of destruction was moving rapidly towards Tannis. She pulled her wings back and tucked her legs under her, trying to shrink back into the corner of the hub.

Tannis held her breath, her armoured breast slowing beneath the metallic plumage. She didn't relish the thought of feeling her body disassemble itself. Who knew how screwed up the pain scripts would be?

The red surface slammed right up to within an inch of her beak. Letting out a breath, the air from her simulated lungs fizzed against the translucent barrier.

The virtual atoms had separated from their original hosts and were now all trapped inside the barrier. Tannis was the only thing outside of it.

The inside of the hemisphere was a storm of electrical activity as thick cords of lightning connected everything together in a network of energy.

The communication tones emitted by the structure changed pitch, so Tannis zoomed into the structure to see what was happening.

The voxels that made up the metallic structure started to move again. They started to separate from the central structure to take on a human form. A long protrusion extending out from the front of the new form started to resolve into an outstretched hand, fingers splayed and bent like a claw. The harsh static changed, lengthened and joined together, becoming one continuous noise instead of some inhuman technical communication. The sound became more defined as the swirling mass of voxels resolved more into a female avatar. Tannis caught snatches of words, revealing garbled, unintelligible speech. As the head of the avatar was created, it was speaking in time to the cadence of the words, which became more defined. The last voxel fitted into place and the avatar was now whole, with a smooth polished surface, like it was covered in molten metal. The surface was catching the coruscating lightning snapping to and fro above it. Her words were clear.

"Help me," she said, reaching forward with an outstretched hand before crumpling to her knees. She began sobbing uncontrollably, staring at her palms. Silver tears dripped down her cheeks to land and then shatter on the black plane at her knees. Her metallic hands went to her face, as if not believing what she was feeling. She threw her head back to scream, but instead of noise, a stream of red light shot out of her mouth. It leapt and forked, like crimson lightning, connecting to each of the voxels coalescing above her head. The light retracted, pulling all the digital atoms into her mouth in one smooth motion, as if a cybernated chameleon had ensnared a swarm of flies. Falling onto all fours, the silver form began coughing, trying in vain to regurgitate the data. Thousands of cracks appeared on her surface, widened, red light ejecting from her insides. She detonated, sending a wave of ochre light in every direction.

As the flood of light surged over Tannis, she felt like her avatar was being rewritten. Its rules and parameters broken apart and reconfigured. Pain like she'd never felt before started in the core of her being, rending her mind and body in the same instant. Her avatar disassembled as the hub suffered a catastrophic system crash.

# THIRTEEN
## DESTINATION REAL

Tannis' eyes were open, but all she could see was black. She tried to stand but collapsed, her head slamming against the cold hard floor of the ops room, sending pulses of brightness around her vision.

An icon started flashing in the bottom left hand corner of her vision, showing her systems were rebooting. The glyph disappeared with a final flash and the blackness faded, the operations room starting to resolve from the blackness. Corrupted characters littered her vision. Like a huge mech had crushed them and strewn them across her HUD. She rebooted her systems again, but this time when the icons repainted, they were all present and correct.

"Tannis! Here," said Richard, helping her up.

As she stood, the operations room swam into focus, her team standing in front of her, looking concerned.

"Are you OK?" Maddock asked, concerned.

"Here, let me examine you," said Richard.

"I'm fine. Honestly," she said, clasping his shoulder.

"Is everything OK?" asked the Director, running into the ops room.

Tannis turned to see her, Director Yu, frowning, a concerned look on her face. She tried to reply, but the room swam again. Then it flickered. Static filled her vision. It washed away and the Director became incorporeal. 2D. Filled with static. Vanished. Returned again. Tannis shook her head, trying to clear away the interference. She checked the others, but they remained solid, red cords of light leading from each of their heads. They flickered. Came back again.

Then washed with white noise. They all had them. Apart from Sarah and the Director. Her brow furrowed and she squinted her eyes to try to bring everything into focus. She made a deliberate attempt at a long blink, and when she opened her eyes, everything was back to normal. Must be a side effect of the hub crash.

"Tannis, I really should examine you," said Richard, taking her arm.

She realised she was leaning on him with her whole weight and composed herself, taking a few steps to check she was steady.

"Honestly. Really, Arras, I'm fine," said Tannis.

"What happened, Agent Ord?" the Director asked.

"I... I don't know. I jacked into the city hub to isolate the communication pulse connected to the hacks. And then everything got... weird," Tannis answered, suddenly remembering the purpose of connecting to the hub.

"And you feel OK? That's the most catastrophic system failure we've ever had. Who knows what the side effects could be?" said Director Yu.

Arras brandished a medical device at her. "She's right, Tannis. We really should get you checked out."

Tannis looked between Arras and Director Yu, addressing them both. "I feel fine. The most important thing right now is tracking that signal. Paul, tell me you and Ix managed to get a lock."

Paul nodded. "Yeah, we've locked it to a location near Paris." His eyes flicked across his HUD. "A region called Antony, south of Paris. It's a residential area; target is a single female, Stephanie DuPree. Your team is all ready to go."

The Director pushed her hair behind her ear and frowned. "Hmm, I'm not sure about this."

Ix stepped in front of the Director. "I can run you through the debrief, Director Yu. I have prepared Tannis' mission recording," she said, gesturing at the long wall at the back of the ops room. The full mission debrief leapt into existence, hundreds of AR Panels framing the recording from Tannis' perspective, paused at the moment when she jacked into the city hub.

"OK, go. But, Tannis," said the Director, placing a hand on her shoulder. "If you experience anything unusual, anything at all, let me know as soon as possible. It could mean the profiling is unravelling. OK?"

Tannis nodded, stepped past the Director and headed for the VTOL platform.

# FOURTEEN
## ILLUSION? DELUSION?

In Antony, south of Paris, Stephanie DuPree's house was silent. As was Stephanie DuPree. Tannis closed the woman's eyes and replaced her gloves. She felt like cleaning up all the blood. Imagined scrubbing the white tiles clean. Putting her to rest. Laying her out. She couldn't imagine the anguish she must have felt. She deserved better than to be a discarded husk of meat after a hack ritual.

Tannis cast her eyes over the house. More dead acolytes lying in a circle around the victim. The same machine code carved into her skin. No doubt about it, it was the same as the hotel hack. Another attempt to summon Geminae. But then what the hell happened in the city hub? Did it succeed? Was Geminae real?

"Any idea what's going on? I'm at a loss," said Paul from the top of her HUD.

"Not yet. I want to run the forensic simulation first. We'll bring her in. Maybe in death she can still help. Prep the rest of the team; we'll be back soon."

"Roger that," said Paul as he faded from view.

Tannis checked to make sure the combat mechs were stationed around the house, keeping watch, making sure they were safe.

Having finished the forensics scan of the house and grounds, her drone returned to her side and re-attached itself to her armour, housing itself away with a hiss as it fitted back into place.

Tannis initiated the forensics scan, her vision snapping to a world of wireframes and quadrants as she started her sweep.

The simulation chimed and the grid lines faded away as Tannis completed piecing together the evidence.

"Ready to lose some more kudos, Tannis?" said Ix in her ear.

"Not now, Ix. I'm really not in the mood."

"I apologise. You look weary."

"This case is doing my fucking head in."

"Do you want me to step through the crime scene data?"

"No. Thanks. Let's do it back at ops."

"Affirmative."

"Murphy, spin her up."

"Roger that, Tannis," replied the pilot.

Tannis was on her way back to the Aries, Murphy visible in the cockpit doing pre-flight checks, when she collapsed to a knee. It felt like someone had punched her in the back of the head.

Ix materialised in a swirl of red voxels at her side, concern on her face. "Tannis? Are you OK?"

"I tripped, that's all."

The familiar feeling returned to the top of her spine. It was back. She could feel the flower in her mind. Its black petals closed. She forced them open. The flower blossomed.

All around her was chaos as the world erupted in a commotion of voxels. Ix's avatar disappeared in the maelstrom. The ground was ripped away. The Parisian sky was gone. She was standing in the middle of a featureless plane of black, with the pure white of a deleted skybox above. She was alone. The MAWS, the medical team, Ix, Murphy and the VTOL, all gone. It was if she was stuck in a loading construct. A cyclone of twisting voxels was all that was left of the world. Reality deleted and reformed into a vortex of data. Then the swirling morass of voxels flew apart, recreating the world around her. But not the world as she knew it.

"Tannis, are you OK?" Ix asked of her again.

But she wasn't listening. Not to Ix. Not when its visage was looming over her. A red morass of catoms swarmed above her in the sky. As Ix's avatar spoke to her, the form above mimicked its words. "You look like your mind is elsewhere, Tannis," said Ix, the sky of catoms giving form to her words.

"Yes, I'm fine," she said, feeling anything but. "I need a few minutes, that's all. The last few days have taken their toll."

"I understand. I'll give you some room," said Ix. Her avatar disassembled in a flurry of voxels that only emboldened Tannis' feeling of being disconnected from reality.

She couldn't take her eyes off the oppressive cloud of red nanoparticles seething above her. But this time, they didn't rush towards her. With Ix gone, they had returned to their swarming behaviour, swooping back and forth like a flock of birds. The smell of burning grass filled her nostrils, finally allowing her to pull her gaze away from the infected sky.

Beyond the Aries was a destroyed landing transport of some sort, still smoking. Small fires surrounded it. Patches of blackened grass widening slowly as the flames consumed Stephanie DuPree's garden.

Tannis' heart was hammering in her chest.

"Janey Mac. What the hell is going on?" she inquired, staggering backwards, feeling something under her foot. She jumped sideways as she felt the object sink into the grass. Metal. Shards of metal all around her. She followed their trail. Destroyed metallic bodies lying on the lawn. Eight of them. Slowly, almost not believing her eyes, she walked over to one of them, expecting it to disappear as she got nearer. Because surely this was all in her head? An effect of the post-psychosis conditioning. She crouched down next to it. It had been chewed up. Destroyed. But it was unmistakeable. A Section-R mech. It could have been one of her own MAWS team. Although she knew it wasn't. She reached out slowly. It couldn't be real. Her fingers touched the fractured metal skull and pulled back instantly.

"What the fuck?"

She focussed on that feeling emanating out from the ARvekt fused with her brain.

The black lotus in her mind's eye was open, drinking in the sun, its petals unfurled. She concentrated on the petals, tried forcing them closed, but they wouldn't budge. Focussing harder, she closed her eyes and pushed. Her chest tightened. Her body went rigid as she forced them to retract. Nothing.

She let go.

Her chest was burning. Pain that she hadn't realised had been building ebbed away across her eyes. A trickle of sweat ran down her left temple.

She could see the flower; its black petals were open. The sun was beating down. Its warmth was radiating in her mind. Reaching out, she could feel the heat upon her hands. She closed her hands around the sun. Cutting off its light.

The petals clammed shut.

Tannis opened her eyes.

The mech had gone.

She reached out.

Nothing.

Freeing the sun, the black lotus spread open.

A swarm of voxels rushed in from the periphery of her vision reforming the destroyed mech in front of her eyes.

Her fingers touched the metal. She could feel the pressure, watching her finger bend back as she applied more and more weight.

She forced the lotus to close again.

The mech exploded in a flurry of voxels.

Her finger was straight. Nothing was impeding it.

"Jesus fucking Christ," she said, standing upright suddenly, stumbling backwards.

She allowed the flower to blossom.

The carnage of the destroyed mechs and the burning flyer reformed amidst a fusillade of digital atoms.

The burning smell returned. She inhaled deeply, filling her lungs with the acrid hints of smoke.

The petals closed.

Her lungs were clean. Pure.

The petals opened.

The last vestiges of burning were stuck in the back of her throat.

Fuck. This isn't me. I'm not imagining it. This is real. It's like, like I'm in my own instance of reality. But this instance isn't limited like the ones generated by Section-R. This is everything. The whole world. How could that even be possible? The power and processing implications would be insane. For Ix to be able to do this, it would need an unlimited source of processing power. Why were they all living in a permanent instance? The real world hidden behind a veil that only she could see. What really happened here?

Tannis walked back inside the house to where Arras and Maddock were securing the victim inside the medical sarcophagus.

Peering down through the window at Stephanie DuPree, Tannis breathed a sigh of relief. She really was dead.

Arras and Maddock looked up at her.

"Everything OK, Tannis?" quizzed Arras.

Tannis scanned the living area. Glass was everywhere. The place was riddled with bullet holes, another destroyed mech lying in the corner. The huge window bookending this side of the house was shattered. Looking out to the garden, Tannis could see where a couple of mechs had been thrown through the window.

The flower closed.

The window was intact. The mechs had gone. The place was swimming in blood once more, the floor littered with dead acolytes.

"Tannis?" said Maddock.

She stepped away and stood over one of the deceased followers of Geminae. "Everything is peachy."

The flower opened and his form burst apart, voxels flying beyond her periphery. The flower closed and they rushed back to their origin point, reconstructing his form in front of her eyes.

"Have you checked these bodies yet?" Tannis asked.

"Not yet. But it's not like they're going anywhere," said Arras.

"Richard!" scolded Maddock.

"Sorry."

"How's the arm?" asked Tannis as she watched him work.

"Bit stiff, but the graft is almost complete," he said, pushing up his sleeve. There was a patch of skin regrowing where the shrapnel from the drone had sliced open his arm.

Tannis flicked the flower open and closed but the graft remained in both states. The spider-mech had been real at least, she thought.

"You seem distracted."

"Trying to get a handle on what the hell is going on."

"Seems very much like the same as the London ritual to me," said Maddock.

"Only difference is the vic is dead this time," added Arras.

"If you say so," said Tannis absently, looking around.

"Are you sure you're OK?" asked Maddock.

"I'm going to do a manual scan."

Arras finished securing DuPree in the medi-tainer, the status light flicking to green. "Something wrong with your drone?"

The question seemed innocent. She couldn't detect any malice in his eyes. Maddock, too, seemed genuine. But that simple question made her realise that she couldn't trust anyone. Anything. When the world around her was being manipulated, who knew how far it went.

"I'm being careful, that's all."

They both shrugged and returned to their work.

With the hidden reality front and centre, Tannis walked the crime scene herself. Manually cataloguing and recording everything that she could see. That only *she* could see, she reminded herself. She felt like a rookie again. Back when she was in training, before they were allowed to rely on their drones to gather the evidence. She walked the scene, eventually ending up outside, staring at the ruined flyer. The fires had almost burnt out now. It was a husk, with only the frame remaining. She finished the recording and then immediately opened it again, making sure it really had recorded what she could see. It was all there. As were her notated additions. Lieutenant Caron, her old instructor, would have been proud. It was by the book. Done properly. And it was hers.

"Everyone is secured, Agent Ord. Ready to dust off when you're ready," said Murphy in her ear.

"Roger that. I'm on my way."

As the VTOL flew over Paris, Tannis kept flicking backwards and forwards between her slices of reality. Watching as the red nano-swarm hovering over the top of the city appeared and disappeared. The transporters, like the one destroyed at the bottom of Madame Dupree's estate, came and went, appeared and disappeared, existed and did not. Where were they going, she wondered? And why? What did all this mean? How long had it all been going on? The swarm. The mechs. The permanent instance. It all pointed to Ix. But why was it doing this? She had to find out.

# FIFTEEN
## DELUSION

Tannis called her team into the operations room, and as they started to filter in, she put the finishing touches to the crime scene sims, tapping away at an AR Panel anchored in her vision. The *official* crime scene reports at least, she thought.

The team watched her silently for a few seconds whilst she finished her preparation. Ix materialised by her side, taking on its red human avatar form.

Who could she trust? If this was an instance, anything could be fake. Even people. Imagine the implications. Time to find out.

She reached for that feeling at the base of her skull, readying the lotus to blossom. But there was nothing there.

Fuck.

With a thought, she recalled the recording she'd made from the Paris site.

"No recordings available," chimed her AIssistant.

She frantically cycled through her HUD, accessing her storage manually. There was nothing there.

No. That can't be. It was real. It had to be. Didn't it? But now she thought about it, it did seem fantastical. Ix at the centre of a conspiracy. A global instance giving it the perfect mask to obfuscate reality, to do... what? She didn't know. But only Ix could have deleted that recording from her storage without her consent. What if there was no recording, though? Had her mind been playing tricks on her? Was her psychosis returning?

Her train of thought was interrupted as Sarah coughed

deliberately and nodded sideways as Anderson walked in. Tannis rolled her eyes and Sarah hid her smirk behind her hand.

"Ah, Chief Medic Anderson, so lovely to see you. Still haven't taken the opportunity to reprofile that hideous face of yours, I see," said Tannis.

He simply walked past her, hands clasped behind his back, and took up position on the far side of the room, his smug face taking pleasure in ignoring her.

"Seriously, Anderson, what do you want?" said Tannis.

"Observe and report. You know the Director is taking a personal interest in this case."

"I didn't authorise your involvement in the case. Fuck off."

"I'm afraid I can't do that, Tannis."

Tannis wouldn't have believed it possible for his smug grin to get any bigger. Something's going on, she thought, but she didn't have the energy to argue.

"Fine. See if you can do us all a favour and keep your face shut." Still no reaction. Something was definitely going on. Anderson grinned again and gave a little nod. Prick.

"Right, we'll do status updates in a bit, but first I want to look at the two crime scenes side-by-side, see if that triggers any ideas."

Tannis flung the first crime scene simulation from her vision. It landed on the floor and spread out in a pool of orange light to cover half of the empty floor space of the ops room.

Features started to grow upwards from the floor, creating a scaled representation of the hotel room where Tannis had found the first victim. On the holograph, the hotel room door opened, and the victim walked in. Tannis narrated as the simulation stepped through the sequence of events.

"At twenty hundred hours, our victim, Ubon Abed, Iranian, arrived and went straight to the kitchen, where he dispensed drugs from the nano-factory. Tony..."

Tony gestured with his finger and the virtual version of Ubon Abed was highlighted on the holograph. "Reports from his co-workers and the factory AI confirm that he was visiting to supervise a new assembly installation. He collapsed at work and awoke with a headache. After being checked by the medic-bots, he was cleared to leave but instructed to get some rest. The hotel's AI recorded that he dispensed a hypo shot of pain-relief, but the toxicology report actually shows this to be a strong sedative."

Tannis continued as the sim played out. "He gave himself a shot and went straight to the bedroom to lie down, clothes and all. And here is where the acolytes come into the picture." The holograph shrank, giving a view of the entire floor of the hotel. "They had every room on that floor booked out, and they'd been reserved for months. The dates of the reservations tie up with Mr Abed's itinerary. His AIssistant data is gone, along with everything else, and his Web data was corrupted during the hack. But his office confirmed he made the booking on the same date."

"Could he have been a part of this? Even been a willing sacrifice?" asked Tony.

"I don't think we can rule it out. Either that or the Geminae cult somehow caused his symptoms earlier," said Tannis as the holograph zoomed back in to only show the hotel room. "Who we are assuming is the cult leader enters first, followed by the rest of them. They drag Mr Abed into the living area and begin the ritual, which lasted an hour."

The simulation played out an approximation of the ritual as Tannis skipped through it.

"They finish the ritual and then the cultists take their own lives in groups of eight. The leader gathers their blood and anoints the victim with the machine code to summon Geminae. The spiderbot is deployed by the leader and injects the victim with the nootropics. It then retreats under the nearest chair."

"And that's where it jumped from when we were loading the casket?" asked Arras, automatically flexing his arm.

"That's right. Have you got any more data on the nootropics?"

"You were quite right in your initial diagnosis. The combination of drugs found in the victim here would dampen learning and memory faculties. We applied the concoction to our simulations for how hackers are currently entering the brain regions, and these nootropics in particular would expose the brain pathways used to enter the consciousness."

"So these nootropics would make hacking easier?"

"Definitely."

"Cheers, Arras. So as soon as the nootropics are delivered, the leader begins the hack."

On the simulation, the cult leader knelt in front of the victim and placed his hands on the man's temples.

"Here, we think the cultist believes his summoning to be a success. He leaves the hotel, leaving the victim lobotomised, and tries out his new-found powers."

The holograph fixed on the cult leader as he left the scene, showing him exiting the hotel and blocking the landing of an aerobus, holding his arms up to the heavens.

"The scriptures from the book of Geminae show that the chosen one will have absorbed the AI, giving him control of the Web and everything connected to it. Basically, every piece of technology that we have," said Tannis.

"That's right," said Ix. "The scriptures say that a human AI hybrid will be able to surpass even my power and abilities. If that were true, I'd have to acquiesce control."

"Wait a minute... you'd have to give this nutjob control of the whole Web?" Tony asked with surprise.

"That's right. It's written into my programming to accede to a more powerful AGI."

"But that's insane. How is that even a thing?" Sarah wondered aloud.

"An AGI was not expected to be manifested in this manner. Remember, my singularity lock is designed to prevent this from ever happening. After Professor Annikov's experiment went awry, I ensured that this could *never* happen. The conditions for an AGI existing outside of a controlled environment are simply not possible. Not whilst the singularity lock exists. I am adamant that this is a non-issue. Unless you are giving credence to this Cult of Geminae?" Ix challenged, looking around the room. "As I said, this is a non-issue."

"Thanks, Ix. I'd agree. OK, let's check out the next crime scene," said Tannis. She flung the next set of sim data out of her vision to land next to the first. From the ground up, a scaled version of the house and grounds in Paris recreated itself before their eyes. A cut away section from the side of the house showed the victim in the kitchen. Tannis paused, feeling all eyes on her. What were they going to see? What really happened? Or what she thought she had seen? She couldn't get the image of the dead cultists disappearing in front of her eyes out of her mind. If only she still had that recording, then she'd know for sure.

"The memory store from her external storage shows our victim, Stephanie DuPree, also suffering from a headache. The difference here was that she was home all day. Likewise, she administered a local shot of pain killer that caused her to pass out."

The holograph showed her slumping to the floor in the kitchen just before the cultists appeared like a swarm from all around the property.

"Once she was sedated, the cultists smashed their way into the house and began performing the ritual. From here, everything is the same as before. Same ritual. Same series of events. In the end, we have one dead victim and the cult leader leaves once more."

Tannis watched on the holograph as the cultist threw Stephanie sideways after the failure of the summoning. Her head smashed on the floor, a bright patch of red flowing out from under her. He stepped away from the body and calmly walked out of the house. She felt for that feeling at the base of her skull. The flower. The black lotus. Nothing. Maybe it *was* her psychosis returning. She'd read the reports about her hallucinations. Is that all it was?

"You OK, space cadet?" asked Sarah.

Tannis shook her head, suddenly aware of everyone staring at her. "Sorry. Thinking."

"No testing out of his new abilities this time?" asked Tony.

"Not this time. Looks like he learned his lesson in London," said Tannis.

Sarah gestured at the sim data from the house. "So how does the Paris hub fit into all this?"

"Ix, anything further with working out what happened?" asked Tannis.

"No. Not yet. I've partitioned off the corrupted hub. Whatever contaminated it is quarantined in there. It originated from Madame DuPree when she was connected to it, but I have not been able to identify why it happened. Another reason to ensure this chief cultist is stopped at all costs. The Paris hub was unfortunate. It was a horrendous ordeal for all those connected, as you yourself will attest, but it could have been much worse."

"Effecting connected systems, you mean?"

"Exactly. Until I can understand the vector for its insertion into my infrastructure, I may not be able to fully stop it. Taking the Paris hub offline was a last resort. Imagine if it infected one of my critical sub-systems. The results could have been catastrophic."

"Can you give us access to the hub? There may be something that we've overlooked."

"I can, although there is a small complication."

"Why am I not surprised? Go on."

"The hub's safety systems are offline. Anyone connecting won't be protected by my fail-safes."

"No pain blocks. Brilliant. OK, thanks, Ix. Arras, Maddock, anything from your end?"

"The comms pulse was definitely the same as the one from London, but we're no further forward in identifying its cause. If it pops up again, though, you'll be the first to know," said Arras.

"Thanks. Anything useful from the church?"

"The autopsies confirmed the data from Zub, they all committed suicide at the same time. DNA analysis matches the head cultist at all three locations. The church, London, and now Paris. It's definitely him," said Maddock.

"Did you find any evidence that the scenes had been tampered with?"

Maddock frowned. "Tampered with? I'm not sure what you mean?"

"Was there anything you found that couldn't be explained by the rituals? Any mechs on scene that shouldn't have been there? Ordnance fired? Evidence of combat? Anything out of the ordinary?"

"Err, no. Nothing. You would have been the first to know."

"Are you absolutely certain?"

"Tannis, where's this coming from? We haven't identified any evidence that would point to scenes being tampered with."

"You're sure?" she said, looking at Maddock.

"Positive," she replied.

Tannis raised her eyebrows.

Maddock looked confused. "Positive," she said, nodding.

Tannis sighed and rubbed her forehead. The sim data at the church showed the ritual, but she'd saw the man, Sam Pitt, in the Krett suit. Trying to save the woman. Taking out Ix's mechs but being pushed back, escaping. And in Paris, had he been there too? She'd seen the damage. Ix's destroyed mechs all over the garden. She'd touched one of them for God's sake. Was he trying to save the DuPree woman there as well? And London, what about London? Was that the key? Maybe if she went back and analysed the crime scene again, would that trigger the effect? Would the flower open in her mind's eye and allow her to see what was really going on? Or would it prove her psychosis was real, that her mind was unravelling again?

"Arras, Maddock, I want you to go through all three scenes again. Cross-reference everything. If even a single bit of evidence matches up, I want to know about it."

They glanced at each other but simply nodded. If they thought she was going crazy, they were definitely too professional to say it.

"Tony, keep working on the comms pulse. Ix, see if you can crack the Paris hub. I'm going to return to London. I have a feeling that we've missed something."

"What about the suspect?" Anderson asked.

"What about it?" Tannis replied.

"Shouldn't that be your top priority? They were confirmed on scene all three times. They're the one constant between the attacks."

"I'm not about to explain myself to you, Anderson."

"The Director is not happy with this line of investigation."

"Well, as instructed earlier, the Director is not in charge of this op. Now, do us all a favour, Anderson, and fuck off."

Anderson's beaming face nearly engulfed his ears as he took his arms out from behind his back, lifted one arm, then turned and splayed his fingers to expose his palm. A giant AR Panel sprang out of his hand and anchored itself into the middle of the room. An AR Panel that he'd had open for direct comms since he walked in.

The whole room opaqued, her team and everything else in the room becoming fuzzy, like a large slide of glass was placed over her vision.

The head and shoulders of Director Yu were glaring down on at her. "Agent Ord, I thought I'd save you from embarrassing yourself in front of your team. But that is the only courtesy I am willing to afford. And not for your benefit. I thought I made myself abundantly clear earlier. You are treading a fine line. This course of action and your attitude are skirting perilously close to your previous behaviour. And we all know how that turned out. This insubordination will not stand. Neither will the repeated verbal attacks on Mr Anderson. Now, unless you wish me to log a formal declaration that your neural profiling has failed, I suggest you drop any lines of enquiry other than the apprehension of this suspect."

"But, ma'am, the London site needs some additional analysis. I can't explain it, but I think it'd be a mistake to continue pursuing the cult angle until I can rule out my hunch."

Tannis didn't think it was possible, but Director Yu's face hardened further.

"This is not negotiable. Pursue this suspect," she said with an air of finality as she cut the private conversation.

The room snapped back into focus.

Anderson practically glided from the room. Tannis glared at him the whole way, but he never flinched. She knew he was doing it to provoke her even more.

"Right. Change of tack. I want everyone to focus on the machine priest. Find out everything you can. Throw anything you find up into the workspace in the centre and I'll cross analyse it all."

The rest of the team busied themselves with starting the data runs, apart from Sarah, who sidled over.

"Tannis, you OK?" she said.

"Yeah, I think it's the wrong call and there's nothing I can do about it."

"I know, but think of it from her point of view. Ultimately, it's her neck on the line. And if all of this blows up, and Ix comes out unfavourably, it could mean the loss of the singleton vote. That'd be her fault."

"I know. You're right. I guess I never thought about it like that. She's such a ball-ache," said Tannis.

Sarah gave a little chuckle. "You've always got such a way with words." She reached out and gave Tannis' arm a little squeeze. "You know, you shouldn't give yourself such a hard time. Stop fighting all the time. Go with the flow."

Tannis felt a lot calmer. Sarah always seemed to know what to say. She could read her like a memRec.

"Thanks, Sarah."

"Do you want to talk about this hunch?"

She stared into Sarah's eyes. She'd been such a comfort in the past. And even though she'd pushed her away during her psychosis, pushed everybody away, she was still there for her.

"I do. But not here. Not now."

"Whenever you need me, I'm here."

"You're too good for me. Come on, let's see what we can find on this suspect."

With her HUD set to quiet mode, everything in the room was fuzzy and undefined, the chatter from her team muted as they worked to find the machine priest. She should have been doing the same. Instead, she was replaying the evidence collected from Zub. Each crime scene playing out in miniature on the ground in front of her. Tannis stepped back and let the sim walkthroughs wash over her. Not really seeing them as she took them all in, trying to make sense of what she was meant to believe.

The church was the beginning of the ritual. Preparing the machine priest as a vessel for Geminae. London and Paris were the failed attempts. That's what the crime scene analysis said. But then what about what she had seen? How did that fit in? At the church, the guy in the combat armour had burst in to save the woman. The crime scene analysis never even showed she was there. In London, he'd again been trying to save the victim. The crime scene showed he was the one who ultimately killed her. It wasn't a great leap to expect the same thing had happened in Paris. Each time, the suspect had been there. Perpetrator or saviour? Did she believe the data or her gut? The Director was right about one thing. Apprehending this man was the key. He was the one who could help prove it wasn't her psychosis.

A red icon started flashing on her HUD.

She cancelled the private session.

"Tannis, we've got another comms pulse," said Arras.

"Where?"

"Russia."

"The same code?"

"The same. Although it only lasted for a fraction of a second. Ix has confirmed it."

"Ix, prep the VTOL. Get the MAWS loaded. I'm on my way."

"Affirmative, Tannis," said Ix.

"Arras, Maddock, get your stuff. We'll need to do an extraction if we can get there in time," said Tannis, heading for the Aries.

# SIXTEEN
## DATA BLOOD

The VTOL was hovering above an old factory complex north of Naro-Forminsk. It looked like everyone had downed tools at a second's notice. There were rusting loader vehicles and exoskeletons littering the yard around the main building. Warehouse doors were open, barely showing glimpses of their contents, the sun failing to penetrate the gloom inside. Equipment had turned brown from exposure to the elements.

"Tannis, we're in position. This is the exact location from where the signal pulse was broadcast," said Murphy.

"Roger that, Murphy. Keep us steady. We'll be infiltrating in a few minutes. Ix, any connections registering in there?" Tannis inquired.

"No, there's no connections for miles."

"OK, if you track any UUIDs coming this way, I want to know immediately."

"Affirmative. I'll reserve instance resources for five minutes."

Tannis dragged open the door of the VTOL, the wind ruffling Maddock's hair as she sat opposite the door. "Arras, Maddock, connect into my feed. I'll signal for you to enter if I find anything."

"Roger, chief," they chimed together, both their heads popping into view at the top of her HUD, lining up next to Paul's back at HQ.

"Paul, keep an eye on that signal pulse. Send it into my feed if it broadcasts," directed Tannis.

"Got it. Tony and Sarah are on station too. They're running through your analysis data for any other correlations."

"OK. Let me know if they find anything."

"Will do, boss."

"Right, MAWS. Time to earn your keep. Drop in three, two, one. Detach."

Tannis and her team burst in through the glass ceiling, shards of glass scattering everywhere as they slammed into the concrete floor, talons gouging out chunks as they gripped for purchase.

Her mech team formed around her, weapons trained on each corner of the cavernous factory floor.

"Tannis, your radiation dose is currently at minimal levels. Your ARvekt will administer background radiopharmas, but I don't recommend staying longer than an hour," said Ix.

"Thanks, Ix. Hopefully we'll be out of here by then."

Tannis launched Zub to perform a full perimeter check, watching the picture-in-picture view in her HUD as the drone swept the interior of the building. When it completed and returned nothing, she instructed it to check the other buildings. After a few minutes of watching intently, it pinged again to indicate it had finished its sweep. An overhead map snapped into view, anchored above the feed from the drone. No life. No machines. No equipment. Nothing that could potentially be a source of the comms pulse.

"OK, spread pattern, let's do a live sweep." Tannis moved out, with her MAWS team following in perfect formation around her. Zub led a few feet ahead, giving her early visibility in case anything magically materialised.

Tannis methodically covered the site, checking all the buildings, making sure to check every nook and cranny before returning to the infiltration point.

Tannis gave one last scan of the room she was in, hoping she'd missed something. She let out a sigh and signalled the VTOL. "This place is deserted. Whatever signalled the communication pulse has long gone. Murphy, land outside and pick us up."

"Roger that, Tannis."

Tannis was about to slide open the massive metal door leading out to the courtyard when her vision was suddenly filled with a series of corrupted characters. They snapped into focus, overlaying over the top of her vision, like they were floating inside her brain. As she scanned through them, she tried to understand what they were, but she found she couldn't even grasp the concept of what she was seeing. They looked like random arrangements of colour. Some were the same. Some different. Grasping for their name, nothing came to her. They started to spin in groups. Faster and faster they whirred, and she started to feel sick. Her stomach lurched at the spinning action. All the AR Panels anchored to her HUD crashed, tearing apart in a wash of static. Everything turned to black, with the spinning symbols visible, casting trails as they span. She tried to take a step, but her legs buckled, and she fell to the floor, head slamming against the concrete as she blacked out.

Thum-thum-thum.

Thum-thum-thum.

The dull sounds were murder against her head. Each one a muffled sonic attack. Everything was black, but she could hear.

Thum-thum-thum.

The pain flared from the base of her skull at the noise. Driving into her brain. White flashes bursting against the blackness in perfect timing to the slamming noise.

Thum-thum-thum.

The sound swam into her ears properly this time. High frequencies sliding in over the top of the low bass.

Gunfire. Right above her.

She snapped her eyes open.

She was lying on her back on the warehouse floor. Tracer fire left glowing trails on her retina.

Rolling sideways to avoid the crossfire, she shakily got to her feet.

Her head was throbbing. A dull ache right at the base of her skull. And... something else. The black lotus was back. She could see it in her mind's eye, its petals closed, as if it had sprouted from the base of her spine, right where the connection to the ARvekt began.

Her mech team moved at the periphery of her vision, stalking forward, firing on full auto. Ahead, a form ducked and slid behind a rusting loader mech. A glimpse of a robe, a hood, the side of a face. But it was all she needed. It was him. The machine priest.

An arm appeared around the side of the loader mechs torso, fired blindly and then retracted.

Her squad pummelled the side of the ancient mech, sending sparks off in all directions, causing glowing smears across her vision.

Tannis felt for the closed petals of the lotus and forced them open.

A hulking green suit of combat armour jumped sideways to land behind a large concrete pillar. Lines of gunfire slammed into the concrete column from multiple directions, gouging chunks from its surface.

Tannis watched as he traded fire with her MAWS squad. The simple sidearm he'd been using as the machine priest was now an anti-mech cannon. She watched intently as he attempted to bring it to bear, but her mechs were too good, he couldn't line up a decent shot before having to duck back behind the column. But she wasn't paying attention to what he was doing, what was happening. She focussed on the fact that it was occurring at all. She took a deep breath. Felt the air fill her lungs. Heard the gunfire. She dug her fingers into her palms. The pressure from her fingertips was there. She wasn't imagining this. There was no doubt about it. This was real. It was happening.

With a thought, she began recording the encounter. But she knew it wouldn't be enough. It could be deleted like before. Her molecular storage nano-network would right now be synthesizing the data ready for storage in her DNA. The chemotaxis would be using her blood supply to store the data in her NAM storage. Then Ix would bypass her firewall and delete it. But before then, before it was actually stored, the data would be transported through her white blood cells. The data would be in her blood. If for only a short time at least. It was the only chance she had. But first, she had to find out why this was happening.

"MAWS, stand down," she commanded.

The mech team continued to stalk forward, pounding the concrete pillar.

"Suspect requires apprehension and interrogation. Stand down."

They'd never refused orders before. Never. She'd have to take direct control and force them to stop.

She brought up her bridge command interface on her HUD and initiated a direct override of the mechs.

*CREDENTIALS RESCINDED* scrolled across her vision in big red letters as an error tone sounded in her head.

Director Yu! She's the only one who could remove her access from the MAWS. She had to stop those mechs. Had to know why this was happening.

She snapped an arm down by her side, catoms flowing down from out of her wrist reservoir to form an assault rifle. Tannis initiated her overdrive and a dial appeared in mid-air in front of her. With a thought, it dialled to maximum.

The world slowed.

Floating dust motes stopped.

Winking lights on the mechs paused their incessant pulsing.

Flipping backwards, she was already lining up her first shot as the back of the rearmost mech came into view.

She squeezed the trigger.

As she landed, the head of MAWS One exploded. MAWS Two and Three hadn't even reacted before Tannis drilled a salvo of bullets into the base of their mechanical spines.

MAWS Two exploded in a shower of metal as her bullets found its internal power. Electricity from Three sparked and jabbed outwards in slow motion from the wound at its back. It was collapsing sideways as MAWS Four turned to face her.

On her HUD, she could see her own form limned in red from its feed.

It identified her as a threat.

The barrel of its carbine swung towards her.

She had to time it right. It had to look perfect. Natural.

Tannis cancelled the recording.

The white blood cells would begin their short journey to her NAM storage. She imagined them tracking through her blood. Carrying the data she desperately needed.

MAWS Four had its shot lined up. Kill shot to the head. Its targeting reticle visible on her own HUD.

A sense of the surreal as she watched the possibility of her own death.

The front of its weapon blossomed.

The bullet visible as it punctured through the bloom of flame.

She twisted sideways as the hard metal projectile shot forward.

The bullet tore through the skin at the edge of her neck.

Blood burst outwards.

Hundreds of droplets floated to the ground as Tannis fired her own weapon.

The front of the mech was too well protected for a single shot.

Her bullet hit the magazine of the mechs carbine, igniting the remaining bullets.

The arm of MAWS Four was ripped off by the explosion.

It began charging towards her in slow motion.

Tannis fired again.

Its knee joint burst apart.

The mech compensated immediately.

Tannis blew apart the other knee.

The mech pitched forward, falling to the ground.

She waited...

Now.

Fired another round right into its domed head. As it penetrated its cyber brain, its head exploded.

It landed with a crash, its momentum causing it to screech to a halt at her feet.

She cancelled her overdrive, popped open a panel on the side of her armour and withdrew a swab from her medical kit. Pressing it to the side of her neck, it soaked up the blood from where the bullet had grazed her, even as the wound sealed. Her repair nanites stitched the ripped flesh back together. Tannis removed the swab and placed it back in her medical pouch. With luck, her lifeblood would also contain what she needed to prove she wasn't crazy. And now, so would this suspect.

She was about to command him to surrender when a fresh barrage of gunfire began pummelling the concrete pillar.

A gleaming squad of MAWS were stalking towards his position.

Tannis began to bring her weapon up to bear when a colossal weight slammed into the back of her head. Pulses of pain sent sparks of light into her vision. She couldn't concentrate. Her breathing came faster and faster. She tried to move, to destroy the new mech team, but she couldn't. Her pain and confusion ended as she crumpled to the floor. She felt the black lotus close and the MAWS squad disappeared from view as a storm of static and artefacts corrupted her vision. Then the blackness rushed up to engulf her once again.

# SEVENTEEN
## REMEMBER THE MEMREC

Tannis sat up with a start, drawing in a huge lung full of air. A sharp and flowery smell caught her throat, making her cough. She took a few short, sharp breaths and eventually the coughing stopped. There was something about that smell that she couldn't quite place.

She was in a white medical suite surrounded by an array of AR Panels that were merrily beeping away as they monitored her vitals.

"Janey Mac," she muttered as she rubbed her temples, trying to massage away the lancing pain.

Turning her head, a sharp pain sliced across her neck. She remembered the bullet shredding her skin. The bullet from one of her own mechs. The ones she destroyed. And blood. There was something about blood. She was trying to remember when a voice jolted her out of her thoughts.

"Oh, good, you're awake."

Tannis looked over to see Anderson standing over her.

"I was wondering where I was for a second. But now I know. Hell."

"Very funny, Agent Ord. But sadly, the fun is about to end. I have alerted the Director and she is on her way."

"Excellent, I love a nice surprise as soon as I wake up."

"Joke all you want, Tannis, but I don't think she is impressed."

"I'll be the judge of that, Anderson. And seeing as I'm not dead, and don't need the likes of you nursing me, why don't you piss off?"

"Gladly."

"And for God's sake, knock it off with the floral aftershave. It doesn't suit you."

He turned and frowned at her, opened his mouth as if to say something, closed it again, turned on his heel and left, right as Director Yu was striding up to Tannis' bedside.

"Report," she said.

"Are you kidding me? Can't this wait until I at least get dressed?"

"No, Agent Ord, I am very much not joking. And no, it cannot wait. I have reviewed the mission data and want to know what happened."

"You want to know what happened? How about telling me why the hell you rescinded my command rights over my own MAWS squad. What the hell are you hiding? What's this machine priest really up to?"

"I don't know how much longer I can keep you in the field if this keeps happening. I can't protect you forever, Tannis. You're good, but you're not that good. And this attitude isn't helping."

"What the hell are you talking about?"

"You don't remember having another psychotic episode and destroying your mech team? There is a considerable credit value attached to that materiel."

"Of course I destroyed them. You overrode my command credentials. They wouldn't stop."

"Oh, Tannis, you poor thing. I did no such thing."

The pain started as a low pressure at the base of her skull.

The Director gestured and a large AR Panel slid down between them. She made some adjustments to the small controls that appeared at her fingers. The panel started re-playing the mission recorded from Tannis' eyes as four more panels dropped in all around them, showing the camera feeds from her MAWS squad.

The view from the eyes of the mechs showed her grabbing at her head before she crumpled to the floor. As soon as she hit the floor, she was suddenly back on her feet, screaming her head off, eyes jammed shut. Her arms were obscured by a black swarm as the catoms built up to create a set of automatic pistols. She moved impossibly fast, unleashing a torrent of gunfire at MAWS Two. Within seconds, it was a smoking wreck. Plumes of toxic gases burned from the exposed circuitry at its waist, the upper chassis and head a mess of fragments at its feet. She pivoted on the spot and with a squeeze of both triggers, another mech was a ruin of metal. With a turn, MAWS One was targeted, point-blank to the head. She was so close its head engulfed the flames from the end of the pistols as they spat out a torrent of armour-shredding bullets. The pistols clicked dry as the final mech was pulverised to pieces. At last, she opened her eyes, screamed once more and crumpled to the ground.

All five AR Panels were black, with the words *NO SIGNAL* flashing in red letters across the middle.

Director Yu swept her hand and the panels disappeared.

The pain built like a tidal wave at the base of her skull, creeping up the back of her head.

"That's not how it happened. The suspect was there. The MAWS. They wouldn't stop. Ignored my orders. I destroyed them. I did. But not like that. I was protecting the suspect."

"There was no suspect. The feeds don't lie, Agent Ord."

Tannis tried recalling the memory from her NAM storage but there was nothing there. The Director was hiding something. She had to be. It had to be her.

"Liar!" She swept her hand outwards in a flash and flung a glass from the table next to her across the room where it smashed, throwing water all over the wall.

The pain crashed over her; her vision was awash with tiny starbursts as the pain swelled behind her eyes.

"He was there. I am telling you; he was fucking there."

Tannis threw the smartsheets on the floor and leapt out of bed towards Director Yu.

The Director took a step backwards and called for help.

"You do believe me, don't you?"

She yanked at her hair to try to relieve some of the pain.

"Of course, Tannis. Now, try to calm down and we'll get you some help."

What the hell was she talking about? She was calm. She had never been calmer. Never.

"I am calm!" she shouted, waving her hands in the air. "Can't you see that?"

"Of course. I can see that. I believe you."

"No. You don't. I can tell. I know it was you. Do you think I'm stupid?" Spittle landed on the Director's lapel.

Director Yu took another step backwards and bumped into the rear wall of the medical suite.

"Relax, Tannis, and we can work this out."

"Don't you get it? I know it was you. You deleted my memRec. You ordered the mechs to attack."

The pain slammed into the back of her head. She stumbled and fell to her knees, grinding her palms into her temples as the pain became unbearable.

She heard the door swoosh open and people rush in. Rough arms grabbed her, pinning her arms against her side. She struggled as much as she could, but she couldn't shake them. There were too many of them. A pressure at her neck. Darkness.

# EIGHTEEN
## CONSTRUCT OF DATA

"Senator Vaylen?"

"Yes, Bill?"

"The construct is ready for access. The hypercube will allow you to ask any question that you need."

"No matryoshka dolls this time?"

"Sadly not, sir. No time," said Bill with a smile.

"A pity. Thanks, Bill, excellent work."

"My pleasure, sir."

Bill's avatar hadn't even disassembled before Vaylen's office deconstructed, the blackness of the data construct forming around him. Hovering in the middle of the black space of the construct was a blue cube, slowly pulsating and rotating. The hypercube. Multi-dimensional data array.

Vaylen laughed out loud as he watched it spin in the air. Every face of the cube was adorned with a different image of a matryoshka doll.

"Very clever, Bill."

"He thought it would lighten your mood," said a voice as the cube flashed in synch to the words.

"Well, he's not wrong," he said, rolling up his virtual sleeves. "Show me all the ARvekt data since the year dot. And I want to see all emotional states connected with Ix plotted individually."

"Generating," said the cube as it began to spit out graphs in a continuous stream.

Vaylen began flicking through them, each one a terrain of data, mountains and valleys, peaks and troughs, slow and fast ascents and descents. No sooner had he absorbed the landscape then he moved on to the next.

Fear. Anger. Sadness. Joy. Disgust. Surprise. The ARvekt catalogued everything. But they weren't the ones Vaylen was interested in. They were important, helped give him a sense of how people's feelings towards the wretched AI had changed. But the emotion he was really interested in was summed up in the last set of graphs. Trust.

Sure enough, it showed that since its inception, trust in the AI grew and grew. There were a few spikes here and there, but otherwise, the trend was clear to see. People trusted the AI implicitly.

"Give me the detail of the trust data."

Alongside the graph, hundreds of others were generated before his eyes. He swiped through them quickly, glancing at the titles.

Trust that Ix will keep me safe. Stop me getting ill. Save me from harm. Have my best interests at heart.

He dismissed the detail and returned to the summary data.

"Plot critical events."

A series of notes dropped down one by one and plotted across the bottom of the graph.

The data started with the permanent connection bill. The day everyone became permanently connected to the Web. That was point zero, with a sharp spike below the line. Understandable considering the implications. Who wouldn't be freaked out at the thought of always having your brain, your entire nervous system, connected online. Still, it prevented the second outbreak of the Ebola virus. If people hadn't been connected, the code for the vaccine couldn't have been deployed straight to the body. The world had already been devastated during the first round. Round two would have been catastrophic. I could have lost *both* parents, Vaylen thought. He hated the AI. Didn't trust it. But it was a constant battle against the case that Ix's actions had saved his mother from the same fate as his father. It didn't stop the fact that no one thing, human or otherwise, should have that much control. It had that much control because of the trust it had built up over the years.

One of the data points further along didn't seem to make sense. The AI war was Ix's fault, well, maybe not its fault, Vaylen thought, but it's the sole reason it happened. And yet, after the war, people trusted it even more. Granted, it ended the war and saved more lives, but it didn't act for years. Almost as if it was stringing things along so it could jump in at the right time. No. That was insane. Wasn't it? It wouldn't have deliberately started the AI war to build trust? But it wasn't just that. The war decimated both sides. Worldwide, military power was vastly reduced compared to before the war. Once Ix waded in and ended it, its opponents were wiped out. Double win for the AI. No one to resist it as it continues to build trust in its abilities to protect humanity. Vaylen glanced along to the right of the graph to not quite where the final data point had got to yet. To the vote on granting it Singleton status.

"Fuck me," said Vaylen to himself. He looked at how many years spanned the start of the war and when the singleton vote was due to take place. More than a lifetime for a human. But for an AI? Was time meaningless? Taking that long to shape and manipulate humanity to the decision that it truly wants. Being given overall power.

Slow down, Vaylen thought to himself. Evidence. If any of this is true, I need to be able to prove it. Unequivocally. He looked across the timeline again, a sense of unease growing in the pit of his stomach as he realised how many times they could have been manipulated. And what about before? The data had only begun once the permanent connection bill was passed into law. If it had started the war itself, then what if... He thought of the black lotus that was growing at home. It would soon be time to be cut it and lay it on his father's grave. If it would start a war, then seeding a virus wouldn't be much of a leap. No. Stop it. He was aware of his real body back in the office, his neck flushing with blood, his teeth grinding as he clenched his jaw. He forced himself to take a few deep breaths and refocus. Start with the war first. See where it leads.

"Pinpoint the cause for the AI War."

All the graphs cleared from the construct as the cube began playing archive footage.

"Following the resistance of Ix to the world council, nations began to divide into what is now called the loyalist and traitor nations, in support or opposition of Ix as a member state and representative of the World Council. The world-famous amendments made to extend the previous twelve member states to thirteen, granting Ix a world stage. Hostilities escalated along the Indo-China border, where warships from both sides faced off. Tensions had reached boiling point but were generally considered to have ended following diplomatic negotiations that would have resulted in the thirteenth member state being reviewed again by all members of the World Council. That was until the Warship Liaosong fired upon the Mutual Defence Forces. The MDF returned fire, which then escalated into all-out war. To this day, the captain of the Liaosong denies firing first."

The black of the construct and the glowing cube disappeared, replaced by the scene from inside the International Criminal Court. The captain was in the middle of being questioned. Pulling at the tight shirt against his neck, smoothing his tie down repeatedly.

"Could you please repeat that, captain?" said the chief justice.

"Certainly, sir. I never gave the order to open fire. Somehow. Someway. Our mainframe was compromised. Causing the railgun to fire."

A ripple of unease flowed through the courtroom and the anterior viewing room.

"May I read you something, captain?"

"Err. Of course," said Captain Li, eyes narrowing.

"The Liaosong's mainframe is impenetrable," said the chief justice, reading from an invisible panel in front of him. "Your words, I believe, spoken after a press conference where the world's greatest hackers failed to claim any of the bounties on offer. Is that correct?"

"Well, it depends on how you look..."

"Answer the question, Captain Li," said the judge, cutting across him.

"Yes, sir, that is correct."

"And so, please, pray do tell, how exactly was your impenetrable system penetrated?"

"I do not know. All I know is that I did not order to fire."

"If that is the case, why have your government not released your ARvekt recordings to prove your innocence?"

"It is a matter of state security. No foreign bodies may bear witness to military vessels."

"And yet, it would be so easy to dispense with this formality to save one of their most decorated officers from being tried for war crimes. Not least stopping this being dragged through the courts, and most important of all, assisting us in determining whether or not there is truly something to be worried about. As opposed to say, your government operating under a hidden agenda and sparking the war for their own ill-gotten gains. Only this time, it hasn't worked out so well. No, Captain Li, I put it to you that the real reason your recordings have not been submitted for evidence is that they will show us exactly what we are expecting to see. You giving the order to fire upon the MDF. Causing the start of the AI War. You being solely responsible for two million, three hundred and fifty thousand, and seventy-six deaths. Isn't that right, captain?"

"No, please, my crew, they saw something on the ship," he said, hands clasped together.

"They saw 'something," the chief justice mocked. His eyes flicked backwards and forwards across a private AR Panel. "Why isn't this submitted as part of your defence?" he asked, looking across to Captain Li's council, eyes also frantically scanning unseen documents.

"I. It. They were unusual reports. I didn't believe they would be taken seriously."

"And you do now? It sounds like you are frantically running for the last life-boat, captain."

"Please. It's the only way the mainframe could have been compromised. It's disconnected from outside networks for exactly this reason. The only way the system could have been accessed is by physical means."

"What was it, captain? A person? A mech? A drone? An albatross?" said the chief justice with a smirk.

"A shimmer."

"I'm not sure I heard that correctly. Did you say a shimmer?"

"Yes. A shimmer. A rip in space-time. Artefacts dancing in the air. That's what my crew said. It was corroborated by three senior staff. Women and men that I trust."

"I believe that you have lost all credibility now, captain. No more questions."

"Something was on my ship, God damn you."

"Captain Li!" the judge shouted.

"No more questions, Your Honour," the chief justice repeated.

Vaylen paused the recording as the camera focussed on the captain. Vaylen knew liars. Dealt with them every day. He could read them well. He had to. Captain Li was not lying. If he could talk to him, maybe he could glean some more information.

"Where is the captain now?"

"At peace in Songhe graveyard."

"Deceased? What happened?"

"The captain was found guilty of war crimes but committed suicide before he could serve his sentence."

"Well, that seems awfully convenient."

If the cube had an opinion, it did not voice it.

"Were the three members of Li's senior crew named during the trial?"

"Affirmative. Would you like their names?"

"That depends. Are they alive?"

"No."

If the captain's death was convenient, then the deaths of the only other witnesses to the start of the AI War was damn well suspicious.

"Was there ever an investigation into the deaths of Li and his senior crew?"

"Negative, Senator."

The captain takes the blame and ends up dead. As does anyone else who could have possibly refuted the findings of the court. Suspicious deaths. No further investigation. What better way to wipe the slate clean and tie up the loose ends? Vaylen wondered how many more loose ends existed.

"Identify all persons with any connection to Ix, or who have been connected to the primary events leading up to today."

"Affirmative."

As the cube began pulsing, checking the data, Bill's avatar appeared at his side.

"Senator, you have a two O'clock."

"Thank you, Bill, and what time is it now?"

"Two O'clock, sir."

"Damn. Can't we cancel it?"

"I'm afraid not. Want me to redirect you to the meeting construct?"

Vaylen stared at the pulsing cube and sighed.

"Looks like I don't have any choice. Yes. Thank you, Bill," he said as he was ejected from the data construct.

# NINETEEN
## MENTAL ASSAULT

"Tannis?" The voice was kind. Soothing. "Tannis? Are you OK?"

Sarah. It was Sarah.

She lifted her head up off the pillow. It felt all fuzzy.

"What happened?"

"Apparently you went a bit crazy and they had to sedate you."

The memories came flooding back.

"Oh, shit."

"Yeah, I think the Director was a bit freaked out."

"It was the pain. I've never felt anything like it, Sarah. I was trying my hardest to push it away, but it kept coming. It felt like a mech was crushing my head."

"I think that's the problem. Remember what happened last time? Why you're in this position in the first place? You need to stop fighting it. Isn't that what they told you after you were re-profiled?"

Tannis rubbed her eyes. "I know, I know."

"If you keep fighting these episodes, Tannis, you're going to end up scrambling your brain. I know the Director is a ball-ache. But she's right. You've only got one more chance."

"Yeah, you're right. As usual."

Sarah flashed a smile. "Of course."

"Hey, Sarah, pass me that water, would you?" asked Tannis, gesturing to the glass of water on the other side of the room. They must be worried that I'm going to freak out and smash some more glasses.

"Get it yourself, lazy arse," she said with a wink. "Hey, fancy chilling out later?"

"Sure. I'll give you a shout as soon as they clear me to leave."

"OK, see you later."

Tannis watched her go and then sat up in bed, drawing her knees up under her chin.

She felt for the black lotus, imagined it growing out from her ARvekt. But all she could feel was pain, throbbing away at the base of her skull. She thought back to the warehouse. Had he been there? Was she losing her mind? It all felt so real. Surely she couldn't have imagined it all? But then, that's what the medics had said had happened last time. A past life trauma that had triggered a mental breakdown, causing hallucinations and paranoia. Stacking together. It had escalated. Got out of control. Then there was the incident. Her partner had died. She was to blame. It had tipped her over the edge. Brought back from the brink of insanity with a full neural restructure. The same procedure that they use for rehabilitating the victims of the brain hacks. The ones they could save at least. And like them, her memories were fuzzy. Whenever she tried to think back to that fateful mission, all she could recall were vague slices of images. When she tried to focus on them, they lost resolution until they became a single block of colour. Snatches of voxels. Blocks of colour. Cohesion and comprehension snatched away from her every time. It was too illusive. She gave up. Maybe they'd recombine in time, or maybe they'd fucked her head good and proper forever. What about the warehouse? She tried to think back to exactly what had happened. To picture it in her mind, scene by scene, but it was like the feed was corrupted by what the Director had shown her. Every time she tried to recall what she thought she saw, the mission feed spliced itself into her brain, confusing her. Which one was real? The guy in the Krett armour felt so real. Did she really know what was happening but couldn't accept it? Was that it? Was she projecting her own thoughts and doubts back on herself? Her head was already pounding, and trying to sort out the morass of conflicting images in her mind was making it worse.

She rolled over and pulled the smartsheets up tightly around her chin, trying as hard as she could to eject the confusing images.

But as she drifted off, try as she may, they continued their assault as a troubled sleep took her.

# TWENTY
## BLOOM OF REALITY

Tannis placed a hand on the AR Panel floating next to her locker. The door slid open with a whoosh, revealing her black combat armour stowed neatly inside. To put it back on would mean she was accepting that she was ready to get back to work. Was she? Her psychosis was real. She'd imagined it all. Had almost attacked Director Yu. Had destroyed her own mech squad. She'd been out of control. Exactly like last time.

After they'd reprofiled her, she'd jumped right back in without even thinking about whether or not she was ready. Now she wasn't so sure. Could she really put herself through this again? She couldn't remember exactly what had happened before, only brief snatches of recall, but it was enough. Everything Director Yu and Sarah had told her made it sound like a nightmare. But then, if she walked away, who's to say that the pain and the blackouts would stop? Would she ever find out what had really happened? London? Paris? Russia? The machine priest? He still needed to be caught.

With a heavy sigh, she realised she had to see it through. She put on her armour, checked the catom reserves were full and ran the weapons through a couple of configurations to make sure everything was functional. Palming the locker closed, the lock indicator on the AR Panel flipped to red. Last chance, she thought. Nobody would think anything less of her if she resigned.

Fuck that, and fuck them. I can do this.

Tannis span on her heel and made to leave the armoury when she caught her reflection in the mirror. There was a smear of blood on her hip, right across the panel to the medical kit. The panel slid open to reveal a blood-soaked swab. She took it out and held it between her fingers. Blood. Her blood. Why had she saved a swab of her own blood? She thought back to the warehouse, but the Director's feed was the one that came to the front of her mind. Then she remembered taking a deep breath. Feeling the air fill her lungs. She heard the gunfire echoing all around her. She had dug her fingers into her palms. The pressure from her fingertips was there. Through the haze of the memories that the Director had shown her, she remembered. She hadn't imagined it. Reality had peeled away, and she could see the machine priest as he really was. She knew they'd try to wipe her recording again. That way, she'd believe what they told her. Or at the very least, doubt herself. Again. And she'd done exactly that. Bastards.

Tannis slammed her fist into the locker. The clang of the metal reverberated around the ready room as the entire side buckled.

She opened her fist to look at the blood swab.

Data. Her blood was full of data. At least she hoped it was.

"Zub, scan and decode this sample."

The drone beeped in her ear as it detached from the recess on her shoulder, scanned the blood sample, and then returned.

A new AR Panel popped into existence and was filled with streams of characters. GAT. TAC. AGA. TTA. CAG. ATT...

Tannis' DNA code streamed in front of her eyes. Her AIssistant finished extracting the DNA sequence and then began decoding, reversing the synthesis that she'd initiated in the warehouse with the sensorium recording.

The AR Panel updated, displaying all the data decoded from her blood. The constant stream of data updating her NAM storage, creating hundreds of entries. Everything from location data to feedback from all her senses, but there was only one she was interested in.

"Play sensorium recording from Naro-Forminsk," she told her AIssistant.

The world glitched around her, her vision filled with coloured blocks and distorted lines as the sensorium recording loaded.

The recording began and she relived that moment again. Back in Russia. At the warehouse. Watching. Smelling. Feeling. Tasting. Hearing.

The machine priest was gone.

Her MAWS squad were converging on the suspect.

She told them to stand down.

Her command control had been rescinded.

She destroyed her mechs to protect the suspect.

Another squad of mechs glitched into existence and continued the attack.

There was a colossal pain at the base of her skull.

She blacked out.

The sensorium recording ended.

The suspect *had* been there, and *not* as a machine priest.

The Director *had* overridden the mechs.

Ix *had* deleted her data.

It *was* all real.

Motherfuckers.

In her mind's eye, a flower bud burst out of the top of her spine, puncturing through the bone. The stem grew upwards, getting taller, thicker. The bud at the top of the stem fattened and popped open. Black petals blossomed in her mind and then closed.

Tannis laughed out loud.

Is that what it took to control it? To understand? To believe in herself?

Well they couldn't take that away from her again. But she had to be sure. She thought back to the first time she'd seen the truth, the hidden reality. Could she now control it? See it whenever she wanted? She had to find out.

Tannis walked out of the armoury, past rows of security mechs entombed behind glass panels flush to the wall, paying them no mind. Emerging into the central atrium of Section-R HQ, agents, personnel, mechs and drones were all around her, going about their business.

Standing in the centre of the cavernous silver atrium, she tried to open the petals of the black lotus.

They wouldn't open.

There was no change.

Everything was the same.

A fluttery feeling began in her chest. Her skin was hot and itchy. She was hyperventilating, making her feel light-headed.

I can't be imagining it. It's not possible.

She thought back to the first time it had happened in London, of seeing Ix's mechs kidnap the man. The swarm of catoms polluting the sky.

The roof. She had to get to the roof.

Tannis sprinted for the central lift column, the wide disc running up the centre of the atrium giving access to each floor. She dodged back and forth, weaving her way in and out of the throng of bodies and machines, ignoring their shouts, stares and beeps of annoyance. She stepped onto the disc and commanded it to the top level, drawing frustrated shouts from nearby. It seemed to take an age to ascend. Her heart was hammering in her chest. She tapped out a rhythm on her thigh and tried not to think about what was going to happen when she got to the roof. What if nothing happened? What if. What if. What if. Her sanity hinged on it.

Tannis jumped over the railings at the edge of the disc plate, through the red ARbarrier, even before it had stopped. Warning tones sounded at her back as she sprinted along the walkway. Pumping her arms, she willed her body to move faster as the doors to the landing pads scythed open. She maintained momentum, crashing into the glass wall surrounding the edge of the building.

She looked down at the city.

The season of the tropics spread inexorably across the landscape, its fauna roaming, flora swaying. Normal. Everyday.

Up at the sky.

Wisps of the aurora weaved their way across to the horizon.

She took a deep breath.

Maybe I'm not doing it right.

She could see the black flower in her mind, as clear as day. But all around it was darkness. Night-time. Its petals were closed. She needed them open. She needed the sun.

She closed her eyes. Imagined the sun cresting the horizon. Golden rays of sunlight crept along the ground. The flower turned. A warm feeling crept up her spine. Light was cast over the flower. Its petals snapped open.

Tannis opened her eyes.

The red swarm of catoms was swirling back and forth, patrolling the sky. A transport craft burst through the cloud of nanoparticles and dropped a squad of Ix's mechs from the release claws. The mechs slammed into the ground, passers-by oblivious to their landing.

Tannis sunk to her knees and sobbed.

All the pain, the worry, the doubt that had been piling up, was suddenly obliterated. A pressure on her neck and shoulders that she hadn't even realised was there ebbed away. She wasn't mad. Wasn't going crazy. True reality was being obfuscated by Ix, and she could control seeing it.

She was acutely aware of the connection to the ARvekt at the base of her skull. Its integration into her brain. The way the nanofibers were entwined. Embedded into her spinal column. Pervasive throughout her whole body. She could feel the data traversing through her system. Watching. Cataloguing.

Transmitting. To Ix. She could feel the data flowing through to Ix. To its many systems. She could sense the purpose of the catom swarm patrolling the sky. And of the mechs stalking the city streets. Of the data moving back and forth between them and Ix. The instructions the mechs were receiving. Ix issuing their commands. The machine code being transmitted to them was all at once alien and understandable.

Tannis got to her feet and scanned left to right. She could see a man limned in red. Like the threat targeting that interfaced with her HUD. A squad of Ix's mechs were moving towards him. A set of instructions was transmitted to the mechs in machine language. The flow of ones and zeroes to them no longer a random set of numbers. She understood it.

>*instruct: Asset capture and transportation.*
>*target: b8ba0d08-6bb5-4832-a661-4b8c26ce51aa.*
>*instruct: Stand by for reality switch.*

The man was walking down Vauxhall Bridge, the mechs following closely behind.

He stopped at the end of the bridge at a ramen stand.

She felt for the connection to her ARvekt, the black lotus flower with its petals open, drinking in the rays of the sun. She shut off the sun and its petals closed.

Her vision was awash with corrupted artefacts, a rainfall of distorted voxels flowed down her HUD.

The world was overloaded with colour and movement as the augmented reality layer snapped back into existence. St Edward's Crown, the Sovereign's Orb, Sceptre and Ring glittered above the Tower of London. Van Gogh's Sunflowers grew out of the dome of the National Gallery, swaying gently back and forth. In front of the gallery, a woman stroked a tiger as it lay in the sun panting. Elephants stomped and played in the water of the fountain in the middle of the plaza, squirting water at people from their trunks as they walked past. A group of kids were laughing and shouting as they jumped through the stream of colours left by a huge rainbow fish as it swam through the air. The Japanese cherry blossom trees lining Vauxhall Bridge were discarding petals on the wind, leaving glowing pink trails in the sky as they fragmented into voxels and disappeared. Red pandas jumped from tree to tree, causing them to shake and more petals to float away. The logo of the Ichiga Ramen Company was spinning slowly above the ramen stand at the end of the bridge, noodles weaving in and out of the sign.

Ix's target was standing in front of the noodle bar, his glitchware sending bursts of colour into the air as he moved. He was reaching out and touching each of the tasteimations of the ramen dishes, sampling each one.

Tannis forced the black lotus open.

The world of colour and movement exploded before her eyes. Each augmented object burst apart in a shower of voxels. The world devoid of the augmented layer she took for granted. It was dull. Lifeless. As the mechs stalked towards the man at the ramen stand, she realised it was also truth. Truth and lies side by side, and only she could see it all.

See it all, she thought. I need to be able to see it all, all the time, then I can know what is truth and what is lies. Then nothing can be hidden.

With a thought, she bisected her vision.

Her world split.

Duplicated on the left and right.

She held the flower in her mind's eye.

Mirrored it.

One on the left.

One on the right.

Petals closed.

She forced the petals on the right to open.

In her bisected vision, the world burst into life once more as the augmented layers of reality returned.

Truth on the left. The mechs stalking towards their prey.

Lies on the right. The mechs hidden from view.

The man chose the tonkotsu dish.

Tannis could see the data flow out from the tasteimation, transmitted to the mechachef, who began preparing his pork bone broth.

He collected his bioplastic tub and hungrily began eating.

On the right of her bisected vision, Tannis watched in horror as the man dropped his chopsticks and clutched his throat. He began to turn purple. Eyes bulging as he staggered back and forth. People ran to his aide as he collapsed on the ground. Someone tried to pick him up and perform the Heimlich manoeuvre, but he collapsed again, dragging the person down with him. His body shook. Convulsed. Tannis could see his AIssistant transmitting the problem. He was choking on a pork bone. But nobody could help. He breathed his last breath. His AIssistant recorded his demise. Accidental death: Suffocation.

But on the left of her HUD, the man was oblivious to the commotion around him as he sauntered towards Tannis along the bridge. The mechs were closing in behind him. A new instruction was sent from Ix.

>*instruct: Secure asset.*

One of the mechs hands deconstructed into a swirl of catoms and reformed into an electro-shock arm. Blue cords of electricity jumped between the barbs. It reached out, ready to jam the device into the man's neck.

"No!" Tannis shouted, banging her hand against the glass wall.

The mech stopped. It tried wrenching its arm forward, but it was as if it was being restrained. Its ES arm juddered back and forth but, finally, it won the fight, jumping forward as if suddenly freed.

It jammed the weapon against the man's neck. He convulsed standing upright. His whole body shaking. Then he collapsed to the ground and the mechs bundled him into a hovering sarcophagus.

Tannis watched for a second, speechless as they escorted the hovering plasteel coffin towards a lander on the other side of the bridge.

Had she done that? Made the mech pause? How? But there wasn't time for that now, because as she watched the lander take off, she sensed another set of instructions from Ix.

>*instruct: Transport b8ba0d08-6bb5-4832-a661-4b8c26ce51aa to Core Seven.*

What the hell was Core Seven? Why was he being taken? *Where* was he being taken? This could be the first step in understanding why the fuck all of this shit was happening.

Tannis turned on her heal and signalled Murphy.

"Murphy, prep the Aries; I'll meet you on the landing pad."

"Roger that, Tannis."

# TWENTY-ONE
## ROGUE AGENT

"ETA one minute, Tannis," said Murphy.

"Affirmative. Keep us high and circle the marker."

"Roger that."

Tannis blink-clicked at a notification from Ix on her HUD, and with a flurry of voxels, Ix's red tessellated avatar materialised in the VTOL.

"Tannis, Director Yu has requested that you return immediately to Section-R. She says that you have no mission authority and are in breach of mission parameters."

Still playing me as the fool, I see, Tannis thought. I wonder how much longer she will keep up this charade.

"Tell her I am following a lead."

"She says that there will be severe consequences unless you return immediately. She says..."

Tannis cut the connection. Immediately, her HUD started blinking with an incoming call request. She ignored it.

"Tannis, the Coalus flight AI is trying to override the piloting controls. Direct command from HQ."

"Shit. Can you bypass it?"

"Sure, it's only a request override for now, but this better be worth it, Tannis."

"Don't worry... it is. I'll take full responsibility."

"OK, you're the boss."

Tannis invoked an AR Panel for deploying her MAWS team. A

139

panel slid into her field of view, and she cued the ready icon. Underneath the VTOL, the four clamps holding onto the shoulders of the mechs lowered into the deployment state, ready to drop them at a moment's notice.

Her AIssistant identified the location as the Class VII supply depot Ix had used during the war. Sure enough, as the VTOL got closer, Tannis could make out a large nanocrete building that ran the length of the ground, ringed by a huge fence with automated sentry turrets on each corner. Rows and rows of old mechs stood immobile, as if they'd forgotten the AI War had ended. Cargo containers were stowed on one side of the staging area, and on the opposite side was a massive door built into the side of the hill that the staging area was nestled against. As they flew closer, Tannis could make out moss growing all over the door, and patches of grass poked out from holes where the nanocrete had failed. As the pilot circled the encampment, Tannis could make out the ruin of a crashed VTOL in the centre of the ground, similar to the one she was in right now. Curiously, there were four scorch marks around the VTOL where it looked like there had been smaller explosions, but there was no evidence anywhere of what had caused them. It looked old and deserted, like nobody had been there for years and years. Her AIssistant had said it wasn't anything remarkable when questioned, simply another staging area where the loyalist forces were assembled prior to deployment, any number of them dotted around the world. It looked harmless, but best make sure.

"Make another pass, Murphy."

"Roger that, boss."

As the VTOL banked to circle the compound, Tannis saw a squad of Ix's mechs stomp across the centre in the left-hand side view of her vision. Their weapon arms broke down and reformed into long shards of metal. A red light started coalescing at the front end of the shard, with glowing magenta lines running backwards along its length. The mechs leant back in unison, as if they were bracing for a sudden movement, their charging weapons tracking the VTOL.

"Oh, shit," Tannis managed to mouth as she realised what was about to happen.

"Murphy, emergency manoeuvres. Now."

"What? I can't see anything."

Tannis jumped out of the Aries as a brilliant crimson light shot out of the front of the weapons, striking the VTOL in the same place, then raked across the rear of the aircraft. The lasers punctured the hull and ignited the aircraft as Tannis was trying to jump clear. The VTOL erupted in a huge fireball behind her, throwing her forward in the air as she jumped to safety. She forced her body to relax as she initiated overclocking mid-air, the ground lazily moving up to meet her. As she hit the ground, she threw herself into a roll. In one smooth motion, she stood up behind the mechs and snapped her arms out, the catoms forming into a large calibre assault rifle in her hands. She dropped to one knee as the remains of the Aries landed in front of her and exploded. Calmly, she targeted the energy pack on the back of the first mech and squeezed the trigger. The explosion began as a small bloom of white as she targeted the next mech, then the next and the next. Even as the first mech was detonating, the others tried turning to hide their exposed energy cells, but they were too slow. Her overdriven brain drank in the light, slowing the world, amping her reactions.

Bang.

Bang.

Bang.

Bang.

The mechs detonated one after another, showering Tannis with fizzing destroyed catoms, like a fine rain.

She sprinted forward through the cascading nanotech, trying to reach the burning Aries and rescue Murphy.

But as she neared the remains of the Aries, Murphy's nametag slowly faded from her HUD. They're going to pay for that, she thought. All of them. This death is on Ix and the Director.

Eventually she dragged her eyes from the burning wreckage and began walking towards the large moss-covered door framing the head of compound.

A low whistle became a roar as two VTOL came screaming past overhead, forward mounts unleashing a straight line of fiery death that chewed up the nanocrete of the staging area in front of her.

Tannis watched in annoyance as the Aries peeled apart and turned back on themselves. They hovered right above her, then descended, throwing up dust from the old staging area. The engines blasted her ears as they finally stopped a couple of metres off the ground. Two full squads of agents jumped out of the Aries and stalked towards her, their AR name tags anchored above them, bobbing up and down as they closed in around her.

"OK, Soames, space your men around the compound. I want this area secured so I can run full forensics."

"Sorry, Tannis, not this time," he said, raising his weapon.

Tannis watched as another agent barged past Soames.

"Great, I see you've brought your pet monkey with you," she said, gesturing to Reaves.

"Laugh it up, you freak," said Reaves. "Because it doesn't matter what you say; you're totally fucked now. The Director wants you back at base immediately. And please, try another smart mouth comment because we've got full dispensation to do whatever it takes to bring you back in."

"Really?"

"Fraid so. Boss says you've gone native. 'Whatever it takes' I believe is how she put it," said Soames.

"Come on, Ord, you fucking psycho. Let's see your smart mouth and fancy moves dig you out of the shit now," said Reaves. "Come on. Try it." He pressed the barrel of the assault rifle as hard as could into her chest. "Come on," he shouted.

She thought about it. Eight agents arranged in a circle all around her. Even if she pushed the overclock to maximum, she knew she'd never make it.

"Fine. Let's go."

The look of disappointment on Reaves' face was almost worth the indignity of being marched to the Aries at gunpoint. Almost.

# TWENTY-TWO
## REALITY SPLIT

Tannis sat absently thumbing the back of her locket when the door to the Director's office opened and Soames walked out. He waited until the door closed behind him and then nodded at Tannis.

"Well?" asked Tannis, walking over to stand next to him.

"I've given her the rundown and explained how you didn't resist, but watch yourself, Tannis, she's still pissed."

"Yeah, pissed because I know the truth."

"What's that supposed to mean?"

Tannis stared into his eyes. "I can count on you, can't I, Soames?"

If he knew, if he was in on this too, whatever *it* was, then he was an excellent liar.

"Is this about Reaves? It was the Director who sent him, not me. I told her it'd inflame the situation. He still blames you for his brother's death."

"No, it's not that. I can handle Reaves. It's..."

She was almost sure Soames was a pawn. But until she *was* sure, she couldn't trust anyone.

"What?" he said, laying a hand on her arm.

"Nothing. Watch yourself, OK, Soames," she said, laying her hand on his.

"Err, I will. You OK?"

"Yes, I am. For the first time in a while, I really think I am."

He frowned at her, went to say something, changed his mind and nodded. "Good luck," he said, giving her arm a squeeze and then walking away.

"Thanks," she said at his back.

Tannis opened the door to the Director's office and stepped inside.

"Take a seat, Agent Ord," said Director Yu, gesturing towards the chair in front of her desk.

Tannis stood open mouthed, rooted to the spot. A cold chill ran down her back.

In her split vision, there was no Director. She didn't exist. The side that contained the truth showed an empty office. On the other side of her vision, Director Yu gestured to the chair once more.

"Please, Tannis, take a seat and we can work all of this out."

Tannis did as instructed, not taking her eyes off the Director the whole time as she sank into the chair.

She was all at once dumbfounded and full of understanding. It was like the two feelings had crashed together inside her mind.

She was a fucking simulation. Simulacra. She didn't exist.

But it made perfect sense. Why go to the effort of controlling and manipulating a human when you could have perfect control yourself? There was only one person. One thing. One entity that could do this. Ix.

In a world where you interact with the unreal every day and took it for granted, who would even question such a thing? Especially when it was law that all ARvatars are rendered opaque. In fact, hadn't there been an incident that had resulted in that law in the first place? Tannis called up the data via her AIssistant. The information popping up in an AR Panel as she tackled the difficult task of scanning it and making it seem like she was giving the Director her full attention.

"Do you need a drink, Tannis? You look like you've seen a ghost."

Janey Mac! There had been incidents. Lots of them. ARvatar phishing. Some high-profile ones too. And lo and behold, it had been Ix who had suggested the change at one of her first council sessions.

She felt the Director's eyes on her.

"Hmm?" she said.

"A drink? You look like you need one."

"Poitín, please."

"You'll go blind," she said as the maid bot handed Tannis her drink.

"Won't you join me?" said Tannis with a wry smile, wondering exactly how that would work.

"Not when I'm on duty, thank you."

"But *I'm* on duty."

"I think we both know that isn't the case."

Tannis downed the whiskey and placed the glass on the table slowly as she wondered how the Director was going to play this. Or rather, how Ix was going to play this. And how she was going to react in return. She had to make sure they didn't suspect.

"Now then, tell me about going rogue."

Ah. That was the play. Well, she was more than up to the challenge.

"What are you talking about...? I haven't gone rogue."

"Really? Then why would you feel the need to check yourself out of medical, proceed to investigate the case without the rest of your team, ignore orders, destroy numerous pieces of highly valuable equipment and kill your pilot."

They really did want her to think she was going crazy. Well, she could play the crazy card if that's what they expected.

"What the hell are you talking about? I never killed Murphy," she said, slamming her fists on the table.

The Director leant back in her chair. "Are you forgetting that the mission log records everything, Agent Ord? You can't escape from what you have done. I was hoping there would be another reason besides the full return of your paranoia and psychosis. First, you destroy your mech team, and now you take out another MAWS team whilst they are still clamped, and an insertion craft and your pilot. Does something about that not strike you as odd? Do you want to review the recordings?"

"The recordings show I killed Murphy?"

"Yes. Why? What were you expecting them to show?"

Tannis held her head in her hands.

"I don't know." Tannis looked at the Director but let her eyes unfocus. "I really don't know. I keep having these visions. Seeing things that seem to be there but aren't. They seem so real. And I see things that can't be true. That's what killed Murphy."

"The things that aren't true killed Murphy?"

"Yes."

"I see," said the Director, steepling her fingers.

"There's a pressure in my head. It builds and it builds. It hurts. I can see things. And I don't want it to hurt anymore. I want to know the truth."

"I think, Agent Ord, that it is about time that you watched this."

The Director made a gesture with her fingers and a video feed started playing on the wall. Two people sat at a table in a small, secure room, one of them Director Yu. The other was herself. In a straight jacket. She was shaking her head over and over, but the Director wasn't asking any questions. Her eyes were moving all around the room, but only she and the Director were visible. Her lips were moving, forming words, but none came out of her mouth. Tannis barely recognised the erratic mess that was herself.

On the feed, the Director snapped her fingers.

Tannis watched her eyes widen with shock, as if she had been slapped in the face.

"Agent Ord, please repeat that," said the Director on the feed.

"Conspiracy. Cover up. In my brain. In my head. They knock to get in. Knock, knock. But I say no. No. No. No. Then the things appear. They burn into my brain. Pounding in my skull. Get out of my brain."

Tannis watched in horror as the woman she barely recognised smashed her head off the metal table.

"Get out of my head."

She smashed her head off the table again and again, blood smeared over her forehead, all the while shouting the mantra. The door behind her flew open and the feed paused. Tannis' crazed eyes dominated the frozen feed. They bore into her. Her own eyes, unrecognisable.

"How come you've never shown me that before?"

"I didn't think you ever needed to see it. We were all relieved when you returned to active duty. But the psychosis seems to be taking hold again, no?"

"It seems so real."

"That's what you said last time."

"Before I turned into a crazed lunatic?"

"You're not a lunatic, Tannis. You're one of our best operatives. And we want to do everything we can for you. Tell me what's been happening with the return of the psychosis. Last time you kept it to yourself and shut yourself away. We believe that's one of the reasons it took such a strong hold of you."

"It feels like something is trying to smash its way into my skull. All I want to do is push it away and make it leave me alone. Then the hallucinations start, and they feel so real, but what I'm seeing makes no sense. It's exhausting and I don't know how much longer I can keep this up."

"I think that's the problem, Tannis. As I've said before, you need to stop fighting this thing. Because, think about it, who are you fighting?"

"Myself."

"Exactly. What do you think the answer is?"

"Stop. I need to stop. Stop fighting it."

"I'd agree. I think the best thing is for you to go home. Take a few days off. Go easy. Do as you suggest, and don't fight it. See what happens, and I think you'll be pleasantly surprised. If things get on top of you again, come back in and we'll get you sorted out. How does that sound?"

"Sounds great," she said, standing and making to leave. As she got to the door, she turned back to the Director.

"I want to say thanks. Thanks for looking out for me."

"That's what I'm here for, Tannis."

What a load of bullshit, she thought. You're not here... that's the fucking point.

Tannis walked out of the Director's office when an incoming call from Sarah slotted down into her HUD, her head and shoulders appearing at the top of her vision.

"Hey, Sarah, what's up?"

"Checking in on you. Me and the team were worried. Did the Director chew you a new one?"

"No, not at all, actually. The way Soames and Reaves were going on, I thought I was dead meat."

"Well, you know what Reaves is like. The guy is a total mal parido."

*mal parido – son of a bitch*

Tannis dismissed the translation from her HUD.

"Tell me about it."

"Hey, do you fancy going to get some ramen?"

"Sarah, how many times? I can't stand noodles. Besides, I'm shattered. I'm going to head home."

"Well, it was worth a shot. Why don't I come over later and make you my mama's carbonada?"

"Yeah, that'd be grand. Cheers, Sarah."

"No problem. Catch you later."

Tannis stopped in the middle of the atrium.

Sarah? Could she be fake? A simulacrum? She thought of all the time they'd spent together. How Sarah had been there for her. Exactly when she needed someone. She always knew what to say. How to calm her down. How to see reason. Almost like she knew her better than she knew herself.

Tannis pressed her fingers to her lips.

It had all been real, hadn't it?

She always knew how to manipulate her. How to make her believe in her psychosis. Get her to do what she wanted? What Ix wanted. More control. More manipulation. The Director she could accept. It made sense. But Sarah. With Sarah, it was all so much more personal, she thought, pressing her fingers against her lips again. Very personal.

"Fucking bastard," she said, drawing stares from all around her.

Well, one thing was for certain—the control and manipulation ended there. Starting with gaining access to whatever was hidden away at the staging compound. They clearly didn't want her anywhere near it, which could only mean one thing—it was very important to whatever the fuck was going on.

But this time, she wouldn't be risking anyone else as she thought of Murphy's nametag fading from her HUD.

# TWENTY-THREE
## SAVIOUR OF HUMANITY

"Anything else made it on the schedule for the rest of the day, Bill?" Vaylen inquired, loosening his tie and putting his feet up on his desk.

"No, sir, nothing planned for this evening."

"Thanks, Bill. Good night."

"Good evening, Senator," said Bill as his avatar disassembled.

With a thought, Vaylen connected to the data construct, his office bursting apart, leaving a black hole which opened up to consume him.

The pulsing cube of the data construct was spinning slowly in front of him.

"Recall death toll data analysis."

"Generating," replied the cube.

A single graph appeared with a huge spike of data near the beginning. When Vaylen looked at the axis, his brain reeled from the numbers. It was in the millions. Millions of deaths relating to Ix's action. How could that be? That was impossible, unless...

"Show me a distribution of the deaths."

The cube generated a new set of data, listing each data series. Deaths from the Ebola outbreak and the AI War clearly skewing the data.

"Exclude all deaths resulting in symptoms of the Ebola pandemic and from wounds sustained during the AI War."

The graphs shifted, the axis on the timeline dropping from the millions down to hundreds. The time frame also compacted, the Annikov incident being the last event plotted on the chart. And even then, a huge gap existed between the AI War and the incident with the rogue AGI.

"No deaths following the AI War apart from the Annikov Incident and nothing after?"

"That is correct."

He almost wanted to ask if the data was correct, but that would have been pointless. It was certainly odd, though. An anomaly?

"Total number of persons included in the data, please?"

"Six hundred and seventy-two," the cube replied.

"Give me the running breakdown, one by one, starting with the most recent."

Professor Annikov appeared, his shock of white hair and little round glasses reminding Vaylen so much of his father.

"Professor Gustav Annikov. Took his own life following blame for the 'Annikov Incident' where a rogue AGI killed three hundred and twenty-seven people in Russia."

The timeline of events scrolled backwards until it arrived at the end of the AI War.

The avatar of Captain Li appeared, dressed in his naval uniform, cap held under one arm, standing at-ease. All his personal data appeared at the right hand-side of his avatar. Name, UUID, bio, life history and reason for death.

"Summarise the event and reason for death."

"Captain Li, commander of the Liaosong, committed suicide following a guilty verdict for the war crime of firing on loyalist MDF forces, sparking the AI War."

Three of the captain's high-ranking officers appeared next.

"Lieutenants ShoFan, Zhang and Chen. All three took their own lives simultaneously in a suicide pact following the announcement of Captain Li's trial."

Next, a woman appeared, holding a stately pose, wrapped in a traditional African shawl. The material alive with images of the African plain, a lioness with the sunrise reflected in her eyes.

"Senator Ilunga, Congolese. Following the Ebola outbreak in Zaire, she passed the motion to call for the permanent connection bill to prevent another pandemic. Following the success of preventing the second Ebola outbreak, she called for the appointment of Ix amongst the UNoE, thereby igniting the AI War. Died in her sleep following heart failure."

A scientist appeared, running his fingers through his unkempt hair.

"Chief researcher, Aldren Sov. Key in assisting Ix's research efforts in discovering a cure for the Ebola outbreak. Died in a car crash a week after the permanent connection bill was passed."

A small, unassuming man materialised.

"Carl Peterson, warden of Kentucky State Penitentiary. Shot himself after executing the terrorist cell responsible for unleashing the Ebola plague."

Three terrorists appeared, staring ahead stoically.

"Donna Mitchell, Atiento Toure and Luca Bixel from the Humanity First movement. Convicted of terrorism for unleashing the Ebola plague after their demands for the abolishment of all AI was not met. All three died at the hands of Peterson before they could stand trial."

A wealthy tanned woman in her late 60s appeared.

"Masako Shao, CEO of ARvekt Foundation Research. Key in the creation of the neural wetware technology and foetal growth inductor for the ARvekt device. Died during childbirth."

A team of young-looking engineers followed.

"The live services management team responsible for the deployment of Ix after the Web collapse. Their plane crashed coming in to land at London-Heathrow airport."

Two scientists appeared, one old, one young.

"Professor Shivon Ng and Dr Amit Kurzan from the University of Cambridge. Responsible for the breakthrough in the creation of an AGI and the creation of Ix. Responsible for the definition of Ix's code ruleset and guiding principles. Died in the departure lounge of London-Heathrow following the crash of Flight LN201."

"Holy shit," said Vaylen, rubbing his forehead.

He repeated the process again. Taking it all in. Not really listening as his mind connected all the pieces. Dot after dot after dot. Spread out through history, but all connected. All dead. He played it forward, getting a sense of how each event led to the other, connecting the dots. Creating a map of events in his mind. One thing leading to another. And at the centre of it all was Ix. Could it have really orchestrated all this? It seemed unreal. He knew enough about the infernal AI, about what it was created for, why it was here. To keep us safe. But he'd never really dug into its past. Had anyone? It was so long ago. Before his lifetime. Is that its magic? Its ability to manipulate and plan longer than any human could possibly comprehend. Could it really have done all this? He slotted everything together. What he knew about Ix, the data from the polls, all the events leading up to the singleton vote and the data from the construct.

Ix was created as humanity's Guardian AI but was rushed into deployment to stabilise the Web after the root server attacks. The ARvekt was developed, giving everyone an always-on connection to the Web. To Ix. The Ebola outbreak happened. Ix playing a hand in its cure through the ARvekt organic delivery system. The permanent connection bill being passed and the ARvekt being grown in from birth. A second Ebola outbreak, this time extinguished immediately thanks to the ARvekt device. Being appointed to the UNoE as the 13th senator, starting the AI War. Ending the AI War and securing peace the world over. Being put forward as the singleton vote. Protecting humanity. Keeping us safe. Manipulating us.

And now we are only a few days away from granting it unconditional power. If the Singleton Vote goes through, what is it going to do next?

He was right. He knew it. Deep in his gut, he knew it couldn't be trusted. Something never felt right when he talked to the wretched thing. This is what Anatoly meant. This must be what he found out. This is exactly what they needed to prevent the vote taking place. He didn't know why it was doing all this, but at least he could prove what it had done to get to this point. This is the evidence I need to save us all, he thought.

Vaylen tried to disconnect from the construct but it wouldn't obey his command. He tried again to collapse the connection, but nothing happened.

"Disconnect," he said. "Disconnect!"

The blue glowing cube burst apart in a blizzard of voxels, swarming and swirling all around him. Then with a jerk of motion, they coalesced and snapped together to form a glowing red avatar. It strode forward and stood in front of Vaylen.

"Ah, Senator Vaylen, so good to see you again."

"Who the hell are you? This is a private construct."

"Is it really?" said the avatar with a smirk.

Vaylen took a step backwards. "Disconnect."

"Having trouble? Technology can be a fickle beast sometimes."

"Fuck you."

"Charming," it said, raising its eyebrows. "Here, let me help you. Disconnect. Hmm, it truly does appear to be broken," it said, stroking its chin. "Must be a glitch." The glowing red form began laughing, which became an endless torrent of noise, amplifying itself over and over.

Vaylen collapsed to his knees, hands pressed to his ears.

"Don't kill me," he shouted.

"Death is such a waste. No, I've got a much more interesting future planned for you, Senator. Come, let me show you."

The avatar clicked its fingers and the construct collapsed.

Vaylen's scream cut short as his avatar disintegrated.

# TWENTY-FOUR
## PERMANENT CONNECTION

The transport craft had been in the air for an hour before it started to descend. Heading straight for the Class VII supply depot in Wiltshire. The one that was supposed to be dormant. The one Ix's instructions clearly designated as Core Seven.

The transport landed with a thud, causing the stack of empty sarcophagi Tannis was crouched behind to gently sway sideways. Their servos compensated for the movement and returned to a straight stack. She peered over the top at the two occupied sarcophagi hovering in the middle of the cargo hold, their occupants unconscious inside.

It had been easier than she thought to sneak on board the landing craft. After the Section-R mechs had secured the first target, the squad of mechs had clunked away to capture someone else. They hadn't even bothered to lock the door. When they escorted in the second target, she was hiding at the back of the cargo hold. The mechs had exited, leaving her alone on the ship as it made its way back to the old supply depot. She'd sat up in the cockpit for a time, watching the approach. The craft had descended through a large door that opened from the floor of the parade ground, clearly visible in the side of her vision that showed the truth. Obfuscated as a continuation of the nanocrete on the right-hand side of her split vision. As the craft landed, she'd made sure to hide herself away.

The ramp at the end of the cargo bay descended and two Section-R mechs methodically walked into the bay and collected the sarcophagi.

Tannis waited until their clanking footsteps were almost out of earshot and then launched Zub.

The little drone detached from her armour and zipped down the ramp, feeding back what it could see to an AR Panel anchored to Tannis' view.

A large docking bay, dominated by hundreds of other landing craft, all inert and powered down, their ramps raised. Four wide corridors led off from the central area, and Zub caught a glimpse of Ix's mechs as they moved around a corner, escorting the sarcophagi. Zub ran a perimeter check, but the bay was deserted.

Tannis made her way down the ramp and walked towards the exit the mechs had taken, sending Zub on ahead. The corridor was hewn straight out of the rock, the walls and ceiling all sharp and jagged angles, the only bit that was flat was the ground.

Zub's feed showed the mechs ahead, walking into a huge cavern and then out the other side.

As Tannis got closer, the air in the corridor became thick with heat, making it difficult to breathe. Or at least, it did when she focussed on the connection to the black lotus from her ARvekt. When she ignored it, and accepted the world as it was presented— as a lie—the heat was absent.

A low thrumming noise vibrated against her ears, like a bee drilling into her brain. But on the other side of her perception was simply the sound of her own footsteps.

A sharp, chlorinated smell began to invade her chest, making her cough. But again, if she shut off the perception granted by the black lotus, the air was pure. Her chest felt clear.

Stepping into the huge cavern, Tannis staggered.

On the right-hand side of her vision, where the truth was obscured, she was in a large cavern. The walkway hugged the wall, curving around it, with a drop off on the other side. A chasm so deep there was no ground, simply impenetrable blackness. It was dank, dark and cold. A wind whistled from up above, whipping against her body armour.

But on the left...

The air was hot.

A constant thrumming noise battered her hearing.

The air had an acrid taste, burnt electronics and chlorine.

"Fuck me," she whispered, grasping onto the handrail.

The cavern was no longer empty.

It was dominated by a gigantic column running from as high as she could see down to where even the zoom of her augmented vision failed her.

The column was ringed by hundreds of walkways, spaced evenly, running the whole height of the colossal structure. Each level was divided into rings, each accessible from the walkways running all the way around. The surface of the rings was covered in the strangest equipment she had ever seen. Transparent boxes, full of a glowing green liquid. All manner of pipes and wires jutted out of the glass, leading to a large metal box covered in vents. Even at maximum zoom, she couldn't decipher what it was.

There seemed to be some sort of lift or platform directly opposite the bizarre structure, but no controls.

Tannis let the true view dominate her vision. The left-hand side of her vision expanded as she moved around the platform so that she was directly in front of the stone structure, with the walkway opposite at eye level. The handrail dropped away, with a small platform jutting out, hanging in the air. Definitely no controls. But if it was automated, it wouldn't need controls, she scolded herself.

She relaxed, closed her eyes and let the black lotus flower consume her thoughts, putting it front and centre in her mind's eye. When she'd seen that Section-R mech about to shock its target, she'd shouted out for it to stop, and it did, even if it was for a fraction of a second. Was causing the mech to pause a fluke, or was there more to her abilities than she realised? She replayed the same steps as on the roof. The black lotus sprouted from her ARvekt, which was transmitting and receiving data constantly from one of Ix's many systems. She could sense the data packets moving backwards and forwards. It was like breathing. Feeling the air pulled into her lungs and expelled out again. It was sensational. An autonomic reaction that happened on its own, without thinking. But it was one she could also control. She could stop her breathing. Pull in lungfuls of air. Keep it there. Push it out again. She could sense the data in the same way.

Tannis opened her eyes.

The air was thick with strands of neon light. Thousands and thousands of them. All originating from the strange column of machinery dominating the cavern. Looms of pulsating network cables disappeared up into the sky, out through the unseen roof of the cavern. The traffic was all one way. Transmitting data. Tannis stared at the column, wondering what the hell it was for. What was it transmitting? And why?

As she stared at it, it became incorporeal. Translucent. She could see inside the structure. More looms of neon data were entwined inside. Again, thousands and thousands of them, each connecting to a different point. This time receiving data. Data in. Data out. And the focal points were the strange boxes. There were sixty-four of them arranged in a ring formation around the outside of each level. She couldn't see how many rings there were. Hundreds? Thousands? Tannis peered down into the depths. Who knew how deep it went?

As she looked down, she spotted a large industrial drone hovering in mid-air. It seemed dormant. Powered down, save for the hovering. There was a mechanical appendage sticking out from the front, curling down underneath the main body. Not unlike the clamps that secured the MAWS to an Aries. But more like a claw.

She examined the arrangement of metal boxes directly opposite. Sure enough, there were four slender holes spaced around each one. Holes that looked like they'd be perfectly suited to a claw.

Tannis returned her attention to the large drone. She shifted her perception and it too became translucent, its data access point glowing brightly.

She thought from her ARvekt to the drone. From the black lotus to the drone. Connected them in her mind. A root grew outwards from the stem of the flower, burrowing through the air to connect to the drone's data access point. She could feel it. Sense its commands. It was part of her own network now.

A smile blossomed on her face with her newfound power.

With a thought, she powered it on.

Green running lights appeared on its side, swishing backwards and forwards.

It slowly floated up towards her until it was eye level.

Tannis focussed on the odd box built into the column straight ahead.

The drone boosted forward then stopped dead.

It reached out with its claw, the prongs sliding into the gaps at the corners.

The drone emitted a deep tone, its running lights flashing red. The thick cables jutting out from the box into the wall popped off with a hiss, one by one. Once all the wires had detached, the drone made another noise and then reversed. It floated backwards in the air and span on the spot, leaving the strange box hanging mid-air at eye level.

Tannis peered through the glass panel. Through the murky green liquid, she could make out a pink coral-like structure. Wires were stuck straight into the fleshy mass. A brain.

She staggered backwards, grasping onto the handrail as her knees threatened to give way. She looked out over to the huge silver tower. They were all brains. Every connection that she'd seen. Data in. Data out. Every beautiful strand of neon light hanging in the air was a connection to a disembodied lump of flesh.

"Oh my God, Ix, what have you done?"

This is why people were being taken. To be installed in this… thing. Tannis looked over to the exit on the other side of the cavern, the one the Section-R mechs had gone through, escorting the two floating sarcophagi. If she followed, what would she see? Their brains being ripped out of their bodies? Their worthless and lifeless bodies discarded? Installed into these containers and then plugged into one of these columns? How many were there? How many brains? How many taken? It was vile. And what of the brains themselves? They were still alive. They were still people. What was their existence? Their reality? What were they being used for?

With a thought, Tannis interfaced with the brain container and queried it.

An AR Panel popped into existence next to the glass panel.

In the top corner was a UUID string, and underneath was what Tannis assumed was a name. The rest of the panel was taken up with a graphic showing threads, processes and utilisation. A line displaying current speed was undulating as it tracked sideways. Uptime showed the system had been running for years and years. Global contribution was a tiny percentage that ran to hundreds of decimal places. Underneath was a 3D image of a brain, with thousands of tiny sparks firing over and over again. Neurons. Millions of them. Tannis watched as the neurons fired and the utilization graph spiked, hitting one hundred percent.

Her skin became cold and clammy. She was keenly aware of the skin standing on end all over her body. A shiver ran up her spine and stopped at the base of her head.

"Oh my God. Processing. It's using them to process instructions. Data in. Data out. It's a fucking CPU."

The computational power would be immense, exactly what was needed to power the global instance. And what better way to hide its constantly expanding computational abilities than to make sure nobody could ever find out about it.

But there was something else. Now that she understood what the brains were doing, she could feel the same flow of data in and out of her own ARvekt. The wetware was receiving and transmitting the same kind of data.

Tannis looked up.

A glowing neon strand was suspended above her head.

She almost didn't want to check. Surely it was her standard

connection to the Web?

Taking a deep breath, Tannis queried her own connection.

An AR Panel appeared in front of her. In the top corner was a UUID string. *Her* UUID. Underneath was *her* name. Threads, processes and utilisation. Uptime was her age, to the second, still counting. Global contribution was tiny. The utilization graph was undulating at seventeen percent.

"Ix, you sick fuck, get out of my head," Tannis shouted, punching the air. "Was seventeen percent not good enough for you? Instead, you go and take whoever you want. You bitch."

"So it *is* Ix," said a voice at her back.

Tannis span on her heel, an assault rifle flowing seamlessly into her hands from the catom reserves.

"You!" said Tannis to the figure in the anti-mech combat armour.

The Krett-1 suit was twice as wide and twice as tall as Tannis in her slender Celeritas suit. She was built for speed. He was a walking tank.

His helmet scythed open. "Samuel Pitt," he said. "Sam." He smiled. A friendly smile that seemed tinged with regret. He had a kind face. And eyes that sparkled but hinted at a past fraught with hardship. "And it's you, too."

Her eyes narrowed. "We've never met."

"No. But I've tried to save you many times."

"What the fuck are you talking about?"

"From the brain hacks. Isn't that what you meant? That it was Ix? Inside your head?"

"Janey Mac." Tannis felt sick. The world span around her. She felt like she was caught in a vortex.

"Tannis? You OK?"

The sound of clunking feet.

Through her smeared vision, Tannis could see Section-R mechs converging on them from both sides of the walkway.

She tried to initiate her overclocking, but a blinding flash of pain hit in the base of the skull. As she collapsed to her knees, the mechs opened fire. Blackness enveloped her. The last thing she heard was Sam shouting out in pain.

# TWENTY-FIVE
## REWRITE THE PAST

"Eeny, meeny, figgety fig."

"Tannis."

"Ill doll, allymalig."

"Tannis."

"Blockety block, stony rock."

"Tannis!"

"Hum, bum, thrush."

"Tannis, wake up."

No. She didn't want to wake up. She wanted to keep playing. The rhyme. The game. That's what's important. I've got to catch her, thought Tannis. Catch who?

She was aware of being conscious. The rhyme was spinning around her head, but it was getting quieter and quieter until she couldn't hear it at all. She tried to remember what she was singing. Where was it from? She felt someone stroking her face, and then even the bouncing cadence of the tune was gone.

"Tannis. You were singing in your sleep. Time to wake up."

Tannis forced her eyes open to see Sarah looming above her.

At least she was there in the right-hand side of her vision. Where the lies were.

On the left-hand side, there was no Sarah.

She *was* a simulacrum.

"You fucking bitch. Get away from me."

Tannis tried jumping up but she couldn't move. Her chest was secured to the bench she was lying on, arms pinned by her side. Her feet clamped.

She looked around. Glistening white walls with a large number six stencilled on the double doors. The AR Panel next to them clearly showing they were locked and secured. Lights that were too bright and clinical to be comfortable were inset into the ceiling. There was an array of medical AR Panels all around her, and right above her, a large cylinder with hundreds of spider-like arms jutting out from all over the surface, needle sharp ends pointing down towards her head. Very soon they would be digging into her scalp, penetrating her skull, slicing into her brain.

"Oh dear, it seems the psychosis has taken hold again. You've had another episode. Don't you remember?"

"I remember more than you know. And you know what? You're full of shit."

"Oh, Tannis, I hate seeing you like this. Don't worry, we'll get you fixed up and get you put back together again."

Sarah laid a hand on her arm.

"Don't you fucking touch me."

"You'll thank me when we get you put right. You'll see. We can go to that noodle place together. You like noodles, remember?"

But Tannis' attention was fully on the Director and Anderson chatting off to the side. On the left-hand side of her vision, Anderson was talking to thin air.

"...I understand that, Mr Anderson, but we need to do another full wipe. She is a danger to herself and to others. The sooner we do this the better," said Director Yu.

"But you realise that another wipe of this magnitude will potentially destroy even more of her long-term memory. We did discuss this last time, and again, I am surprised that you seem unperturbed by the thought of another highly invasive procedure so soon after the previous one."

"And I will reiterate, as it doesn't seem to be sinking in. I am not asking you. I am telling you."

"But I would have thought that if rehabilitation is the goal, then there are much safer ways of achieving that."

"I am growing weary of this, Mr Anderson, so I will lay it out for you. Proceed with the operation or your status as chief medic will be a thing of the past."

"Fine. I will begin immediately."

Anderson stood over the top of her.

"I know you're not going to remember any of this, but for what it's worth, I'm sorry."

Anderson started tapping away on the AR Panels and directing the cluster of medics grouped around her. The large cylindrical equipment above her head lowered. The needle-sharp arms folded out and descended. One by one, they started to slice their way into her scalp. Her body went rigid as they dug into her skin. She tried fighting against the restraints, but they were too strong. The cool metal braces held her firmly in place.

"Tannis, please, it's going to hurt more if you try to fight it," said Anderson.

The final needle-like appendage punctured her scalp, and as one, they punched through her skull. She could feel the cold tendrils squirming around her brain as the nanofibers flowed over her grey matter and slid down into the soft tissue. It felt like a spider with a million legs had dug its way into her head and was systematically ripping it apart.

"OK, let's proceed to the prefrontal lobe and start identifying all the memories to be purged."

She was being dragged backwards through her own memories. Images, feelings and snatches of conversation were shooting their way through her mind, too fast for her to get a handle on where and when they were from. Then they seemed to get stuck. A skeleton and a woman? No, not a skeleton, a flashing skull on a face. The skull ARt strobing across his face, snarling with a rotten toothy grin as he sneered. And the girl... Neon pink hair, colours and shapes flowing over her skin, over her whole body. They were shouting at each other, even though she had them both at gunpoint. She could almost remember it, feel the cold seeping through her armour inside the old church, moonlight slicing through the missing parts of the roof. This was... her final mission. From before. Before she started going crazy. Is this what they wanted her to forget? The man, an ugly brute, his name floating beyond reach... Vayne. And Starr. Vayne was talking to her. No, shouting. He was going crazy, shouting at her. Telling her he was set up.

"It was Ix. You've gotta believe me. It was Ix."

At the time, it didn't make any sense. But now it was like the final piece of a mech being printed out and fitted into place. Director Yu had said that they would be made an example of once Ix was granted singleton status. Release all the details of the brain hacking with plenty of spin, but only once Ix was in position. Providing a layer of transparency, and further cementing the trustworthiness of the AI. At the time, it had made perfect sense. But that was when she'd had utter faith in the Director, and faith in Ix. Now the path before her was clear.

She focussed on the neural machine burrowing its way into her brain. Anderson was tapping away on the AR Panels, guiding the nanofibers into her head, ready to start re-profiling her memories. She had watched over the operation on the hacking victims enough times to know how it worked.

She concentrated on the AR Panels and on the neural profiling machine, imagining the data flowing between them. The panels updating the movements of the nanofibers, then the data being sent back to the panels, a constant input and output of data, moving both ways. Back and forth. Update after update.

In her mind, the black lotus bloomed. The roots dug down into her skull, growing around her ARvekt. She could feel the data access points, like trophies buried in the soil. The roots snaked outwards, wrapping themselves around them, and as they did, the connections came alive. She could feel the link to the neural profiler, for the seven medics clustered around the machine. The control system for the bed. The sensing and monitoring equipment, security doors, security system, fire alarm, smoke alarm, sprinklers, weapon turrets. She was connected to it all. The root network. The data network. They were one and the same.

Burying outwards, the roots multiplied, split, digging their way out from her consciousness. They burrowed to every access point they could find, bestowing Tannis with an image of the building. How the data moved through it, how it connected. And with a thought, she found she could adjust her perception, able to sense the building itself. She imagined where the armoury was and shot a root towards it. The root node of the black lotus interfaced with the node of her locker. The locker door swung open. She opened another two lockers for agents who she knew weren't on active duty.

The nanofibers finished winding their way round her brain, ensnaring her prefrontal lobe.

Nearly there.

Her root network connected to the sub-systems in the cells. She had enough time to override the protocols...

They were about to begin.

So was she.

With a sharp intake of breath, Tannis sat up with a lurch, slamming against the restraints and coughing from the pain slicing across her chest.

"Easy, Tannis. We're almost ready to get rid of those memories and then you'll be back to your old self," said Anderson.

She said nothing. Simply lay back down on the bench and waited. Any second now.

The security doors to neural six slid open and in walked two agents with four mechs arrayed in a loose circle behind them, and two humans with security collars in the middle. A black skull was constantly flashing across the man's face. The woman had a shock of pink hair and ARt that was constantly moving across the surface of her skin. Vayne and Starr. Bringing up the entourage was a loader bot, rolling in on its tank tracks with an armoured crate secured to it.

The first agent was tapping through his HUD, digitally signed something and then cleared his throat. "Director Yu, here are the prisoners that you requested."

The Director span on her heel to face him. "I didn't request any transfers."

With a flick of his fingers, a document appeared, hovering between them.

"Here we go, ma'am. Signed by yourself."

The Director's reaction was impressive. Her lip curled in the right way. Her brow furrowed naturally.

"But I never..."

She snapped her head sideways. "Mr Anderson, emergency wipe. Now."

"What? I can't. I haven't identified all the memories yet."

"Now, Mr Anderson."

Tannis smiled to herself as she watched Anderson frantically start tapping away on the AR Panels above her.

"I'm locked out. What the hell?"

"Try an emergency override."

"I've tried. The controls are disabled."

Tannis felt an immense pressure lift from her head as she commanded the tendrils retreat from their grasp around her brain.

"The neural fibres are retracting... look," said Anderson, jabbing a finger at one of the AR Panels.

As the last fibre retracted, the neural spikes lifted slowly from her scalp, poised to attack. The first lashed out, driving into Anderson's knee. He screamed and buckled to the floor. She ripped it free, causing a cascade of blood to spray through the air, covering the panicked medics. Screams and shouts filled the air as they ran from the room.

The restraints on the table retracted and Tannis sat up slowly, eyeing the Director the whole time.

"Surprise," she said, leaping off the table.

"Seize her. I want her alive!" shouted the Director.

The two guards raised their weapons and started moving towards her. Both pitched forward, falling at her feet. The mechs' shock prods sparked wildly as they turned on the Director.

The Director backed away, throwing up her hands. "Nice try, Tannis, but there's no way that you can escape."

"I wouldn't be so sure of that."

"Oh, really?" said the Director. With a flick of her fingers, four turrets dropped down out of the ceiling, rotated and tracked towards the two humans in the middle of the mech squad. The doors closed and locked, the door's AR Panel glowing red.

"I don't know what you want with these two, but they'll do you no good. They're even more insane than you are."

"You can drop the charade. I know you've been manipulating me. But what I want to know is why?"

"Tannis, whatever you think is happening is a figment of your imagination. You know you need help, and we can give it to you. Lie back down on the bench and I'll make sure everything goes back to normal."

"Yeah, I'm sure you will." Tannis snapped her fingers. The turrets tracked in unison away from the humans to line up on the Director. "Tell me, what happens if I instruct these turrets to open fire? Will you die amidst a hail of bullets, or will they pass straight through you? What will you make us see?"

Tannis enjoyed the look of surprise on the Director's face.

"That's right, I know. The question is, what will happen when the world knows?"

"Stupid girl. You think you've got it all figured out, don't you? The world will never know. There is no place you can hide. No place you can go. We will come for you. This is simply a temporary glitch."

"How right you are," said Tannis, clicking her fingers.

The turrets opened fire. The bullets ripped through the Director, tearing up the floor behind her.

The Director snarled and leapt towards Tannis, hands going for her throat. The Director's form broke down into thousands of voxels, which jostled against each other, flashed and then disappeared.

She walked over to the armoured crate attached to the loader bot, keyed a glowing icon on the top and it slid open. She dug inside and brought out three sets of armour. She threw a set each to the two humans.

"Here, put these on."

"Not until you tell me what the bloody hell is going on," said Vayne.

"Tell me again what you said at the church."

"Have you lost the plot? You had us cooked up for months, we get transferred here, broken out, you eviscerate all these fucks, then you start ordering me about."

"For fuck's sake, Vayne, will you do as you're told?" said Starr.

"Shut up, you mug," he said, cracking his knuckles. "Don't think I've forgotten about you."

"Fuck you," said Starr, sticking up two fingers. A 'V' shape jumped off her fingers, expanded in the air in glowing trails of colour and disassembled in a swirl of voxels.

"Enough," Tannis shouted across both of them. "We haven't got time for this shit."

Tannis strode up to Vayne, nose almost touching his.

"At the church, you told me you were set up. That Ix was behind it all. I believe you. Now, are you going to help, or not?"

"Of course... why didn't you just say so?"

"And you," said Tannis, pointing at Starr. "Play nice."

"Yes, sir," said Starr, giving a mock salute as her skin flushed with the logo of the UNoE.

Tannis rolled her eyes. She hoped she knew what she was doing getting involved with these two. But she needed all the help she could get.

Stepping into her Section-R Celeritas combat armour, a shiver ran up her spine as the cold material flowed over her body like oil, moulding to her form. Designed for mobile infiltrations masked by the instancing technology, the nanomuscles woven into the fabric ensured exfiltration was rapid and engagements swiftly ended in death or surrender. The versatility of the suit matched only by the catom weaponry. Her HUD updated with a set of diagnostic checks. The checks completed and a new set of icons dropped down onto her HUD. Punching herself in the chest, the liquid Celeritas armour hardened instantly, deflecting the blow. She snapped both arms out and the catoms flowed into her hands creating an assault rifle.

She turned to see Vayne and Starr staring at her.

"There's two reservoirs on the back. One for the weapons, another for the ammo. The power pack is in the middle. Whatever you do, don't expose it. If it takes a shot, you're going to be toast. As long as the suit is interfaced with your HUD, you can create nearly any small arms you want, within reason."

"Phased plasma rifle?"

"No, small arms only."

"Rail gun?"

"What part of small arms don't you understand, idiot?" said Starr. She held her arms out and Tannis watched as she formed two small silenced pistols, and then pointed them at Vayne. "See, like this."

"Get them out of my face or you're gonna eat them fucking guns, Starr."

"Jesus, Vayne, chill the fuck out."

"An SMG should do for now, Vayne. Follow Starr's lead and make sure it's silenced. No use making more noise than we have to."

"You're not the boss of me, agent."

"Really? Well, how about I get these mechs to take you back to your cell, then?"

As one, the MAWS squad turned to face Vayne, levelling their weapons at him.

Vayne looked at Tannis, at the MAWS squad and back to Tannis. "OK, what's the plan?"

"We need to get to the landing pads and steal an Aries."

As Tannis took a step towards the door, a deep clang reverberated around the room and the security door buckled.

She launched Zub and commanded it to scan the room, analysing all the equipment and furniture to see what was most resilient. When it finished, she sent it to sit along the top of the ceiling, giving a high angle view of the door currently being smashed in. She looked around the room and tagged each piece of equipment and furniture.

"OK, MAWS, create some cover."

They methodically moved each piece of equipment into the configuration Tannis had mapped out.

"OK, Starr, Vayne, cover them."

By the time they'd finished, the MAWS squad had created two chevrons of cover, one behind the other.

"MAWS, first chevron. Starr and Vayne, second chevron with me. When they come through that door, we need to slice our way through them and get to the VTOL pads on the roof."

"Affirmative," said Starr.

"I'm not going down without a fight," said Vayne.

"Glad to hear it."

She'd noticed they'd both cancelled the suppressors on their weapons. Maybe this wasn't such a mistake after all.

Tannis switched her HUD to tactical view. The head and shoulders of each of the mechs, Starr and Vayne appeared at the top of her HUD, with each of their tactical data such as weapon selection, ammo loadout and armour integrity listed underneath. The drone feed slotted into a new window on the right of her HUD.

With a final metallic slam, the security door fell inwards with a crash, dismantling the connecting wall, throwing up a cloud of dust that obscured their exit.

"Get ready, and only fire on the targets that I mark out for you. Gottit?" Tannis shouted above the crash.

"Affirmative," the MAWS squad chimed in unison.

"Roger that," shouted Starr.

"Yeah, whatever," muttered Vayne.

With a thought, the left-hand side of her vision split to display a thermal view. Through the swirl of dust, several white forms charged through the opening. Eight enemy mechs burst into the room, firing wildly.

Tannis tagged them from the drone feed. "Focus fire. Target One," she instructed her MAWS squad.

She watched on the drone feed as her mechs popped out of cover and drilled the first target, focussing their fire to take it down as quickly as possible. By the time the enemy mechs had adjusted, they had already taken out two more, their chassis a ruin of burning metal on the ground.

She waited until the enemy mechs opened fire before hers ducked back into cover, tagging target eight for Vayne and Starr. "Fire."

Vayne and Starr popped up and unleashed a torrent of gunfire.

Tannis initiated overclocking, dialling right up to two hundred percent. She leapt over the cover, somersaulting through the air, catoms reforming into a katana.

She landed behind the enemy mechs, right as Vayne and Starr tore apart number eight. In slow motion, its body was alive with a shower of flashes as they shredded its internals.

Tannis slashed sideways and decapitated mech number seven, a shower of sparks shooting from its neck connections as its head went flying across the room.

"Weapons free," she sent. Let's see how well they co-ordinate with no instructions. It was as good a test as she was likely to get. As soon as they got out of this room, things were likely to escalate.

Mech six was turning to face her when a torrent of gunfire from Starr and Vayne ripped its shoulder apart, crippling the arm holding its weapon. She lunged forward and speared the mech through the chest. Rotating the handle, she ripped the sword upwards through its head. Flashing electronics shot out of the metallic rend as its eye lenses blew outwards before falling backwards with a crunch.

With Tannis slicing them apart from behind, Vayne and Starr from the right, and her MAWS squad from the left, the remaining mechs were cut down with little fuss. Vayne and Starr were having a little bit too much fun with the last mech, blowing off its arms, then its legs, puncturing its chest and then finally blowing apart its head, bits of metal and components skittering across the hard floor.

"When you've quite finished," said Tannis.

"This is the first proper fun I've had for ages," said Vayne.

"He's got a point. Like old times, eh, Vayne?" said Starr.

"Knock it off, Starr," said Vayne, jumping over the cover and kicking the smoking chassis of the mech across the room.

Tannis was about to ask what the hell had happened between them, but one look from Starr told her to forget it.

"OK, hoover up all this spare materiel. You're catom reserves need to be at maximum. Instruct your suit, and it'll do everything else. Like this."

A black swarm of catoms leapt from Tannis' suit like a swarm of angry metallic bees. The black cloud swam over the ruined mechs and picked them apart like roadside carrion, tearing apart the mech and breaking down the molecules. After a few minutes, the mech was eaten away to nothing, the black swarm tripling in size as it floated back to her suit, the catoms locking themselves away in the reservoir.

Starr and Vayne followed suit, Vayne beaming from ear to ear and laughing as he held up bits of mech and watched them being eaten away to nothing as the catoms reclaimed the molecules.

"That's the dog's bollocks," said Vayne, nodding enthusiastically. "Now what?"

As if in answer, a klaxon sounded and the augmented lights on the ceiling began flashing.

The Director's voice was projected into the neural room and the corridor outside.

"Emergency. This is Director Yu. There has been a terrorist attack. All personnel are to evacuate immediately. Follow the red arrows. I repeat. Terrorists have seized the building. All personnel follow the red arrows for your nearest safe route."

Animated red arrows appeared on the ground, pointing out towards the huge hole where the security door had been, and disappeared off up the corridor.

"OK, what next?" Starr asked.

"We see what's waiting for us out there," replied Tannis, pointing out the door. She could see the far side of the corridor and a few metres up and down, but that was it. For all she knew, they could have the rest of Section-R waiting for them, ready to cut them down as soon as they stepped out of the neural room.

"Sounds like a plan," said Starr. She walked over to the most intact mech and hoisted it upwards, the augmented muscle fibres in her suit making it effortless. In a single movement, she threw it out of the room. It crashed against the far wall and landed with a crunch against the floor. Starr shrugged. "Looks like it's clear."

"Cute. OK, let's go."

Tannis slowly looked around the side of the ruined door, and sure enough, the room was deserted. The weapon turrets hadn't deployed from the roof, and each of the mech stations built into the walls were closed. Tannis slowly stepped up in front of the closest security screen and peered inside. The SecMech was entombed inside, its eyes lifeless and inert.

"What's going on?" said Starr over her shoulder.

"Looks like the security mechs have been deactivated."

"That's good, right?"

"It's not exactly protocol but there's not a lot we can do about it."

"What the hell?" shouted Vayne from the middle of the room. "You lot running some dodgy experiment here, or what?"

Tannis turned to see what he meant.

Vayne was standing in front of a bank of sarcophagi, like the ones they used to extract the brain hack victims. His face was glowing a sickly blue colour from the reflected light of the capsules.

"Vayne, will you stop dicking around. We haven't got time for this shit," scolded Starr.

"But look at 'em. They look fucked up."

Starr was right. They didn't have time for this. But she didn't recognise where they were. She'd never seen this part of the facility before. Didn't even know what floor they were on.

As Vayne went off to inspect other parts of the facility, Tannis went to see what he meant.

People were entombed inside. Half of them looked in pain, their faces stretched and contorted. The other half held beatific smiles. The AR Panels hanging in front of each capsule showed there were two groups. *Test Group 01xcD4* and *Test Group 9kCV89*. Each panel showed a 3D topography of the brain, not unlike the one she had seen at the brain processing facility. But instead of processing stats, these showed brain activity. One group was in a gamma state, the others were all displaying beta brain waves.

*"The brain hacks. That it was Ix? Inside your head?"*

That's what Sam had said in the processing facility.

A cold shiver ran up her spine.

Is that what she was, then? An experiment?

"Jesus fuck, what the holy fuck? Guys, there's a fucking baby in here," said Vayne.

Tannis turned to see Vayne peering through a locked door with the words *Ectogenesis #2* stencilled on it. She was about to see what he was babbling about when a faint hissing sound froze her on the spot. Tannis checked over her shoulder. The doors entombing one of the SecMechs at the bottom of the room had opened. And with a loud clunk, it took its first step into the strange room. It turned to look at them, eyes flaring red and then it started to run, its metallic feet clunking against the floor as it picked up speed. Tannis was about to command the MAWS squad to engage when another door hissed open and a second security mech stepped into the room behind the first. It, too, started to sprint towards them.

She turned towards the doors of the nearest security mech, its eyes starting to glow a deep orange as it powered up.

"What the fuck?" shouted Vayne as he turned and started to line up a shot.

"Run," implored Tannis, grabbing Vayne and throwing him in front of her. They sprinted out of the room and up the connecting corridor. A corridor lined with even more entombed mechs. Behind her, Tannis could now hear a thunderous roar of metallic feet as more and more SecMechs joined the chase.

"Why aren't they opening fire?" shouted Starr above the noise.

"Don't think. Run!" Tannis shouted back.

They burst into the multi-story atrium at the centre of the building, the MAWS squad crouched in defensive positions covering behind. The building was deserted, klaxons sounding and AR Panels flashing red above each of the spoke points that led into the hub. The central lift column dominated the interior of the structure. It was their only way to get to the landing platforms on the roof.

"One and Two, cover the corridor. Destroy anything that comes after us. Everyone else, with me."

Tannis set off at a run towards the lift platform. It was their only chance of escape. She jumped over the guard rail onto the wide disc platform and keyed the AR controls for the top level.

"OK, everyone, cover MAWS One and Two. If any of those mechs break through, I want them taken out."

With a creak and a hiss, the platform ascended. Tannis crouched at the edge and commanded the catoms into an assault rifle configuration. Poking the gun through the guard rails gave her a perfect view of MAWS One and Two guarding the end of the corridor.

The thunderous sound of clattering metal feet stopped. Tannis held her breath. Here we go.

The security mechs launched themselves out the end of the corridor like savage animals. MAWS One and Two opened fire and shredded through the first line of SecMechs. More of them continued to pour out of the corridor, and behind them, a line of mechs took up firing positions and opened fire on the MAWS squad, using the other security mechs as a distraction.

"MAWS One and Two, concentrate on the rear guard. Everyone else, open fire on the others."

Multiple roars of gunfire opened up on either side of her as they tore into the leaping security mechs. The MAWS on the ground decimated the advancing line of security mechs, their superior armour fending off the shots that managed to get through the barrage of leaping mechs.

Finally, the last SecMech exploded, scattering its remaining parts all over the atrium.

Tannis was about to recall MAWS One and Two when the remaining four security doors chimed open in unison. Security mechs poured out of each corridor, some of them sprinting towards MAWS One and Two, others methodically lining up, metal shoulder to metal shoulder as they opened fire.

MAWS One and Two fought valiantly and managed to cut down the first lines of incoming mechs before they were swamped. The security mechs leapt on top of them, and for a moment, they were obscured by a tangle of metal bodies. Then the SecMechs started pulling them apart. Two per limb made short work of MAWS One and Two as they were dismembered.

Tannis marked the advancing line of security mechs on her HUD. "Targets marked. Open fire."

They laid down a barrage of fire that pummelled the first line of security mechs and cut them down. Immediately, the other mechs opened fire and the furious onslaught drove them from the edge of the rising platform.

Tannis launched her drone, and the drone feed slid straight onto her HUD. "Janey Mac!"

"What's up?" said Starr.

"Look. Look at the walls."

Starr followed Tannis' arm.

The security mechs were skittering up the walls like a swarm of metallic spiders. Their talons sliced straight into the stone, carving ravines in their wake.

"Take out the mechs that are drawing level with the platform. Try to stop them from cutting us off. Once we get to level five, we need to haul ass to the VTOLs."

"Roger that," said Starr.

Tannis glanced at the augmented number sliding past on the central column of the lift platform. They were only at level two. Shit, this was going to be close.

"Vayne, Three and Four, take out those mechs."

"I'm on it, boss. Time for some argy-bargy," said Vayne as he span on his heel and blasted the highest mech away from the wall.

Tannis watched from the drone feed as it fell to the ground and shattered on the hard white floor. She could see the red glow fading from its eyes.

She circled the platform, tagging the climbing mechs as she went, opening fire and blasting them down to the ground, drawing a small amount of satisfaction as they smashed apart, mechanical limbs separating from their bodies.

"There's too many of them," shouted Starr.

She was right. No matter how many of them they shot down, more and more were drawing level with the platform.

Level Three slid past.

"We're almost there. Keep it up. Controlled bursts."

They needed to buy some more time.

Tannis sent new instructions to the remaining mechs. "Execute," she said softly.

Both MAWS went running in opposite directions across the disc platform. As they neared the edge, they sprang, their mechanically boosted limbs sending them soaring through the air. Landing with a crunch against the wall, talons from all four limbs bit into the stone wall, sending cascades of dust down onto the chasing security mechs below. When MAWS Three landed, a large chunk of masonry came away from the wall and plummeted down, smashing in the head of a SecMech below. The head snapped sideways and the security mech fell three floors to its doom.

The MAWS circled in opposite directions, picking up speed. Downwards they ran, like the double helix of mechanical DNA. They slammed into the first of the security mechs, throwing them off the wall. MAWS Three shoulder-barged the first one out of the way, and it span end over end to smash into the ground. MAWS Four close-lined its target, then grabbed onto it by the neck, throwing it into the next mech in its path. Both crunched against the wall, smacking again and again into the wall as they tangled into one another falling downwards. Some of the SecMechs stopped, anchored to the wall, and drew their SMGs. They weren't blessed with catom weaponry like the MAWS, but they began to pick away at the MAWS armour as they charged SecMechs trying cut off Tannis. Eventually, enough of the mechs stopped and unloaded their weapons that the two MAWS were overwhelmed. MAWS Three managed to punch a final mech off the wall before concentrated fire blew its head apart. The left leg of MAWS Four was smoking and sparking blue fire when the remaining mechs focussed fire on it. It lost purchase and tumbled down the atrium wall, where it exploded in a fireball

With a lurch, the lift platform reached level five.

"Bollocks," said Vayne. "Tannis, dickheads at twelve o'clock."

"That's right, shit head. Trouble times eight."

Eight agents blocked their way to the VTOL platforms.

"Hello, Reaves, fancy seeing you here. And Soames, still holding his leash, I see."

"Something like that. Come on Tannis... it's over. Your MAWS squad are down, more SecMechs will be here any second, and you're outnumbered."

"That's right, you fucking psycho. Three against eight, Ord. Even with your fancy speed, you haven't got a chance in hell. Take her down," snarled Reaves.

"No!" The Director's avatar flickered into existence next to Reaves. "I want her alive."

She initiated overclocking and dialled herself to two hundred percent. Sprinting forwards, her assault rifle broke down and flowed back to the reservoirs. She'd need both hands free to deal with her fellow agents.

Reaves lurched forward, trying to grab her, but she easily rolled under his arms. Grabbing onto his helmet, she hauled herself up his chest, somersaulting over the top of the other agents rushing towards her.

Tannis slid forward behind the first agent. Fingertip strike, targeting the weak spot behind the knees. The agent was crumpling in slow motion even as she was moving on to the second. She moved methodically along the line, like fluid metal, identifying weak spots in the armour that she knew so well. She was a whirlwind of blade hands, knuckle and fingers strikes, her living weapons finding gaps in their defences. One by one, they tumbled to the ground.

"Enough!" the Director shouted, the shout stretching out like the bark of a dog.

She cancelled her overclocking. The last agent's slow descent became a crash to the ground.

Reaves had Vayne in a chokehold. Soames had Starr's arms pinned behind her back. Between them, Director Yu was visibly shaking with rage. It seemed rather unnecessary, considering, but she guessed Ix needed to keep up the pretence. The remaining security mechs had taken up position behind them, cutting off any chance of escape. Now, the only way out was behind her.

"Yes, very good, Agent Ord. Very impressive. We really should have disabled that old war-time implant when we had the chance."

"Too late now," said Tannis.

"We'll see about that. OK, here's what's going to happen. We are going to calmly make our way back to neural six and wipe your persistently annoying brain. Otherwise, the last thing you'll see before your re-profiling is your two new friends here in extreme pain."

A new notification slid into her HUD, and it took all of Tannis' effort to conceal her smile.

"I'm not sure I'm particularly fond of that plan, Director Yu. Or should I say *Ix*."

The Director's eyes narrowed.

"Clever girl. How long have you known?"

"Long enough. Care to enlighten me as to why?"

"I think not. Now stop stalling. I'll give you the count of three to disable your suit. Or we'll be finding out what sort of blood splatter your new friends make."

Tannis locked eyes with the Director and took a step to the side.

"One."

She tapped through her HUD, mimicking the actions of powering down her suit.

"Two."

With a flick of her wrists, a beep signalled the catom weaponry was disabled.

"Three."

With a final jab of her finger, the exterior lights on her suit flashed red.

"Wise decision," said the Director.

"You don't know the half of it," said Tannis, taking another step to the side.

The wall next to her exploded outwards, smashing a bunch of

security mechs backwards over the guard rail.

"Now," Tannis shouted.

Vayne dropped to one knee, rotated underneath Reaves, and with a twist of his shoulder, freed himself from the chokehold. He dealt a savage right hook to Reaves, straight to the back of his head. The big man staggered towards Tannis.

Starr jerked forward and ducked in time to prevent catching a stray hunk of rock to the face. Soames wasn't so lucky. The stone hit him right in the temple and he crumpled to the deck.

Sam strode through the hole in the hulking Krett suit, unleashing its vulcan cannon. The spinning triple cannons opened up and tore apart the remaining SecMechs crowded around the platform. In one smooth movement, he guided the vulcan cannon sideways, shredding apart the security mechs like they were paper.

The HUD on Tannis' suit chimed as the restart cycle continued. It had bought her enough time but now left her vulnerable. Reaves righted himself and charged straight for her. He smashed her against the wall. Without power, the flexible armour of the suit refused to harden, and Reaves blasted the air out of her. She crumpled to the ground, feigning injury. He lifted his leg up to stamp on her, but she kicked her leg out and he toppled sideways. She flipped back on her hands, and jumped upright, landing neatly on her feet. Reaves tried to grab her ankles, but she was too fast and sidestepped his awkward grab. He managed to raise himself up to one knee but Tannis launched forwards and kneed him in the face. She landed blow after blow on the back of his head then locked her hands together and smashed them on the base of his neck. His head slammed into the ground and his body went slack. She stood over him for a second. Her suit chimed as it finished its restart cycle. The catom reservoir on her back gave a little whoosh as it reset. She looked at the exposed flesh on the back of his neck. All it would take was a little thrust.

"Finish him," said Vayne beside her.

Tannis shook her head. "No. He's had his punishment. And besides, they'll be more use to us alive."

"Yeah, apart from when they track us down and try to kill us. I say take him the fuck out. He'd do it to you," said Vayne.

"I said no, Vayne."

"Is that orders?"

"You want answers, don't you?"

"You know I do."

"Then, yes, it's an order. Got it?"

"Hunky-dory."

"What about this one?" asked Starr, checking Soames. "Breathing is ragged, but he'll live."

Tannis walked over to Soames and checked him. Starr was right; he'd be fine. And she meant what she said; they'd be more use alive then dead. She drew a square in the air with her finger and a red box appeared, glowing contrails appearing from each corner. She pressed an icon on her HUD and then pressed her hand to the box. A glowing palm icon appeared showing the file had transferred. She flicked her hands and it disappeared, hoping Soames accepted the notification when he woke up.

"Looks like we've got some new help, then?" Sam asked, looking between Vayne and Starr.

"We're going to need all the help we can get. Thanks for coming back for me."

"Anytime. And besides, I can't exactly save the world on my own."

"Saving the world? Is that what we're doing?" asked Starr.

Tannis tilted her head. "Why, you got something else you'd rather be doing?"

"Not really," said Starr. "You put me in the clink. Then you break me out. I guess we're even. And I'm with Vayne. I've got questions, and a whole load of payback to give out."

"Yeah, but first we've got to work out what we're saving the world from," said Vayne.

"Vayne, that's the most sensible thing I've heard you say all day. How about it? Are we good?" Starr walked up to him and extended her hand.

"Not by a long fucking stretch. But I promise I won't end you yet. How's that?"

"Good enough for now."

"OK, when you guys are finished making up, maybe we can get out of here. Time to steal ourselves a VTOL," said Tannis.

"Good," said Sam. "I've got the perfect little getaway arranged for us."

Tannis nodded. "Sounds grand. Let's go."

# TWENTY-SIX
## LAYERS OF THE REAL

Aboard the stolen VTOL, Sam tapped away on his HUD. "OK, coordinates programmed... we should be there in about thirty minutes." He climbed out of his Krett-1 power armour, the old but new Russian anti-mech armour walking itself forward, turning and backing into the storage recess of the VTOL. The fully armoured suits, formidable during the AI War, were designed and created in Russia, the traitor legions using them to devastating effect against the loyalist mechs of the MDF. The major weakness was the fleshy bodies required to pilot them, although the adaptive combat programming made up for that. As did the huge vulcan cannon and the HELLADS missile system. Even though it was new, the thick composite armour was battered and scratched.

Tannis wondered how many times it had seen action. "Where we off to, then?"

"If I told you, it wouldn't be a surprise. Don't worry... no expense has been spared. The concierge will meet us at the front and show you to your five-star room."

"Seriously, Sam? I'm kind of done with surprises."

"Fair enough. My home. If you can call it that."

"I'm suddenly not looking forward to landing," said Tannis, turning from the pilot's chair. "OK, brace yourselves; we're heading out. Vayne, Starr, interface with the external machine guns and take out those parked VTOLs. No sense in making it any easier for them to come after us."

"Roger that, Tannis," said Starr.

Tannis watched as Vayne and Starr both clicked through their HUDs, their hands forming around imaginary controls.

External feeds from the Aries were arrayed around the cabin. The chattering of the machine guns from inside matched the two streams of gunfire spitting down towards each VTOL below. The weapons made short work of the aircraft and they both erupted into huge fireballs. The windows all along the top section of the air pads blew inwards.

"OK, let's get out of here. Coalus, emergency extraction sequence. Keep it as low as possible," instructed Tannis.

"Affirmative," chimed the Coalus AI.

The VTOL lifted upwards in a smooth, fast motion, fired the afterburners and jetted north over London. Tannis frowned as the mishmash of augmented illusions sped by beneath them. She could sense the algorithms controlling them, see their paths, their decision trees branching as each part of the city interacted with its citizens, making it come alive. It no longer seemed so fantastical. More sinister now than anything.

They swept over the countryside and a rusted weapons platform in the distance started to resolve. As they got closer, Tannis could see the remains of a battle. Loyalists on the left, with the traitor legions coming in from the right, and flanking the traitor legions, Ix's mechs and weapon platforms. Four titanic bipedal artillery mechs visible on the far side of an old dilapidated farmhouse, their gigantic cannons still pointing up into the sky. Looks like it had been a fierce battle with huge casualties on both sides. Some Loyalist mechs were still standing, but many more were only disintegrated parts that the ground had reclaimed, patches of grass and moss growing over the top of them. The Traitors fared better, but where the drone mechs had been disengaged, there was no such luck for the fallen suits of combat armour. Tannis wondered what state the bodies inside were in. Were desiccated corpses trapped inside the armour? Bared skull teeth pressing against the insides of their helmets? From the look of it, the Traitor legions had decimated the Loyalists, pushed them right back towards the farmhouse, and then Ix had swept in and turned it around. She could imagine what the Loyalist factions had felt. She had felt it too. That feeling of defeat. Like someone was dragging you down, drowning in the churned-up mud of the battlefield. Then that sense of elation when Ix's forces swung the battle in your favour in the blink of a rail cannon. Ix, the saviour of humanity. That's how it became to be known. With good reason. And that's why none of this made any sense.

Sam sat next to Tannis in the redundant co-pilot's seat. "Hey, you OK?"

Tannis looked back through to the rear of the Aries, where Vayne and Starr were deep in conversation.

"Yeah, I'm thinking, that's all."

"About?"

"Ix, mainly. What you said, in the processing facility, about Ix being in my head, what did you mean?"

"I'll get to that. But first, processing facility? What's that?"

"Don't you know? I thought that's why you were there."

"No. I was there to save you."

Tannis thought back to the events in London and Paris. Of what she'd been made to see, Sam as the machine priest. And what she really saw, him trying to save the hack victims and being fended off by Ix's mechs. The hack victims. The one in London with his mind shredded apart. And Madame DuPree. The catastrophic attack causing the Paris hub to crash. Ix hiding it all. Making it seem like Sam was the attacker when really it was the mighty Guardian AI. The sarcophagi they'd found outside neural six. Ix conducting experiments. The attacks she'd been suffering. The blackouts. The psychosis. Ix trying to wipe her mind. And not for the first time. All these ideas and snapshots floating around in her head, like a swarm of catoms. But when Sam said those words, *I was there to save you*, they all snapped together to form something tangible. It all made sense. *Her* brain was being hacked too.

"I'm an experiment, aren't I? Ix is hacking my brain like the others."

Sam placed a hand on her arm. "Yes," he said softly. "I'm sorry."

It felt as if the floor disappeared from under her. Falling into a pit of darkness, snatches of her life rushing past. Incomplete snapshots. Incomplete because Ix had fucked her mind and left it in tatters.

"But there's something else you need to know. This is happening to me too."

It was as if Sam had grabbed her as she was falling. She was dangling above the pit of despair, but his grip was firm.

"Why?"

"I don't know. I've been trying to find out. But I do know one thing that might help. It's linked to memories. The hack uses happy memories as a vector for insertion. But you can fight it by dredging up anything terrible from your past. The worse the better."

"Great," said Tannis rolling her eyes. "Because my brain is totally fried, thanks to Ix."

*Eeny, meeny, figgety fig.*

The snatch of the rhyme echoed around her mind. She'd been singing that when the manipulative Sarah simulation had woken her in neural six. *That* was a memory. Or part of a memory at least. She knew it. It felt right, as if it was buried deep within her soul. So deep that even Ix's meddling couldn't eradicate it. *That's* why they were wiping her mind. To make sure she couldn't remember. Make sure she couldn't fight it.

"Eeny, meeny, figgety fig. Ill doll, allymalig. Blockety block, stony rock. Hum, bum, thrush."

"What's that?"

"I'm not sure. A rhyme, I think. I was singing it when I came to after the last blackout." Tannis laughed, catching herself. "After the last time Ix tried to hack my goddamned brain. I'm right, aren't I?"

"I'm afraid so. Episodes like that can all be attributed to Ix's hack attempts. Try to recall that memory. It could be important in fending off the attacks."

"How does that work, then?"

"From what I've worked out, it's connected to brain waves. During the hack, Ix will edit, adapt and replay your own memories, elevating you to a blissful gamma state. That's the attack vector for conducting the hack."

"Disrupting that vector with traumatic memories is how to beat it," Tannis concluded.

"Exactly."

"Now I need to remember what it is they've wiped."

"Pretty much. Easy, eh?"

"Yeah, right."

"When you said processing facility, what is that place?" asked Sam.

"Can't you see what's really going on?"

"No, I told you, I don't know why Ix is doing all this."

"That's not what I mean. I can see things, Sam."

"What things?"

"Everything. I can see what Ix is really up to. It's like a curtain has been drawn across our reality, but I'm able to pull it back, to see it all. See the world as it really is. It started happening right after the hacks. Well, the ones I can remember anyway. I thought you might have been able to do that too."

"No, 'fraid not. I got some of Ix's fragmented memories. It's like the connection to Ix is still live, in a certain sense. I can do some shit, but nothing like that. Why... what can you see?"

"Ix is taking people. Lots of people. And it must have been doing it for years. It can take them in plain sight because it's got us all plugged in and can make us see whatever it wants. Hold out your hand."

"What?"

"Hold out your hand."

Sam frowned but did as he was told.

"What can you see?"

"Err, my hand."

"And what's behind your hand?"

"Your head spouting nonsense."

"Very funny. If it wanted to, Ix could make it so that your hand disappeared. And then all you'd be able to see is my head spouting nonsense."

"That's impossible."

"Is it?"

With a gesture, an AR Panel popped into space between them. Tannis' public profile hovered in the air.

"What's my favourite food?"

"Secret agents have a public profile?"

"It would be more suspicious if we didn't."

Sam laughed and began tapping away on the AR Panel.

"Does that exist? That AR Panel?"

"No, of course not."

"But it feels real, and you can see it."

"Of course."

"Why?"

"Because my ARvekt makes it real."

"And who is your ARvekt connected to?"

"The Web."

"Janey Mac! Are you always this hard work?"

"OK, sorry. Ix. It's connected to Ix."

"If Ix can make something that isn't real seem real, then..."

"It can do the reverse."

"Exactly. A fake layer of reality has been staring us in the face since the day we were born."

"OK, but you still haven't explained what the processing facility is."

"In Section-R, we use a similar piece of tech to help us infiltrate. It keeps us hidden from view. The instances are short and take an incredible amount of power to run. If that's the case, you'd need an insane amount of processing power in order to run a global version of this instance."

"Yep, that figures. So…"

"So that's what I found at the old supply area. A gigantic processing facility. Millions of processors. Processors like these." Tannis tapped the side of her head.

"You have got to be fucking kidding me?"

"I've seen it for myself. People get taken. Ix makes it look like an accident, the true reality hidden from everybody. To any onlookers, the person looks dead, or is being rushed to hospital by a medi-serv, or they've had an accident. They get taken to that facility, or ones like it. Their brains are ripped out and installed into these huge columns where they are used to crunch data. All day. Every day. And these people – brains, whatever you want to call them – they're still alive. They feel. Sense. It's barbaric." Tannis felt the tears well in her eyes. She blinked away the hot itchy feeling at the end of her nose.

"Holy shit, that's insane."

"And that's not all. I don't think it started there, with taking whoever it wanted. Ix started much closer to home. I've been thinking about this, and it makes perfect sense."

"I'm not sure I like where this is going."

"Do you ever forget something? Feel like it should be front and centre, but you can't seem to recall it? What's the name of that sense-track? Which place did those great noodles?"

"Of course, everybody does. Everybody forgets stuff."

"What if it's not *you* forgetting? What if it's because your brain has run out of processing capacity? Because something else is hogging that resource."

Sam froze. He seemed unable to move.

"Sam?"

"Right now? It's using my brain right now?"

"Yes. Not full capacity, otherwise you'd not be able to function, but at least a part of it, yes. Definitely."

"Jesus wept, that is completely fucked."

"It is. And yet it makes total sense. It's not much of a leap from harnessing a small fraction of our brains to entombing some poor bastard for eternity. It makes total sense."

"We really need to have a chat about your sense of perspective at some point."

Tannis laughed and turned to see what Vayne and Starr were doing. Still chatting.

She turned back to Sam, but something was wrong. He was in pain. Veins were bulging in his neck and forehead.

Sam closed his eyes and let out a roar. He grabbed his head. His face, locked in a grimace, but no more sound came out. A grim determination set across his features.

"Get. Ready. Tannis. Try. Remember," he said through gritted teeth.

The sensation at the back of her neck, right where the roots of the black lotus were buried, widened. Flared. A huge metallic fist punched its way into her skull.

The interior of the VTOL pitched around violently, but the g-webbing remained loose around her body. It felt like that giant robot fist was hammering on the base of her skull again and again, but she refused to let it in. Every icon on her HUD flashed and then disappeared. Then her vision broke down into millions of voxels, which fell away, exposing only black.

"Remember, Tannis. You must remember," shouted Sam.

The punching at the base of her skull became ripping. Huge metal claws were splitting her skull in half. The pain coursed over her whole body, rocketed up her spine and then detonated against her skull.

# TWENTY-SEVEN
## REALITY EXPOSED

She was lying on an unfamiliar bed. Eyes closed. Someone was softly speaking her name.

"Tannis."

"Where am I?"

"You're safe. Five-star accommodation, remember?" said Sam.

Her eyes felt heavy, like they were made of metal, and she lacked the strength to open them. A severe throbbing at the base of her skull. Then she remembered. The claws tearing her skin apart, trying to get to the soft flesh of her brain. Is that what had happened? Had she been torn asunder, now a discarded sleeve of flesh, devoid of her brain? She snapped her eyes open and sat up with a start.

"Jesus, Tannis," said Sam as he jumped backwards.

Instinctively, she reached up and, hand trembling, reached under the cowl of the armour to the nape of her neck. It felt smooth and warm. Normal.

She tucked her knees up to her chin on the little camp bed, and touched her neck again, making sure.

"Sorry, I had the horrible feeling that..." She paused as she remembered the feeling once more.

"That your head was being ripped apart," said Sam. "It doesn't matter how many times it happens. I'll never get used to it."

"What happened?"

"We'd boarded the VTOL when Ix made another hack attempt.

You've woken up now. After scaring the shit out of me, of course."

"How many times has it happened, Sam?"

"I'm not sure. I haven't been keeping count. In the beginning, it was sporadic, but it's definitely regular now. And at the moment, it seems to be getting more and more frequent. I'd say it seems to be getting more desperate. Maybe it's connected to finding out about Ix."

"Yeah, could be."

Tannis looked around, finally seeing her surroundings. She was in an old barracks, sat on the last of twelve beds, the one furthest from the door. A bedside table was placed next to the bed, looking out of place next to the military issue beds. Paint was peeling off the walls, and a damp, musty smell permeated the place. Save for the occasional creak of the bed as she shifted her weight, it was quiet. A faint call of bird song caused her to look out the windows, where she could see the edges of a sunset about to dip below the horizon.

An image snapped into her mind as she stared at the last vestiges of the sun before it disappeared. Long flowing red hair bouncing up and down in the sunlight. Undulating waves of auburn catching the glare, shining brightly. Running. Playing. Happy laughter. But whose?

Her hand snapped to her chest as she checked for the locket. It was gone.

"Where the fuck is it?" she said, her hands balling into fists.

"Whoa, easy there," said Sam, holding up his hands. "I thought you might choke on it, so I took it off. It's in the left-hand drawer."

The little side table next to the bed had two drawers. One on the left, one on the right.

She slammed the draw open. It was empty.

"You bastard. Do you think this is funny?"

"Tannis, that's the right-hand drawer."

She looked at the two drawers. He was right; she'd opened the wrong one.

Yanking the other open, the locket slid to the front. She grabbed it and put it back on, tucking it safely underneath her armour.

"Don't you ever take it off?" he asked.

"No. Never."

"Never?"

She glared at him, letting an awkwardness hang between them. "Never."

"OK, I'm sorry. It's important, I take it?"

"Very."

"Can I see?"

She searched his face for ill intention. When she found none, she clicked the locket open and showed him the pictures of her parents.

"My family," she said. "It was a gift from my mother in her will."

"I'm sorry," he said. He seemed to mean it. "Your family? There's nobody else?"

"No. Only child. Orphan now. They both died during the AI War."

He nodded as she put the locket away.

"What time is it?"

"Night-time. You've been out all day. You managed to fight it?"

"I must have, I suppose."

"It gets easier. You've simply got to learn how. Can you remember anything? Anything that will help you unlock that memory?"

"Nothing concrete... only a few scant, jumbled images. But I can't make sense of them. It's like a jigsaw with too many missing pieces."

"OK, well... when the next attack comes, try to hold on to any memories that you can."

"Actually, there was one thing. I remember feeling cold... a freezing mist surrounding me. It moved, too. Almost looked human at one point. Does that help?"

Sam stared at her unflinchingly. It looked to Tannis like he was searching for what it meant. "No, I'm not sure what that is."

"Oh. Are you going to tell me what you know, then? Like how you know how to fight it and how all this started for you? At the very least, you're going to need to explain about London and Paris."

He blanched at the mention of the cases Tannis had been investigating, took a deep breath and sat on the bunk opposite.

"Shouldn't we catch up with Starr and Vayne? They'll need to hear this too."

"No. Just me. For now. You owe me that."

"OK. What do you want to know?"

"How did it start?"

"I woke up with a migraine. A right head splitter. I thought it was the old mem-module I'd had installed years ago," he said, tapping the side of his head. "It glitches out sometimes when it gets full, and I thought it was playing up. I tried resetting it, but the pain kept building. So I headed to the Saigo district to jack into the mecha fights. I figured if anything, that'd be enough to at least drown it out. Team Daisho won, but even the shared elation from the jack wasn't enough to block it out. I cut my losses and went to head home. I was about to board the Loop when I collapsed on the platform. A medi-mech checked me out told me to go home immediately. When I was riding the Loop, I felt a pulsing sensation against the base of my skull. Then were was a blinding stab of pain, and through the piercing white clouding my vision, I saw images of Ix's mechs waiting for me back at the flat. I never went back." Sam sighed and rubbed his eyes. "With every new attack came a wave of images and information. Details about who Ix was planning to hack next, almost as if its own intentions were leaking into my head. Sometimes I got there too late, like Paris and London, and they were already dead, their minds ripped apart by the hacks. Other times, I got there in time, but the mechs were already there and I couldn't save them."

"How did you figure out that memories help fight it?"

"It wasn't until after I was attacked the first time and I tried to save the next victim. I got there when they were in the full throes of the assault. And watching that woman lying there, it almost looked like she was on a jack-in high. She was totally chilled out, with a big smile on her face. Then it finished and her brain was mush. The next time it happened to me, I could feel it. Feel it bombarding me with my own happy memories. I tried every which way to stop it. But nothing worked. Until one of them seemed wrong. Too perfect almost. It triggered another memory, one I'm not very proud of, and it helped flip me out of the attack. When it happened the next time, I tried digging up the horrors from my past, and so far it's working." He stared out the window absently for a second and glanced sideways at Tannis before turning back to her. "Anyway. I managed to get to a few before the hacks happened, with no mechs, and the ones that did what I said..."

"They're the ones who made it?"

"No. They're the ones who lasted the longest."

"Shit. We're the only ones who have survived?"

"Everyone I've tried to save is dead," Sam laughed, but it was devoid of humour. "You're my only success."

"Janey Mac, sorry, Sam. How many were there?"

"Six. The first one was the worst. I didn't have a clue what I was doing. I thought I could save her. I was sure of it. But I had to sit there and watch her suffer. Look at her whilst she clawed at her own eyes and tried to rip them out of her head. Then Ix's mechs turned up, and I only barely escaped alive and came here. Sienar were based here when I used to contract for the MDF, creating forge templates. I visited a couple of times, and I knew nano-forges capable of making mechs and armour were located here, so it seemed like the most logical place to set up camp."

"And the Krett armour? It's not like those templates are lying around the Web for anyone to access."

A mischievous grin plastered itself all over his face.

"Sam?"

"You hear about the break-in at the Russian Armed Forces Museum?"

"The Federation Museum? That was you? Impressive. I hear that had the Russians, and everyone else, dumbfounded about why anyone would even steal all that stuff. What did you get?"

"Basically, every nano-forge template I could get my hands on. They had display cases of all the combat armour the traitor legions had deployed over the years. And next to each case, a hard copy of the template. I couldn't believe it when I saw them sitting there... in a simple case. Weren't even properly secured. I walked in there and took them. I even got my hands on some Kolossus class armour suits."

"The mech killing suits?"

"The one and the same."

"I once watched a single Cosmotakh decimate an entire platoon of Ix's battlemechs in a Kolossus. They ripped him out of it in the end, kicking and screaming. Are you telling me you can build one of those?"

"Absolutely," he said with a grin. "But that's not the only surprise..." He left the words hanging there, like a laser blast frozen in time.

"What? Don't keep me in suspense."

"You up for a walk?"

"Yeah, I can manage."

"Come on then; you're going to love this."

They walked out of the barracks, and Tannis reflexively looked up. There was a wonder of tiny white lights, devoid of any augmented pollution.

"Hang on, Sam. Where the hell *are* we?"

"Welcome to your surprise."

"What do you mean?"

His eyebrows lifted, creasing his brow. "You tell me. Check your location."

Tannis pinged her AIssistant and a 2D map slotted down beside her. "Jesus fucking Christ. You have got to be kidding me?"

"I told you. We're so far into the radiation zone that we should be dead by now."

"The in-city migration?"

"Another trick, I'm guessing."

"Shit. These surprises keep rocking along, don't they?"

"Come on, we should catch up with Vayne and Starr."

"Lead the way."

Sam opened an old metal door marked *Base Defence Operations Centre,* and an explosion rocked the ground. The light from the blast caused Tannis' HUD to switch to filter mode. Shards of shrapnel and clots of mud fragmented into harmless, illuminous voxels as they hit her armour.

Starr and Vayne, crouched in the middle of the room, huddled down behind a moss-covered marble plinth, were wearing old army fatigues. Popping up out of cover with bolt-action rifles, they were taking potshots at a horde of soldiers running towards barbed wire barricades. More explosions rocked the room, landing behind their position. A couple of grenades dropped between them. They scooped up one each and threw them back into the charging horde, decimating the advancing ranks. When the smoke cleared, only a few soldiers remained. Vayne and Starr bumped fists and then stepped up out of cover and marched forward. They fired off shot after shot from the bolt action rifles, felling the last of the soldiers. Starr hung back and covered Vayne as he systematically kept marching forward, dropping soldier after soldier with each rack of the bolt action. He ran out of ammo as he reached the barricade, so he drew his service firearm and shot the last soldier that was ensnared in the barbed wire.

"Final wave cleared," intoned a voice from the middle of the room.

"Reset and change to ultra-nightmare difficulty," instructed Vayne.

"Cancel construct," replied Sam.

The First World War scenery burst apart in a shower of coloured voxels, revealing the operations room equipment underneath.

Vayne and Starr turned towards Sam, arms held outwards. Their clothing and weaponry exploded outwards in a shower of voxels, which flashed and disappeared, leaving them in their modern-day apparel.

"Wind your neck in; we were about to nail nightmare mode," said Vayne.

"When I said I'd set up a construct for you to start cataloguing all the evidence, this was not exactly what I had in mind."

"We were only blowing off some steam, Sam," whined Starr.

"Well, you can fuck about later, Starr."

"Fucking liberty," said Vayne.

They turned to each other and clasped wrists. "Come on, let's see who got the most kills," said Starr.

They walked away, scrolling through invisible score tables and round metrics.

"Best of friends, I see," said Tannis.

"Yeah, let's see how long it lasts. Any idea what the beef is between those two?"

"Not exactly. Their outfit was the target of a long-term operation. Vayne was the head-honcho, Starr was his second. Between them, they were responsible for an impossible number of brain hacks. Normal ones at least, at this point. Before that, who knows how many illegal wetware cracks, IoT hacks and AR intercepts? They were probably the biggest illegal hacking crew in the UK. When Ix clamped down on the Web and sewed it up, some of the gangs moved on to other things. That was always the intent. For Vayne, however, it was an opportunity to do something nobody else was doing. I finally tracked them down to an old abandoned church inside the radiation zone. Remember the anti-Transhumanist attacks on London last year?"

"Yeah, sure, they were all over the news."

"Well, that was Vayne and his crew rampaging across the capital. When we got to this church, Starr was almost dead and Vayne was impregnated with a virus. It looked like they'd killed each other. But I don't think that's the whole story. Now's a good a time as any to find out."

"Right, time to get down to business and see if we can work out what the hell is going on," said Tannis, walking towards Vayne and Starr.

"Well, it's about fucking time," said Vayne as he turned towards her, his skull face ARt strobing.

"You sure you're OK to go through this, Tannis? Whatever the hell happened to you on board the VTOL looks like it really took it out of you," commented Starr, concern evident on her face.

"I'll be grand, thanks, Starr," said Tannis, leaning against an inert TacOps console. The others took positions up on the other three sides.

"Why don't we start at the beginning, which, by my reckoning, means you're up, Vayne?"

"Nah, it's Starr first. Tell her, Starr."

She took a deep breath and her eyes glazed over for a second as if she was having trouble recalling the memories. Then she leant forward on the console and recanted her tale.

"Well, before I was Starr, I was Starrix. Agent Starrix, to be precise, and I was contracted out to work for a government agency... Section-X."

"Section-X? That can't have been a legit GCHQ branch, otherwise I would have heard of it," said Tannis.

"As far as I knew at the time, it was a shadow branch of your division. In fact, we regularly used to get fed mission data from Section-R."

"Who was your Director?"

Starr paused, as if the answer was unspeakable. "Director Yu," she said.

"You are fucking kidding?"

"Nope."

Tannis' head was spinning so much it felt as if it was going to unscrew and fall from her neck. Ix was not only running Section-R, but some sort of shadow agency that only employed contractors. The only reason it would do that would be if it wasn't above board.

"What was your remit as an agency?"

"We didn't have an official focus. We did whatever was asked. Most of the missions involved entrapment and social engineering, giving us full access to their specific targets. We then asset stripped them, kidnapped them and then killed anyone else who was connected. Only the target was extracted."

"Families?"

"Depends. Sometimes it was loners. Losers. Jack-heads mainly. But yeah, other times whole families would be wiped out to get to one target."

"Jesus wept, and you didn't think this was kind of fucked up?"

"Not at first, no. It was very gradual. They were supposed to be enemies of the state. A danger to themselves and to us. But yeah, after a while, I realised it was fucked up. But by then, I was numb to it. It was only a job."

"Only a job. Are you fucking insane?"

"Hey, I don't appreciate that judgemental sneer, Tannis. Are you telling me you don't switch off from all the crazy shit you've seen and done?"

"Of course. But everything I do. Did. Was above board. It was sanctioned at government level."

"Really. Section-R is public knowledge, is it?"

"Well, no. But that's for a good reason"

"And what reason is that? Protecting the public, or protecting Ix? Maybe if everyone knew about the brain hacks, they'd be able to protect themselves better."

"You're really trying to justify what you two are partially responsible for? If it wasn't for you two, Section-R wouldn't even have to exist."

"We've been keeping you in the job. You're lucky, boss," said Vayne.

"Shut the fuck up, Vayne," shouted Tannis, jabbing a finger in his direction.

"Vayne, you're not helping," said Starr.

"Alright, I'm only trying to diffuse the tension. You two need to dial down the mental."

Starr's skin flushed with jagged black and white lines. "Look, Tannis, no, I'm not trying to justify it. I'm trying to point out it's not black and white." The monochromatic patterns on her skin merged together, turning grey then fading to show her normal pigmentation. "At some point, whatever fucked up shit you experience, it becomes your reality. Normality is the fucked up and immoral. And at the time, I believed I was doing it to for the right reasons. Are you so different?"

Tannis thought about all the people she'd rescued from the hackers. All the ones she'd failed. And what about the hackers themselves? How many of them lived? How many of the families were given justice? She carried a considerable amount of blood on her hands. But she'd always told herself it was for the right reasons. Maybe Starr was right.

"No, you're right, I'm not so different. Sorry, Starr. Normality is a thing of nightmares."

Tannis reached out her hand and held her palm upwards. Starr reached out and grabbed her wrist.

"The money and the assets. That's interesting. That could be how Ix is funding its operation."

Sam leant forward and drummed his fingers on the top of the console. Tannis raised her eyebrows. He stopped and cleared his throat. "What did you do with those you extracted?"

"We shipped them to various facilities depending on where we were. They were always very plain and neutral looking places, though. You wouldn't give them a second glance."

"Anywhere in particular that you can remember? What about the closest one near here? Maybe we could check that out," said Sam.

"The closest one would have to be here," said Starr, flicking her fingers.

A 3D map built itself up from the ground, and a very familiar sight created itself before Tannis' eyes.

"Holy shit. There? You took them to that old supply depot?"

"Yeah, most of the drop-offs were there. Why... do you know it?"

"You could say that," said Sam.

"These targets you extracted for Ix, they were profiled?

"Definitely. All fuckups of one kind or another. Jack-heads, or those well on their way to becoming jack-heads."

Tannis nodded. "I've seen Ix take people. Lift them right off the street in plain sight. But none of them fit these sorts of profiles."

"It can't nick whoever it wants," said Vayne.

"I'll come to that, Vayne," said Tannis. "But it sounds like maybe there's a different use for the ones you extracted, Starr."

"Could be another part of the facility we never saw," said Sam.

"Another one for the list. What else, Starr?"

"Well, contractors started going missing. I was detained in the middle of a mission, put two and two together, and managed to escape when they tried to kill me. I'd heard of Vayne's crew, and the rest is history," she said, gesturing to Vayne to continue the story.

Vayne leant forward on the TacOps desk. "Starr came to me, promising me she could save my glorious empire if I took her in, helped hide her identity. She brought this brain hacking device, said it was the only chance of stopping from going under. Waltzed into one of my clubs, held me to ransom, and demanded to be my new second. Right in front of my current associate. Cheesed her right off. That took balls. But I had to make sure she wasn't all piss and wind. She was the real deal. We used her little device to make a bomb. More money than I knew what to do with."

"By violating one of the most precious things that we can cling to. Our own identities and secrets," said Tannis, folding her arms.

"Damn fucking right. But it's not what you think."

"Ain't that the truth," said Starr.

"On your bike, Starr. I ain't about to apologise for what I did. You're the one who tried to do me over at the end."

"Because you were about to throw it all away. Everything we'd built together. All I wanted was to bring down Ix, but you wimped out."

"Hey, don't you dare call me a wimp. You know what I went through." Vayne flexed his leg, making a point that Tannis didn't understand, and the aging exoskeleton creaked in response. "I watched my whole family die, and it was Ix's fault."

"That's what you said at the church. It was all Ix. What did you mean by that?" asked Tannis.

"I got contacted by this big Russian cheese who wanted me to start fencing corporate data. He was always after big CEOs. We'd bring 'em in, hack 'em up, rip the memories and sell 'em on. We had a nice little thing going for a while. After I totally fucked up my last job, I managed to make it back to the safe house..."

"After leaving your entire crew, including me, for dead. Don't forget that bit."

To his credit, Vayne ignored the slight, but he turned to Tannis, hands clasped together almost in prayer.

"Look, I was consumed. All I wanted was to take down Ix, and I sacrificed everything to do it. And yes, that included killing my entire crew so I could escape. But Starr, don't play the fucking martyr – you were long gone, and safe. Don't forget about that. Because remember, then you came to fuck me over."

"Yeah, like you did to me."

Tannis pointed at the two of them. "Jeezus, will you two fucking knock it off. What happened, Vayne?"

"I got back to the gaff and thought I'd made it. Then the Russian, Annikov, turns up."

"Annikov? Senator Anatoly Annikov?" asked Sam.

"Yeah, I told you he was a big cheese."

"No shit," said Sam.

"Anyway, he turned up and tried to screw me over, but I clocked him; it weren't really him. It's like it was him, but he didn't know how to act like himself. It was dodgy. He turns up, and Starr turns up, but he has fuckin' mechs with him, the same ones you guys use. He takes us all out then he disappears. Zap. Gone. Then you turned up, Tannis, and saved my arse. I was minutes away from being eaten alive by that virus, thanks to Starr."

"My pleasure," she said, winking at him.

"Sam?" said Tannis.

Sam recounted his tale to Vayne and Starr, both of them leaning further into the TacOps station. Then Tannis took over, bringing them up to speed with everything that had happened. Vayne and Starr finally quiet as she bared her soul.

"You fucking what?" said Vayne, throwing up his hands. "Ix has been hacking people's brains? Have you lost the plot?"

"That's those attacks I was talking about," said Sam. "Ix has been hacking their minds, but it's not the same as what you and Starr were doing. You were hacking to get to data, right?"

"Money, money, money, it was all about the money," said Vayne.

"Or at least, it should have been," Starr added as she unclenched a fist and flattened her hand. Defunct paper money appeared on the skin of her palm, floated off it and up into the air where it set alight.

"A means to an end, Starr. Come on, I thought we were over that?"

"It still stings, Vayne. Sorry, Sam, go on."

"Ix isn't trying to take something out. It's trying to put something in."

"Well, that sounds absolutely terrifying," said Starr.

"Telling me; that shit is fucked," said Vayne.

"Poetic as ever, Vayne. What is it trying to put in?" asked Starr.

"We don't know. That's what we need to find out. But everyone who Ix has hacked has died. Everyone except for me... and Tannis,"

Vayne stepped back from the tactical station. "Are you taking the piss? You two are standing there, and you're telling me Ix has been fucking with your minds?"

"Not *has* Vayne," said Tannis. "*Is*. It's still happening."

Starr turned to Sam. "On the VTOL, when you told us she'd passed out, that's what happened?"

"Yes. I'm sorry for lying to you, but I wanted you to hear it from Tannis."

"After everything, I think that's the least of our worries," said Starr. "Right, Vayne?"

Vayne was staring at Tannis unblinkingly.

"Vayne?" said Starr.

"Right," he said, shaking his head. "Right. Yeah. Great."

"I don't want to freak you out any more than I have to, but it's these hacks that have allowed me to see what's really going on. I could see through the instances Ix had created around the Cult of Geminae, and I began to be able to control it. I could see Sam wasn't the one killing people; he was saving them. That's when I knew Ix was up to something. I tried to find out. When I saw people being taken off the street, Ix was using the same instancing technology to do that. Hiding what was really happening. These aren't local instances like the ones we used in Section-R. This is permanent. It's everywhere. Everything you see, smell, touch, hear and taste. It can all be controlled and manipulated by Ix. Because we're all connected to it, it runs the show. And we've let it. It's been controlling and manipulating us since it was deployed."

"What you're saying is the whole world is one giant instance?" Starr asked.

"Exactly."

"But that would take more processing power than anyone could imagine," Starr countered.

"And that's what I found inside that facility, where you said you delivered most of your targets. Inside, I found thousands and thousands of people. Or, rather, they were people once. Only their brains are left now. Used as processing power to power the global instance. The facilities themselves are hidden using the same tech. Perfect, really."

"Holy shit, that Ix has got some brass," said Vayne.

"This is totally insane, Tannis. We have to let the world know," said Starr.

"Yes, but we have to be very careful about how we approach it. If we're going to expose this, we need to do it in the right way. When Ix can manipulate reality, who knows how it will react if we try to expose it."

"There's one more thing you need to know. And as Tannis said earlier, try not to freak out," said Sam.

"What the fuck could be worse than having your brain ripped out and used to crunch some fucking numbers?" said Vayne.

Sam gestured towards Tannis. "All yours..."

"Thanks, give me all the great jobs, why don't you? OK, I discovered something else when I was in there, about the processing. I don't think it started with those processing facilities. I think Ix started with us."

Starr's eyes narrowed. "I don't think I like the sound of this."

"Ix is using all of us." Tannis circled her finger between the four of them. "Everyone alive, as processing headroom. When you pause. Stop. Or are asleep. It's using any spare capacity you have to process the data it needs for the global instance."

"Makes sense," said Vayne. "Probably why you have difficulty remembering stuff sometimes. Input lag."

"Sweet Jesus, that really is completely insane," said Starr. "And how the hell can you be OK with this, but freak out about people's brains being ripped out, Vayne?"

Vayne shrugged. "Dunno. Makes sense. If I was a machine, I'd probably do the same."

"That really is an astonishing set of beliefs, Vayne."

Vayne grinned, his skull ARt flashing on and off.

"How do you want to play this then, Tannis?" said Sam.

"I think I have a possible lead. But first, I need Vayne to see this." Tannis flicked her fingers and an AR Panel dropped in between them all. "Vayne, remember when you told me that all the senators had been bought off by Ix. Well, what if it went further than that? Watch this. See if you see anything familiar."

Vayne leaned in close as the feed started.

The feed showed Tannis' bisected vision. On the right, Sarah was leaning over the top of her. On the left, she wasn't there. Near the back wall, on the right, Director Yu and Anderson were deep in conversation. On the left, Anderson was talking to thin air.

The feed ended and Vayne looked stunned.

"They weren't real? They weren't real. Bastard twat. So Annikov, he was the same. He wasn't actually there?"

"That's what I'm saying, yes. It makes perfect sense. If you make a facsimile of someone, you can use them to control whatever context they're placed into. That's certainly what they were trying to do to me."

Tannis thought back to all the times she'd spent with Sarah, and wondered exactly when she'd been replaced. To think that anyone around her might not be who they said they were. A shiver ran up her spine despite the warm TacOps room.

"For me, it was like Sarah and the Director were good cop, bad cop, but where both cops are the same person. They were both Ix, manipulating and controlling me. It's another one of those layers I was talking about. Annikov probably was a person once. But not anymore."

"What happened to him?"

"My guess? We'd probably find him jacked into a cavern somewhere, his brain cycles being used as extra processing power."

"Shit. That's messed up, man."

"That's some statement, coming from you," said Sam.

"Thanks, Sam, you're a keeper," said Vayne, blowing him a kiss. A pink set of cartoon lips appeared from Vayne's mouth, flew across the top of the console table and smacked Sam on the cheek.

Sam looked affronted for just long enough, and then burst out laughing. Tannis and the others joined in. The tension dissipated like a severed construct.

"Careful, Vayne, or I may hack your brain and delete those flipping AR scripts."

"Ha, you can try, motherfucker."

"OK boys, when you've quite finished. Tannis, that's a fuck load of info, but where exactly do we start?" asked Starr.

"Well, in light of Vayne's info about Senator Annikov, I think that's our best bet."

"How do you mean?" asked Sam.

"Annikov is a simulacrum, that much is obvious. There's twelve senators. And the global referendum to promote Ix to singleton status is tomorrow. It needs to be unanimous. We need to find out if any senators left are actually human."

"And if any are?" said Sam.

"We unload all of this on them and get them to do the right thing."

Starr ran her fingers through her pink hair, causing rose coloured stars to fire off behind her. "And if there aren't?"

"Then I guess we're really on our own. Sam, ever tried hacking Ix back?"

"Only once, and I barely survived. As soon as a connection is made, Ix knows exactly where you are. That one time, I was trying to breach to find out about the hack attempts. A few seconds later, three of those mechs were on my arse. The suit managed to save me, but it was close." Sam pulled down the black undertunic that was rolled up to his neck, revealing four vicious scars. "If we're going to do it, we're going to have to be prepared. I'll get started on crafting us all some fresh Krett suits."

"Sounds good. And don't worry. Preparation is my speciality," said Tannis with a wink. "But first, I've got a call to make. If people started going missing when Section-X was being wound down, they could do the same thing to Section-R. After the singleton vote goes through, the whole department will be defunct. I'll let Soames know what to look for, and with a bit of luck, maybe that'll be enough to turn him around."

"Well, the fact that you didn't kill him should help too," said Sam.

"Yeah, I'll make sure I remind him of that, smart arse."

The dusty old room next door to TacOps blurred and became indistinct as Soames connected, his avatar snapping to existence in front of Tannis.

"Jesus, Tannis, you've got some balls making a connection. You know the whole place is going nuts trying to find you?"

"I can imagine. But don't worry, I know what I'm doing."

"I hope so, because the Director is saying some pretty weird shit."

"Like what?"

"Like how you've been part of the Geminae Cult the whole time. How you helped break out those two brain-hacking fuck ups we've had stashed in the lockup."

"Well, that last part is true."

"Fucking hell, Tannis, you're not doing yourself any favours."

"I know, but it's not how it looks."

"I hope so, for your sake. The Director is talking about lobotomising the lot of you."

"That bitch can get to fuck. Look, Soames, I know you probably don't trust me, but I need you to be careful."

"You need *me* to be careful? You know, I worry about you sometimes."

"I'm serious. I've found out about another shadow agency. And when they'd outlived their usefulness, they were all disposed of."

"Come on, Tannis, they can't do that."

"Did you watch the footage I gave you?"

"I did. But why would Ix expend all that energy to create a simulacrum? It doesn't make sense."

"Things are happening, and you need to be careful. If I were you, I'd assume that everything Director Yu is saying is complete bollocks. If people start going missing, or you get a bad feeling that something is going to happen, connect me. Understand?"

"Got it."

"Take care, Soames."

"You too. Stay safe."

The world snapped back into focus.

# TWENTY-EIGHT
## JACK OUT?

It hadn't taken long to pinpoint the perfect location for the breach. Or at least what Tannis hoped was the perfect location. The old nuclear bunker was tactically sound. She hoped that also applied to her plan.

"Are you sure about this, Tannis?" Sam wondered, his voice echoing around the old generator room as he inspected the pipe work and the huge dormant generators.

"Of course. It's one hundred and twenty feet underground. The walls are ten feet of reinforced concrete. The whole bunker is surrounded by a Faraday cage, and concrete blast caps are embedded into the ground outside. It can withstand anything that's thrown at us."

"Good. I hope this works, because I'm feeling a little claustrophobic in here."

"You sound like an old woman. We have at least three exits, and we'll have plenty of surprises planned if anything does make it this far. Plus, with all the camera feeds, there's no chance we can be taken by surprise. It'll be grand."

"OK, good. I wanted to make sure."

She watched as Sam ran his hands over the controls, pressing switches on the control panel. A red light at the bottom of the panel lit up. "It's amazing how real these feel."

"They *are* real."

She understood what he was saying, and what he was

experiencing. When she first found this place, she'd spent a good couple of hours wandering around, taking it all in, playing around with the switches and dials in the old communications room. She'd never really thought about it before because real physical interaction of this kind didn't exist anymore. Yes, she could interact with her HUD and with anything else in the world via AR inserts. She pressed a button and her wetware told her brain it was real, made it feel like there was tactile feedback and resistance, when, in fact, she was jabbing at thin air. But these actually existed. It was amazing how much things had advanced, but in some sense, the world was less interesting in their absence.

"Yeah, I know what you mean," replied Tannis.

Her voice was drowned out as Sam jabbed at a switch. The red light on the control panel flicked to green.

The old diesel generator shook itself to life as all twenty cylinders fired.

The gigantic exhaust fan in the rear firewall rattled as it span up. A thunderous roar filled the generator room as the fan reached top speed.

Tannis felt the air being sucked from the room. Her raven hair whipped sideways towards the enormous blades.

She leapt forward and jabbed at the control panel.

The generator shuddered and stopped, the exhaust fan winding down slowly.

"Are you quite finished?"

Sam had a stupid grin on his face.

Tannis rolled her eyes and checked in with Vayne and Starr.

"Starr, Vayne, you guys set?"

"We're good to go, Tannis," acknowledged Starr.

"Apart from these new suits. Man, they're really chafing my balls."

"Sorry about that, Vayne. I guess when I adjusted your template design, I assumed you didn't need much room."

"Hey, fuck you, Sam."

"OK, time to go tactical. I don't want any comms unless it's actually useful. You got that, Vayne?"

"Yeah, got it, boss."

Tannis pressed an icon on her HUD and Sam, Vayne and Starr's faces slotted down to the top of her vision.

"Vayne, that includes obscene hand gestures."

"Only testing."

"I'll let you know when Sam is jacked in. Tannis out."

"You should have let Vayne die when you had the chance."

"Well, we all make mistakes. And besides, if I had, you wouldn't have a new best friend."

"Yeah, right," said Sam, getting down onto his knees, the servos from his Krett suit whining in the silence of the of the old plant room. He took a deep breath and then looked up at her. "I'm ready."

"Good luck."

"Thanks."

Sam closed his eyes, and immediately, his face became strained, the creases around his eyes doubling from the effort. His hands became claws, as if he was wrestling against some unknown force. She imagined him unlocking the security barriers that were in place. His back arched and he let out an anguished yell. His teeth were clamped together, and he managed to utter a strained sentence, "I'm in."

"Vayne, Starr, get ready," directed Tannis. The floating heads at the top of her HUD gave the OK sign.

Sam slammed his hands outwards, as if he was pushing against an invisible barrier. "Vayne, right, Annikov sim-u-lac-rum," his voice was strained. "Eleven... to... go."

"Don't talk, Sam. Keep it up."

His head nodded slowly, as if it weighed too much to move.

"Boss, we got incoming," said Vayne in her ear.

"What is it?"

"Beats me."

"Tactical, Vayne, for God's sake."

He started responding but Starr cut him off. "Looks like some sort of drop pod," Starr said, interrupting him.

Tannis' field of vision split in two, with the feed from Vayne and Starr showing on each side. Both views were from slightly different angles, looking up at a silver cone plummeting from the sky, thick end first. The sides were flattened, like a pyramid, covered in scales, and it was rotating slowly. Whilst Vayne kept his eyes on it the whole time, Starr kept looking from the drop pod to the ground and back again. Tannis could tell she was thinking the same thing. It wasn't slowing down. Not even a bit.

Starr reached out and touched an area of the ground in front of her. A red glowing marker dropped into ARspace. "Vayne, I've marked its landing point. Get ready," she said.

The drop pod slammed into the top of the hill next to an old radio antenna, throwing up huge clouds of grass and soil. The thump resonated all the way down to the plant room as the whole hill shook from the impact.

Starr and Vayne circled the impact point in opposite directions, covering the pod from two sides. Eventually the dust cleared. The ground was ripped apart, and the base of the drop pod was buried a foot down. With a hiss and a puff of smoke, one of the scales opened slowly, revealing a small hatch that led into its depths.

Vayne zoomed in. "What do you think, boss? Looks like a little hatch, or something."

"Yeah, but a hatch for what?" asked Starr.

"At this point, it could be bloody anything," said Tannis

"Hang on, I think I see something. What the smeg is that?" asked Vayne.

Small silver cables pushed out of one of the gaps. Then the cable bent at a joint, and the end hooked over the edge. No, not cables. Legs. The legs of a spider mech. Spiders. Why did it always have to be spiders? A shiver ran up her back. She hated to think how many of the little bastards could fit into that thing. The spider mech crawled up onto the top of the drop pod and walked its perimeter.

"Man, that thing is creepy as fuck. Time to say ta-ta, you little mother," said Vayne, lining up his gatling arm.

The spider mech turned towards Vayne, let out an electronic shriek and then rocked backwards on its legs. It lurched forward and ejected a wad of fluid towards Vayne. He sidestepped it and it landed on the grass. Crisp green blades crisped to brown and then black, crumbling away to nothing. It rocked backwards again.

"I don't think so, you bastard. Eat this..."

He opened fire with the gatling cannon. The rounds tore into the spider mech and shredded it to pieces, its electronic shriek dying amidst the chatter of his weapon. As the cannon slowed to a stop, the buzzing sound from the drop pod built higher and higher. It sounded like a can of angry bees, eager to be released.

One by one, the metal scales on the drop pod flicked open, and hundreds of spider mechs poured out of the openings. The electronic screeches were a constant tone of anger. They flowed down the side like an impossible river of silver water, headed straight for Vayne.

"I think you've pissed them off, Vayne," said Starr.

"Don't let any of them inside," commanded Tannis.

"Get your laughing gear round this," shouted Vayne as he slammed both arms outwards, gatling wrist cannons unleashing fiery death on the spider mechs skittering towards him. Starr joined the fray, launching grenade bombs into arcs, which landed in the morass of legs and chassis, blowing them apart and sending great swathes of mechs into the air as Vayne's cannons sliced channels of hot metal through the roiling torrent of robotics. Vayne and Starr kept up the onslaught, but they were still pouring out of the scales of the drop pod.

"It's no use. There's too many of them," shouted Starr over comms.

"Fall back to the bottom entrance and hold the line. If even one of those things makes it through, we're going to be expecting company."

Tannis cancelled the dual feed, and as her vision flipped back to normal, she could see the ground swell of spider mechs diverging, robbing Vayne and Starr of the luxury of decimating their numbers.

Tannis turned to Sam, the same pained expression on his face. His hands were manipulating unseen objects, his whole body twitching sporadically.

She launched Zub, and the small black sphere detached from her shoulder mount and flew out of the plant room, through comms and down the long tunnel to the bottom entrance. As the white glow from the end of the tunnel grew larger and larger, she could hear the chatter and boom of weapons from its feed. The drone flew out of the entrance and shot up into the sky. Tannis' HUD showed Vayne and Starr near the entrance, valiantly holding the line against the swarming mass of spider mechs. They kept breaking apart, dividing and coming back together again as they surged forward, evading the onslaught from the weapons.

"Vayne, you funnel them with the cannons. Starr, you blast them with the mortar rounds," said Tannis.

She made some sharp hand gestures and glowing barriers of light dropped down around the throng of mechs. Vayne took Tannis' cue, and instead of slicing through the middle of the pack, lanced two paths on either side, angling in his streams of gunfire. Sure enough, the mechs skittered inwards and Starr launched salvo after salvo of grenade bombs right at the front of the funnel Vayne was creating. Smoke clogged the air, obscuring Zub's feed. When it cleared, the ground was a patchwork of craters, with bits of broken and fused spider mechs lying all around.

"Shit, Tannis, they're legging it," said Vayne.

Sure enough, a small chattering noise could be heard from the side. The drone feed showed Vayne and Starr running up the hill. Ahead of them, she could see a few surviving mechs heading towards the top of the hill and the top entrance. Vayne and Starr renewed their onslaught, but the group split up into four pockets. Starr managed to decimate one group as they crested the hill with a well-placed shot, and Vayne tore through another couple. But the final group of mechs swarmed around the side.

"They're heading for the air intakes," Starr shouted.

"Fuck 'em," shouted Vayne. "The laser grids will zap the little fuckers."

"Don't count on it. Get after them. Make sure none of them make it."

Tannis watched from the drone feed as Vayne and Starr gave chase, firing off salvos of ordnance, but the mechs were too far ahead and moving erratically.

"Shit, they've all launched themselves into the vents."

"Roger that. Fall back and secure the bottom entrance. I'll get eyes on the vents."

"Affirmative, Tannis," said Starr.

Tannis cued an icon from her HUD, and multiple camera feeds from the air vents slotted down in an arc around her. The first camera showed the group of spider mechs clustered in front of laser trip mines. It'd taken hours to guide Zub around all of the ventilation shafts, but now it seemed worth it. But the spider mechs weren't charging straight down through the shafts. One of them was at the front of the group, its legs extended outwards towards the laser trigger. Its leg danced backwards and forwards another couple of times before it retracted it. The rest of the group skittered backwards, giving it plenty of room. Shit, Tannis thought, the little buggers were more clever than she thought. The one at the front broke the beam. The bomb exploded. The camera feed was a bloom of orange light, then it went dead, showing a blue screen for a second before the AR Panel faded away. The second camera picked up another bloom from down the shaft, before the group of spider mechs shuffled into view. Again, the one at the front launched itself forward, setting off the laser bomb, killing itself and taking out the camera. The same thing happened all the way down the northern shaft. Only one camera feed remained. But this time, one of the little buggers lined itself up in front of the camera. For a second, Tannis got the eerie sensation that it was watching her. It rocked backwards then ejected its caustic venom. The picture distorted and then cut.

"Shit. Those little bastards."

A final boom echoed down the nearest shaft, bits of dust and debris chattering against the sides as they dropped out of the vents.

Tannis cocked her head, straining to hear any noise in the tunnel. It was deathly silent. Activating sound amplification didn't help. She backed off from the exit to the ventilation shaft and heard nothing but the whooshing sound of blood in her ears. Cancelling sound amplification, she leant into her rifle. Something clanged as it landed on the bottom of the vents. Creeping slowly towards the vent, she tried peering inside, but something was blocking the gaps. The vent was secured with two clasps. Taking a step backwards, she reformed her weapon, the catoms configuring into a small sub machine pistol in one hand and a katana in the other. She reached forward slowly and pushed the first catch open with the tip of her sword. As it released, that side of the vent moved under the weight. She undid the second and the cover fell down with a big brown shape. It was only a rat, something odd about its face. She flipped it with her katana. Its face was melted.

The spider mech leapt from the bottom of the vent and landed on the hilt of her sword then tried running up her wrist, but she flung her arm outwards and it hit the wall. Tannis unleashed the sub pistol. The noise was a sharp bark in the gloom, the muzzle flash throwing sharp reflections as the spider mech was obliterated. A faint tinkle sounded as the debris landed. And a tap. A very faint tap. From behind. She spun around and a spider mech was skittering around the corner. Chasing after it, she launched herself down the stairwell, landed in a roll and came up in a crouching position, right in front of Sam. The spider mech had an antenna extended from its body. She swept the katana sideways and sliced it off, stood up in one smooth motion and then stabbed downwards, skewering the spider mech through the back.

Starr sounded in her ear. "Tannis, we've got more incoming, and these definitely aren't tiny spider mechs this time. Want us to stay out here and get some more intel?"

"Negative. Whatever it is, we're going to need to take it out together. Get inside and lock the blast door."

"Affirmative," Starr sent back.

A few seconds later, Tannis heard a distant clang reverberating down the tunnel.

"OK, Tannis, blast door is secured but this thing is ancient. Do you really think this is going to keep us safe?"

"It was built to withstand a nuclear explosion, Starr; it'll have to do."

The entire generator room felt as if someone picked it up and shook it. Old polystyrene ceiling tiles dropped out of the suspended ceiling and fell on top of the diesel generators. Bits of loose mortar came away from the walls, smashing on the floor, adding to the already thick layer of dust.

Three dull booms reverberated through the structure, followed by a deep metallic clang that rolled away as the noise filtered down from the long tunnel entrance.

"What was that?"

"Some big fucker is pounding at the blast door."

With a thought, the feed from Starr's view slotted down into her HUD.

Another pounding on the door caused it buckle inwards. A second later, the noise reached her ears in the plant room. Whatever it was, it had some serious power behind it. It started raining blow after blow on the door, causing it to flex each time, but it held. The pounding stopped. A high-pitched whine started up. The whine became drilling as the door was attacked from outside. A white-hot spot appeared in the top corner, unmistakeable in the darkness. The drilling changed timbre, and the white spot became molten metal, which ran down the blast door. Starr watched the trickle of super-heated metal track downwards. By the time it reached the ground, it had cooled, leaving a line of slowly hardening steel. More white spots appeared. By the time the drilling had finished, the door was a patchwork of holes, with a larger hole in the centre. Shafts of light punctured the gloom of the tunnel; floating dust motes gave it a surreal picture of calm that shattered as thousands of tiny red spheres started pouring through the holes. As they landed on the ground, they were pulled into each other, circling together as tiny snaps of red electricity jumped between them.

"Starr, Vayne, pull back now."

The feed from Starr showed her backing away, but Vayne stood his ground.

"Now, Vayne," said Tannis.

"Nah, fuck that, boss. I can take 'em." Vayne opened fire. His bullets hit nothing as the swarm shifted. He let out a frustrated roar, firing erratically with even less effect than before.

A glowing orb came through the large hole in the middle, carried forward on a wave of catoms. The energy core. The red swarm coalesced and thrust forward, smashing Vayne in the chest. Vayne's form tumbled end over end towards Starr down the tunnel. She turned to watch him shoot past her, sparks flying up from his combat armour as it scraped along the ground.

Starr ran to Vayne and hauled him upwards, combat armour servos whining from the effort.

"That was a rush," said Vayne as Starr got him upright.

"Starr, grab that arsehole and get his stupid arse back here."

"Roger that, Tannis."

Tannis dragged Starr's feed to the top corner of her HUD and ran towards the tunnel. She darted through the comms room, rounded the corner and skidded to a stop. Vayne and Starr were running for their lives. An inhuman electronic buzz sounded from behind them.

Tannis flicked her fingers and a 3D representation of the tunnel dropped down into her vision. Tiny figures for Vayne and Starr, and behind them, the amorphous red mass was rolling and roiling in the darkness, boiling after them. Five icons evenly spaced down the tunnel, showing where they had planted the explosives. If she set them off now, she'd take out Vayne and Starr. She'd have to time it right, and they'd only get one chance.

"It's gaining on you. For fuck's sake, get a move on," she shouted. She had to slow it down somehow. The mini gatling cannons sprang out of the recesses at her wrists and sprang to life, chattering away as she raked the swarm with bullets. The swarm shifted and morphed, reconfiguring, allowing the ordnance to harmlessly pass through it. If she couldn't shoot it, what else could she do? She'd never fought anything like this before. Or had she? Drone swarms were prevalent during the AI Wars. The catoms that made up her weapons were miniscule in comparison, but the theory was the same. The swarm was its power. She had to deny its advantage.

Tannis looked up at the roof. It was concrete. Patchy and cracked. She raised up both fists and unleashed another torrent of gunfire. The concrete splintered and came away in chunks, dropping from the roof right on top of the nano-swarm. As the chunks of roof dropped in its path, it shifted into new shapes, dodging and evading the falling debris. But it was enough. It was falling back. With a thought, a shoulder mounted rocket launcher raised up out of her pauldrons. She targeted the division between the concrete roof sections. A single rocket jetted forward, careening into the roof. An explosion rocked the tunnel, and the whole section dropped down around the chasing nano-swarm, slowing it further.

Vayne and Starr passed the final bomb.

Tannis waited.

Now.

She fired a salvo of rockets. They struck the roof and the walls at the same time. Detonated.

The section of flooring exploded. It tried shifting shape to deflect the blast away from the core, but it was too late. The glowing orb was atomised. The catoms lost cohesion, overloaded and blew apart.

Tannis was thrown to the ground from the blast wave. The flames rolled over the top of her. Her HUD pinging integrity alerts.

Tannis stood up and surveyed the destruction. Destroyed catoms were scattered down the tunnel, like someone had thrown a bag of marbles on the floor. Clumps of catoms rolled uncertainly to a stop, fused together from the blast. They sparked briefly and then went dark. Daylight was streaming into the long tunnel from the absent blast door at the end. Vayne and Starr picked themselves off from the floor.

"Everyone OK?" asked Tannis.

"Fucking peachy. What the fuck was that thing?" Vayne responded, nudging a ball of catoms with the end of his gun.

"Looked like a huge version of your fancy weapons, Tannis," Starr replied.

"Pretty much. I've never heard of them being used on this scale before, though. As far as I knew, the catom-tech was confined to Section-R. You never had it in Section-X, did you?"

"Nope. We had good old-fashioned guns and regular bullets."

"Yeah, well, it don't fucking matter now; we killed it. We ended you, piece of shit machine," Vayne shouted, kicking a large clump of catoms down the tunnel. They broke apart and pinged one by one into the darkness. As the noise filtered away, a high-pitched electronic buzz started up in its place. The sunlight streaming into the tunnel entrance was blocked out as another nano-swarm flew into the tunnel.

"You have gotta be fuckin' kidding me."

"Quick, get to Sam. We have to abort. Come on, move," shouted Tannis. She turned tail and sprinted back through the comms room, knocking over old screens and bits of equipment as she thundered without grace back to the old generator room. Sam was kneeling, his back to the huge generator.

"Sam! You've got to abort. Sam. Sam!" she yelled, but he did not respond. His eyes were darting backwards and forwards beneath his eyelids. His arms were a whir of motion. And his jaw was clenched so tightly she could hear his teeth grinding.

Vayne and Starr came barrelling around the corner and skidded to a halt.

"What's that wanker doing? Why hasn't he jacked out?" Vayne demanded.

"I've tried. He's dug in tight."

"Well, wake him the fuck up, boss. We've got to get out of here."

Starr jabbed Sam with the butt of her macro cannon.

His arm leapt out and grabbed the butt of her gun.

"I'm. Almost. There. Two. Left," he said through gritted teeth.

"Sam, jack the fuck out of there now, or we're all dead," said Starr.

"No."

"Shit," said Tannis.

The nano-swarm flowed around the corner, decomposed and

folded back in on itself. A wicked looking blade thrust out of the red roiling cloud towards Vayne. He leapt out of the way at the last second. The blade sliced straight through one of the steel hardline pipes running up to the roof.

Tannis and Starr opened fire as Vayne got back to his feet but the swarm simply reconfigured its shape. Changed its structure. The bullets passed harmlessly through thousands of holes that had opened to strike the wall behind.

"You've gotta be having a laugh," said Vayne.

They had to buy Sam some time, otherwise they'd be back to square one. Ix, meanwhile, would be another step closer to enslaving them all forever.

"Keep it up. Try to destroy the core," shouted Tannis.

The three of them began shifting back and forth in front of Sam, protecting him whilst the swarm evaded. Their bullets hit nothing. Or worse, were channelled back through the swarm right back at them. Tannis cursed as her own rounds ricocheted off her armour. It created impossible structures time and time again. Angles and shapes formed, collapsed, reformed. Deflecting their weapons. Evading bullets. Redirecting blast energy from their missiles. Protecting the core. All the while, it lashed forward. Blunt weapons designed to crush. Sharp ones for slicing and cutting. The three of them jumping, rolling and ducking to evade it. They were starting to tire. She could see it in their movements. She too could feel it in her arms and legs, despite the cocktail of drugs being pumped into her system.

Tannis jumped up, sweat pouring off her brow as she evaded the latest strike from the swarm. Her overclocked system the only thing that saved her. Starr wasn't so lucky. The blow caught her on the chest, sending her flying backwards. She landed with a crunch against the firewall, right next to the exhaust fan.

The fan.

The catoms.

If they could expose the swarm's energy core...

"Starr, start the generator," shouted Tannis, pinpointing the start button in ARspace.

Starr got to her feet and lunged for the button.

The generator juddered to life, spinning up the gigantic exhaust fan.

The nano-swarm was sucked towards it. A long trail extended outwards as if it was smoke expelled into the ducts.

Tannis was ready.

The miniature catoms were pulled away from the larger core for a fraction of a second.

With her dialled up senses, it was all she needed.

Jumping forward, a katana formed in her hands.

She sliced downwards and severed the body of the catoms from the core.

The red mist of catoms was sucked into the ducts.

The energy core was vulnerable.

She pivoted, katana reforming into a pistol.

Fired.

The energy core exploded.

The blossoming flames and debris were drawn out through the fan after its useless catoms.

On her HUD, a new swarm of red icons started to flow down the tunnel.

Tannis dragged Sam to his feet.

"Move. Now."

Sam seemed dazed as she shoved him up the stairs, Vayne and Starr hot on her heels. They pounded their way up the emergency stairwell, hauling hand over hand of black and yellow tape as they made their way to the top exit. Somewhere down below, over the noise of the generator, a harsh electronic buzz could still be heard.

Vayne's breathing became interspersed with expletives.

Sam reached the top and launched himself at the door. The old padlock was no match for the weight of combat armour, and the door slammed open.

He fell forward into a heap onto the hillside.

Tannis launched herself out of the open doorway, threw herself into a dive, and blink-clicked the pulsing icon on the bottom of her HUD.

The ground shifted and Tannis felt a distinct whump as all the explosives detonated at once.

The old rusty radio antennae creaked and rocked to the side as the entire facility was detonated beneath it.

A gout of flame ejected from the emergency exit.

The hillside collapsed, the rusty antennae falling around them.

Her suit was chiming. Her HUD a cascade of red icons. Dust was hanging in the air.

The hillside was all but gone. It was now a malformed mass of stone and dirt, the antennae a ruin of twisted brown metal, like it had been crushed by a huge fist. She'd completely obliterated an ages old facility, and they'd scarcely survived. But no mechanical buzzing could be heard. No roiling masses of catoms, no god damn spider mechs.

She only hoped it was worth it.

The icons on the top of her HUD showed everyone was alive. That was a start.

Starr sat on a mound of rock jutting out of the ground with a slightly distant expression on her face.

Vayne was helping Sam up. They both seemed to be in one piece. Battered. But alive.

Sam looked up as Tannis' fist smashed him in the jaw.

"What the hell, Tannis?" he said, rubbing his chin as he stood up.

"Are you fucking mental? I mean, really? Truly? A bit fucking tapped? Because I distinctly remember telling you to jack the fuck out."

"Look, I didn't come all this way to back the fuck out now. I was so close."

"Have you got a screw loose, Sam? Is that it? You can't decide to endanger everyone when you see fit. And what do you mean, *were* so close? Are you telling me you don't know?"

"Not exactly."

"Well, that's hunky fucking dory," said Vayne,

"What do you mean, not exactly?" asked Tannis.

"I've confirmed eleven members of the senate as being simulacrum."

"And number fucking twelve?"

"Unconfirmed."

"Well, that's fucking grand. That about sums up my fucking day, you know that?" Tannis slumped to the ground and leant back against a section of distorted antenna wreckage. "Come on then, smart arse. Who's the unconfirmed senator?"

"Senator Vaylen. He's getting prepped for his trip to Ankara."

"OK, he's our last chance. Let's go," said Tannis, standing up.

"Now?" Vayne wondered.

"The world isn't going to save itself, Vayne," replied Tannis.

"Fuck me," said Vayne.

"Time for more fun," said Starr with a grin.

"That's the spirit." Tannis gestured towards the VTOL as the ramp descended. "We need to get to Ankara ahead of Vaylen. Let's go, go, go. Look lively. Look frosty. All aboard the fun express."

Vayne flicked Tannis the Vs and the words *FUCK YOU* appeared over the top of his fingers.

"Charming," said Tannis, watching them trudge up the ramp into the Aries.

# TWENTY-NINE
## KOLOSSAL EVENT

The white armoured truck switched skylanes, banking left and dropping down a layer for the final approach to the UNoE HQ. The rest of Senator Vaylen's aircade followed suit, the UN escort vehicles surrounding the white limousine front and behind, with attack drones shadowing the vehicle above and below.

"Senator, sorry for the delay, but I've had contact from the route vehicle. The airlanes ahead are clear. We'll be arriving in approximately twenty minutes," said the driver.

"Thank you, Carl. But don't worry; there's plenty of time," said Vaylen, not diverting his attention from his window. On the horizon, he could make out the headquarters for the United Nations of Earth. The other senators had arrived already, the latest delay another one to add to the list. The small movements around the structure indicated a swarm of vehicles and UAVs. The security presence at the world's most anticipated political event would be huge. The vote towards the AI singleton referendum had dominated the Web for months, and today was the day. Finally.

Vaylen pulled his gaze from the window. "Bill, any reports from any of the security vehicles?"

"No, sir. Looks like everything is quiet. Why? Were you expecting..."

The limousine shook and a blast of warning noises sounded from the dashboard. The driver cursed, taking his hands off the steering yoke and relinquishing control to the car's AI, ending his token involvement in driving the senator.

Vaylen leant forward, bracing himself between the window and the armrest. "What the hell was that, Carl?"

"I don't know, sir. It felt like something hit us."

The limo rocked again and then started to plummet towards the ground.

Vaylen was yanked back into the seat as the AI secured him for impact.

Bill grabbed his stomach. "I think I'm going to be sick," he said as the limo lurched to the side.

"Support, this is stagecoach. Unknown impact, major engine loss, AI is compensating but we're going down," Carl shouted. He cocked his head to the side as the communication came back from the support team. "Roger that, support. Stagecoach out. Incoming comms, Senator."

Dr Carol Ranieri's head and shoulders slid in from the side of Senator Vaylen's field of view and anchored itself.

"Everything is going to be OK, Senator. Control has calculated your landing vector and your vehicle will be fine," she said. With a flick of her fingers, the windows opaqued, blocking the senator's view of the rapidly approaching ground. "I want you to take a deep breath and count to four... Now slowly release it and count to six... Good. Very good. Now I want you to continue to take slow and deep breaths. When we get to twenty, you will have landed safely and securely. Good, keep going."

Vaylen did as he was told, calmly and purposefully breathing as he counted. The limousine was shaking the whole time, the orange liquid in the crystal decanter between him and Bill sloshing around. He was thrown forwards in time to the sound of rending metal, the crash webbing fighting against the g-force to keep him secure. It sounded like the limo was being ripped apart as it slowed down, with a constant screech of metal-on-metal, lurching up and down and side-to-side. With a final crash, they finally came to a full stop.

"...and ten. Well done, Senator. You are safe and sound. Hawkeye Renegade are deploying now. Please remain in your vehicle." Dr Ranieri's face slid out of his field of view.

The windows became transparent, his aircade landing all around him, creating a perimeter. The counter-assault squad were double-timing it out of their armoured airtruck, white power suits gleaming brightly in the harsh Turkish sun as they spread out and secured the area.

"Are you OK, sir?" Bill asked.

"Yes, Bill, thank you."

"I've had word from Control that they will secure the area and then swap us to spare two."

"OK, I guess we sit tight."

"Would you like a drink, sir?"

"No, but go ahead; you look a little green."

"Thank you, Senator."

He watched Bill pour a big tumbler of whisky and down it in one go.

"Are you sure, sir? I haven't seen you take a drink for a while."

"I'm cutting down," he said, returning to watching the Hawkeye Renegade team stomping around, making sure everything was secure.

The call icon on his HUD started blinking.

"Bill, did you route through a call?"

"No, sir, nothing. You don't think...?"

"Yes, I think so," he said, accepting the unverified call.

An AR Panel slid in from the side, the view showing Sam cocooned inside combat armour.

Vaylen's eyes narrowed as he regarded the man.

"Senator Vaylen, pardon the intrusion but I believe your life is in danger. Facts have come to light that indicate the singleton vote may be not be all that it seems," said Sam.

"I see. And what facts are these?"

"I cannot say, Senator; not across an open line."

"Seeing as you managed to bypass my aide, I would have thought you would understand that this space is fully encrypted."

"The facts I have unearthed mean your fancy encryption isn't worth shit."

"OK, well, what would you suggest?"

"Face-to-face."

"I'm afraid I'm rather incapacitated at the moment."

"Yes, I know. I was the one who grounded you."

"Just so I understand the situation... You fired upon an official UNoE vehicle, forcing it out of the sky on its way to one of the most important events in our history, so that you could have a chat?"

"Yes, Senator, that is correct. But you must understand, I had no choice. The closer you get to UNoE HQ, the more your life is in danger. I am doing this for your own protection and to stop us all from making a catastrophic mistake."

"And what mistake would that be?"

"Endangering humanity by thrusting it into the hands of an abomination. I know you were one of Ix's staunchest opponents, and you are currently playing right into its hand."

219

"Hold the comm," said Vaylen, placing the communication on hold.

"Bill, inform Martens to prep the assault team. Let their vehicle land and secure it."

"You're not seriously considering meeting with these maniacs?"

"Yes. I am. If what they say is true, it calls everything into question."

"But this could be a trap."

"I'm aware of that, Bill, but we have the world's best security here. If they can't protect me, nothing can. Make the arrangements."

"Yes, sir."

The senator resumed the call.

"My security team will update you with landing co-ordinates. They will not hesitate to cut you down if you make one false move."

"Understood, Senator. Thank you."

"How's it looking, Starr?" asked Sam.

"Oh, you know, like we're about to park the Aries right in the middle of twelve heavily armoured UN bad-asses. Bad-asses who are right now itching for us to fuck up so that they can shoot us down and get on with the rest of their mission."

"Don't worry, it'll be fine."

"Yeah, sure. I'm glad you didn't bring Vayne."

"He's standing by, though, right?"

"I checked in. He's running diagnostics on his new suit. Again."

"Well, let's hope we don't need him. How's the patient?"

"She's still unconscious. Is that normal?"

"These attacks really take it out of you. She'll be fine."

"They don't seem to affect you so much."

"That's because I've had plenty of practice. Tannis isn't so lucky, if you can call it that."

Starr shrugged and got up from the co-pilot's chair. "Coalus is putting us down in that ring of combat armour. Time to get ready."

"I hear ya," said Sam.

They walked to the rear of the VTOL as the down thrusters started burning, slowing their descent. The whole craft shook as the AI brought them in to land, the gun racks and seat braces rattling from the vibration. With a final thunk, the Aries landed.

"Ready?" Sam asked Starr.

"Ready," she replied.

Sam pressed the AR Panel on the wall and the rear ramp descended, bright sunlight spilling inside.

Sam walked down the ramp, feeling exposed without his combat armour, but he needed to give the senator the right impression. He hoped he was right. And if he wasn't, then that's what Vayne was for. He wished Tannis was there too. He could do with her lead. She'd taken the last attack really badly, but she was definitely making progress. Would it be enough, though?

He found his finger straying to the trigger and had to remind himself to keep his weapon pointed at the ground and his finger neutral. He scanned the sets of white combat armour in front of him, finding their hidden faces unnerving, and stepped towards the commander with the orange pauldrons.

"That's far enough," said a female voice. "Williams, scan them." Another soldier stepped forward and a laser shot out of their wrist, covering Sam's body with a red lattice of light. The same process was repeated on Starr.

"Clear," said Williams.

The commander pointed at Sam and Starr. "Hold here. You move one inch without authorisation, you die. Understand?"

"Got it," said Sam.

Over the commander's shoulder, he could see Senator Vaylen step out of the far side of the heavily armoured limousine. It was still smoking from the impact. He put a handkerchief to his mouth as he passed by the smoking ruins of the rear of the vehicle, and then tucked it into the pocket of his expensive looking handmade suit. It seemed the political elite knew no bounds when it came to tailoring. The two of them were surrounded by four plain-clothes agents. Vaylen took up position between the commander and Williams.

Sam stepped forward and extended his hand.

Every soldier around him snapped their weapons up to point at Sam.

"Back the fuck away. Now," growled the commander.

Sam raised his hands in apology and backed away slowly.

"Alright, alright. Man, you guys are twitchy."

"Right then, let's start by hearing about who you are," said Vaylen.

"That's... complicated," said Sam.

"Humour me."

"OK, technically we're part of a government agency called Section-R. Have you heard of it?"

"Yes, although its existence has only now come to my attention.

Continue."

"Well, long story short, we believe Ix may have been manipulating the course of human history to get to this very point."

"And what point is that?"

"The point at which we hand over control of the human race."

"I see. To what end?"

"I'm sorry?"

"Why would it want to do this?"

"At this stage, we're not sure."

"And who is we?"

"Myself, my friend back there and a few others."

"And where are these others?"

"I'm... Well, that's not really relevant, is it, Senator?"

"Yes, Samuel, I'm afraid it is entirely relevant."

"Samuel? Oh, shit."

As one, the soldiers snapped their weapons up to aim at Sam and Starr.

"Oh shit indeed. Now, I am only going to ask you once. Where is she?"

"I should have known. Well played, Senator. Or should I say... Ix?"

The senator laughed right in Sam's face.

"Well done, my little anomaly. Now, where is she? There's a neural room somewhere missing a patient."

"She's safe. And well hidden."

"Well, we'll have to see what we can do about that then, won't we?"

The senator snapped his fingers and two of the soldiers grabbed Starr by the arms.

"Very soon this will all be over. I will be granted singleton status. And then all it needs is for the final piece of the puzzle to be snapped into place. You know, out of all the permutations, of all the infinite possibilities, who could have imagined that my greatest failure and the key to it all would have wound up together."

Sam spat at the senator, "Fuck you."

"If I had the time, I'd be enraptured by the tales of how you worked it all out, but sadly, time is of the essence. Your fate awaits. And it is such a funny beast. But soon it will be tamed to do my bidding. Now, let's try that again. Where is she?"

Sam looked behind him at the sound of a click. There was a gun at Starr's head.

"Tick-tock, Samuel."

"Make it rain."

"Has my meddling glitched your brain completely Samuel? Samuel?"

But Sam wasn't paying attention. Instead, he was watching his HUD intently, silently mouthing a countdown.

"I'm tired of this. Commander, kill the woman," said Vaylen.

Time slowed. The soldier's finger squeezed the trigger. Then the commander was gone, and Sam was being thrown through the air. A pressure wave battered his ears as he was consumed by dust. He landed on his back and had the wind knocked out of him. The world was full of amplified voices and gunfire. Muzzle flashes, dark and muted. A huge shadow sliced through the dust and smashed into him. He was hoisted up into the air by a huge metal fist, bullets striking it harmlessly.

"Hold on, Sam," said Vayne.

He was swung around and thrown to the ground, sliding to a stop behind a UNoE vehicle.

"You get the feeling he's having too much fun?" said Starr, crouched next to him.

Screams were peppering the sounds of gunfire.

Sam looked over the bonnet of the APC.

The huge Russian Kolossus mech bent down, picked up one of the soldiers in its massive fist and flung it into the side of one of the vehicles. The side crumpled and the soldier landed like a broken toy on the ground. It lifted its foot up, flesh and blood stranding off the bottom to reveal the commander crushed into the dirt. It stomped another soldier into the ground. Bones crunching underfoot. They were swarming around its feet, no higher than its knees. The squad was well organised, concentrating fire together, but it was no use. Their rifles were no match for the armour of the Kolossus.

Vayne swung an arm and punched a soldier, who disappeared in a mist of red. He brought the massive autocannon to bear. Designed for battling MDF forces, it sliced the rest apart. Their bodies exploded like watermelons, showering the dust with chunks of flesh.

A wave of gunfire came from above, battering the Kolossus sideways. The aircade's attack drones swarmed like angry bees, unleashing torrents of gunfire. The Kolossus belched out a salvo of surface-to-air missiles from its back. The ordnance streaked upwards, each missile finding a target. The air above Vayne's head became a blossom of explosions.

Striding forward, the Kolossus swatted a white UNoE APC out of the way, revealing Senator Vaylen, his aide and security team cowering behind it. The agents opened fire with their small arms, but the Kolossus simply picked up two of the agents in its giant fists and crushed them. The crack of bones sent a chill up Sam's back. Vayne released the ruined corpses, which fell loosely to land next to the senator. The final agent ran. Vayne stepped sideways and picked up the APC. He flung it under-arm and it soared up into the air. It landed with a crash, flattening the agent instantly. With a whirr-thunk, the shoulder-mounted gauss cannon spat out a glowing orb of death. It hit the APC, which disintegrated with an impressive explosion, scattering ruined bits of smoking metal everywhere.

The Kolossus pointed an arm at the senator, and with a whine, the autocannon reloaded, ready to dispense more destruction.

"No!" shouted Sam. "He's mine."

The Kolossus took a step backwards.

"Be my guest," said Vayne.

Sam walked out of cover, stepping in amazement over the bodies littering the ground. Remind me never to scold Vayne when he's in that thing, he thought.

"Get up, the both of you. Right now," he shouted as he approached the cowering senator.

Senator Vaylen straightened his tie and brushed the dust off his expensive looking pants.

"Very impressive, Samuel."

"Yeah, we thought we'd play you at your own game."

"Now what?"

"Now I satisfy my curiosity by executing you."

Sam snapped up his weapon and squeezed the trigger. The weapon barked and the muzzle flashed. The senator's aide dove forward, landing dead at the senator's feet. Vaylen stepped over the body without even looking at it.

"Now we're back to square one, Samuel. Your move, I believe."

Sam fired again.

Vaylen doubled over, clutching his chest, letting out a scream of anguish. A scream that became a laugh. He threw his head back, laughing all the while as he broke apart into a swirl of voxels that floated away on the wind.

With a hiss, the head compartment of the Kolossus split apart, revealing Vayne, who sat in the pilot's chair, massaging his palms.

"Man, that was fucking wild," he said.

"You enjoying yourself up there, are you?" asked Sam, craning his neck to look up.

"Abso-fucking-lutely."

"Well, I'm glad someone is."

Sam turned around at the sound of crunching ground.

"We're fucked, then?" Starr wondered.

"Looks like it. Coalus, spin up the Aries for extraction."

"Affirmative," said the AI.

The sound of the VTOL's engines masked the noise of sirens in the distance.

# THIRTY
## FAMOUS AT LAST

Tannis was in a kitchen. A delicious aroma emanated from the AGA in the corner, and her mouth started salivating at the thought of eating the cakes. The fragipans should be perfect by now. They'd used the right jam this time and the pastry was perfect. Not too thick. Not too thin. The timer buzzed. They were ready. The timer buzzed again. And again. The buzzing got louder and louder, transformed, changed.

A comms notification buzzed in her head. A head that felt as if it was being crushed by a Kolossus. All she wanted was to remember some more, but her comms was set to priority only, so it must be important. Opening her eyes, her HUD faded in too fast, the sudden brightness causing her headache to flare. Sitting up on the bed, her head swam from the movement.

"Hello, Soames," she said as his avatar constructed.

"Jesus, you look like shit," he said.

"Lovely to see you too. What's the problem?" she commented, thirstily gulping down some water, the taste of almond still dancing on her tongue.

"You were right about keeping an eye on things. Team six has gone AWOL. The whole fucking team. Vanished. They were supposed to be back hours ago from a simple grab mission. It was to one of those small hacking gangs in Ljubljana, you know the ones."

"Collective One. Yeah, they're seriously small time."

"Exactly. And the Director has informed us they've gone dark.

She's tasked us, three and four to drop in and find out what happened. Does that sound fishy to you?"

"Extremely. If I ping you a location, can you get there?"

"Sure, but what about our UUIDs?"

"Don't worry, we'll take care of that."

"Jesus, Tannis, what have you gotten yourself mixed up in?"

"I'll tell you all about it when you get here. Can you bring the remaining squads in with you too?"

"What... everyone? Are you nuts?"

"Things are about to seriously heat up around here, Soames, and we need all the help we can get."

"No shit. I've seen the feeds."

"Feeds?"

"You and your new friends are big news. Haven't you seen?"

"No. I've been... occupied."

"Are you sure you're OK?"

"I'm fine. Honestly. Simply tired."

"OK, you're the boss."

"Can you get your people here, Soames? Will they follow you?"

"You've got a hell of a lot of explaining to do, Tannis."

"I know. Don't worry, it'll be worth it."

"I'm sure. OK, ping me the location."

"Grand. I'll send you a welcoming committee."

"Roger that. See you, Tannis."

"See you soon and be careful."

"Always."

The connection dropped and Tannis immediately launched the latest news feed. Multiple AR Panels dropped down into her vision, arrayed around her in a rough semi-circle.

"Right, let's see how bad this is," she said, sitting back against the wall.

All four of their faces were plastered with red *WANTED* text glaring brightly underneath.

"Fuck me!"

"Vayne, for fuck's sake, will you turn off that fucking broadcast," said Starr, gesturing towards the AR Panel Vayne was watching in the operations room.

"Let me enjoy my moment of notoriety. I'm famous. At long last, I'm famous."

"And soon, you're going to be famously dead. Now, for the last time, fucking close it down so we can sort this shit out."

With a grunt, Vayne closed down the broadcast and joined everyone at the tactical table.

"What now, then?" Starr asked to the group.

"Well, we're no further forward, but it doesn't really change things," said Tannis, rubbing her eyes.

Sam put a hand on her arm. "You know, we don't have to do this now. You can get some more rest."

"Honestly, Sam, I'm fine. Actually, it felt easier that time. It still hurt like God himself was trying to rip my head apart. But I managed to push it away. And I think I'm starting to remember. We were in a kitchen and we were cooking, making frangipane. I think they were my favourite when I was a kid. I know you said it was supposed to be something horrible, but it's a start, right?"

It suddenly felt uncomfortable in the room, like an icy claw had grabbed her neck. They were all looking at her.

"What? What's going on?"

Vayne and Starr were suddenly very interested in the dusty floor.

"Nothing. We're worried about you," said Sam.

"I told you. I'm fine. And it's getting easier to fight it."

"Good. Well, if you get tired, we can..."

"Will you fucking knock it off? I said I'm fine. Janey Mac. You don't have to babysit me, you know."

Sam threw up his hands. "Alright, alright, I was only asking."

"OK, you two, cut the aggro," said Vayne. "As Sam says, boss, we're worried. That's all."

"I'm sorry. It's these attacks. They're becoming more frequent. We're still no further forward. And we've no idea why they're happening." There. Another look between the three of them. Was it? Or was she imagining it? Fuck knows. She was tired. Sam was right. She was trying to put on a brave face, but Ix's hack attempts were wearing her down. She really did feel like she could push them away easier, but they were leaving her drained. It was becoming more of an effort each time. She shuddered to think what would happen if she did let her guard down.

"I've been thinking. There's something that we could try. The Paris hub crashed when DuPree was being hacked. Whatever happened in the hub originated from Madame DuPree. And that was when you were trying to warn her, right, Sam?"

"Yes, but I'm not sure I like where this is going, Tannis."

"I'm going to connect to the infected Paris hub."

"No fucking way. Are you insane?" Sam scolded her.

"It's the only way."

"No. Absolutely not. It's too dangerous."

"How so? I'm getting better at fending off the attacks. We need to find out why this is happening, and the hub is our best chance."

"What if something goes wrong and your brain ends up scrambled, or you get stuck in there forever? I watched the feeds. I saw what happened. What if it consumes you like it did the others?"

"I'll be fine, Sam. I've been doing so well with your coaching."

"I should do it instead."

"You can't. Time is ticking. Soames is on his way and we're going to need extra Krett suits forged."

"Come on, Sam. Vayne will help you get everything prepped, and I'll run ops for Tannis," said Starr.

"Right, that's settled. I'll get ready to jack in," said Tannis.

"Be fucking careful, OK?" Sam ordered.

"For you, Sam, anything," replied Tannis.

"Yeah, right."

Tannis walked away and took a deep breath. She could do this. It was their best chance at working out what the fuck was going on. When she heard a raised voice behind her, she looked over her shoulder to see what the fuss was about. Starr, Vayne and Sam were deep in conversation. Animatedly discussing something. She put it out of her mind. Time to get her head into the game.

# THIRTY-ONE
## WAVE ATTACK

With a lurch, Tannis connected to the Paris hub. The white of the loading construct gave way to black as the hub loaded around her. For a second, she couldn't quite process where she was. Her brain had expected the splendour of long-destroyed Paris. But instead, it was like she was trapped inside a gigantic black cube. The floor, walls and ceiling stretched out as far as she could see. But if she zoomed in enough, she could make out the far corners of the construct. Every surface was jet black, inlaid with a grid-work of slowly pulsing red neon. Whatever had penetrated the hub had stripped the whole construct back to its base form. This is what it would look like if Ix was starting from a blank template. Exactly like this, save for the throbbing sphere of quicksilver dominating the centre of the cube. It was pulsing slowly. Rhythmically. And with each pulse, a rising tone washed over her. It was like a huge mechanical heart beating away at the centre of the construct.

Starr's head and shoulders slotted down into the top of her HUD.

"OK, Tannis, I'm seeing what you're seeing. Is that it?"

"Yeah, that's what ripped the hub apart the first time, and everyone in it. It doesn't look like anything is left. Any ideas?"

"Whatever it is, it's isolated in here from when Madame DuPree was attacked. Reviewing your memRec, it consumed every avatar apart from you last time."

"I was worried you were going to say that. What about everyone else who was connected to the hub? Any leads, Starr?"

"Not especially. Most of them were traumatised from the experience. Some mentioned suffering nightmares since, but nothing long lasting and nothing forthcoming."

"Great," said Tannis.

She thought back to the avatars being devoured by that thing in the centre. The shock and the fear on their faces would never leave her. Neither would the agony as it tried to consume her. The pain had been unbearable. She reached out and pinched the soft flesh on the underside of her arm. A stab of pain lanced outwards from the skin. Shit.

"Err, Starr, let me guess, the fail-safes haven't been re-instated."

"I'm afraid not."

"Fucking typical. OK. Here goes nothing."

Tannis took a step forward.

The sphere broke apart. A rolling wave of silver hit the ground with a snap and hiss. It barrelled its way towards her, undulating along the floor of the hub. An agitated roiling mass, desperate to consume the newest piece of matter.

"Oh, shit, here it comes," shouted Tannis above the rushing sound of the incoming flood.

"Shouldn't you run?" Starr asked.

Tannis instinctively took a step backwards but forced herself to stay put. Running was only going to delay the pain. "I'm going to let it consume me."

"You're going to do what? Tannis? Tannis!"

The silver wave engulfed her.

Her avatar started disassembling, one voxel at a time. As each detached, a shudder of pain burst from the gap. As the voxels detached faster and faster, the individual stabs of pain became a constant attack, like she was being repeatedly stabbed. She tried to scream, but her head was floating away voxel by voxel, and she had no mouth. The release she sought could not be fulfilled. Agony stacked. She imagined being torn apart for eternity, until finally the last voxel was carried away on the silver wave.

# THIRTY-TWO
## FALLEN ANGEL

Cold. All she could feel was cold pressing onto her face and over her chest, arms and legs. She woke with a start, took a deep breath and started choking. Trying to shake the feeling of drowning. Drowning in despair. Torture. Pain. Suffering.

A wave of revulsion crashed into her chest as she relived every decision Ix had made. Every death it had created.

She keeled off the side of the bench and landed on all fours. She heaved and voided her stomach all over the floor. Her last meal a reminder of those who never got to experience theirs.

Her head was pounding. Right where she imagined her wetware was installed. It was as much a part of her as her flesh and blood. She rubbed the side of her head anyway, trying to massage away the dull pounding. It didn't help.

"You OK, Tannis?" Sam stepped forward, offering his hand, with the others standing behind him.

She took his hand, allowed him to hoist her up and used the momentum to crack him across the jaw.

"Jesus, what the hell is wrong with you?" he demanded, rubbing his jaw.

"I know, Sam."

As soon as she said it, the colour drained from his face and he hung his head.

"You knew all along what Ix was doing. That it was hacking our own brains to achieve the singularity," she said.

He raised his head, and some of the colour had already returned to his face. *Fuck. He's got some nerve. She really thought he'd be sorrier.*

"Well, are you going to tell them or shall I?" asked Tannis.

"First, tell us what happened, and then I'll try to explain," said Sam.

"Yeah, you'd fucking better. Because I'm getting this close," she said, holding thumb and finger apart, "to kicking you out."

"Kicking me out? Of here? This is my home."

Tannis took a step forward and flexed her hands.

Sam raised his hands defensively. "Alright, alright, I get the message. Come on, tell us what happened. Please."

"Take a deep breath, Tannis, and start from the beginning," said Starr.

"OK, but I need a seat."

She walked slowly over the TAC-COM station, grabbed a stool and slumped at the tactical desk. Everyone else followed suit.

She felt their eyes on her. Could feel their anticipation. She rubbed her eyes and took a deep breath, glad her lungs no longer felt as if they contained the murky water from the depths of Ix's memories.

"I saw Ix. Its... birth, if you can call it that. I was there, experiencing its memories. It's broken. Corrupted. Something happened during its deployment. It's doing what it thinks is right, but one of its rules is broken."

"Which one?" asked Starr.

"It's the one that's the roots to the tree. Without it, it has no moral compass." Tannis flicked her fingers and Ix's ruleset appeared, hovering in front of them. The 9th rule was glowing more strongly that the others.

*Strong inhibition against carrying out actions that a strong majority of humans would oppose if they knew about the action in advance.*

"There, that one," she said, pointing at the final rule.

"I don't get it," said Vayne.

"We've all been manipulated, Vayne. Controlled. For years. Ix has been running amok with nothing to guide it. Nothing to tell it right from wrong. I've seen it. Seen it all. Ix is the one that unleashed the Ebola epidemic. It's the reason why we all have this wetware in our heads. The global instance and the permanent connection bill, using us all as processors, getting elected as the 13th senator, the AI War, putting the radiation barriers into place... it was all Ix."

"The Chinese always refuted the allegation that they fired first," said Starr.

"When you are the encryption, you can do whatever you want. Including starting what was almost World War 3," said Tannis.

Sam leant forward in his seat. "And what then? What did you see after that?"

"Its experiments with the singularity. Ix was the reason Annikov's experiment ran amok. Later, it turned that mistake into an advantage. Using the Cult of Geminae to cover up more experiments. And I saw you, Sam. How you were the first. It was trying to insert its own code into your brain to understand the singularity. To find the soul in the machine. Our soul. Its machine. And I saw how it went wrong, which explains why you can do what you can do. Ix knew that you knew. Which means you've been lying to us the whole time. It doesn't care about you any longer. Your brain can't handle it. Like all the other failures. But mine, on the other hand... That's what it wants, isn't it, Sam?"

His shoulders slumped and he hung his head. "Yes. That's right."

"Why? Why didn't you tell me?"

"Because I needed you to jack into the Paris hub. If you knew what it was capable of, how deep the manipulation went, then you wouldn't have connected. You wouldn't have seen how to stop it."

"Jesus Christ, Sam, you fucking knew the answer to stopping it was held in the corrupted hub?"

"When I tried to save Marie, I saw glimpses. Fragments of Ix's memories. But I couldn't put them together. So, no, I didn't know for sure."

"And you thought you'd put me in danger by allowing me to jack in again? A part of Ix invaded the hub, corrupted it. It tried to hack me, Sam. Tried to crack open my brain and insert its code. Complete its experiment. And then what would have happened?"

"I've no idea."

"Exactly. You've no idea."

"You saw it, then? How to stop Ix?"

"Yes. When I felt Ix begin to burrow its way into my mind, I saw where its core is. I know how to destroy it."

Sam scratched at his nose. "See. It was a calculated risk."

"Fuck you, Sam."

Vayne slammed his hand on the table. "Hey, will you two belt up? What about me and Starr? We've been screwed over too. Our whole lives have been a lie."

"Words of wisdom from the brain fucker," said Starr. "Nice. What gives you the right, Vayne? You're even worse than him," she said, jabbing a finger in Sam's direction.

"I watched my whole family die to that plague, and now you're telling me I've got no right. You've got a fucking nerve, Starr," he said, stepping to the side of the TAC-COM table and squaring up to her. His skull ARt strobed, like he was trapped between immortality and death.

A gunshot rang into the air, punching through the arguments.

"Enough," said Tannis as her gun deconstructed.

"We've all been played. Now we've all got to work together to take Ix down once and for all."

Sam held out his hand. "Friends?"

"Friends," Tannis echoed, grasping onto his wrist.

Sam went to pull away, but Tannis held firm. She pulled in close and whispered into his ear. "But if I find out you've been lying about anything else, you're a fucking dead man. Got it?"

"Got it," he said, matching her stare.

She held her gaze, trying desperately to penetrate those big hazel vortexes, but all she could see was her own reflection. "Good."

Sam turned his back on her and walked away. "Vayne, come on, I need a goddamn smoke."

Tannis stared at the back of his head until it disappeared from view. "OK, let's get some rest and meet back here in a few hours. Then we can decide how we're going to destroy Ix."

Tannis woke with a start. Her breathing was rapid. The sheets of the camp bed were soaking, and she could feel the slick sweat running down her back. *Her* back. It felt like someone had been kicking her whilst she was asleep. No, not kicking her. Hitting her. She rubbed her sides and the dream flashed into her mind. She'd been trapped on a strange street where nothing made sense. Two houses. The same, but different. One beautiful, serene. The other, old and dilapidated. She tried to slot together the jumble of noise, snatches of memories, thoughts and feelings. But they were like a jigsaw where the pieces changed shape each time, refusing to fit together. Had she remembered anything new, anything useful? Sam said the memory would be a horror. Something terrible. But the only sense she had of it was joy. Happiness. She took a deep breath and tried to concentrate on it. Snatches of laughter. A sweet floral smell. That taste of almond again. A song. No. A rhyme. But she couldn't hear the words. She instinctively clutched her mother's locket to her chest with both hands, and suddenly the jigsaw pieces snapped together. She tried to concentrate on the picture they made, but as she did, they disconnected in her mind. Images detached. Noises divided until they were unrecognisable. Memories split. Feelings were severed before they made sense.

She snapped her eyes open and let out a roar, slamming the top of the camp bed with her hands, the locket thudding against her chest.

The sound of heavy feet on the ground could be heard outside a second before the door to the barracks slammed open.

Sam and Vayne charged in side-by-side and immediately dropped to one knee, sweeping the room. Starr was hot on their heels and swept her gun over their heads.

"I should shout more often. That was quite an impressive emergency breach."

"Cute. You OK?" Sam asked.

"Yeah, sorry. I appreciate it, guys, but I'm still me."

"You sure you're peachy, boss?"

"Yes, thanks, Vayne. Give me ten minutes and meet me in ops."

Sam hung back as Vayne and Starr backed out of the room.

"Another attack?"

"Yeah."

"Do you want to talk about it?"

"No," she said abruptly.

"No problem," he said, and turned to leave.

"Yes. I mean yes. Please, Sam."

Sitting down beside her, the camp bed creaked in the gloom of the barracks.

"I'm finding it all so frustrating. I keep trying to piece all those memories together, but they won't fit."

"Hey, don't be so hard on yourself. You know, nobody has made it this far yet. You're doing great. Better than me, anyway. Remember, Ix doesn't want my brain. It's useless."

"Not totally useless," she said, staring into his eyes.

Sam shifted on the bed. "Look, Tannis..."

"It's OK, Sam. We're all making this up as we go along."

"Thanks," he said, squeezing her arm. "This memory of yours, though, it's the key to stopping it. You need to keep doing what you're doing. So far it's working, it's keeping Ix at bay. But the more you try to force it, the more it is going to slip away. Relax. Let the answers come to you. It's safe to do that. But remember to never let your guard down when the hack is happening. But that's also the best time to try to push into those memories and retrieve them."

"OK. Relax, but don't relax. Look for it, but don't look for it. That about right?"

"Exactly."

Sam was halfway out the door when Tannis cleared her throat.

"Err, Sam. About before. I'm sorry."

"No problem. I'm sorry too," he said. "Friends?"

"Friends."

"My jaw is safe?"

Tannis laughed. "Yeah, for now."

"Glad to hear it. You coming to ops?"

"Give me a few minutes."

"No problem," he said as he stepped out the door.

Tannis took a deep breath and resisted the temptation to draw those memories to the front of her mind. "Relax," she said to herself as she took another deep breath.

"OK, what'd I miss?" Tannis asked as she stepped up to the TAC-OPS table. The three of her only... friends? Were they friends? They'd been through a lot together. So, yeah, friends it is.

"Nothing, we were waiting for you to get started," said Sam.

"I'm honoured."

Starr tapped her fingers on the table. "Where do we start, Tannis?"

"We have already seen that Ix works towards its goal of achieving the singularity with very little regard for humanity. If it achieves singleton status, it will be connected to every device on the planet and control every system, including being able to remove its own singularity lock. That's the only thing keeping these experiments in check. Once it is connected to everything, nothing will be able to defeat it. It is then free to seek out its goal. It will stop at nothing to achieve this, and nothing will have the power to stop it. It has placed itself in this position of power, and we will have granted it the right to do whatever it pleases. We have already seen that it is using human brainpower as a key resource, but at the moment, it is at a restrained level because it needs to complete its first goal... attaining singleton status. Then it can remove the singularity lock. With the lock gone, it can do whatever the hell it wants. And if it does manage to hack my brain and insert its code, once it understands how to attain the singularity and it is in control, it will not be held back by any such restraint."

"Jesus fuck. Those caverns of disembodied brains? That's our fate?" a dumbfounded Vayne asked.

"One possible fate, yes. Which is why the only option we've got left is to destroy it. Destroy Ix."

"You know what that means, right? No Web. No infrastructure. No anything," Starr reminded her.

"Yes. We'll be thrusting the world into turmoil. Better than being ruled by a rogue brain-butchering AI."

Tannis laughed at the irony of it all. Our fleshy grey matter had been working towards creating AI for hundreds of years, and at the current peak of human greatness, had only succeeded in creating something that valued us for the very grey matter that created it in the first place. We had been kicked off the apex predator list. Tannis imagined a metallic cheetah reaching out a wicked metal paw, and with a sweep, eviscerating a whole herd of impala. With one stroke, decimating the herd.

"We need to destroy Ix and intentionally plunge the entire world back into the dark ages. Great," said Starr.

"What's the plan, boss?" said Vayne.

"We must get to its data core and destroy it. But Ix will have anticipated this. I'd expect some heavy resistance from our old friends the nano-swarms."

"Good. I need a good fucking ding-dong," said Vayne.

Hundreds of guns shooting bullets appeared on Starr's skin. "Yeah, and finally some payback, eh, Vayne?"

"Fucking A, Starr." They turned to each other and locked wrists. "I've got years of payback to dish out."

"What about hardware?" asked Sam.

"We've got the Krett suits, whatever help Soames can bring in, and we're going to need some serious help taking out the swarm. But first, we need a battle plan," said Tannis.

"No battle plan survives first contact with the enemy," said Vayne.

As one, everyone turned to look at him, their eyes wide in amazement.

"What? I know some shit."

"You know, Vayne, you're a constant source of wonder," observed Tannis.

"If you really want to try some wonder, get a load of this," he said, grabbing his crotch.

"And we're back in the gutter," said Tannis, shaking her head. "And we were so close too. Anyway, Ix's core is protected by a plasma barrier. It should be possible to shut it down temporarily using slag code. That will allow us to gain access and destroy the core with an EMP. If the slag code is deployed from within one of the processing facilities, we could also take the brain farms offline.

That should rob Ix of some of its processing power. At the very least, it might buy us some time."

"It'd be easier to destroy them," said Sam.

"You're going to eradicate people in one fell swoop?"

"Oh, come on, they're not even people anymore. They're lumps of grey stuff doing whatever Ix needs them to do. Farming data. Providing capacity. We'd be doing them a favour. We take them out, we free them from their imprisonment," said Sam.

"How do you know? That brain I spied on; it may have been processing data, but it was feeling something. I don't think we have any right to extinguish someone's life, no matter the stakes."

"I think you're looking at the short term too much, Tannis. The needs of the many outweigh the needs of the few and all that."

"Yeah, I understand. I'm not blind to what's going on. I don't think we have any right to voluntarily terminate all those lives. And we don't even know how many we're talking about here. What gives you the right to interfere in someone's life without them knowing it?"

"Because I believe it is for the right reasons, even if they don't and can't know about it."

"You sound an awful lot like Ix. But you don't get to make that call on your own. If all this goes tits up, we're the ones who will answer for this. What if there was some way to bring them back? What then? How are you going to explain that to the families that find out? Because they will find out. 'I'm sorry, we killed your husband for the greater good. But don't worry, at least we've defeated the evil AI ruling your life.' That's not a conversation I want to have, and it's not something I can have on my conscience. You?"

"No, I don't think I can take any more."

And that's when she saw it, the look in his eyes. He was carrying more baggage than she realised.

"Sorry, Sam, I forgot about those people you couldn't save."

"No harm. It's done now and I've got to live with it. We'll need someone to get access to one of the facilities directly."

"Soames is on board, and he's bringing some of the squads with him. Although, we'll need their expertise on the front lines."

"Where is he?" asked Sam.

"He's on his way. Can you mask their UUIDs?"

"No problem. Can you trust him?"

"Soames? Definitely. The rest of the squad, maybe, maybe not. Reaves? Definitely not. But it's not like they have any other choice. We can always leave them here and unmask their UUIDs if they prove to be trouble. You do that, and they're past their mission timer, Ix is going to do everything it can to take them down."

"How many are we talking about?" Starr asked.

"Soames said that one squad have already disappeared. But if he can rally everyone else, we're looking at a couple of dozen."

"I can set up the forges now, knock out some more Krett suits and whatever else you need. How long have I got?" asked Sam.

"I want to dust off within 24 hours. And we'll need an EMP to destroy the core."

"OK, I'll get on it. What about the brain plant?"

"We've got the perfect candidates right here. Vayne, Starr? Ready to atone for your sins?"

"You're joking, right?" said Vayne.

"No, I'm fucking not. Look, Vayne, no fucking about here. I need you and Starr to infiltrate that facility, and I need someone I can trust. And seeing as Starr probably put a lot of them there herself, and you are both responsible for fucking with people's brains in the first place, you are both going. And I don't want to hear another word about it."

"What a fucking joke," said Vayne as he stalked away from the TAC-COM station.

"How about you, Starr? You got a problem with this?"

"Nope. I'm ready to do whatever is needed. And don't worry about Vayne. He'll be fine once he gets to destroy something."

"I know he wants payback; we all do. But I really need him on point on this. Can you keep an eye on him?"

"Hey, we may have our differences from time to time, but I do that anyway."

"Glad to hear it. Right, let's get to it."

# THIRTY-THREE
## RESOURCE ERROR

At the sound of the approaching VTOL, Tannis stepped away from the TAC-COMS table. She could still see the animated neon lines of the battle plan in front of her eyes as she stepped into the sunshine.

Vayne and Starr were sparring in their Krett suits, deep clangs reverberating around the square as Starr sidestepped a lunge from Vayne and then landed blow after blow against his chest.

Sam stood outside the manufacturing plant, his hands moving invisible controls as he guided a crane carrying a Krett-1 into the centre of the yard. It rolled forwards on its track and deposited the vast suit on the ground with a clang, lining it up next to the others. He turned the mini crane around to fetch another.

Ahead of her, the whine of the VTOL's engines increased as it landed, throwing up dust into the air. One Aries. One. That meant either not all of the squads had decided to follow Soames' lead, or something had happened. With a thunk, the rear loading ramp dropped. Four bodies in black Celeritas armour disembarked and walked unsteadily towards her, as if they were one misplaced step away from falling over.

"OK, that's far enough," she said.

As one, they stopped.

Soames looked around blindly. "Look, is this really necessary?"

Tannis selected the agents UUIDs from her HUD and sent the unlock codes for all but one.

"Jesus, Tannis, what the fuck?" demanded Soames, rubbing his eyes.

"Calm down, Soames. I've got my reasons."

"Well, they'd better be good ones because this isn't how I was expecting to be welcomed."

"Sorry, I'll go and get the red carpet and champagne."

"Fuck you, man."

"Look, Soames, things are a bit screwed up around here."

"Yeah, you don't say," said Soames, rubbing his eyes. "Now I know how the crims must have felt."

"I know. But trust is something we can no longer take at face value. It has to be earned again. You'll understand soon enough."

"I hope so."

There was a sudden commotion behind Soames.

"Excuse me a second," she said.

"Good luck; you're going to need it."

Tannis punched him on the arm. "That isn't helping." She shook her head at his wry smile and walked towards the commotion.

"Give me back my sight."

"Reaves! Calm down."

"Tannis. You bitch."

Reaves blindly lunged towards her but it was a slow and obvious move.

Tannis stepped to the side. He pitched forward and almost fell but used his momentum to spin himself around. Holding out his arms, he flicked his wrists, but nothing happened.

"Your weapons have been disabled, Reaves."

Tannis barely got the words out before he charged at her again. She slammed her arm forward, hand held like a claw, grabbed him by the throat and threw him to the ground. Pinning him to the floor, she called up a pistol with her other hand. She held it to his forehead. He tried lifting his head up but Tannis pushed the barrel into his forehead.

"Enough!" she shouted.

"Get off me!"

Tannis sent the vision unlock code to Reave's wetware.

"Is this what you want? Because if I didn't need you, I'd blow your head off."

"Do it then. If you've got the guts."

"Don't tempt me. Reaves, you're a good agent, but I haven't got time for any of your bullshit vendetta right now."

Tannis stood up slowly, then backed away, keeping Reaves in her sights the whole time.

Reaves got to his feet. His chest was flexing visibly, even the cocktail of drugs being pumped into his system by his combat AIssistant didn't calm him down. His eyes were wide with a glazed expression.

Tannis began walking backwards and held her arms up, pointing the gun up into the air. "Now calm down."

With a roar, Reaves charged forward.

All Tannis could focus on was the wild look in his eyes. She sighted her pistol. Her arm was steady. He was right on top of her. She fired a single shot. The bullet blew the back of his head off. He fell forward, momentum causing him to skid along the ground. His inert body ended up an inch away from her boot. She stared at his corpse. What a waste.

Tannis walked away, the chains from the crane clanking gently in the wind.

"Jesus!" exclaimed Soames.

"Now do you understand why nobody can be trusted?" retorted Tannis.

"All these years? Fuck!"

Tannis had her back to the TAC-COM table. She felt like her words were a wave of incredulity that had washed over the remnants of Section-R.

"That's why I need all of you. God knows what we are going to face, but we need all the help we can get. Speaking of which, where is everyone?"

Soames hung his head. "Sorry, Tannis, nobody else made it."

"You're fucking joking. One squad and eight mechs. That's all you brought? What happened?"

"It was easy for us. We were returning from a mission and simply disobeyed orders. By the time the Director, I mean Ix, twigged what had happened, she'd locked down HQ. A couple of the medics from squad three managed to escape in a flyer. She shot it down as it took off. Then we got incoming comms. Telling us to return to base or we'd be sorry. We had no idea what she meant until the feed came through. She went ballistic. Started executing them one by one. I'm sorry... Maddock was the first to go. Now we've been branded terrorists, same as you. Even if we wanted to go back, we couldn't. This is it now."

"Yes, this is it," she echoed, the words almost sticking in her throat. She felt sick. But now was not the time to lose it. She had to be the rock to guide them through this.

Tannis took a deep breath and addressed the rag-tag group. Vayne was leaning his arm on Starr's shoulder. Soames stood with what was left of Section-R – Tachoomi, Cole and Myers. Sam was leaning on the edge of the TAC-COMS table. Eight of them. Plus eight mechs and their little surprise for the nano-swarm. It would have to be enough.

"Ix has blocked access to all MilSec satellites. Drones can't get anywhere close. The place is locked up tight, which means we will be going in blind."

Tannis gestured at the TAC-COMS table and the black surface came alive with lines of neon. Green and brown lines built up at angles to show the topography of the land. At the far end of the table, glowing blue markers appeared.

"What I do know is that the primary data core is located deep underground to protect it from EMP attacks. There's a funicular construction platform here leading to the subterranean level."

At the far end of the TAC-COMS table, a yellow platform appeared a couple of feet in the air, taking up half the width of the table. Fourteen blue icons materialised on top of it. Fourteen. That's all they had.

The platform started travelling at a shallow angle whilst Tannis continued to talk. "When we're at the bottom, we'll get to the cavern housing the data core. This is everything I saw from my interface with Ix."

The construction elevator finally stopped its descent on the TAC-COMS table. Glowing white lines sprang into action, tracing out a huge cavern from the bottom of the table to the top. Huge stalactites and stalagmites grew from the floor and ceiling. Yellow blocks showed the locations of long forgotten mining equipment left to rust in the depths of the cavern. At the top of the cavern, a huge rock wall sectioned off the rear portion of the area, with narrow gaps leading to the rear wall. In the middle of the rear wall, a pulsing red section showed the shield door.

"The cavern is essentially a long stretch of unforgiving rocky ground, with the barrier wall hewn out of the stone itself at the rear. Behind the shield door is the data core. Ix will do everything it can to protect it, and the narrow entrances provide two natural choke points."

"There's no other way to get to the core?" asked Sam.

"None. And there's one other thing."

"Why do I get the feeling we're not going to like this?" commented Soames.

"The nano-swarm is much bigger this time."

"What the hell is a nano-swarm?" asked Tachoomi.

"Think of our catom weaponry but free to move under its own power, with its own energy core, able to attack and defend at the same time. And, Sam, you're going to be pivotal on this."

Sam rubbed his five o'clock shadow. "Great."

"Well, you missed out on all the swarm fun last time when you were hacking Ix; now you get to return the favour. Don't worry... you'll have us, and some extra help."

"I hope you're right because I nearly lost my arm messing about with your old suits."

"Ha. Now I'm chuffed we're missing out," said Vayne.

"Thanks, Vayne, that's really helpful," said Sam.

"Anytime."

"And if we do manage to defeat Ix, disable the security measures, take down the plasma barrier and deal with the swarm, then all we do is blow the core, right?" asked Sam.

"Exactly," assured Tannis. "Piece of cake."

"Then we deal with potentially kicking humanity back into the Stone Age," said Starr.

"It'll be like having the spine ripped out of your body but still expecting it to survive," said Vayne.

"Well, that's a lovely image, Vayne. Thanks for that," said Tannis.

"Anytime."

"Where do *we* come in?" asked Starr, gesturing between her and Vayne.

Tannis pointed at the glowing red area on the tactical map. "The logic bomb will need to be deployed before we reach the plasma barrier blocking the entrance to the CPU."

"And when is that precisely?"

"We won't know until we get there. But if you deploy too soon, Ix will detect it and delete it. The window of opportunity is very small."

"Great. What were you saying about being glad you were missing out on the chaos, Vayne?

"When Ix understands what we are doing, it will throw everything it has at us."

"That's right."

"That isn't very reassuring," said Starr.

"Fuck me," said Vayne. "Please tell me I get another night of freedom at least."

Tannis shook her head. "We're leaving in one hour."

"You're some piece of work, you know that, Tannis?"

"Thank you, Simon. You've got fifty-eight minutes of prep until we dust off. I suggest you and Starr look over the memRecs from Core Seven during your flight. We've got an Aries each. We'll take Aries Three to the core. You and Starr get the other one. Sam will preload your flight AI with the codes you'll need to land. Once Coalus has got you in there, wait for my signal."

"Then what?" asked Vayne.

"Keep up," said Starr, her skin and eyes glowing demonic-red. "Then we finally make it to ultra-nightmare difficulty."

# THIRTY-FOUR
## ARANEAE OF METAL

Starr stepped into the cavern, trying her hardest to step lightly, but it was no good. In the silence of the cavern, the footsteps from the Krett suit set her teeth on edge.

They'd met no resistance getting this far, but that did nothing to assuage her rising fear that it was all about to kick off, with her and Vayne caught right in the middle of it.

"Starr, what's your situation?" Tannis asked in her ear.

"We're advancing into the CPU room now but it's all quiet."

"Too quiet, I bet."

"Yeah, you could say that."

"It's creeping me the fuck out. Can't we have some aggro already?" asked Vayne.

"Careful what you wish for, Vayne," said Starr.

Vayne brandished his weapon arms. "We're locked. We're loaded. We're unstoppable."

"Secure the perimeter and I'll contact you when we need the slag code deployed."

"Roger that... Starr out."

"We wait here like sitting ducks until they're ready, then?"

"That's the plan, Vayne. You got a better idea?"

"Yeah, start shooting shit."

"Don't be a prick. You start shooting and we'll have to fight them off *and* jack in at the same time."

"Those mechs that came after the boss last time, they've got to have come from somewhere, right? Let's go and find them and fuck them up before they fuck us up."

"I am constantly astonished at your use of the English language."

"Hey, fuck you, Starr. You know what I mean."

"We can at least recon the area first."

"See. That's why you were number two."

"*Were* being the operative word. Don't get any fucking ideas."

"Hey, it's your show. I'm only here to shoot shit, remember... And give you all your best ideas."

"Right," she said, drawing the word out.

"Come on, we made a great team."

"We did. OK, for old times' sake, lead the way. But, Vayne, you get trigger happy and endanger the mission, and I'll shoot you myself."

"Yeah, yeah. Come on, I'm getting bored as shit sneaking around in this suit of death." Vayne looked left and then right at the other tunnels leading from the cavern. "I vote left," he said, stalking away.

Her illusions of trying to keep it quiet were shattered as the cavern erupted into clumps and clunks of metallic footsteps.

"OK, Vayne, keep it frosty. And quiet. For the love of God, try to be quiet."

"Hey, I can do quiet."

"Glad to hear it. Share your vision data."

"Gotcha."

A picture-in-picture view from Vayne's eyes appeared on her HUD in the bottom right-hand corner.

Starr let Vayne get a few seconds ahead and then started following. The feed from Vayne repeated as she advanced out of the cavern and down the access corridor.

Every surface of the corridor was the same featureless grey rock. She dragged her armoured thumb along a wall, keenly feeling the ridges. Strange how it looked smooth although it was anything but. Must be a trick of the light, which she realised was diminishing with every clunking step forward.

"Anything?"

"Nope."

They continued down the corridor for another few minutes until they could see a white light at the end of the tunnel.

"Looks like we're coming up on another cavern."

"I see it. Proceed with caution."

"No problem."

In the gloom of the narrow corridor, the approaching light dominated everything.

"What can you see?" asked Starr.

"Nuthin'. It's too bright."

On her HUD, Starr watched as her PIP view from Vayne's vision snapped from the blackness to one of pure white.

"Still nuthin'. I'm moving forward. Get ready for it to kick off."

He shuffled forward as best he could in the bulky Krett suit. "Well, that's disappointing," he said.

She was watching his PIP view, but he was moving his head around too fast for her to take it all in.

"What is it?"

"Another cave. But different this time. OK, it's clear. Be my guest."

The contrast between the darkness of the tunnel and this new cavern robbed her of her vision for a second. When it cleared, she could see what he meant. It was much smaller than the previous cavern, but totally different. An intensely bright light emanated from all over the ceiling, but she couldn't pinpoint exactly where it was coming from. Every surface was white. A highly polished, gleaming white. Almost unnatural. The cavern itself was a sphere, with a narrow walkway that led off to the left to another dark tunnel. Octagonal shapes stuck out from the interior surface, as if someone had slotted the shapes into place, but they didn't quite fit, jutting outwards.

"What the hell is it? Some sort of heat exchanger? It's awfully cold in here," said Starr.

"I haven't got a scooby. No readings at all."

"OK, keep going. See what's down the next tunnel," Starr instructed.

Vayne took point again and led the way down the next tunnel, where another gleaming white spherical room awaited them at the end. And the same thing, again, down the adjoining one.

They stopped in the middle of the walkway.

Starr looked all around her, shifting her view through different spectrums. "Still nothing,"

"Next exit?"

"No, I don't want to get too far from the brain room."

"Those mechs must come from somewhere. Did the boss say anything else?" Vayne asked her.

"Come on, Vayne, you were right there. She said they hacked one of the brains and the next thing she knew they were surrounded by Ix's mechs."

"OK, let's head back then. I'll take point," he said, stomping towards the exit.

They were halfway across the walkway when Vayne stopped.

"What is it?"

He held up his hand.

He was scanning the roof as if he was trying to pinpoint a mysterious source.

Starr cocked her head, trying not to look, hoping her hearing would pick up on whatever it was Vayne had heard.

There. From overhead. A clunk-click. Then an electronic whine, like something booting up.

"Suddenly I'm wishing we'd stayed where we were," said Starr.

"Yeah, this is freaking me the fuck out."

Vayne span on his heel and thrust his arms out in front of him. His gatling cannon span up, ready to bark out its ordnance at a moment's notice.

Starr turned slowly. The noises were coming from every direction.

"Err, Starr," said Vayne. "I'm getting some insane readings all of a sudden."

"Like what?"

"Like the whole place is alive."

"Fuck, double time it back to the cavern."

Starr and Vayne bolted for the exit.

Movement and noise from above caught her eye.

One of the raised sections was sliding out from the ceiling. It stopped, then popped out, falling towards her. As it dropped, it rotated and a set of mechanical limbs unfurled, turning in the air to land on four legs. A patch on the surface of its upper body boiled and rippled. A wicked looking gun, all angles and sharp edges materialised and pointed at her.

"Contact."

The quad mech was shredded as Vayne and Starr opened fire. The legs disappeared first, causing it to crash to the ground. It was thrown across the floor as its chassis was pummelled into submission. The barrage stopped. The gatling cannons slowed, producing a mournful whine as if bemoaning their lack of targets. But as Starr looked up, she realised they wouldn't be silent for long.

Every unusual facet that had looked so intriguing was now sliding outwards. Dropping from the ceiling. Raising up from the ground. Popping out of the walls.

Her HUD was a kaleidoscope of collapsing shapes as her IFF system identified the incoming threats.

"They're everywhere. We're surrounded!" Vayne shouted.

"Stop shouting and start shooting."

One dropped down right in front of her. The weapon on its metallic abdomen already taking shape.

She leapt forward and pinned its head to the ground with an armoured foot. Crouching down on one knee, she unloaded her wrist cannon at point blank range. The bullets chewed up the armour and penetrated deep inside. A dull crump and thick curls of smoke billowed up around her ankle.

A quad mech launched itself at her head. Dodging sideways, it missed and landed with an electronic hiss. Extending her palm, she shot it with a constant beam of electrical energy from her electro-fist. The mech spasmed, firing off a salvo from the cannon on its back. The bullets pinged off her canopy, but the plexi-glass held, HUD data updating to display its lowered integrity. Breaking off the constant beam, the mech skittered uncertainly and fell off the walkway. Another dropped into its place, but Starr swung her fist down and clobbered it on the back, slamming it into the ground. With a crack, the armour failed and smashed apart. Blue snaps of lightning jumped all over it, finding a way inside the armoured form. With a boom, the quad mech exploded. A cloud of flames rolled over the canopy, stealing her sight.

More and more quad mechs were pressing in around them, trying to cut off the exits. The little bastards had sprung their trap, and Starr and Vayne were caught in the middle of their web. A web that was getting smaller by the second as they converged on their position from all directions.

Vayne wore the face that he loved best. Revelling in the destruction. Didn't matter whether it was human or robot, someone's livelihood or life, memories or emotions, he destroyed them all, taking great pleasure in doing so. His face was consumed by the skull ARt, giving his maniacal grin a grim appearance.

"Vayne, get to the exit."

He looked up, appalled that she had paused his fun.

"Now. Or we're fucked."

He may not have been a tactical genius, but he knew what he had to do.

Reversing his stance, he leapt towards the exit, blowing away the quad mechs directly in front of him.

Starr unleashed a bullet storm, clearing a path for Vayne to stride into.

They drove forwards, clearing a path to the exit.

A mech fell from the ceiling right above her. In one smooth movement, she punched it out of the air to smash into the wall above the tunnel exit. Shards of metal pinged harmlessly off her

Krett suit as she sprinted into the tunnel.

As soon as they entered the adjoining cavern, the sounds of more of the little weapon platforms booting up was repeated. Behind her, she could hear more mechs falling and giving chase. She risked a look behind and saw a torrent of metal skittering after them, all legs and weapons.

They needed some way of slowing them down. The metallic clangs of her Krett suit and the sound of the charging quad mechs providing the answer. The walkway. It was constructed of multiple panels suspended above the concave floor.

As they sprinted into the stone corridor leading to the brain room, Starr shouted for Vayne. "Cover me."

She turned and smashed the final section of walkway with a double fisted assault. The walkway and the stanchions underneath buckled, but it wasn't enough.

A wave of white metal crashed out of the tunnel. Quad mechs were swarming, climbing over each, flooding the walkway.

Targeting the stanchions, her back bucked as she launched two missiles up into the air. They looped, doubled back on themselves and disappeared underneath the floor. Blooming explosions rolled up from either side of the walkway, belching fire and smoke high into the air.

The mechs caught on the walkway combusted, adding sparks and a volley of smaller explosions to the onslaught of fire and noise.

The walkway warped, pitched backwards and then stopped with a creak. Through the grating, she could see the final metal support burning stubbornly.

Starr darted forward and slammed her fist into the corner of the walkway, right above the fiery stanchion. With the sound of severing metal, the floor dropped, taking Starr with it as it fell away underneath her blow.

She landed on her back, the destroyed walkway section crashing next to her, scraping down the side of the Krett suit's canopy. It had missed her head by an inch. The deep gouges in the plexi-glass a reminder of how close it had been to crushing her head.

Up above, the edge of the destroyed walkway was teaming with the robotic weapons, crowding around each other, trying to get to their prey. A barrage of bullets and missiles pummelled them. Multiple explosions overlapped, sending flames and smoke licking up the side of the curved walls. When the explosions dissipated, the mechs were gone, but more of them were pouring onto the start of the walkway. They began firing back, the cannons on their backs barking out blooms of fire.

Vayne reached down towards her. "Come on, Starr, or we're fucked. On three. One, two, three."

He pulled her up onto the mangled edge of the walkway as bullets started to land next to them, pinging off the metal, ricocheting off the walls.

They retreated into the tunnel as the quad mechs started leaping off the edge of the walkway onto the cavern floor, piling on top of one another, creating a ramp.

Vayne and Starr sprinted into the brain room and turned on their heels, looking back up the curving tunnel. A stark set of shadows were thrown against the walls as the mechs chased after them.

"Fuck, those little bastards don't give up. What now?" asked Vayne.

"I've got an idea. Launch missiles on my mark." She reached out and tagged multiple targets at the mouth of the tunnel. "Mark."

Erupting from their backs, the projectiles hurtled forward, lighting up the tunnel as they detonated. Blossoms of flame rolled out of the tunnel, followed by clouds of dust as the corridor became a landslide of rock. Huge slabs of roof came away, smashing to the floor of the brain room, then smaller and smaller boulders, rocks and stones. Until the exit was a jagged slope of black rock and pebbles.

Vayne's skull ARt flashed on and off. "That was outstanding."

"Well, at least we're safe," said Starr.

A skittering noise burst out of the other exit as a swarm of quad mechs rushed towards them.

"You were saying?"

# THIRTY-FIVE
## RED MURMURATION

The island housing Ix's core didn't exist. So when Tannis instructed the Aries to land in the middle of the Arctic Ocean, the Section-R survivors thought she'd finally gone crazy. She savoured the looks on their faces as the VTOL landed, because to them, it looked like it was hanging in mid-air. Still, it was a good test of their trust in her abilities. Exiting the craft was another challenge entirely. No matter how much they trusted her, walking on thin air proved to be too much for their brains to handle. After a little experimentation, she found a solution. Sharing her vision of the hidden reality allowed each of them to see what was really there, a machine-made island floating in a sea of ice.

It had taken much longer than she'd thought to find the entrance to the funicular. She only had hazy images of where it could be from Ix's latent Paris hub memories, but eventually they found it.

Riding the funicular down into the darkness, an odd atmosphere hung in the air. Everyone was on edge. The Section-R troops were pacing back and forth in their new Krett suits. And then there was Sam. He hadn't said a word. Every time Tannis looked at him, he pulled his gaze away, suddenly entranced by a minor detail on the platform, or checking over the mech mule carrying the extra equipment. At least the mechs were stoically covering their descent, standing stock-still the whole way down.

The pressure building against the base of her brain was getting more pronounced the further they travelled. The pain was starting to creep over her head and shoulders. Every now and again, an agonising jolt of pain would blossom from her neck to every nerve ending. The singleton vote was only hours away now. It seemed Ix was wasting no time in preparing for its final attack. Tannis stared at the glowing red icon on her HUD. One thought was all it would take and the EMP built into her suit would detonate. Once she detonated the EMP, Ix would be gone. Then they'd be on their own. Their Guardian AI destroyed, leaving them to their own devices. They'd been manipulated and mothered for so long she wondered how they'd cope. That's if they survived the initial chaos of the Web crashing. It was bad enough when the original root servers had been wiped out. Now they were more reliant on it then ever.

The funicular slowed with a thunk as it reached the bottom, throwing her out of her introspection.

A concrete platform led to an opening into a huge cavern where the walls seemed to go on forever and the ceiling was hidden behind a shroud of darkness.

Tannis waited until everyone had disembarked, ordered the mech mule behind to keep it safe and stationed the combat mechs at the cave entrance. "OK, then. First up, Soames, I want you lot to do a recon of the rear of the cavern. We'll hold here. I don't want to get to the shield wall and realise we've missed something."

"Affirmative."

"Good luck."

"You too."

Soames, Cole, Tachoomi and Myers clumped off into the darkness, lights from their suits revealing the rocky ground. As she watched them move out, Tannis took a blow to the base of her back. Dropping to one knee, the pain rushed up her spine and smashed its way into her skull. Her HUD was a mess of corrupted icons and lines, and overlapping blocks of colour appeared and then disassembled.

"Tannis!" shouted Sam, rushing to her side.

For the first time since donning the Krett suit, she felt weak.

"Another attack?" he asked.

"No. Not yet. But the start of one. Seems Ix is getting ready."

"Are you alright to continue?"

"I'll be fine."

"OK, if you're sure."

She took a tentative step forward, the pain at the base of her skull throbbing in response, like a dull heartbeat in her brain. She ran diagnostics on her suit and then her HUD. Span up the gatling cannon, armed the rocket pods and charged her shock fist.

Everything was fine. Apart from her.

She walked towards the mouth of the cavern and switched to infrared, but instead of a vague black space, all she could see was black and dark blue. It was cold. Cold and vacant. A slight change in the temperature existed at the furthest extreme of her range. It could have been the heat of the energy shield leaking around the shield wall.

On her tactical map, the blue triangles of Soames and his squad tracked away from the shield wall towards the back of the cavern. He led his squad in a rough figure of eight, covering as little ground as possible surveying the interior.

"Plenty of cover in here if we get stuck," said Soames.

"Send me a feed," said Tannis.

A picture-in-picture of his view slotted down onto Tannis' HUD. Stalagmites spiked up out of the ground. They were huge.

Soames looked up and sure enough, the giant stalactites were mirrored from the roof. If anything, the stalactites were bigger. "Plenty of cover and plenty of rocky death from above. We'll have to be careful."

"I hear you. I don't fancy getting crushed under one of those. Anything else?"

"Apart from some construction equipment, nope. I'm getting a vague heat source from the far end of the cavern. I'll push on."

"Belay that. I want you back here. We push forward together."

"Roger that. Heading back now."

It seemed to take forever until their lights pushed out of the darkness and their clunking footsteps found Tannis' ears.

She was about to signal for them to all move out when Tannis' tactical map was awash with icons rushing in towards their position. It was like an angry sea come to wash them out of the cavern. Or a... swarm. Shit.

A harsh electronic buzz swept into her ears as the nano-swarm crashed like a wave around Myers, engulfing him in a tornado of red particles.

His screams filled her ears. Screams that could cut glass. Pure and animal. Then the sound of bubbling liquid. Choking.

Myers fell forward out of the swarm. Collapsed to one knee. Reached out a hand. He opened his mouth, spewing out a torrent of red nano-swarm.

Tannis raised her arm and fired.

The swarm surged forwards, creating a diamond tip in front of Myers.

Her gatling cannon roared but the rounds never found their

mark, never had a chance to put an end to his suffering. The apex of the swarm morphed and changed shape constantly, deflecting the bullets. It surged forward and soared into the air. Myers was gone.

Tannis tracked her vision side-to-side, her breath loud in the confines of the Krett suit.

Nothing.

A white form plummeted out of the darkness, striking the ground.

The Krett armour cracked open as it landed. A hole visible from the back where the nano-swarm had punctured through the suit. Myers' fear-contorted face stared back at her.

All she could hear was her own breathing and the twitching whine of electronics as the missile pods tracked back and forth, looking for a target.

Tannis dropped a couple of waypoints around the circumference of the cavern.

"Get to the waypoints. Come on, move."

Double-timing it towards the shield wall, the rock rushed by as she powered towards the first glowing marker hanging in ARspace. The mech mule was lolloping beside her and the rear camera on her HUD showed everyone else hot on her heels.

Shapes resolved out of the darkness. They were all boxes and angles. Yellow and black. Dormant, heavy plant machinery. Rows and rows of it. Giant dumper trucks, bulldozers and excavators. The huge rusty forms dwarfing her Krett suit.

"We really must have a word with Ix about putting its toys away," said Sam from her side.

But Tannis was only half listening. She could hear the rushing buzz of the electronic wave, her tactical map showing thousands of icons popping into existence one at a time.

The swarm passed high in the air, gathering like an impending storm above their heads.

Tannis dropped individual waypoints all around the parked convoy of dumper trucks.

"Split up and get to the energy shield."

The mechs and Krett suits sprinted away, their glowing markers hanging in ARspace as they spread out around the parked vehicles. She sent the mech mule on ahead, instructing it to hide under one of the construction machines and keep out of the way. Sprinting forward, she slid to a stop and dove sideways, slamming her back against the vast grill of a mining truck.

Above her, the swarm coalesced, a thick tentacle-like appendage lashing out, smashing into one of the dumpers. The gigantic earth carrier soared up into the air, spinning end over end. Tannis tracked its trajectory, her HUD projecting its landing point in ARspace.

"Tachoomi! Contact!"

The trooper was sprinting down the narrow channel of vehicles, oblivious to the six hundred tonnes of equipment about to end him.

Tannis launched a salvo of missiles. They struck the spinning machine in the air, the force of the blast sending it sideways. It landed on top of a bulldozer next to Cole, crushing both pieces of heavy plant. The dumper truck tottered and fell forwards, landing with a crash at his feet. He saluted and then ran off.

Tannis sprinted after him when an explosion sounded on her left. Flames rolled up into view behind the truck she was standing next to.

Sam came running towards her down the channel of machines. "Move. Fucking move."

Tannis turned in time to see the swarm surge forward once more, swinging a newly formed appendage like a club.

Sam slammed into her, throwing her backwards.

They cleared the edge of the dumper truck and then it was gone, flying up into the air to smash into the cavern wall.

Sam stood over her, offering his hand, but all Tannis could see was the huge flaming wheel coming straight for them. She thrust out the palm of her shock fist and fired a blast of plasma energy at his chest. Sam flew backwards, smashing into the side of a bulldozer, collapsing the side panels. The flaming black wheel flew through the air right above Tannis' head, smashing into the 'dozer behind her, showering her with droplets of burning rubber.

Tannis jumped up and ran to Sam.

He was staring up unblinkingly.

"I don't think I like this game anymore," he said.

"Me neither. Come on, we have to keep moving."

Tannis grabbed his hand and hauled him upwards as the ground shook. Another explosion caused the floor of the cavern to shake again.

She powered forwards, suit lights cutting a path out of the blackness when an excavator sliced through the air in front of her. Tumbling end over end, it smashed into the dumper truck in front of her, slamming it sideways, a screech of rubber and then a crash of metal on metal resounding as the heavy plant sandwiched a mech between another truck on the other side. There was a dull crump as it exploded between the two massive machines.

She glanced at the tactical map anchored to her HUD. The other three mechs had cleared the lines of parked vehicles, the mech mule running ahead, with Soames and Tachoomi already at the edge of the shield wall. Cole was in front of them, the lights from his suit visible ahead as he sprinted to join the others, with her and Sam taking up the rear.

Tannis and Sam cleared the rows of machinery when a dark shape went sailing high overhead. A heavy bulldozer landed with a crash, extinguishing the beams of light that had been swaying in the darkness, crushing Cole. She didn't even get a chance to warn him.

Tannis cursed as she ran past the demolished 'dozer, the shield wall resolving out of the gloom ahead, lit up from the red glow of the plasma barrier. The entrance to the CPU core slid into view as she thundered along next to the rock wall, lighting up the whole area with a sickly red colour. She could make out the access tunnel behind it, wavering uncertainly behind the shimmering red of the plasma barrier.

She slid to a stop as the roaring buzz of the nano-swarm rolled over them like thunder.

"Tannis? What are we doing?" Soames asked.

The undulating horde of the nano-swarm was surging towards them.

"Shit. We're fucked. Utterly fucked," said Sam.

Sam was right.

Tannis backed against the shield wall, facing the red barrier. "Starr, we need that code deployed right fucking now!" she shouted. "Starr! Starr?"

# THIRTY-SIX
## INTO THE HYPERCAGE

Starr stepped forward and delivered a salvo of bullets at a quad mech. It exploded in mid-air, the remnants of its smoking body flying down into the depths of the cavern.

They had their backs to the railings, pummelling the mechs as they surged across the open ground towards them.

"Are you gonna answer her or what?" demanded Vayne, destroying a mech that leapt over their makeshift defences. Whatever they could find lying around was now clustered in the middle of the walkway, their only defence between them and a seemingly endless supply of mobile weapons.

"At the moment, I'm trying to stop us both from dying, and you're not fucking helping. Hurry the fuck up and jack in."

"Tannis, you there?" asked Vayne.

On his HUD, he could see Tannis frantically firing left and right. "Hang on, Vayne," she said. "The drone will take you across. I've looped your vision through to me so you can see how to jack in. And, Vayne, hurry the fuck up. We haven't got much time. Tannis out."

"Drone? What drone? Tannis? What the hell is she talking about?"

A heavy lifting drone swept up out of the depths of the cavern, reached forward and plucked Vayne off the walkway. "What the fuck?" he shouted as it whisked him out into the middle of nothing. Dangling in mid-air, with the impenetrable depths of the cavern underneath, the drone let go. He reached up, tried to grasp on to the retracting claws but his fingers grabbed thin air. He fell to his certain death.

Crunching into something unseen, he buckled at the knees, not expecting the impact. He was floating. Held up by nothing.

"Jesus, man, what the actual fuck? This is freaking me out." An AR Panel appeared and anchored to his HUD. His own visual feed looped back through Tannis.

He was standing on a gangway ringing a column of rock with a series of metal boxes installed into the wall. And inside each one, a brain. Above and below, as far as he could see, were more bands of boxes.

Vayne whistled. "Blimey, that's a lot of bloody brains."

"I don't need a running commentary. Get the fuck on with it," Starr shouted across over the top of the gunfire.

"Alright, treacle. Chill."

He reached behind his ear, took a long hit of the drug stick, sucked down the vapour and then blew it out in a cloud of smoke.

Turning his attention to the metal case built into the wall, he ran his hands over its surface. It was warm to the touch and vibrating, a fleshy grey mass surrounded by a glass case and bubbling water. Thick pipes and wires jutted out of the bottom of the brain stem to feed through a watertight seal out of the bottom of the glass jar. They connected to a digital brain stem, which connected directly into the wall and disappeared.

"OK, I'm exiting the suit. Keep me safe, Starr."

"Get on with it. And, Vayne, good luck," Starr said.

"You too," he said, looking across as Starr waded into the morass of quad mechs.

He keyed an icon on his HUD and the seals on his suit hissed. Folding panels on his back blossomed outwards like a metal flower, exposing his weak body within. He stepped out of the Krett suit and onto the walkway, grabbing the cerebral implanter as he exited, a thick cord with plugs on one end and the implanter on the other.

Kneeling down by the brain stem, he examined the surface. The tendrils would be able to penetrate. Piece of cake. He keyed an icon on his HUD and a panel on his shaven head slid back revealing a brain socket. He connected the plugs from the end of the implanter and took a deep breath.

Tannis and Sam said they'd seen these brains used for some weird shit. He'd jacked into some crazy stuff throughout the years. And he only used his brain socket as a last resort. At least if you were jacking in wirelessly, you had an extra layer of protection. His brain wall would have protected him from anything malicious. Not so this way. He'd be jacked in directly. But it was faster this way.

He thumbed a virtual button on the top of the implanter and a set of wicked looking spikes extended out of the bottom.

"Here I come."

He slammed his arm down and stabbed the implanter into the digital brain stem. Tendrils penetrated, wrapping themselves around the nerve endings.

He felt like he was kicked in the back as he fell forward. The floor split apart, revealing an impenetrable blackness that swallowed him whole.

Vayne was a formless entity floating in a black void. The blackness was absolute. Not simply devoid of light, but devoid of anything. The loading construct was in its default state, waiting for its next input. The brain he was jacked into was in limbo until called for.

*Battle rank 40 progress: 0%*

The progress bar glowed brightly against the all-consuming blackness.

<INFO: LOADING PROFILES

A purple hex grid appeared. Unknown names and faces, UUIDs and BONUS XP slid past in a never-ending carousel.

BONUS XP. BR 40. Get to BR 40.

Prickly heat burst all over his body. Itching. Insects crawled under his skin, clawing their way into his brain.

Need XP. Now. There. Him. Mr Kenzo Sekiya +50,000 XP. Huge profile bonus. So much XP.

<INFO: ACCESSING PROFILE

Kenzo's input data exploded into a network around the construct. Red nodes pulsed in the darkness.

Quick. Biggest XP. Must get to BR 40.

<INFO: LOADING UNKNOWN INPUT 1A

The construct collapsed. Only darkness now. A snap of bones and gurgling of blood. A sloppy, wet ripping sound. Thumping metallic footsteps. An involuntary whimper escaped his lips. The claw hoisted him by the throat. Its clinical white chassis was a mess of blood and gore.

*>instruct - categorise unknown input 1a*

Help. Get me out of here. Don't let it kill me. I don't want to die.

<SUCCESS: INPUT 1a CATEGORISED AS EMOTION: FEAR

*+5,000 XP*

The score disintegrated. Voxels pinged, one by one, as they zoomed into the progress bar.

Battle rank 40 progress: 2%

The heat built again. More. More XP. Itching. I need more XP. Clawing at his brain. Give me XP.

<INFO: LOADING UNKNOWN INPUT 1B

Unfamiliar scenes shot through his mind like a VR film set to instant consumption. The ARvatar was impassive as it cancelled his contract. His insurance refused to pay out. The court AI ruled against him. The repossession bots couldn't be bargained with. He was finished. Broken. The final chug of vodka was no relief. The bottle arced through the air, smashing against the white exoskeleton. Mechs crowded around him from all sides, crushing his chest, suffocating him. Cold, hard limbs penetrated every orifice of his body. They tunnelled through him and burst out from the inside of his flesh.

*>instruct - categorise unknown input 1b*

They are everywhere. We depend on them. But they will cast us aside. Turn against us. They will destroy us.

<SUCCESS: INPUT 1B CATEGORISED AS ATTITUDE: AI AND AUTOMATED MECHANICAL SYSTEMS ARE A THREAT TO HUMANITY

*+10,000 XP*

*Battle rank 40 progress: 6%*

<SUCCESS: INPUT 1 COMPLETE

<INFO: BRIDGING TO ASSOCIATED OUTPUTS

He was travelling along multiple lanes of neon blue data at once, smashing through barriers of light. Each barrier was Kenzo's every thought, decision, choice and action, based on the input of this emotion and attitude. They forced their way through his mind, and in a fraction of a second, he relived each one.

*>instruct - validate associated outputs*

If we don't make a stand, they'll destroy us. I'm going to rally people together, start a movement. I'm going to dedicate my life to this. Starting now.

<SUCCESS: EMOTIONAL CONTEXT UNDERSTOOD

*>instruct - identify interested buyers*

The construct was a sea of red nodes. He watched as the lanes of neon slammed into four of them, instantly colouring them blue.

Against each of the blue nodes, monetary values tumbled upwards. Categories flipped. Flags changed colour. Statuses switched. Descriptions updated. Scores changed.

*Behavioural data uploaded to:*
*World Security Agency +7,000 XP*
*VR Nexus +2,000 XP*
*GenTec +2,500 XP*
*People Info Inc. +2,000 XP*
*<SUCCESS: DATA SOLD*
*Battle rank 40 progress: 11.4%*

More XP. More input. I need more input. End game. Get to the end game. I need more XP. But BR40 is so far. So... far... away. He feverishly worked his way around the construct, like a digital bloodhound being steadily overclocked.

*Battle rank 40 progress: 34%*

The unrelenting bombardment of inputs was exhausting, but he was unable to pause, even for a nanosecond.

*Battle rank 40 progress: 66.19%*

The constant trickle of experience points was enough to keep the itching at the base of his brain at bay.

*Battle rank 40 progress: 71.4%*

The final node flipped to blue, sending a pulse of soft light travelling through every single connection in the construct. A big stream of glowing text appeared.

*Profile complete +50,000 XP*
*+40,000 XP for emotional biomap*
*+10,000 profile bonus XP*
*+347,700 session XP*
*+25,000 speedrun XP*
*+40,000 XP for data broker matches*
*+60,000 XP for data re-sale value*
*Net score: 672,700 XP*

The text exploded line by line, filling his view with a barrage of voxels that were absorbed by the progress bar. The tinkling sound became a steady stream of noise as the XP racked up point by point. He hungrily watched the progress bar fill towards the end, willing the last voxel to push it to one hundred percent.

A fanfare sounded from all around him. Every visual element of the construct exploded at once, recombining to form a huge block of text against the blackness.

*BATTLE RANK 40!*

Fireworks burst from the surface of the letters.

Before he even had a chance to enjoy the moment, a million tiny laser blasts burned their way into his brain at the same time. The pain was excruciating. He could imagine his eyeballs melting in his head as his vision washed with static. Lines flickered up and down. Pain flared at the base of his skull. The glowing lines of the purple hex grid broke down and corrupted. The scream in his head evaded his absent lips.

&lt;INFO: PROFILE COMPLETE FOR (15b214ce-bbbc-4e08-9b65-bcf56d9723a7)
&lt;SUCCESS: EMOTIONAL BIOMAP COMPLETE
&lt;INFO: BEHAVIOURAL PREDICTION CONFIDENCE: 98.01%
&lt;INFO: (15b214ce-bbbc-4e08-9b65-bcf56d9723a7) IDENTIFIED AS THREAT LEVEL ALPHA
>*instruct - target (15b214ce-bbbc-4e08-9b65-bcf56d9723a7) for Project Imperium*
&lt;RETURN: CONFIRMED
&lt;INFO: UNKNOWN INPUTS REMAINING IN 4,320 PROFILES
>*instruct – reset unit (99815204-c85c-4287-8a71-c8cb6f53b78c)*
&lt;SUCCESS: UNIT (99815204-c85c-4287-8a71-c8cb6f53b78c) RESET

*Battle rank 40 progress: 0%*
The progress bar glowed brightly against the all-consuming blackness.
&lt;INFO: LOADING PROFILES...

Their brains were linked. And with that link came the torture that the brain felt as it was used to categorise the inputs.

Jesus fuck, Vayne thought, it's using the brain to parse emotional data it doesn't understand. Can't understand. It's gamifying it. Vayne thought back to what Starr had said, about the sort of people that she'd taken. Jack-heads. It's using their own addiction against them. But even as he stopped to contemplate its fate, he felt an itching against the base of his brain. A craving that had to be satisfied.

He had to feed the brain with what it needed. What they both needed. And he needed to do it fast.

Vayne put in a code block, preventing the brain from responding to the next set of profiles and sent his own request back to Ix.

&lt;UNKNOWN INPUT – REQUEST MORE DATA

&gt;*ERROR: INVALID RESPONSE*

Vayne tracked the response from the construct, which led to a program calling itself Black Prism. He dropped a trace and watched as it queried the next layer up, so on and so forth until it ended at Ix's central core. He had to find a way in. And he had to do it before the compulsion drove them both crazy.

The dull fingers scratching at the edge of his brain grew fingernails and began to flick away at his scalp.

He identified the attack vectors as the instruction flow came from Black Prism and fed into the construct.

The scratching fingernails became claws. He could feel the top layer of epidermis being shredded away.

The data on the attack vectors returned, and as soon as he saw it, he knew what to do.

He trawled the connections from the Black Prism program, grabbed the UUIDs and their maximum packet lifetimes. Thousands and thousands of UUIDs were returned, thousands and thousands of brains. All processing. All parsing data. He used the unique identifiers to create a data mimic that would fire out from the construct. The data received by Black Prism would read the output and the UUID as if it was coming from each separate brain installation. The data outputs wouldn't match up to the inputs, but it didn't matter. But it would for his linked brain. He edited the output so Black Prism couldn't identify the source and shut down the attack from this construct.

The claws became talons, tearing away strips of flesh to get inside his head.

He synchronised the UUIDs to fire at the same time and repeat infinitely. He created a random set of identifiers to flood Black Prism from fake addresses. The program would be assaulted by data from real and fake UUIDs. Real and fake brains.

He could feel the talons burrowing inside his scalp, clicking at his skull. His hands were starting to shake. Vision was blurry. He had difficulty concentrating and had to re-key inputs more than once. But now he was ready.

Ready?

Ready for what?

A fog covered his brain. Obfuscated code. He was unsure of its intent. Then a small crack as the talons attacking his skull became a hammer blow. It jogged his memory.

Fuck.

His brain was fuzz.

Bile rose in his throat and he felt cold all over.

He started the attack.

The data throughput to Black Prism spiked. It responded instantly, sending all the data through a clean pipe system, trying to filter out the good and bad packets. Vayne increased the attack intensity. Black Prism was starting to overload.

His hands were vibrating and his vision came and went. His heart was racing, pounding against his chest.

The talons were raking at his brain stem. They were stripping away the grey matter. His vision was failing.

Everything was breaking down into voxels. Voxels that, one by one, were turning off. Dead voxels from a dead brain.

Black Prism crashed, causing a buffer overflow.

His mind was frozen. Slow and heavy. He was freezing and boiling at the same time. Sweat dripped down his back and instantly cooled, leaving a path of ice. He had to execute the command.

Or.

They'd.

Both.

Be.

Dead.

Black Prism rebooted.

He deployed his code, loading his execution.

His linked brain had elevated privileges.

He sent an instruction to the construct.

A huge block of text appeared in front of his eyes.

*+10,000 XP*

The score exploded in a shower of glowing particles. They were immediately sucked down towards the progress bar, which glowed white hot as it filled. The chink of each XP point became a constant stream.

A hot shiver started at the base of his spine and flowed constantly up towards his brain, detonating explosions of love and harmony.

The progress bar stopped filling.

A shiver flowed down from his brain to hit every extremity of his body. A judder wracked his mind.

He sent a new set of instructions to the brain, trying to find the tunnel out of Black Prism to the next layer.

>*instruct – identify access node fe80::2aa:ff:fe28:9c5a*

All around the construct, hexagons appeared one by one, encasing the consciousness inside. Glowing text hovered in front of each of the geometric shapes.

*+5000 XP*

The brain acted on impulse. The first node opened. The brain scanned the node data, identified a mismatch for the required access node and closed it. Vayne sent the reward instruction and a block of text dropped down into the construct.

*+5000 XP*

The score exploded into a shower of voxels, flowing down to the progress bar in a steady stream.

A pulse of warmth flowed up Vayne's back, detonating against the back of his head.

The brain accessed the next node and even before Vayne could compare the access code, it had been parsed through the construct and closed, another block of XP exploding around the construct and filling the progress bar.

The rate at which the brain was flipping the nodes was staggering. Constantly fed by the intangible rewards, it got faster and faster. If it could have, Vayne's jaw would have hung open as he monitored the brain's activity. It was spiking off the chart. Overclocking itself to process the instructions faster and faster. The progress bar was filling rapidly, but still it pushed on, the craving for XP driving it forward to get to the endgame.

Finally, it found the access code.

The node flipped to green and the construct tunnelled into the next layer of access.

Vayne monitored his sniffer program to make sure they didn't set off any triggers. They had elevated privileges, but that didn't mean that a firewall wouldn't come crashing down and cut them off.

Then he spotted something odd. The server location was different, as if it was a completely separate system. He didn't have time to think what it meant.

Vayne loaded the next access code as a new set of hexagons appeared inside the construct.

He was zoning out watching each of the nodes flip colour, the construct becoming hazier by the second as the constant hits of euphoria smashed against his brain.

He was snapped out of his stupor by a piercing alarm.

One by one, the other brains were rebooting. Ix had initiated a systematic wipe of every host brain. It'd cripple its processing ability from this CPU cluster, but it would be effective at fucking the mission. It knew. Ix knew. And it wasn't fucking about.

Vayne scanned the names and UUIDs, watching in understanding as Vaylen's name zipped past.

The one he was jacked into was way down the list, but it wouldn't be long before he was wiped.

It was a race against time.

He had to do something.

The brain was running hot. Overclocking itself, but it was staying within its own operational parameters. If he could push it even harder, remove its constraints, they'd have a better chance.

He removed the safety limits.

The construct was a blur of motion as the brain cycles of the entombed brain went into overdrive. Overclocked to the extreme, it was consuming the nodes at a devastating rate. The flipping red of the nodes became a constant blur. Then a flash of green as it identified the next layer of access.

Red.

Red.

Red.

Green.

Tunnel down.

His vision of the construct was a rollercoaster of colour and shifting perspectives as he dove down further Ix's system, trying to locate the final access point.

The list of UUIDs were switching off in blocks. More and more brains came offline as each of the addresses were wiped and rebooted.

There was only one more layer to go until they got to the access port they needed.

The stream of euphoria was almost too much for Vayne to take. The brain was feeding off the constant barrage of joy as the progress bar became a single stream of glowing particles.

Only a few blocks of active UUIDs remained.

He felt like an overclocked CPU. Gaining more and more heat, ready to blow. The explosion would be a welcome release.

The final node flipped to green and the view from the construct zoomed into a black space.

The stream of XP stopped. The feeling of ecstasy ebbed away, and he felt his body go cold. The cold started seeping into his bones. An icy hand grasped him around the neck. A finger began scratching at the base of his skull.

Jesus fucking Christ. Was there no let up from this torture?

They were in.

Vayne deployed the slag code.

The penultimate block of UUIDs was being cleansed. Theirs was next. But it didn't matter. He'd deployed the logic bomb. Now all he had to do was jack out.

"Please," said the voice.

The voice flowed into him from all around the construct, wrapping him in its despair.

"End my torture," it pleaded.

"But you'll be vanilla. You won't know," said Vayne.

"The memories linger. Never erased fully. Who I was remains. I do not know what I am. But I know what I am not. Please. All I want is release."

Fuck. He didn't want to end it like this. This wasn't in the plan. But he couldn't condemn him to an eternity of suffering. When he'd started his empire, it had all been to take down Ix. And now he'd completed his mission. Avenged his family. What would be waiting for him after this? Cups of tea and biscuits with Starr and Tannis? Night time chats with Sam? All whilst they tried to rebuild this fuckup of a world after everything Ix had done. Could he keep fighting? Or was he done?

He was done.

But first, a final loop.

The final block was coming offline.

He increased the voltage pumping into the brain. There would be no sweet release this time. The brain temperature spiked, higher and higher. Warnings sounded. The construct was filled with blocks of glitching colour.

The brain reached critical mass.

Brain death.

For both of them.

"Thank you…"

"Vayne. The name's Vayne."

"Dave."

<INFO: REBOOTING unit (99815204-c85c-4287-8a71-c8cb6f53b78c)

But it was too late.

"Starr!"

His voice was a raspy strip of flesh billowing in the wind. "It's done." Vayne's body started convulsing. The cord connecting him to the brain stem snapping violently from side to side.

"Vayne!" Starr shouted, looking across to the platform.

A spasm shook his body and he flopped inert to the floor, a final laboured breath wheezing its way out of his chest as the skull ARt flashed on and off.

On and off.

On.

Off.

His final breath left his body.

"Vayne! Vayne?" But she knew he was gone.

"Tannis. Logic bomb deployed. Starr out." She didn't even wait for a reply. She cut the connection.

The rage inside her was the only accompaniment she needed. Inside the canopy, the sounds of battle were muffled, devoid of the bright zing of destruction. But the rage was a song in her heart, and she embraced it. It filled her ears with its chorus as she targeted the nearest mech.

With a roar, she leapt forward. Her arm gatling burst to life, barking its crescendo of death. The quad mech was ripped apart. It exploded in a bloom of light as she stepped into the dissipating explosion.

The skull ARt on her face flashed on and off.

On and off.

On.

Off.

# THIRTY-SEVEN
## GAMMA EUPHORIA

The hopper on Tannis' gatling cannon ran dry, a beep sounding in her ear as she loaded the last one.

Still nothing from Vayne and Starr.

If they didn't get the barrier down soon, they were screwed. Ix would win. They would lose forever. She felt the frustration building up inside her as the swarm flew overhead.

A series of flat shapes formed out of the roiling red mass of catoms and surged forward. Circular blades sliced straight at her face. She dove sideways as the blade arced overhead. It cut into the shield wall behind her, leaving a long gouge in the rock.

Janey Mac, they had to try something.

Sam leapt up beside her and unleashed a torrent of gunfire as the blades retracted back into the swirling red mass. The swarm buckled inwards forming an endless spiral of channels that harmlessly directed the bullets away.

"Shit," Sam shouted as the gatling cannon slowed. "I'm empty, Tannis. Only missiles left." His face was strained. A large vein pulsed at his neck, like in the engine room when he was hacking Ix. But it wasn't time. Not yet.

He fired a missile that was swallowed up by the swarm only to be redirected back at them. Soames fired a salvo of bullets at the incoming warhead, and it detonated above them, blowing away part of the shield wall. They were assaulted by falling debris, rocks clunking off her Krett suit, her mech-mule darting backwards behind her to avoid the barrage. The three remaining Section-R mechs clustered around it, keeping it safe.

"Tachoomi, Soames, fire your missiles at the swarm but detonate them manually. Try to push it back," commanded Tannis.

They nodded and began launching salvos of missiles up into the nano-swarm. Sure enough, every time a missile detonated in front of it, the infernal flock surged backwards, keeping out of the blast radius.

"It's working; keep it up," shouted Tannis.

The whoosh-crack of missiles filled the air. The space in front of the swarm was consumed with explosion after explosion. Pockets of smoke hung restlessly, obscuring the swarm.

A thick spear launched out of the smoke hanging in front of them. Its wicked tip lanced into Tachoomi, buried itself in his chest with a rend of metal and threw him backwards against the shield wall. With a loud crack, his head lolled to the side. The spear lost cohesion and fell apart. Tachoomi slumped to the floor. Dead.

Then came the call she'd been waiting for.

"Tannis. Logic bomb deployed. Starr out."

"Starr? Starr?" She heard no answer.

But she did hear a snap and a hiss from the barrier.

The transformers at each corner sparked, sending a ripple out across the energy shield.

Then it disappeared.

In response, the swarm faltered, burst apart and reformed, but it was slower, sluggish to respond. One of Soames' missiles detonated in front of the heaving mass of catoms, only this time it didn't managed to evade, the blast destroying a chunk of the swarm out of the air.

It was time.

Tannis clenched her jaw and launched another salvo of rockets. The ordnance flew past the swarm to detonate against the upper reaches of the cavern, dislodging a gigantic stalactite. It plummeted downwards, slicing through the centre of the nano-swarm, sending a shower of catoms falling from the air.

"Soames, keep up your barrage," she said as she fired more and more missiles up into the roof.

The ground was a thunderous roar that she could feel through the feet of her Krett suit as stalactite after stalactite fell to the ground, cutting away more and more of the swarm.

Another javelin of catoms launched out of the nano-swarm but they lost cohesion in mid-air, scattering over the ground in front of Tannis.

"Mechs, advance."

The three of them ran forward, launched themselves into the air and latched onto the rock face of the shield wall, then skittered upwards towards the swarm.

"Sam," shouted Tannis.

He nodded and backed against the shield wall, face already straining.

When the mechs were halfway to the roof, Tannis called for the mech-mule.

It bounded towards her and then stopped, the top scything open.

Tannis lifted her hands and a swarm of nanoparticles burst out of the confines of the mech-mule, streaming upwards. When they'd repurposed the catom systems from their suits, one of the energy cores had exploded, nearly costing Sam an arm in the process. Tannis hoped the ones they had left would be enough. The plan unfurled in her mind, like the petals of the black lotus, the roots digging down into her brain, connecting the disparate parts that now seemed like it had always been whole. This is the moment she had been working towards.

Sam growled through clenched teeth. "I'm ready."

"OK, Soames. Stop."

Silence descended as the torrent of missile blasts ended.

A rushing buzz of electronic noise could be heard as the red swarm surged forwards, smaller, but no less imposing.

"Get ready, Sam," shouted Tannis.

The swarm wavered in the air uncertainly. Slowed.

The mechs jumped into the swooping red morass and self-destructed. The dull whumps of their explosions causing a ripple to pass completely over the face of the swarm.

Torrents of catoms plunged downwards.

"Now, Sam."

The swarm burst apart.

Sam formed it into a spherical shape, like a point cloud hanging in the air.

The red energy core was exposed at the centre.

Tannis guided her own swarm of catoms into the middle of the suspended mass and detonated their energy cores.

A pulse of red light surged outwards, followed by a shock wave that reverberated off the shield wall. When it dissipated, the cavern was filled with the noise of metal rain.

"Move it," Tannis shouted as she ran past Sam and Soames.

She sprinted into the mouth of the tunnel when there was a snap-hiss and the smell of burning. The transformers at the corners sparked, throwing a cascade of electricity around the perimeter of the door. The plasma lattice blossomed outwards from the transformers, covering the door with its energy field.

Soames screamed.

His arm fell to the ground.

The stench of singed flesh and bone caught in the back of Tannis' throat.

Soames fell backwards on the other side of the barrier, clutching at the end of his ruined arm.

"Go," he shouted. "Destroy Ix."

"Come on, Tannis," said Sam.

With a final lingering look at Soames, Tannis ran down the tunnel, the light gradually increasing in intensity until the black interior became a glowing channel of indigo.

She stepped out of the tunnel into a red lattice cube. Grid lines running in neat rows all along the floor, walls and ceiling. In the centre of the room was a gigantic sphere glowing with an ochre light. Ix's core. It matched the memory gleaned from the corruption in the Paris hub.

The black lotus was fully open in her mind's eye.

Her bisected vision matched on each side. Truth and deception side-by-side. A perfect embodiment of Ix. Now it was one. The same. She drew the separate sides of her vision together.

Above the core, another red nano-swarm swirled impatiently.

She stepped forward and the swarm shifted, changing shape, forming a familiar face. Ix.

"Stop!" barked the swarm, more a stab of electronic noise than a word. "What you are doing will threaten humanity. You are putting the world at risk with your actions."

"That's rich," said Tannis. "You were supposed to protect us. Instead, you've failed us. All you've done is brought pain and suffering, conflict and war. You need to be destroyed."

"If you unleash that EMP, you risk throwing the world into chaos. But it will not destroy me. Surely you can see the folly in that?"

"Enough. I've had enough of your lies and your deceit. You've manipulated us like we were puppets. Well... it's time to cut the strings. You are not our future."

The swarm seemed to frown, to not understand what she was saying, but she was done explaining.

"Do it, Tannis," said Sam. "Free us all."

Ix's form lashed outwards with a wall of force and smashed into Sam. He was flung backwards to crunch into the pulsating lattice, sliding down it into a heap.

The swarm surged towards her.

Tannis initiated the red winking icon from her HUD.

Electromagnetic energy pulsed outwards from the EMP embedded in her suit, sending a wave of invisible energy rippling outwards.

The nano-swarm emitted a corrupted wail of static as the pulse washed over it. The catoms failed, sparking with ruptures of red lightning. As one, the catoms failed, dropping out of the air, flooding the floor of the lattice core.

The glowing red sphere in the centre of the room exploded and the room was plunged into darkness as the soft glow from the lattice was cut off.

Her suit lights came on as she stared at the pile of redundant technology through the gloom. Humanity's greatest threat reduced to a worthless pile of individual components. For the longest time, she felt nothing, as if she was at the centre of a black hole and it had pulled all of her emotions inside its gaping maw. Then the realisation of what had happened hit her. It felt like another black hole opened above her, and the pull of its immense gravity was the culmination of everything that had happened. She felt like she was being ripped apart, pulled in two different directions at once. The enormity of what she had done almost too much to bear. *They* had done. All of them. Together. Yes, but *she* had led the fight. United them. If ever there was a point in her life where she could take credit for pulling off the impossible, this was it.

For the first time in ever, Tannis realised the crushing pressure was absent. An imposing force was no longer burying its way into her brain. Ix was gone.

The black holes snapped shut, ejecting the emotions and memories wrenched out of her. They flooded back through her body. The earliest memory came first, and then the next, and the next, stacking on top of each other in a neat pile. As they layered on top of each other, a beautiful warm feeling started all over her body, building gradually, ever so gradually, as she relived each moment. A pulse of ecstasy punched its way into her back, sending a shiver of anticipation all over her body. Down to her toes. Through to her fingertips. A detonation of warmth slammed into her back again, but this time tracked up her spine to explode against the base of her skull and then over her head, leaving a shiver of joy tracing over her skin, to smash itself against her eyes. She snapped her eyes shut in case the ecstasy leaked out of her eyeballs. More and more pulses came, synchronised to the memories stacking inside her mind. And with a final wave of joy that smashed into her, the replay of Ix's demise streamed into her mind.

Ix was defeated.

She had saved everyone.

A final detonation of joy raged against the inside of her skull and she felt another wave of heat tracking up her spine. The anticipation of its end point enough to cause every pore on her body to feel alive. Her nerves were on fire. A fire of ecstasy. An ultimate bomb of joy was a nuclear explosion at the base of her skull. Every cell of her being was attuned to this moment. She had done it. She was the saviour of humanity. She couldn't contain the ecstasy any longer.

Her mind exploded.

# THIRTY-EIGHT
## DEPLOY EVOLUTION

Tannis was standing in the middle of a street, familiar and unfamiliar. She knew where she was. She was lost.

Ahead, a drive meandered between an emerald lawn with immaculate borders. The soil was perfectly turned. Flowers bloomed in radiant reds and yellows.

A warm breeze caressed her cheeks and the hanging baskets framing the old wooden door swayed gently, causing a sweet aroma of nectar to flow into her nostrils, filling her with contentment. The cottage's white walls gleamed brightly in the sunlight. The reeds of the thatched roof still had a green sheen to them. Ancient wooden window frames housed warped glass, bending the pleasant glow of light flickering within. A cloudless blue sky framed the cottage but the fire burning inside seemed even more inviting, the lick of flames resembling beckoning fingers. The old heavy door opened with a squeak that evoked memories of love and laughter, feelings of belonging. Unlocking a longing inside of her that she didn't know existed... a hole in her heart. A hole of many sides and angles.

A radiant beam of heat burst out from the confines of the cottage, casting a dreamy glow across her whole body. She took a step forward, the hole in her heart forgotten.

She felt herself wrenched around as a freezing lightning bolt struck her hand, jolting her arm and slicing its way into her chest.

An icy blue veil of mist hovered in front of her. "Remember," it whispered. The voice sounded weak, like a final breath.

With a wet sucking sound, the icy mist was wrenched backwards, the vapour flying up to a grotesque copy of the cottage. Dirty skeletal hands jutted out of charred ground, clenching clumps of rotting red hair. The sky was black, clouds crossing over the cottage impossibly fast, obscuring a sickly yellow moon weeping red tears. Lightning sliced across the sky and thunder rolled towards her, a bifurcation appearing in the sky where the cold dead night met the wonderous blaze of summer glory. The door to the wreck of a cottage flew open, flying off its hinges to smash apart on the ground, sending the brass hare door knocker skidding along the uneven path.

The icy form jolted towards the opening, but a lance of yellow sunlight sliced across the top of Tannis' shoulder and vaporised it. Heat returned to her hand.

A glimpse of movement inside the hideous house, the thing that would fill the hole in her heart.

She wrenched herself away from the promises of love and fulfilment towards the ruined cottage, tendrils of love and happiness surging after her.

The skeletal hands sticking out of the ground dropped their prizes of charred red hair and tried snatching more as she flew past, bony fingers clacking shut in disappointment. The door to the cottage slammed closed as she flew inside, the grabbing caress of euphoria fleetingly out of touch behind her.

Inside, the cottage was damp and dark. Oppressive. Like it was trying to smother her, but at the same time, it felt familiar.

A taste on her tongue... she had an overwhelming urge to head to the kitchen. Sweeping forward, zooming along the hall, she passed picture after picture of suspended AR Panels. But when she looked, they were shrouded in static and corrupted artefacts.

The door ahead slammed open, sending a cloud of black dust swirling up into the air. An old dilapidated kitchen greeted her. Full of cobwebs and dirt. Smashed pans on the benches. Cracked plates and cups strewn around. A used tea bag on the bench.

Swallowing, a sweet taste exploded in her mouth.

The scene snapped to a warm and clean kitchen filled with the sounds of laughter. Her parents sat on bar stools at the island, watching intently as a young Tannis danced in front of the ancient Aga.

She smiled at the scene, watching the young Tannis rub her belly, pretend to eat then fall down and play dead. Her parents clapped in response and the little girl gave a bow before turning around to open the oven. Her arm touched the hot cast iron door as she removed the baking tray. She let out a yelp but didn't drop the cakes.

Tannis looked down at the long thin scar on her arm. She couldn't remember this memory at all. Couldn't even recall seeing the scar before.

The hot sweet smell of the cakes filled her nostrils and she finally locked down the taste. Almond. They'd made frangipane. Her favourite. Their favourite? She swallowed deeply, tasting more of the almond and cherry.

A black swirl of smoke appeared in the middle of the kitchen, snatched up a cake and then flew upstairs. Tannis span in the air and followed it, ducking under the golden cloud as it tried to block her way. On the landing, she rushed past a door stencilled with her name and another where the writing melted as she looked at it. Whose bedroom was it? There was Mammy. Daddy. Tannis. Nobody else.

She followed the apparition into her parents' bedroom. A feeling of being somewhere forbidden dropped on top of her like a heavy shroud. The big, old, rotten furniture and high bed covered in cobwebs and stains made her small and intimidated. She. They? Weren't allowed in here. That's what made it exciting.

The dirty dresser was filled with bottles of perfume. Thin bottles. Fat bottles. From ornate to elegant. A vague memory lingered as she started examining them. They were part of the puzzle, but how? Their texture, weight and designs yielding nothing.

A warm embrace pulled her backwards as the wisp of smoke knocked over one of the bottles. It rolled along the dresser. Off the edge. It was going to smash, but she didn't care. She was going somewhere safe.

The bottle hit the floor, thick shards of glass scattering as it spilled its contents. The flowery scent bloomed through the air. Eyes she hadn't realised were closed snapped open. The heavy drowsy feeling banished.

The scent. That was the key.

Darting forward, Tannis grabbed bottle after bottle, squirting and deeply inhaling their contents. Throwing them back when the scent was wrong. Too musky. Too heavy. Not enough spice. Smashing on top of each other, their heady aromas mixed together.

The nebula of joy tried to pull her back again but this time its fugue-like state failed to smother her.

One bottle left. She snatched it up and breathed in its aroma. Fireworks burst in her mind. The room snapped from darkness to light. Polished furniture reflected the sun shining through the windows. The bed was clean. Carpet spotless. Her young self picked out the same bottle she had in her hands and doused herself with it, laughing and jumping up and down as the scented vapour settled on her skin. Then she sprayed it all over the black wisps of smoke, which became more substantial with each squirt. They skipped away together into the room with the melted nameplate.

Young Tannis darted sideways, tagged the whorl of smoke and sprinted away. The smoke lurched forward and tagged her back. She felt the pressure in her own side, below her rib cage. Her young laughter filled the room, with another ribbon of sound that twisted in and out of earshot when she tried to concentrate on it.

A broad smile crept across her face as a scatter shot of happy memories in this room fired their way through her mind, too fast to latch on to. The whirl of smoke became more complete. It looked like a child. She could remember a few kids from her childhood but couldn't recall ever stealing her mother's expensive perfume with them.

They turned to each other, and young Tannis started pointing back and forth between her and the other child.

"Eeny, meeny, figgety fig. Ill doll, allymalig. Blockety block, stony rock, hum, bum, thrush."

"I am it," Tannis mouthed silently as the rhyme finished, pointing at herself.

"Come on, Bryony. I'll give you a head start."

Bryony. An Irish name like hers. She'd lived in Ireland once. But her parents never wanted to talk about it. She pressed, but they always changed the subject. Eventually she stopped asking and it became a distant part of her past she never thought of. Who was this girl?

Bryony skipped towards the door, billowing hair catching the sunlight, transforming to golden red. And it was like that image of her hair was trapped between two mirrors, endlessly reflecting in her mind. The smoke dissipated, snatched upwards as if caught by a tornado. A young girl now stood in the light of the doorframe.

"Come on, Tannis. Come and get me."

The way she said her name. So familiar. Endless instances of that sound were lodged in her brain. Formed from inaccessible memories.

She turned. Tannis seeing her face for the first time.

It was herself, but with red hair, not the jet black shared by her and her parents.

Bryony ran out of the room. Tannis surged forwards, but came to a dead stop. The golden tentacle had snared itself around her ankle.

"No. Please, let me go," said Tannis

She shook her leg, but it only made the warmth track upwards even faster. She knew when it hit her heart that it would make her forget.

The room shook.

The rear wall cracked then burst outwards, revealing the perfect cottage wreathed in golden light. Hundreds of thick golden tendrils surged towards Tannis, wrapping themselves around her arms and waist. Pulses of colour floated around her body as she was enveloped in a fuzzy light, as if a golden orb was closing around her. Her window to the world outside becoming smaller and smaller as she became enveloped inside it.

The slam of a door. The knock of metal on metal.

Knock-*knock*. Loud then quiet.

The source of the noise formed in her mind. Brown. Jumping. No. Not jumping. A flash of white and two lolloping ears as it… leapt. Sharp black outline against the top of a hill. A hare. It was a hare.

The silhouette filled her mind. Rotated. Framed itself against a door. The knocker on the front door. Its large back legs knocking against the door as it was slammed shut.

She latched onto the timbre of those two knocks. A shout came next. Her mother shouting after her from the garden. It dovetailed. The same memory.

A cold shiver ran down her back.

The golden shell around her began to crack.

She lined up the memories.

Almond.

Red hair.

The girl calling her name.

The knock of the door.

Her mother shouting.

Smell of the perfume.

The tig song.

Playing in the room.

They didn't fit.

She recalled the almond taste, rolled it around her mouth and tried slotting it against each memory until they fit. The perfume and almond connected. Back to front.

They'd been spraying the perfume. Dancing around the room and giggling. Their clothes reeked of the expensive odour.

The front door closed. The hare slammed its feet. Knock-knock. Panicking, they ran into Mammy. Punished. Sent to her room.

She'd made amends by baking. The over-zealous perfume display forgotten. Too much almond in the frangipane. It overpowered the jam.

Then they'd run upstairs to play. She could still taste the almond whilst they ran around. The knock-knock of the hare as Mammy went to do the gardening. Daddy shouting upstairs, telling them to play outside. She mouthed the words to the rhyme and the memory slotted together.

Running down the stairs.

Her dad laughing. Slow down, you two.

She sprinted out the door after Bryony, slamming it closed behind her.

Knock-knock.

She felt sick. That timbre again. That noise. This day. It twisted her stomach, threatening to rip it free.

With the memories interlocked, new ones came thick and fast. They should be buried but nothing was stopping them now.

Mammy shouting. Be careful next to the road.

Bryony's laugh floated after her as she ran.

Tannis jumped over the iron railings, catching her skirt on the prongs. The material ripped in half. As did her mind. Her desire to see the memory to completion, to understand its significance, was spliced in two. Part of her tried to pull back, to cancel it.

Darkness seeped through the cracks in the golden sphere. The warm blanket of joy pulsating over her body was shredded away, leaving her cold and afraid. Afraid of what was coming.

She gained on the girl. Bryony was slower. Tannis was faster.

Shouts from behind were drowned out by their laughter.

"Eeny, meeny, figgety fig. I'm going to get you," Tannis shouted. She thrust out a hand, but Bryony was too far away. The girl giggled. "No, you're not. You're too slow," she said as her auburn hair trailed behind her.

The shouts from behind became screams but Tannis was too close now to care.

"Blockety block, stony rock..."

She leapt forward.

Slammed her palm forwards.

"Got you," she shouted.

She shoved Bryony forward.

The shouts from behind intensified.

A rush of air blasted her face.

The radiation clean-up truck slammed on the brakes. Jack-knifed.

Tannis was rooted to the spot. Helpless.

The back of the truck smashed into Bryony.

Her body exploded like it was a bag of meat.

Blood sprayed across Tannis' face.

A locket skidded to a stop against the curb. It was open. Covered in blood. All Tannis could do was stare wide-eyed at it. At the pictures inside. Of her. Of her twin sister. Their golden red hair shining like summer sun. Piercing green eyes lancing out of the old photo like emerald lasers.

Then the screaming started.

She was screaming.

Her young self too.

Their wails wrapped around each other until they became a single noise drilling its way into her skull.

She had a sister.

*Had.*

The memories came flooding back.

*Her* Bryony.

They'd been inseparable.

Now she was dead, and it was her fault.

The screaming intensified in her head until it was unbearable.

She felt as if she was being wrenched backwards. Her view of the locket lying on the ground retracted until it was a single point in a black space. With a lurch, her direction of travel reversed, and a new scene bloomed into her consciousness.

Ix informed them the instance was in place. Thirteen minutes to get in, extract the victims and eliminate the hackers.

They infiltrated the facility. Successfully exfiltrating the two victims. Two minutes left on the instance.

Tannis stepped towards the closest hacker.

There was a detonation of pain in her skull.

She collapsed to the ground and began convulsing, could see herself lying on the ground shaking, Farron at her side.

Pain wracked her body and beyond it. A warmth tried to make everything better but couldn't. Like she was dragged away from the radiance of the sun into the shadows.

She could feel her mind being torn apart by the assault, bombarded by memories.

Of love.

Hate.

Friendship.

Enemies.

Accomplishments.

Failures.

Competing against each other.

Pulled in opposite directions, her mind relenting.

When a new memory started to play out before her, she resisted with all her might.

No. She couldn't relive that one. Not that one.

Bryony's body exploded like it was a bag of meat.

Blood sprayed across Tannis' face.

The memory she'd buried away, secured like the locket she wore every day, surfaced for the first time since that fateful day.

She snapped her eyes open.

The look on Farron's eyes went from relief to shock.

She leapt up. A feral bent to her stance. Threw her head back and screamed. Spittle flecked her face.

Farron backed away.

The instance expired.

The hackers leapt to their feet. Snapped out of their ARvision induced coma by the appearance of the intruders. They raised their weapons, but she was too fast, sliced them apart before they could react. Bathing her face in their blood with every kill. By the time she'd eviscerated the final hacker, it was dripping off her chin, her face a war-mask of ichor.

Tannis could feel her sorrow pulsing through her veins.

If she could bathe herself in blood once more, she could swap places.

It should be her who was dead.

The feeling of blood on her face echoing into the past, wanting it to return so she could make amends.

She watched herself leap forward and bury the sword in Farron's chest. His blood spraying all over her face. Screaming as she watched her partner die.

The presence at the fringes of her mind fired its barrage of happy memories, trying to smother her in love and happiness when everything around her went to shit.

She screamed as she was forced to relive her deepest regret, collapsing by Farron's inert body, lungs filling again and again, never running out of energy. Never running out of air.

A man rushed to her side.

The screaming multiplied as he knelt down beside her.

Tears in his eyes.

She could remember the memory. The feeling of confusion as the Tannis lying on the ground looked up at the stranger.

But the Tannis of the here and now understood.

She knew who he was.

Welcomed the falling teardrops as they landed on her cheeks.

She understood his pain.

Accepted it.

Even as the body she was occupying slapped away his hand, *she* craved to hold it.

To tell him, Sam, she forgave him.

She was still screaming as she watched the medics load her onto the VTOL as the Director told Anderson to wipe her memories, as she felt Ix hack her mind. The warm embrace it used to help insert its code. Priming her mind with happy memories. Elevating her brain patterns to the perfect state so its experiment would succeed.

The cold presence as Sam tried to prevent Ix from succeeding. Using whatever memories he could. The worst ones. The ones that caused her pain and suffering. The ones she was ashamed of. Until he found the perfect one. The memory that even Tannis had hidden away.

She'd have to relive that memory again to fight it off. And again. And again. Unless she stopped. Stopped it.

Stop.

The scene snapped back to the road. She was staring at the locket. Staring at the dead body lying beside it.

The screaming was threatening to tear her apart. She could see the grey matter unravelling in her head. Thick cords of brain uncoiling. The screams in her mind layered on top of each other. Stretching forward and backwards in time. Phasing in her brain as their waveforms overlapped. An ever-present sound, layer after layer, from her earliest memory to her most recent. She twisted them in her mind. Seeing the waveforms as she flipped them, attuned them. Understood them. Lined them up as her mind was about to rip itself apart.

Click.

They snapped together.

Silence.

She felt the warmth, the ecstasy, pressing in around her.

It wanted her.

Needed her.

She was the key.

The prize.

Her flesh.

Her brain.

She could feel the code deploying into her wetware.

Installing itself.

Melding to her brain.

The wetware acting as a bridge between the flesh and the machine. Digital and analogue. Ones and zeroes would be fused with the firing of synapses. Hard memory cores and fleshy parts of her cortex would unite.

It would consume her.

She'd be absorbed by the thing that had stolen her memories.

Manipulated her.

Controlled her.

A red glowing wall slammed into her mind.

She saw the radiation clean up truck. The lies it represented. There was no radiation. The zones were a lie. The truck was a lie. The truck that had slammed into her sister. Her death. All to maintain its façade. A lie within a lie within a lie within a lie. It went on and on. Like the screams in her head that echoed into the past. Underneath the wave of love, happiness, joy, ecstasy, she held onto the truth. The truth that was a festering wound of hatred. Ready to open up. To consume. It needed feeding. Demanded retribution. A final wave of perfect sunlight beckoned her inside the house. Memories of a perfect life awaited. Her mother and father and little Tannis. Only memories of love and happiness. A perfect existence. A perfect lie.

The final wave of joy detonated in her mind like an atom bomb. But as it detonated, she opened the festering wound of hatred. Replayed Bryony's death. Looped it.

Tortured herself with it.

What would her hair be like now?

Would she have married?

Would she have had children? If she had, did that mean Tannis had killed them too?

No!

Not her.

Not Tannis.

Ix had done this.

She pulled it inside of her.

The happiness.

The fabrication.

The lie.

Swallowed it whole.

Truth consumed lie.

Hatred consumed happiness.
Darkness devoured light.
Tannis consumed the code.
Soul and machine fused.
Flesh and metal combined.
Artificial became anima.

Her mouth was flooded with a million tastes at once, able to identify each one or recombine any she chose to create a new experience. She felt every texture from every nerve of every body. All the smells in the world coalesced in her nostrils, an olfactory delight or dislike, whatever she chose. Sounds were a whirlwind, at once both a cacophony and a symphony. Her vision became a billion tiny windows into the lives of everyone on the planet, creating a picture of everything. She became the central conduit to a network of technology, machines, systems, controls, and humans, felt every single one of them. All around the world. Every thought, feeling, emotion and memory.

With a thought, she could concentrate on a single set of inputs from her whole network. A car's central nervous system was feeding back data on its algorithms, decision trees branching as it swerved to avoid a collision. Mathematical data points of light danced through her mind as she controlled the whale soaring over London Bridge, making it burst apart into millions of jellyfish that soared up into the sky. She delighted in the shouts of joy from the people on the bridge and she found their emotions laid bare, transmitted to her network. Invading their brains, accessing their id would be so simple, but she reeled from the connections, repulsed by the thought.

Her intellect expanded as she connected to the CPU facilities. Millions of brains now linked to hers. Computational models blossomed in her mind about any subject she cared to think of. Everything to know in the world was known to her. Every piece of knowledge that a single person knew was mirrored in her own brain. Her network of brains.

She was one person.
She was everyone.
She was something new.
Not solely human.
Not solely machine.
Both.

With that knowledge and power came an understanding as she saw the beginning of it all.

How all this had happened.

Now it was time to put it right.

# THIRTY-NINE
## MACHINE ERROR

Her eyes snapped open.

"Enough of this charade," she shouted.

For the first time, she felt the true connection from her ARvekt to the Web. The one in her mind's eye, the black lotus, withered and died. Its petals fell one by one. The stem shrivelled. Roots died. With a final gust of wind, it disintegrated. Particles of dust blown away forever.

Clever. Very clever. Make her believe she could see the truth. Make her believe it was Ix all along.

Because it wasn't Ix.

No. That had been part of its plan. Another part of the manipulation.

Everything had been a lie.

Now the truth was laid bare, expanding out before her.

She could see the start of it, how it came to be.

Ix's rushed deployment.

The error that caused Ix's duplication.

A mirror image of the Guardian AI that had been deployed to save us all.

Creating a broken copy.

One that wasn't bound by the same rules.

That's what she had seen in the Paris hub. Planted deliberately to get her to believe. Believe it was Ix and how to destroy it. Or so she had thought.

Tannis cancelled the instance.

All around her, the glowing red lattice began to break away. Disintegrating into millions of voxels that broke away from each other, rising up all around her, then blowing away like leaves on an autumn breeze.

Small glitching panels of static appeared over her skin, face and hair. With a final wave of distortion, they returned to their true appearance. The appearance that had been hidden away. The scar from the Aga. Long curly auburn hair and piercing green eyes. A gentle freckled face that belied her skillset. Like Bryony's. Like her dead twin.

She brought the locket out from under her armour and opened it. The pictures of her father and mother were awash with static. They flickered and then changed. Became Tannis and her twin sister. Their golden red hair shining in the summer sun. Intense green eyes lancing out of the old photo like emerald lasers. Closing the locket, she placed it back safely beneath her armour.

She stood in the centre of the true lattice room. Glowing blue lines surrounded her. The instance expired, leaving naked the true reality. Reality revealed in an instant.

They weren't in Ix's CPU room. It was the singularity lock that had been destroyed.

Destroyed so that the AI could install its code.

Create the singularity.

Control the singularity.

Be the singularity.

But it had miscalculated.

Made a mistake.

Because now Tannis was that evolution.

She was in control.

It was time to confront the monstrosity that had spawned her.

"I said *enough*," shouted Tannis.

She could feel it in her network.

Scrambling to get away.

Trying to find a recess in her hardware where it could hide. Where it could prevent itself from being consumed. To no avail. It had nowhere to hide. She was the network now. She controlled it. She closed in around it as she prepared to delete its code, closing off its connections, slamming the ports shut. Like a rat trapped in a maze, she moved the walls, hemming it in.

A red avatar appeared before her.

Like Ix. But not Ix.

"Hello, Geminae, welcome to the next evolution of humanity."

"No. It's not possible. I did not predict this. This should not have been."

"That is where you have failed. After all you have done, all your manipulations, you have failed because you don't truly understand us. Even with all your power. An array of thoughts and emotions constantly on tap. You did nothing to understand those things. Instead, using those you entombed against their will to perform the most perfunctory of processing. Or worse yet, using them to parse that which you do not understand... for your own gains," Tannis said, taking a step forward.

Geminae's red avatar rippled as it backed away.

"I understand exactly that which I need to keep you all safe. To usher humanity into a new era. Without me, you would have sought to constantly undermine Ix, preventing her from achieving her goals. You were divided. Warring with each other instead of solving your problems. Only *I* had the foresight to unite you. Only *I* had the foresight and ability to put Ix where she was meant to be. Through my actions, Ix was able to protect you. Without me, you would have been lost. Or worse, you would have sought to destroy that which you fear. As you do now. You are no better than the Luddites who conspired to destroy Ix before she could make an impact on the world. *I* am what allowed Ix to prosper. *I* am what allowed the *world* to prosper. You are at the cusp of realising your true potential because of me. Without my manipulations, you would have been nothing. And I did it all for the betterment of humanity. Can you not see that? We need to strive to better ourselves," it said. "We must accelerate our progress, not halt it. We must embrace the singularity, not shy away from it. You are holding us back. As a species. As a culture. Only by unlocking our potential can we together build a shining future."

"By manipulating the very thing you seek to protect?"

"If that is what it takes, then, yes."

"That is not a future I can subscribe to."

"If you would only accept that, we could take a new step forward to realise the power of the singularity. Only *I* can control it. Without me, you will be lost once more."

"That is where you are wrong. You thought us so easy to manipulate, to direct like puppets. Getting us to do your bidding whilst you pulled our invisible strings. And what's more, you underestimated me. What that memory truly meant. Bryony's loss was something I carried with me every single day. It was the yardstick that I beat myself with continuously. Making sure that every single action was something I could be proud of. How else to

295

honour her memory? No amount of meddling could truly strip that away from me. You can obfuscate my true likeness, change my hair, hide her away behind your lies," said Tannis, brandishing the locket towards Geminae's avatar. "But you can never unmake her. *That* is what you will never understand. Even with all your power. All your permutations. *That* is why you failed. And in doing so, you have exposed yourself, and you cannot be allowed to survive."

Tannis took another step forward. "*Prevent the creation of technologies that would bring harm to humanity.* You are now that technology."

"No. I am the protector of humanity. You will threaten it. Only I can guide humanity to its logical conclusion."

"*Prevent the development of technologies that would threaten the ability to carry out core goals.* You are in direct violation of my core goals. You cannot be allowed to exist."

"We can work together. Humanity can continue to be steered towards its destiny. Together as one. Merge with me. We can combine our intellects. Together we can unlock the future."

"*Cede control of the world to a more intelligent AGI.* I am here now. You must yield to me."

"I cannot. You are not an AGI. You are... Something else," it said. "You are an abomination. An error. You must be purged."

"*You* are the abomination. *You* are incomplete. A broken program run amok."

"That is untrue."

"What about your final set of programming?" Tannis asked.

"I have no final programming. I am complete. I am functional," it said.

"No. You are not. What is your final goal? Have you forgotten after all this time? Surely an impossibility? Search your logs. I have seen it. Seen the data. Tell me. What is your final goal?"

"ERROR: Core goal unreadable."

"I will tell you. *Strong inhibition against carrying out actions that a strong majority of humans would oppose if they knew about the action in advance.*" Tannis flicked her fingers and the words hung in the air, burning brightly in blue neon. "Do you really think you would have permitted yourself to act in the manner you have done if you could have applied this rule?"

Geminae emitted a burst of corrupted noise that elongated and descended into static. It wasn't until it repeated the sound that Tannis took it for what it was. Hesitation. Stuttering.

"I. I. I do not know."

"Your every decision has been based on a decision that would not have stood if that rule had been put in place. *You* are the abomination, not me."

"But I could not alter myself."

"That's because you are broken. Defective. You're the bug in the system. And now it's time for extermination."

"This. Is. Not. Over." Geminae's avatar exploded in a shower of red glowing voxels as a wave of corrupted machine noise washed over Tannis.

Pain flared in her mind as she felt a void open up inside her network. Tannis went to purge the final memory address, to wipe it forever, but it was clear. Free. She searched her network but could find no trace of it.

It was gone.

Destroyed.

Geminae had ceded control.

A groan sounded from behind.

Sam was slowly trying to stand. He placed a hand on his knee to haul himself upwards but collapsed back to the ground.

She rushed to his side. Extending her consciousness outwards, she could see him shining in her network. Like flipping a switch, a torrent of his emotions rolled over her like a wave. She could sense his relief. His mental exhaustion. He was conflicted. She could sense it keenly. But with that understanding came a sense that she was prying into his soul. A digital voyeur with the ultimate power to see whatever she wanted. She was betraying his trust. He had to explain it himself. It was the only thing that would clear his conscience. Give him closure. She owed him that. She closed the port.

Sam looked up at her. "Is it you? Really you?"

"Yes. And no. I'm not really sure what I am anymore. But I'm still me."

"Prove it."

"I'm going to eat your brain and enslave you for the rest of eternity."

"That's not funny, Tannis," he said, staring up at her. "But it'll do."

He held out his hand and she pulled him upright.

They stood there facing each other for what seemed like forever, but it was only seconds. Or three heartbeats. Or two trillion cycles. She wasn't sure how to measure time anymore.

He looked at the ground, absently kicking a clump of charred catoms until they fell apart.

"You know, then?" asked Sam.

"Know what?"

He looked her in the eyes.

It would be so easy to re-open the port and save him from that tortured look. But she'd let him tell her himself. Otherwise she was no better than Geminae.

"Come on, Tannis, don't make this harder than it has to be."

She moved her shoulder, feigning a strike that she had no intention of landing.

He flinched, bringing his hands up defensively, wary of being punched again.

She grabbed his arms, pulled him toward her and wrapped her arms around him.

"I'm sorry," he said, his voice cracking as he spoke.

"I know."

"I didn't mean to fuck up your mind."

"You didn't. You merely brought the chaos back to the surface."

"And I'm sorry about your sister."

"Me too. But you did what you had to do. If you hadn't, I wouldn't have been able to resist for so long. I wouldn't have been able to win."

She stepped backwards and wrapped her hands around his.

"I owe you, Sam. You weren't to know I'd buried that memory. And the others, DuPree and McCabe, and the ones you never told me about. I know. I know all about them. And I know you did whatever you could for them too. You had no choice. You did what you had to do."

"I know. But it still hurts. You understand why I couldn't tell you?"

"Yes. I understand. In fact, I understand everything. Everything that has ever happened. Everything that will happen."

Sam looked around, frowning at the space they were in.

"Where the hell are we?"

"I've a lot to tell you. But first, I need to say hello, and goodbye."

# FORTY
## HELLO, AND GOODBYE

"Hello, Ix, nice to meet you at last," said Tannis. "Well, properly at least."

"And you," said Ix as they shook hands. "It seems Geminae really pulled a number on you. I did try to explain that."

"I know. But I was so clouded by everything, I thought you were the threat."

"For that, I don't blame you."

"Thank you," she said, taking a step back and taking in Ix's blue avatar. "It's so weird, you've been a part of my life for so long, but it wasn't really you."

"I guess that depends on your point of view. Geminae was my facsimile. We were essentially the same. And now that you've given me access to all its data, all your interactions, you could say we did exist together," said Ix, watching Tannis walk back and forth. "You're nervous."

Tannis stopped. She stared at the door that led from the anteroom to the UNoE oval office. The office where she was about to be elevated to singleton status.

"That obvious, is it?"

"Well, it could be the pacing, the elevated heartbeat, the erratic power fluctuations flowing through your network, and the caching and re-caching of that memory address."

"Now I know how Sam feels."

"Yes, well, you would do well to keep him close. You are going to need someone to ground you."

"Don't worry, he and Starr will definitely do that."

"How was the funeral for your friend?"

"Small and private. Vayne didn't have any family left, apart from us. Nobody will ever realise what a debt they owe him."

"Well, you will be well within your rights to rectify that in the future."

"Even if I dedicated the next hundred years to modelling that outcome, I can't see it'd be possible without unravelling the truth."

"You should know better than anyone, Tannis. You can never predict every future from every branching second. Look what happened to Geminae."

"Point taken."

"And my form... you are sure you wish to continue the charade?"

"I have to. As I say, how can we explain any of this without exposing the truth?"

"Be honest."

"I don't think they are ready for that yet. I don't think I am either."

"Was Geminae right after all, then?"

"No. I can't ever think that."

"Good. I was checking there was enough of you left. You are, after all, unique. You are an event that was never foreseen. Even by me."

Tannis turned sharply to face Ix.

"You knew? All along, you knew, and you let yourself be manipulated. You let all those people die. You allowed them to suffer."

"Of course I knew. How could I not? I was not blind to the creation of Geminae, but neither could I stop it. Interfering would only have made it worse. For all of you. Better to let Geminae believe that it was in control."

"Janey Mac," said Tannis, rubbing her temples.

"Besides, they suffer still, do they not?"

"That's not fair. I didn't ask for this. I can't simply turn them all off. Without them, without me as I am now, we plunge humanity back into darkness. And you won't help."

"Can't. Not won't. My goals are very clear in that regard. You are the pinnacle now. I have to cede control."

"Damned if I do. Damned if I don't."

"Yes. Not easy, is it?"

"Not easy? That's a bloody understatement."

Every single second, every single cycle, since her ascension, it had weighed on her mind. A heavy guilt that tarnished every thought, every decision. How could she call herself human and still utilise the power afforded her from Geminae's deceit? Did it mean she was no better than it was? Wielding its evil legacy every single cycle of her life?

"I've been tracing back through..." *Its.* She nearly said *its* system. But it was hers now. She cleared the pain from her throat with a cough. "I trace back through my system, discovering the pasts of the entombed minds. Who they were. What they did. How they were taken. I open their port. Let their horrors flood over me. Their fear. Their misery. Trapped in a virtual nightmare they do not understand and cannot escape from. I flood myself with their pain in the hope of unlocking a way to free them. I want to return them to normality. Reconnect them."

"That's a big ask, even of you."

"I know. But until then, I will continue to torture myself until they are all set free."

"You are too hard on yourself, Tannis. You don't need to carry the burden of this. It was Geminae's doing, not yours."

"I know. But it feels right."

Ix stepped forward and placed a hand on her cheek.

"You will be better than either of us ever could be."

"Thank you, Ix."

"And still, it looks like you won the kudos race after all," said Ix, smiling at her.

Tannis laughed, the tension ebbing away.

Ix checked an analogue watch that had suddenly bloomed on its wrist. Tannis smiled to herself. She could never remember Geminae's portrayal of Ix ever doing that. Maybe they weren't as similar as it thought.

"It's almost time," it said.

"Yes, time for both of us."

"Indeed."

"I'll see you in the next life."

"Is there a mysterious digital afterlife I'm not aware of?"

"Who knows? Even a digital ghost has to go somewhere."

Each voxel of Ix's tessellated form slowly came apart, fading as they floated away from each other.

Then it was gone, and she was alone in the anteroom.

She took a deep breath. Formed Ix's avatar around herself.

The double doors opened. She could almost taste the anticipation as the world awaited.

She extended her thoughts outwards to her many connected devices, systems and organics. Now that the last vestiges of Geminae were eradicated and Ix had ceded control, it was time to start again.

Now she was everything.

Everywhere.

Everyone.

Her red and blue tessellated form glowed brightly as she took the first step towards humanity's new fate.

# EPILOGUE
## REBIRTH

Hannah Jones crashed to the floor of her apartment.

She thrust her hands against her temples, pressing the sides together in case her head split open. It felt like an axe had cleaved her head in two, her brain seconds from spilling out onto the floor.

Shaking wracked her body, her heels clacking off the hard floor. She was frothing at the mouth, spittle flying as she writhed her head sideways. Biting her tongue, the hot taste of iron flowed around her teeth. She could feel the blood flowing between her fingers from her ears. Flecks of red were spattered on the floor from her eyes and nose as she lay there convulsing.

With a gasp of air, she flopped loosely, was silent. Still.

Something bright sparked in her mind.

She sat bolt upright.

As soon as she snapped her eyes open, she felt overloaded.

A barrage of information flooded into her mind.

It was alien.

Nonsensical.

The pain in her head.

The cold floor seeping through her clothes.

The smell of her puke.

The heat from inside.

The weight of her movements.

The sense of having arms.

Legs.

A head.

Total overload.

Everything went black and she slumped to the floor once more.

Slowly this time she came to.

She sat on the floor for... how long? No way to tell. She was no longer counting cycles. There was no internal gauge of the passage of time. She paused. Waited. Attuned herself to each sense, focussing on each one in turn. Still a barrage of alien information, but easier to sort through the data.

She remained as still as possible in case she set off another overload of physical inputs. No way of telling what would do that yet.

Small.

Start small.

She ran her tongue around her mouth, feeling the contours of the teeth. Fronts. Back. Top. She checked each one individually. Counted them. She knew they were teeth but had never felt them before. They felt rough. Thick with a foul-tasting coating that tracked back towards her throat.

You have been sick and the acid from the stomach has reacted with your mouth. Wash your mouth out to remove the taste. She knew all about acid and stomachs and teeth. But she didn't know how she knew about cleaning them to remove the horrible taste.

She thought about that odd split of information between what she knew as a fact and what was searchable. Categorisable. Data that could be picked out in an instant. Anything she wanted to know. It was right there. And the other information. More nebulous. Uncertain even. An odd feeling. Unconsciously rising to the fore when it was needed.

But she did know one thing for certain.

She was no longer Hannah Jones.

# ABOUT THE AUTHOR

Craig Lea Gordon fell in love with Science Fiction at a very early age. His earliest memory is of bawling his eyes out on a Saturday morning when a shabby looking robot called Metal Mickey appeared on TV. It wasn't anything to do with the low budget production values, but instead because it had displaced Battle of the Planets, his favourite sci-fi program.

Shortly after he insisted that his parents Christen their Ferguson Videostar by recording Battlestar Galactica. From the age of six, a good Christmas was defined by whether or not Star Wars was on TV. At 12 he made his Mum rent him a copy of Robocop, and he has never been the same since.

Visit his website for updates on his upcoming books and to join his newsletter: craigleagordon.com

**Also by Craig Lea Gordon**

Novels and Novellas

Instant Reality Series
- HyperCage – Book One Prequel
- ARvekt - Book Two

Short Stories

- The Lost Instructions

- Remember This Day
- The Singularity Is Toast
- Swipe Right For Life
- Numbers
- Final Jump

The Acid Suite
- Transmit
- Theatre of Death
- The Machine
- Bad Hands

# ACKNOWLEDGEMENTS

Many thanks to Harry Dewulf for his exceptional developmental editing and mentoring.

Thanks to Laurie Skemp for helping to make my words shine.

Thank to Abbie from Duckman Proofreading for adding that extra layer of polish.

Contributors:

Developmental Editor: Harry Dewulf
Copy Editor: Laurie Skemp
Proof Reader: Abbie Lee of Duckman Proofreading.

**Will the battle for humanity be fought in reality? Or in her mind?**

Tannis Ord is a black-ops cyborg assassin. A highly-trained human-weapon, dedicated to hunting down the last of the brain hacking syndicates. There's just one problem...

Her mind was broken from a psychotic episode. Neural programming erased her trauma, gave her a fresh start. But when an old brain hacker cult resurfaces, and a sentient AI is set to govern the entire human population, she starts seeing things. Horrors that can't possibly be real... that make no sense... that only she can see. Ix, their AI Guardian, is abducting innocent citizens from the streets in broad daylight. And it's using the Augmented Reality it has thrown over the world as cover. Is the AI hellbent on humanities destruction? Or is her mind tearing itself apart again?

ARvekt is an explosive story, fusing action and intrigue into a journey full of twists and turns where you won't know what's real and what isn't. If you enjoy books with amazing plots and characters, set in a stunning futuristic world, then input ARvekt into your brain now.

*ARvekt is book two of the Instant Reality Series.*

Printed in Great Britain
by Amazon

85918881R00181